~ *The Tesseracts Series* ~

Tesseracts 1
  edited by Judith Merril
Tesseracts 2
  edited by Phyllis Gotlieb & Douglas Barbour
Tesseracts 3
  edited by Candas Jane Dorsey & Gerry Truscott
Tesseracts 4
  edited by Lorna Toolis & Michael Skeet
Tesseracts 5
  edited by Robert Runté & Yves Maynard
Tesseracts 6
  edited by Robert J. Sawyer & Carolyn Clink
Tesseracts 7
  edited by Paula Johanson & Jean-Louis Trudel
Tesseracts 8
  edited by John Clute & Candas Jane Dorsey
Tesseracts Nine
  edited by Nalo Hopkinson and Geoff Ryman
Tesseracts Ten: A Celebration of New Canadian Speculative Fiction
  edited by Robert Charles Wilson and Edo van Belkom
Tesseracts Eleven: Amazing Canadian Speculative Fiction
  edited by Cory Doctorow and Holly Phillips
Tesseracts Twelve: New Novellas of Canadian Fantastic Fiction
  edited by Claude Lalumière
Tesseracts Thirteen: Chilling Tales from the Great White North
  edited by Nancy Kilpatrick and David Morrell
Tesseracts Fourteen: Strange Canadian Stories
  edited by John Robert Colombo and Brett Alexander Savory
Tesseracts Fifteen: A Case of Quite Curious Tales
  edited by Julie Czerneda and Susan MacGregor
Tesseracts Sixteen: Parnassus Unbound
  edited by Mark Leslie
Tesseracts Seventeen: Speculating Canada from Coast to Coast to Coast
  edited by Colleen Anderson and Steve Vernon
Tesseracts Eighteen: Wrestling With Gods
  edited by Liana Kerzner and Jerome Stueart
Tesseracts Nineteen: Superhero Universe
  edited by Claude Lalumière and Mark Shainblum
Tesseracts Twenty: Compostela
  edited by Spider Robinson and James Alan Gardner
Tesseracts Twenty-One: Nevertheless
  edited by Rhonda Parrish and Greg Bechtel
Tesseracts Twenty-Two: Alchemy and Artifacts
  edited by Lorina Stephens and Susan MacGregor
Tesseracts Q
  edited by Élisabeth Vonarburg and Jane Brierley

Publisher's Note:

Thank you for purchasing this book. It began as an idea, was shaped by the creativity of its talented author, and was subsequently molded into the book you have before you by a team of editors and designers.

Like all EDGE books, this book is the result of the creative talents of a dedicated team of individuals who all believe that books (whether in print or pixels) have the magical ability to take you on an adventure to new and wondrous places powered by the author's imagination.

As EDGE's publisher, I hope that you enjoy this book. It is a part of our ongoing quest to discover talented authors and to make their creative writing available to you.

We also hope that you will share your discovery and enjoyment of this anthology on social media through Facebook, Twitter, Goodreads, Pinterest, etc., and by posting your opinions and/or reviews on Amazon and other review sites and blogs. By doing so, others will be able to share your discovery and passion for this book.

Brian Hades, publisher

Alchemy and Artifacts

Tesseracts Twenty-Two

23 Selected Stories Edited by

Lorina Stephens and **Susan MacGregor**

EDGE SCIENCE FICTION AND FANTASY PUBLISHING
An Imprint of HADES PUBLICATIONS, INC.
CALGARY

Alchemy and Artifacts
Tesseracts Twenty-Two

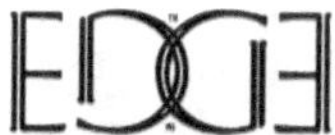

EDGE SCIENCE FICTION AND FANTASY PUBLISHING
An Imprint of HADES PUBLICATIONS, INC.
P.O. Box 1714, Calgary, Alberta, T2P 2L7, Canada

The EDGE Team:
Producer: Brian Hades
Acquisitions Michelle Heumann
Edited by: Lorina Stephens and Susan MacGregor
Cover Art: Cathleen Tarawhiti
Book Design: Mark Steele

ISBN: 978-1-77053-194-9

EDGE Science Fiction and Fantasy Publishing and Hades Publications, Inc. acknowledges the ongoing support of the Alberta Foundation for the Arts and the Canada Council for the Arts for our publishing programme.

Library and Archives Canada Cataloguing in Publication
CIP Data on file with the National Library of Canada
ISBN: 978-1-77053-194-9
(e-Book ISBN: 978-1-77053-193-2)

FIRST EDITION
(20190601)
Printed in USA
www.edgewebsite.com

Contents

Foreword

Lorina Stephens

When Susan MacGregor approached me to co-edit an anthology of historical fantasy for the next Tesseracts series it didn't take a lot of reflection for me to agree. I work well with Susan. While we don't agree on everything — what partnerships ever does, or should — I knew we shared a deep love of historical fantasy and fiction, that we both felt the genre tended to get shunted off into the realms of literature of little import, fluff, pulp for the brainless masses. And we are both uncompromising in our search for excellence.

We both feel historical fantasy very much matters, especially historical fantasy that pushes a reader to think, fiction that takes a concept, a culture, an incident, or an artifact, and launches into rich speculation — what if?

For me, the cultural surround of history has always been profound, because it is through cultural artifacts we glimpse the possibility of what occurred in the past. The artifacts carry voices, warnings, celebrations. They are touchstones and resonate if we only will observe, listen, be willing to learn. Once the creators are dead, the wars ended, the political machines decayed and dissolved, there are the artifacts, the art. Manna.

Ah yes, manna. It is a concept I have long embraced, first coined to me outside of its Biblical reference by an old acquaintance, Darrell Markewitz, who is an artisan blacksmith of some considerable repute, having forged — forgive the pun — a reputation as an expert in ancient Norse metallurgy. Darrell said to me an artisan should strive to imbue manna in the work they create, that by doing so they created something which transcends themselves and their skill, that they created something which would inspire and nourish generations to come.

That concept, that imperative to imbue manna into a work has stayed with me ever since. And so, when it came to selecting stories for an anthology about the alchemy of artifacts, it of course followed those stories must needs be imbued with manna. These stories had to not only use as a touchstone an artifact from history, but then create a story which would nourish those of us wandering in a wilderness. Especially the wilderness of today, in a world which seems determined to plunge blindly and eagerly along a path of hate, destroying all that has been, everything that is true and beautiful and that nourishes our global community, everything that has manna.

So, Susan and I waded through an embarrassment of riches, and finally, after weeks and weeks of reading, discussion, debate, came up with twenty-three stunning stories, all of them with manna.

I am very proud of this anthology, proud to have been one of its curators. I believe, in time, it will be remembered as an anthology of manna, this anthology — Tesseracts 22: Alchemy and Artifacts.

Lorina Stephens

Foreword

Susan MacGregor

I'm one of those people who likes to ask herself why she's drawn to certain things. It's never been enough for me to answer, 'because I am.' I have to delve into my own predilections and analyze them. Why historical fantasy? What is it about the past that intrigues me? And what do I hope to have accomplished in co-editing this book?

I've always found history fascinating — although not so much its dryer aspects. What captivates me instead, are the motivations behind those dates and events, the quest for power, the fight against repression, the sacrifices to a greater cause — in other words, the human drama that reflects the worst and best of who we are. Greed and conquest drive us as much as our need for order, justice, and peace. Our past shows us where we've been and how we are evolving — if, in fact, we are. Above all, our history reflects our human need for *more*. As humans, we are a grasping, driven, hungry, and magnificent species. Which means we live and create wonderful stories, just by virtue of *who* we are.

When we add a fantastic element to such tales, we stimulate two other very human experiences — the satisfaction that comes from sudden insight, and occasionally, awe. When I asked contributors to send us stories that featured the 'hidden' side of history, tales that reflected the magic behind the events, I was hoping to come across such alchemies. There is much that happens in our world that we don't see. The past is no exception. I wanted to get a sense of 'the man' (or woman) who was behind the curtain, the one pulling the world's strings. Or to get a hint of those forces we only suspect are there, but that disturb us with their possibility.

I've often felt that historical fantasy tends to be dismissed by those who favor the purer flavors of the genre, as well as by those lovers of science fiction who look to the future with hope or cynicism. Why bother with the past, when the future is so much more exciting or depressing? Writing historical fantasy demands a whole new level of expertise. All writers world-build, but with historical work, research is critical. You have to know your stuff and work within the past's restrictions and constructs. And then — you weave what you hope is an intriguing story.

Before you are twenty-three amazing artifacts of fantastic historical fiction, filled with the alchemy I had hoped to discover. It's been a pleasure to put this collection together with my dear friend and co-editor, Lorina. May these tales entertain and enthrall you, as they have us.

Susan MacGregor

Cleaning House in Ithaca

Leslie Brown

"Papákis, I've been looking everywhere for you!" The dark-haired boy landed beside him accompanied by a tiny land-slide of shale and dirt.

"I'm here where I always am," Odysseus said and flipped his bait a little farther out into the aquamarine waters of the Ionian Sea.

"Mitéra says you are supposed to be cleaning out the back room of the house. Your useless junk has to go so Giagia can sleep there." The boy started rooting through the crock of worms, pulling one out and then another.

"Leave my bait alone, Poli. You'll put the taste of boy on them and the fish won't want them anymore." Odysseus squinted up at the sun. Penelope had a point. The room containing the souvenirs of his travels was in the gynaecium or women's quarters. There had been space there when he had returned from the war but ever since Telemachus had married, there were more women in the house. And now Penelope's mother was to live with them. Odysseus was expected to dispose of the mementos of his past, as if his achievements meant nothing.

He left early to go fishing in an effort to avoid Penelope, so she sent the boy to do her nagging for her. That wasn't the only thing she'd been pestering him about. She wanted him to speak to Telemachus about how he treated his younger brother Poliporthes, the same who was now rooting through the worms. Odysseus had left when Telemachus was an infant and returned when he was a man. His older son was jealous of his younger brother for having the attention of a father as he grew up. Odysseus felt bad about that, of course he did, but what could he do about it? Ignore the boy to make his brother feel better? It was ridiculous and annoying, and it gave rise to his retort to Penelope, words that could not be taken back: *if he is even my son.*

Odysseus had been a red head in his younger days and Telemachus a reddish blonde. Poliporthes was dark-haired like his mother but his skin was more olive toned than hers. And where did that nose come from? Odysseus had never asked after he had disposed of his wife's suitors, and Poliporthes had been born close enough to the proper time after they had returned to their marriage bed. In all truth, he never would have said anything but for the nagging. *You don't pay enough attention to your oldest son. You pay too much attention to your youngest son. You don't want my mother to live with us. Your useless junk is taking up valuable space. Get rid of it or sell it so we can feed all these mouths.*

Odysseus sighed. He couldn't avoid it forever. "You'll help me clean the room, boy?"

The boy, who might or might not be his, glanced up at him, love and trust shining in his eyes. "Of course, Papákis. I'm strong. I can carry things down to the courtyard."

The heat of midday was upon them and the house was quiet. Odysseus led Poliporthes upstairs to the storage room, glancing ahead to make sure all the women's rooms were decently curtained. He paused briefly beside Penelope's dayroom and then resolutely pushed on. She'd be sweeter once she knew he was tackling the storage room.

He had put a wooden door on this room and had woven an intricately knotted piece of rope looped between two brackets to hold it shut. No one, including himself, had gone in there for five years or more. He cut the rope off with his knife rather than trying to untie the knot. Dust swirled in the air when he pulled open the door. Ah, he had forgotten how much was in there. The stories of shipwrecks and lost valuables were exaggerations. He had loaded up his ship with the treasures of Troy and hadn't exactly come straight home. He had dallied, there was no denying, in most cases to earn him and his men shelter and food. Who was he to say anything if his wife had also done what she needed to do to survive? Ah but Gods, the look she had given him when he had said those unforgivable words. You'd think he had struck her across the face.

The chests were going to be the biggest job. They were stacked from floor to ceiling for half of the room. There was ornate furniture too fussy for any of them, even his wife's mother. That could go, either to be remade into something more palatable or sold to a rich merchant with no taste.

"Poli, let's take these chairs down to the courtyard." Penelope would chide them for doing servants' work, but Odysseus didn't want uncaring hands touching his mementos. By starting with furniture, they could postpone the chests for a bit. There was no gold or jewels in them. He had taken those out before the chests had gone into storage. The money had been put into the house which had desperately needed repair.

They made quick work of the furniture and stacked up three piles in the courtyard: one to sell, one to give away to the villagers and one to have the carpenter simplify.

"Right," Odysseus said, dusting off his hands and glancing upwards. Heads were appearing at the second floor railing then disappearing. Many eager feet were now scurrying to tell Penelope that her husband was finally doing her bidding. "Let's tackle some of the chests."

He knew where everything was, even after all these years. Since he had found new resolve, he and Poli pulled down the most troublesome first. The resin had seeped out of the wood, sealing the lid shut. They pried it open with an old blade. Inside was a wrapped statue, approximately Poli's height. They set it upright and Odysseus pulled off the wrappings.

"Athena," Poli exclaimed with delight, touching his brow respectfully. He knew the stories of how the goddess had favored his father in his travels, and also aided his older brother. She was a favorite of his.

"Not just any statue," Odysseus said, gazing at the lidded eyes and pursed mouth of his patron goddess. "This is the Palladium. Troy could not fall until I stole her from inside its walls. All I had to do was dress like a beggar and speak with a cowherd's accent. They let me in, even with a foreign army camped on their doorstep, the idiots. I heard the city cry out, you know, when I took the Palladium through the gates in a dung cart. But only I heard it. The guards kept playing dice."

"Hah," said Poli in awe and appreciation.

"Such a fine piece as this should go to Menelaus and Helen. We'll bring her down to the family shrine and make offerings until she goes to Sparta. She's probably angry with me for shutting her in a trunk for so long." He set the carved wooden statue aside. She could use a paint touch-up as well. He and the boy would make a mess of that. Best pay an artist.

Poli was already digging around in the trunk. He pulled out a slingshot. "Papákis, may I have this?"

Odysseus took it from him. "Needs a new leather cradle strap or you'll have to oil the old one. If I give it to you, you don't treat it like a toy. It can take out an eye. And no hitting the sheep on the rumps with it. I had my own arse tanned for that when I was a boy and rightly so."

"Thank you, Papákis!" Poli put his treasure by the door so he would not forget it. There was a tap on the door and Iokaste stood there, nose wrinkled at the dust.

"The mistress told me to bring you bread and olives. And some wine." Iokaste's nose was still wrinkled so it was at him, not the dust. When the master and mistress were at war, the servants and slaves chose their sides and usually he found very few on his.

"Thank you. You can put it down there." He gestured at the top of a chest. Iokaste hesitated.

"The boy needs to eat."

"And so he will. Leave the food, Io. We are busy."

Iokaste huffed and, ignoring his instructions, slammed the pottery bowls on the floor, harder than was necessary. Odysseus glanced at her from under his brows.

"Now you've made it so that neither of us can eat that. You've offered it to Pallas Athena."

Iokaste jerked her head in surprise. The bowls rested at the foot of the statue. Odysseus watched her dismissive look turn into something more speculative. Faded and battered as it was, the Palladium had power.

"I will bring more food," she said, curtly. "If my mistress will allow it."

"And tell my wife, while you're begging food for her husband and son, that not everything in here is junk." There, he'd just tossed more fuel on the fire, but it was worth it to irk Iokaste. She had implied it was the Queen who determined whether or not the King could eat.

"Will you hang me then, like Melantho, for speaking with a sharp tongue?"

Odysseus was on his feet so quickly, Iokaste took a step back, eyes wide. "Melantho was not hung for her sharp tongue, although that didn't help her case any. She died for sleeping with the suitors, for money and gifts, along with the other handmaidens Telemachus strung up on the garden wall. You are too young to remember that and thus speak casually of it. Let the older women educate you on the foolishness of bringing that up to me."

Iokaste paled at his anger. No doubt she was belatedly remembering the power men had over women and how an honorable wife could be killed at just the suggestion of infidelity. She gave a jerking bob of her head and left. Odysseus glanced guiltily at Poli. He was oblivious to the altercation between the adults. In his hands was an elaborately carved wooden horse. The paint was still as bright as the day Epeius had made it. The whites of its eyes flashed, and the bared yellow teeth were ready to take a bite out of the boy.

"Papákis, what's this?" Poli's voice was hushed with far more reverence than he had paid Athena.

"The Trojan horse, of course."

"No!" Poli looked up at him, waiting for the joke's punchline.

"It's the truth."

"But!" Poli examined the object he held. It was two man's hands in height and three in length. The boy's fingernails found the little trap door in the horse's belly and opened it.

He held it up to his eye but was no further ahead. The pieces of the horse had been joined so well together that no light could come in through a crack for the men to know when it was dark. That is why two spies had to lie close to the mouth and relay when it was safe to emerge.

Poli put the horse down and glared at his father. "Papákis, all the stories say you hid forty men inside the Trojan horse. You needed that many to subdue the guards before you could open the city gates. This horse would not hold a grain-fattened rat!"

"Think, my boy. What if we had left a giant wooden horse at the gates? For all their faults, the Trojans weren't stupid. They weren't about to pull this box on wheels into their city. And they would have heard the men inside. Neoptolemus always giggled when he was nervous. Thoas' farts could be heard back home, across the Aegean. So, I prayed to Athena for aid. She told me if we made a small horse, she would see to it that we all could fit inside. Then, once we came out, she would ensure that we were in our proper forms for fighting."

"What did it feel like, to be so small?"

"It didn't feel like anything at all. It appeared that we had built a large horse and we simply climbed in and out. Everything was normal. No stones the size of boulders. The walls of Troy looked the same as they did on any day that I stood before them. I've talked to some of the men years later who were in there with me. They don't even remember the horse being small. Perhaps I only do because I snatched it up after the last battle to bring home."

"Will Athena let me go inside it?" Poli glanced at the Palladium.

"Why would you want to do that? Here, give that to me." Odysseus took the carving away from Poli and put it back in its chest, closing the lid. "Enough work for today. Iokaste has forgotten us. Let's go looking for our midday meal."

They barged into the kitchens and Frona, the head cook, scowled at them. With a cheeky grin, Odysseus scooped up an olive oil jar and snatched a loaf from under its cloth. They dodged her half-hearted slap and sat at an old worn table in a side room with the ripening cheeses. Making a farmer's meal of it, they dipped the hard bread into the olive oil. Telemachus came in, sunburnt from supervising the plowing of the fields, and spotted them in the cheese room. He cast the same annoyed, disgusted look at the back of Poli's neck he always did. Odysseus had ignored it in the past, but Penelope was right. It did not behoove a grown man to be jealous of a child.

"Sit with us, Telemachus. We break our fast."

"I still have a whole half field to plow, Papákis. No time to sit and eat."

Odysseus grabbed his son's wrist. "There is always time to sit with family."

Telemachus gave a withering glare at the hand gripping his wrist but plunked down on a stool. Odysseus passed him the bread and the jar.

"Did you hear the story of how I tried to pretend to be mad so that I would not have to go to war against the Trojans?"

"Many times," muttered Telemachus at the same time Poli said "Tell us, Papákis!"

"When I heard about this Helen business, I consulted an oracle on the east side of the island. She said if I went, I would be a long time coming home. Telemachus had just been born and I didn't want to go." He glanced at his older son, but Telemachus' face remained stony. "So I decided to pretend to be insane. Now those mainlanders don't get subtleties, so I had to be dramatic. I hitched a donkey and an ox to the plow and started them up the north hill."

"A donkey and an ox! Now that is crazy. Did you go in circles, Papákis?" Poli bounced up and down in excitement although Odysseus knew for a fact that he had heard this story at least several times.

"Yes, and I yelled at the poor beasts as if it was their fault. And if that wasn't enough, I took handfuls of salt from the pouch at my waist and threw them over my shoulder as if they were seed."

"And then they took Telemachus...." Poli slapped his brother on the shoulder and ignored the black glare.

"Who's telling this story? Yes, Palamedes turned around and walked down to the house. He asked your mother politely to borrow Telemachus and she handed him over. Palamedes trudged back up the hill with your anxious mother a hand's span from his back. He set Telemachus down in my plow's path and then held your mother still when she screamed at all of us."

"And you veered away!" said Poli.

"Of course I veered. My son was more important to me than avoiding a useless war over a woman that dragged on for more years than you've been alive, Poli." While he addressed his speech to Poli, his eyes held Telemachus'. He wanted time to speak with his first born. "Poli, run upstairs and bring the Trojan horse to show your brother."

Then it was just the two of them. Odysseus grasped his son's forearm, man to man. "What can I do to make things better for you? I could stop fishing with Poli, dragging him down to town with me, sparring with him in the gardens. Would that make you feel better?"

"Papákis, it's not the time you spend with him." His son's throat moved in a hard swallow.

Odysseus' brows arched in surprise. Not jealousy? "What is it then?"

"As he grows older, he doesn't look like us."

"My grandfather Autolycus was as brown as a berry. Sometimes I see his features in young Poli." If he squinted and used one eye.

Telemachus leaned forward and gripped his father's arm in return. "Then why are you saying things to Mitéra about Poli's father?"

"Your Mitéra and I were fighting. We say all sorts of things."

"But this," and Telemachus hammered the top of the table with his fist, "this will get Mitéra killed! Is that what you want? I won't do it, you know. I hung those women for you because I knew they slept with the suitors for money. If one, just one of them, had done it to keep them away from Mitéra, I would have argued with you for her life."

Odysseus looked away. "I wasn't thinking," he finally mumbled.

"Not thinking will lose you your family so no more, please, Papákis? Please?"

"No more." There was a time when Odysseus had been so prideful he never would have let anyone speak to him in such a way. But this was his oldest son looking at him with fear and pleading in his eyes.

"Good." Telemachus gave his father's forearm one last squeeze. "So where is this magical horse?"

Odysseus frowned. Unease rippled up his neck making the hairs stand up. "He should be back by now. I hope the women are leaving him alone." He rose and ran upstairs, taking the steps two at a time. All the curtains were still closed to the women's rooms. The door to the storage room was open and the horse was in the middle of the floor. Poli was not in sight.

"Poli," Odysseus roared. He picked up the horse and held it to his ear. If there was a response, he couldn't hear it over the pounding of his heart. He placed the horse down and lay on his belly. With one chipped fingernail, he pried the trap door open. "Poli, come out." He was aware, without looking, that there was a crowd forming at the door behind Telemachus.

The dark hatch gaped empty in the horse's belly. He remembered the spy port in the mouth and peered in there. "Poli," he whispered.

There was only one way this could have happened. He pushed himself up onto his knees and spun towards the Palladium.

"You!" There was so much venom in Odysseus' tone that Telemachus flinched back, and the women cleared the door.

The serene smile on the carved statue was mocking now. Odysseus clenched his fists.

"What do I have to do to get my son back?"

Telemachus grunted, and Odysseus turned his head in time to see his eldest fall backwards through the doorway as if pushed. The door slammed shut, just missing his toes.

A silvery fog began to fill the room. It swirled around Odysseus' face and had the smell of blood and bowels emptied in terror. It smelled like Troy. The room's walls were far away, then vanishing. The horse beside him creaked and grew. It towered above him, higher than the ceiling should have allowed, and it smelled of fresh pine. The clean fragrance cut through the mist's stench. The door hung down from the belly, still a good man's length above him and a rope ladder thwacked him in the face.

"So that's your game? Very well, I'll play." He climbed up into the dark belly of the horse and stood, squinting.

"Close the trap," came a voice from the dark. Odysseus tensed. He didn't even have an eating knife on him. Keeping his head turned in the direction of the voice, he pulled in the ladder and then grabbed the short rope that was tied to the latch. He secured it shut, making the horse's belly impenetrably dark. There was a flare and a torch sprang to life.

An old man sat slouched against the curved wall of the horse. Shoulder-length white hair was held back by a jeweled band across a forehead engraved with deep furrows. A close-cut white beard fringed the jawline. But it was the eyes that gave her away. Vast and incomprehensible, the Goddess Athena stared at him from one of her favorite forms, Mentor.

"Did you miss me, Odysseus?"

"Like I would a boil on my arse. Give me back my son."

"Such ingratitude after all the help I've given you. It was you who caught my attention, you know, when you unwrapped my Trojan effigy. It was as if you had tugged hard on my chiton. So I came to see how my favorite trickster was doing." Athena produced an orange ball, seemingly from thin air. She snapped her fingers and a small knife appeared between them. She peeled the ball in one continuous rind and Odysseus saw the juice drip from it.

"Would you like a piece? It's called an orange, obviously enough, and you won't see another in your lifetime."

"No, I just want my son." He steeled himself for the burn of his next word. "Please?"

Athena popped a piece of orange into her mouth and chewed with obvious pleasure. "Are you sure you want him? A few hours ago, you were casting your doubts as to his parentage."

"It was an intemperate comment brought on by my wife's tendency to treat me as a small child instead of the King of Ithaca."

With startling suddenness, Athena flung the remains of her orange at him, hitting him on the forehead. Sticky pulp trickled down his face. Odysseus left it rather than wiping it away with a hand.

"That was for comparing me to an ass boil. You are King of Ithaca because of me, ungrateful whelp. Telemachus is alive because of me. Penelope is your wife because of me. What more do you want, Trickster? Another war to go to because you are bored of a peaceful happy life?" Athena spat a pip at him for good measure.

"I have no objection to a peaceful life," Odysseus grumbled, scrubbing a sandal against the rough wood.

"Just not a boring one?" Athena's form flowed and shimmered in the torch light. A blonde woman blinked at him and then gave him that dear crooked smile. "Would life have been more interesting if you had stayed with Circe?" Mist swirled around her hips and three children appeared. Two looked close to Poli in age, the other a bit older. "And watched your offspring grow up?'

Odysseus chose silence and fingered a loose strap on his sandal.

"You can't even look at us, can you?"

"Lady, I cannot change the past." He swallowed and squinted at her. "I did not know about the last two."

"Twins, in the womb when you left her."

"Ah."

"All boys."

Odysseus covered his eyes with a palm. "Lady, enough. Can you take another form?"

"Better?" Mentor was back with his kindly face.

"Much. My thanks." Time to get this back on track. He had to distract Athena from his faults and get her to give Poli back.

"Lady, let me make this right. I'll send your Palladium to Menelaus and Helen. They will do you fit honor in a temple of gold. Better than anything we poor farmers can do."

"Pah! I am not my sisters, taken with gold and fawning kings. And I have no desire to be housed with Menelaus and *that* woman." Another orange appeared in her hand and it was peeled with as great efficiency as before. Odysseus prepared himself for another onslaught of pulp. Instead, Athena handed him the fruit and he bit into it obediently. Sweet and succulent. Something about the matter-of-fact, kind gesture made Odysseus' eyes well up.

"I'm not used to having everyone angry with me." He swallowed the last bit of fruit and spat the pits onto the wooden planks.

"Everyone except Poli. He's never angry with you."

"Yes, except Poli. A temple in Ithaca? I cannot promise much gold in it but I can put it at the top of the pasture, so you can see out over the sea."

"And a new coat of paint for the Palladium."

Odysseus laughed. "Yes, a new coat of paint done by an artist."

Athena nodded to his left. "He's up at the mouth."

"My thanks." Odysseus stood and was surprised at how stiff his legs were.

"He's not your son." Athena's voice froze him in place. "Peisander hid in your marital bedchamber the night before you came home. He offered Penelope a necklace and when she refused, forced himself upon her. She killed him as he slept and hid the body in a chest. After you killed the suitors, she managed to throw his body in amongst them."

Odysseus did not turn around. "You are not known as the Goddess of Truth."

"But I am of Justice. You have the right to know. What shall you do now, son of Ithaca?"

Odysseus swallowed hard and blinked the wetness from his eyes. "Poliporthes is my son. None shall say otherwise."

"As you wish, Odysseus. I will bid you farewell. Do not be slow about building that temple."

He crawled up through the dark, feeling for the rough handholds that had been nailed to the planks. He climbed for a long time, further than would be required to reach the horse's mouth but he grimly kept at it. As he went, the hard, icy lump in his chest that had formed when Athena revealed the truth about Poli started to melt. Finally, a glimmer of light appeared ahead of him. As he got closer, he could see a boy lying on his stomach, peering out.

"Poli," he said as he lowered himself down beside his son.

"Papákis. I've been watching. Is this Troy?"

Odysseus looked out through the narrow opening. It was early morning, with just a glimmer of light coming over the horizon. The light he had seen climbing up the throat of the horse came from dozens of torches driven into the ground around the Greeks' offering as it rested on a makeshift altar. He could see the dark forms of his men creeping around the square, slitting the throats of the Trojan guards as they lay passed out from celebrating the end of the war.

There was the remembered clamor as someone less drunk realized what was going on and raised an alarm. The gates creaked as they opened and then there was the full-throated roar as the Greek armies poured into the sleeping city. Time seemed to be going faster as the warriors moved at a blurring speed. The sun rose quickly, and it was full day. The Trojan men were dead, and their women were bearing the brunt of surviving.

"Poli, let's not watch anymore. Your mitéra will be wondering where we are." They turned away from the cries of all those sheltered, pampered girls and women. Their safe world had vanished in an instant. Most would end up as slaves in Sparta or Athens. It was a lesson to him on how transitory things were.

The journey down the throat was a lot shorter than his trip up it. The belly was empty although the torch was still there. With the help of its light he found the trap door and helped Poli out. Mist swirled and the horse shrunk behind them to its former size. Odysseus hugged his son.

"Some adventure, huh? Did you see Athena?"

"No, the horse was empty when I climbed in."

"A pity. Maybe she will come to the temple I am going to build on the hill."

"That's the north pasture, Papákis. Telemachus isn't going to be happy about that."

"Your brother will learn to live with it." Odysseus pulled the storage room door open and the whole household stood on the other side. Poli was snatched away from him and sucked into the loving crowd.

Odysseus was face to face with Penelope. She had been crying, the eyes under those winged eyebrows red and bloodshot. He pulled her close and whispered in her ear.

"I'm sorry for being a bored, grumpy, careless old man."

"I'm sorry I nagged you," she whispered back.

He kissed her and remembered why he had struggled so hard to come back to her.

"When are we going to finish cleaning the room, Papákis?" asked Poli, tugging on the bottom of Odysseus' tunic.

"Cleaning that room has caused enough trouble," said Penelope. "I'll put my mother somewhere else."

* * *

>>> *We all know the story of the Trojan Horse. The Greeks built a giant wooden horse, hid warriors inside, and the Trojans obligingly towed it inside their city walls. No narrative tells us what happened to that horse, nor is there mention of the fate of the Palladium, the statue of Pallas Athena that had to be stolen out of Troy before it could fall. Odysseus, King of Ithaca, trickster and thief, wouldn't have left any portable treasures behind. This story asks, what if the horse wasn't all that big and what happens when Odysseus is asked to clean up his man cave?*

Leslie Brown

Leslie Brown is an Ottawa-based writer of science fiction, fantasy, horror and romance. She has published short stories in *On Spec, Neo Opsis, Strange Horizons, Tesseracts 15, Tesseracts 20* as well as other anthologies. She has recently retired from the National Research Council as a research technician in the field of Alzheimer's disease.

http://www.leslieannbrown.com/

Caligula's Eagle

Tony Pi

The madness of Caligula should have died with him, but my nephew would leave me one last atrocity to bury: what he did to Jove's eagle.

Seneca had found what remained of the creature in the bowels of Caligula's temple, somehow still alive. It struck such terror into the philosopher he begged I alone should come see. Though no stranger to Caligula's depravity, I dared not imagine what misdeed had survived him.

"An insult to the gods, Claudius Caesar!" said Seneca.

By the light of his lamp I saw a glistening web of feather, sinew, and entrails strung between pillars. Caught like a fly was the skeleton of a grand bird, its heart still beating within a cage of bone.

I stammered. "G-g-gods. What m-m-monster—"

"A legion captured it in the Caucasus Mountains," answered the Stoic. "They say it's the divine eagle Jove sent to punish Prometheus."

Seneca seemed to know too much for him to profess innocence in this.

I knew the myth he told. For stealing fire and giving it to Man, the Titan Prometheus was bound in chains so that Jove's eagle could eat his liver anew each day. "But didn't Hercules shoot the eagle?"

"What eats of an immortal gains a measure of life eternal, or so Caligula believed," said Seneca. "He consumed the eagle's flesh; bathed in its blood. Those are the least indignities our Emperor had visited upon it, and yet it survives."

My nephew had believed himself a god. This deathless eagle must have fanned the fires of that madness.

I limped forward.

What I thought was a bauble on a string was a living eye.

I couldn't stop shaking. The *aquila* was more than a symbol of Rome's might; it was the divine servant of Jove. By dissecting it alive, Caligula must have angered the gods and cursed us.

Then there was Seneca. "You knew of this?"

"I did," Seneca whispered. "Caligula made me devise the first cuts to his plaything. When I could bear the eagle's cries no more, he threatened to execute me, but decided my age would kill me first. Forgive me, Caesar."

"No one told Caligula no and lived. I am well aware."

I never wanted to be Caesar, yet the Fates made me so. It fell to me to appease Jove for the sins of my kinsman, for surely Rome would burn with godly wrath for this. But could I undo the harm done to this noble creature?

No. I couldn't scrape away the past. What the eagle once was, Caligula had broken forever.

And yet—

"Send for a *haruspex*."

Seneca was perplexed. "A divination? Certainly, none of this bodes well?"

"I don't need a *haruspex* to read these entrails. I need one to put them back right."

~ ~ ~

Jove's eagle was slowly sewn back together.

The *haruspex* fussed over how the intestines should fold, while Seneca paired feathers to wings. I held the light for Seneca's pupil as he stitched up the great bird's neck. "A st-st-steadier hand than mine, lad. Pl-Pl-Plinius, is it?"

"Gaius Plinius Secundus, Caesar." The young man continued to sew, his hands stained red.

"The blood doesn't bother you?"

Plinius washed his fingers. "The eagle lives, and it may yet fly. That matters more."

"Fly?" My hands twitched. "That's the hope, but what if we make a cripple like me?"

"But, Caesar, what if it lives to be emperor of the skies?"

"Let's pray." I met the eagle's eyes, now tucked back in its skull. "Forgive us this pain, *aquila*."

We did what we could, the four of us: eight hands, sixteen nights to remake Jove's eagle. No kingly specimen our handiwork, but it was whole once more, developing an insatiable appetite for livers.

Would its broken bones mend? Might the stitchings hold? That was for the gods to say.

Only Seneca feared to approach it. It might have been Caligula's cruelty, but it had been Seneca's knife, and the creature did not forget.

We freed Jove's eagle on a moonless night. When it tasted open air, it screeched and struggled to climb the sky.

I turned to the lad. "I hope you learned something from this, Pl-Pl-Pliny."

"Yes, Caesar. No matter how dark the day, there remains hope. We must help those on the brink of death. Always."

I nodded. "Then some good has come of this."

The eagle continued to circle the Palatine Hill.

"A good omen, *haruspex*?"

"I arranged its entrails most auspiciously. A private word, Caesar?"

I allowed it.

"We who touched its blood will not be spared," he whispered. "We will suffer long and die infamous deaths, all of us: poison, ash, fire, suicide."

Which death is mine? I almost asked, but thought better of it.

"As for Seneca, Caligula's crime against the gods taints him most," the *haruspex* said. "He cannot remain in the city, lest he dooms us all."

I understood.

I hobbled to Seneca's side and gripped his shoulder.

He startled. "It hungers for my liver, I know it."

If only his death would be that simple.

For the good of Rome, I had no choice but to exile Seneca on a false charge.

"Tell me, Seneca, do Stoics believe in noble sacrifice?"

* * *

>>> *Emperor Claudius would be murdered by poison in 54 A.D. As for Seneca the Younger, Nero would falsely accuse him of being involved in a plot to kill him in 65 A.D. He ordered Seneca to kill himself by severing his veins and bleeding to death. Pliny the Elder became a naturalist, and would die in 79 A.D. from inhaling poisonous fumes at the volcanic eruption of Mount Vesuvius, as ash fell from the sky.*

Dr. Tony Pi

Dr. Tony Pi is a writer in Toronto with a Ph.D. in Linguistics from McGill University. A finalist for the John W. Campbell Award for Best New Writer in 2009, he is also the winner of 2015 Aurora Award for Best English Poem/ Song. He loves myth, magic, and history, in particular the Greek and Roman periods, and the Tang and Song Dynasties. He's fascinated by Pompeii, and was thrilled to have visited that buried city on a trip to Italy. That and the TV series *I, Claudius* inspired this story.

www.tonypi.com

Blood, Lead, and Torchlight

Cat McDonald

Aquila, known to his peers as Aquila the Phoenician, sat in dim lamplight with a half dozen of his fellows, deep in a pile of scrolls both clean and ink-stained, his forearm cramped from a day's work and his eyes beginning to strain. He glanced back and forth between a history commandeered from a Greek ship that morning and his half-finished copy; the script blurred in his tired vision. To save the Greeks from his mistakes, he took a moment to look at the wall and stretch the cramps out of his hand.

Melanthios the Younger, who could always tell the moment anyone else looked up from his work, spoke up. "So many ships coming in from Rome lately."

"You always give me the Latin books anyway," Aquila said with a laugh. He spoke fluent Latin, Phoenician, Aramaic, and — a particular source of pride, since he shared it with their exiled Queen — Egyptian. His Greek was passable, but he didn't dare try to pass the work off to someone who might not get it done by day's end. Though he was called the Phoenician, Aquila's mother was Egyptian by way of a Phoenician grandfather, and his father a Roman. Aquila was all of these things, but he was something much worse — he was an Alexandrian, born and raised in the shadow of the Pharos.

"I can't give them all to you! My entire workload today is Latin!" Melanthios sold himself short; his Latin was near-perfect, though he was more comfortable in his native Greek.

Festus, the Roman who never allowed anyone to pass their Latin off on him, sighed and stretched his long, sinewy arms out in front of himself. "Pompey the Great has been routed, or so I'm told."

"So the Civil War's ended? Can't imagine the grain farmers will be happy now that there's no army to supply." This time, Melanthios did go back to his work, though he only wrote a few lines before looking up again.

Aquila continued staring at the wall, watching the dance of the orange lamplight while waiting for the ache in his eyes to subside. "That's not what he means. Pompey is a close friend of the Pharaoh, right?"

Festus nodded somewhere in Aquila's peripheral vision. "Exactly. And he has few friends remaining in the civilized world. Should he arrive here, the civil war may arrive with him."

"Ugh, Romans. Present company excepted, of course."

Festus shrugged. "You're Egyptian; I don't expect you to have restraint."

"Alexandrian," Aquila corrected and went back to his work. His eyes had cleared, but now his mind saw the text through a thick fog. Rome, which had always seen his homeland as a grain store to be alternately plundered and protected, had only been disinterested in Egypt because of other, more pressing concerns. With the Queen in exile building an army, the last thing Egypt needed was legions complicating things.

He dipped his pen and copied a few more words, and as he traced out Greek letters onto a fresh scroll, he began to recognize the text. Herodotus: if a heavily adapted version which Aquila hadn't seen before. It only became familiar to him when he read of Xerxes, the Persian King of Kings, demanding earth and water from the Greeks as a token of submission.

What would Rome demand, when the dust of its internal strife had settled?

The rest of Aquila's work went by quickly, because his mind was elsewhere, and his hands couldn't sit still.

~ ~ ~

The Library of Alexandria housed original copies of texts from all over the world, in numberless languages and subjects a single mind couldn't begin to list. Histories, both factual and fictional, lined its walls, as did manuals of tactics and strategy, philosophy and art and religion and food. A ship could come to Alexandria from anywhere, and when it did, its books were taken and copied, the copies returned to the owners and the originals kept for study. Aquila had copied the comedies of Aeschylus of Greece, Persian treatises on astronomy and mathematics, and Latin misunderstandings of Plato.

In the near-silent library, by the light of a dim little lamp, he traced a descending path. A set of marble stairs led into a chamber, a little tomb concealed beneath the comedies, guarded by a carving of Thoth, who seemed to watch the scribe pass with quiet concern.

Down there, in a space too small for any sound to echo, Aquila found the Library's collection of mystic texts pilfered from the world's sages. The Book of the Dead of his own people, selected works of the alchemists of Persia and further east, and accounts from the mystery cults of Greece all sat neatly alongside one another.

Some time ago, Aquila had copied one such text, and having stared at it for hours, he could recognize it instantly. A Greek text, claiming to contain the secrets of the Goddess of Witchcraft and laying out several very definite rituals. Aquila laid a hand on it, and felt a familiar tingling in his hand, the ominous sensation that had pricked at him the entire time that he'd spent copying it.

Alone in the silence, in a tiny oasis of light, he unrolled a blank scroll and began to make another copy. He didn't have time to copy the entire thing, so he read over the text, shivering, until he found the section he had been looking for.

To repel an unwanted guest:

~ ~ ~

The next day, Aquila had gathered everything he needed. He sat at the small desk in his room, flanked by two torches instead of his usual oil lamp, to honor the Queen of Crossroads. His pen and papyrus had been replaced by a stylus and a sheet of beaten lead that shone grimly in the unstable light, the ink by twin bowls, one full of dark wine and one of blood from a sacrificial sheep. At a glance, he couldn't tell the difference between them, and the scents of wine and iron and lead blended together in front of him.

He took a deep breath to quiet himself, and as he did, he could hear his city in the background. Shouts, some in one of his own languages and some foreign, and the crashing of waves against the center of civilization. Whenever Aquila tried to quiet himself, he found that waiting behind the quiet was Alexandria.

He raised his stylus to the lead and started pressing Greek letters into its surface, stopping after every line to take a breath and look over at his scroll to make sure he made no errors in the foreign alphabet, and the dim light, and unfamiliar instrument, and the surging feeling in his chest.

Then, when he had finished, he placed the lead tablet first in the blood, which crept up and stuck to his fingers, and then in the wine, reading it aloud as he did so.

"O Hekate, tender-hearted, bright-haired, and all the gods who look over travelers, hear my plea. Prevent Pompey, who is called Magnus, from crossing the threshold of this place. May the door reject him, may the earth disappear beneath his feet rather than suffer him to tread. May he wander a thousand years rather than arrive here, and may this banishment remain until I have excavated this writing and read it again aloud."

Then, taking up one of his torches, he went to find a crossroads in which to bury the thing.

~ ~ ~

Days passed, and the frantic feeling of the spell slowly ebbed from his heart. While burying it, he had barely been able to stop his hands from shaking, but days later he was working at his usual pace, without having to take regular breaks to stare at the wall and wonder what, if anything at all, he had done.

Aquila copied out a Persian book of poetry, one old enough that he couldn't read it as he copied it, and he took regular breaks to stop and pay attention to what he was copying, to feel the lush verses trying to drag him away somewhere green, rose-scented and decadent.

A shout went up, some frantic rumor whirling from one person to the next among the scribes and record-keepers. It came in splinters, *sails* one second, *Roman* another, and every piece of information stiffened Aquila's back and soon made it completely impossible to focus on his work.

Festus looked up from his work with the stony, tired, decidedly Roman expression of an old man who had seen many such minor disasters.

"I'm going," Melanthios said, already halfway through putting his work away.

"I'll join you," Aquila offered.

Festus just sighed.

Together the scribes made their way out of the dust and shade of the Library into the brilliant Alexandrian sun. It shone off the waves, searing the horizon in a ribbon of light that stayed in Aquila's vision no matter how many times he tried to blink it away. At midday, Alexandria was deafening, its streets stuffed full of people and animals and goods.

Melanthios said something in Greek that Aquila couldn't hear, and eventually just gave up and grabbed Aquila's hand as they dove into the press of people. He soon surrendered the lead, stymied by the body of a stranger everywhere he turned, and let Aquila lead the way. Turning sideways to get around a small group of people and darting between a man and a donkey, Aquila found an alley that took them to a building on the seaside with a solid earthen stair leading up to its rooftop, where people had already begun to gather.

A proud Roman trireme, true to the rumors, waited outside the harbor.

"It's definitely him, isn't it?" Melanthios leaned forward against the wall, shielding his eyes from the glare.

"It can't be."

"Hm, you're wrong there, my Phoenician friend. That's his standard if ever I've seen it. And there's a rowboat on the way in. Come to seek audience with the Pharaoh, or I'm a cow."

Aquila watched the little boat work its way toward the city, and soon enough he could see the sun glinting off a metal breastplate and the brilliant violet robe of a Roman general; his nostrils flooded with the scents of lead and blood. His heart retreated back into itself, crushing the feeling out of him, as he watched the general approach.

The boat reached the shallows, and one of the soldiers stood and got out of the boat.

Before their visitor could do the same, a flashing blade came down upon him, and Pompey, called Great by the

Romans, was hacked to death in the Alexandrian surf. On the distant warship, someone cried out in anguish, piercing the capital, and Aquila could, in that moment, hear nothing else.

"We'll be copying out accounts of this moment for the rest of our lives," Melanthios said when the scream had faded. The soldier kept hacking, and when Aquila realized he intended to take the general's head to the Pharaoh, he turned away.

~ ~ ~

After the killing, Alexandria, knowing full well that the Pharaoh had opened her doors to Roman occupation, grew tense and wary. Soldiers walked carefully, all too aware that their presence in the wrong place at the wrong time would give birth to bloodshed. Aquila took back roads in his walks home from the library, keeping his distance from the most flammable places.

This new path took him past the crossroads where he'd buried the tablet, and he couldn't look at the place without a desperate, paralyzing uncertainty grasping at him.

It hadn't been his doing. The Pharaoh had given the order, and surely would have done so regardless; it was beyond the power of a single scribe to influence a Son of Ra.

He walked past the exact spot where the tablet was buried, the disturbed earth now trampled flat by a day's worth of passing feet, and stared at it, wondering, as always, if he should dig it up and destroy it.

Torchlight blossomed out onto the road, driving his shadow away behind him.

He had to move his head to see her; she stood on the edge of the road as if she had been there all along. She was a fair woman, Greek, with curly black hair bound up behind her head in a dignified style like he'd seen on old statues. Her clothing, too, was old and simple, a dress pinned together at the shoulders, though it caught the torchlight and shone as if made from silver. Red light flickered in her dark brown eyes, not just in reflection, but as if a fire kindled just behind their surfaces.

"You seem troubled," she said to him in stiff Greek, and, though she seemed no older than eighteen, her voice sounded somehow like a grandmother's.

"Sorry! I nearly ran into you," Aquila said. He didn't know what else to say, not the least because his limited Greek tied his tongue down.

"Not at all. Is there something here?" She tilted her head sideways without breaking her gaze, and the effect was like that of a watching cobra. "Something buried here?"

Aquila blinked. "Why would you ask?"

"Buried... here?" She lowered her torch until the fire burned directly above the spot where the tablet had been concealed, her slightly pointed teeth now bared.

Aquila said nothing.

"Ah, it was you."

"Who are you?" Aquila took a step backward, but heard a dog snarling somewhere in the dark periphery around them, and froze.

She didn't move a step from her place at the edge of the road. "We are the Lampades, handmaidens to the Queen at the Crossroads. Tell me, how did you learn this?" Silence crept in between her sentences, as though she had to choose her words carefully. Perhaps she could tell he wasn't a fluent speaker of Greek.

"I... why? What will happen?"

"How did you learn this?" She leaned forward, and the firelight reflecting off her gown foretold disaster. "To touch history in this way? How did you learn?"

Aquila looked over his shoulder, and the dogs he'd heard were nowhere to be found. So, his heart lashed by panic, he broke into a run from the crossroads, into a dark side street, and down the street alone.

When he realized that he couldn't hear pursuit, he stopped and let the silence rush in. No feet, no dogs, no voices, just his own breathing and, beyond, the surf.

He followed that narrow alley until it met another. Panic choked him when he saw the orange torchlight leaking around the corner.

When he stood in the place where the two alleys met, there she was, still watching him with her eyes flickering red.

"Where? Tell me, Egyptian."

When he ran from the crossroads again, she was gone.

Aquila, now only a couple streets from his home, squeezed himself between buildings and clambered over walls rather than face her so close to where he slept.

~ ~ ~

On his normal route to work, Aquila would walk through thirty-eight crossroads. At every single one, even in bright daylight, he saw the light of her torch and the shine of her garment. Her voice stabbed through the city's thousand voices, found him in the crowd and spoke only to him. If he hurried, he could make it out of the crossroads before she finished speaking, and then her voice would vanish like a popping bubble.

"You cannot flee me for—"

"Tell me where, Egypti—"

This carried on for days. Aquila managed to find a road to work that only passed twenty-two crossroads, and hurried through them so her words were scattered. Then, she learned, and the little shards of her threats came together over the course of his walk.

"This was not ev—"

"—er meant for you, do—"

"—you know what you have taken—"

"—and from whom?"

Aquila kept his head down and hurried past her. He didn't know, of course. He had known that Alexandria would be in grave danger if she became the battleground for Roman siege engines and trench-diggers, and little else.

"I have seen—"

"—your entrance to the—"

"—Library."

Aquila stopped, and the crowd carried on without him. The nymph sat on a jar of oil by the roadside.

"Ah. I've stopped you."

"What do you want?"

"I've already said. Tell me who taught you the arts of the Queen." She rested her lit torch across her lap, and the flame didn't seem to bother her.

Aquila watched the way the fire approached the oil, and said nothing.

"Unless, Egyptian, no one taught you. Unless, somewhere in that tomb of books, someone has committed the words of the Queen to papyrus in defiance of her wishes." Like any predator, she watched his hesitation unblinkingly, and crept forward to match his slight retreats. Slowly, she stood, though she kept the head of the torch lowered. "Does such a thing exist?"

Aquila said nothing, only because the trembling in his jaw and tension in his breast smothered his words to death.

Still, she advanced, until she stood within arm's reach, until her nose almost touched his and he could smell rich wine and wood smoke coming from her dark hair and see the chaos behind her eyes. The heat from the torch singed the hair from his arm as she leaned up to him.

"Bring it to me, Egyptian. Bring me the papyrus, or I will seek it myself." For just a second, she glanced back at the oil.

~ ~ ~

Work had continued at the Library of Alexandria, but the number of books coming in had dwindled to nearly nothing. Following the death of Pompey, the general's adversary had come to the city to demand retribution for the death, and occupied Alexandria with a single legion.

And Pompey's allies now hurried to Egypt, and would doubtless lay siege. Martial law had already been declared, and Alexandria strained against the bonds like a wild horse, lashing out just to demonstrate its power before letting the riots settle back into the background chaos of the city.

Aquila, slowly, copied a history written in the vivid, pious Hebrew tradition, reading as he went a rich account of a battle Babylon had described in a single terse sentence. The record-keepers of ancient Judah had rendered it with such color and life and love, and such accounts were precious and hard to find. Any scribe would count himself blessed to have been able to see it, or the works of the obscure Persian poets, or the letters of the first Roman kings, or any number of the other treasures that passed under Aquila's hands.

That the nymph intended to burn the scroll was obvious to him. So was her threat against his city.

When his work for the day was finished, he excused himself to return to that tomb beneath the comedies. The marble Thoth watched him enter, cold white in the library's shady interior.

There Aquila sat, staring at the scrolls, his gaze settling on the scroll containing the Greek sorcery and refusing to leave it for any reason. People shuffled around above him, and he could faintly hear the city even down here in the cold earth, but the only thing on his mind was the papyrus.

He'd done it for Alexandria. Now, she found herself occupied in spite of his best efforts. He had repelled one Roman and got a legion in exchange, and now the nymph waited with her torch.

He reached forward and pulled out the scroll. No one had touched it since he had copied it; it was still in exactly the same position. The time-worn papyrus rustled softly against his hand with a barely-perceptible sound of reeds, and his lamp-light dully illuminated the fading text. Now that he knew, he could see that it had been written in a hurry, drops of ink and stray tails coming off letters betraying the panic of the scribe as he committed the sin of preserving the words of the Queen.

What sin was it to merely record? Aquila stood beneath a temple of records, a high priest in the worship of the written word. He had devoted his life to preservation of humanity's knowledge.

If he gave her this scroll, he thought, he would never see another like it. More than that; no one else would. The knowledge would be scrubbed from the world, would disappear like smoke.

He couldn't.

Aquila returned to his desk to find his colleagues had also finished work early and left, so he set about making another copy of the scroll.

~ ~ ~

It was past dark when he finished, but when he stepped out into the cool night, he carried a copy of the scroll under his arm. The original was safe in the basement, far from the nearest crossroads.

As soon as his path met another street, she was waiting for him.

"Have you brought it, Egyptian?"

He extended the scroll to her, and she took it in her free hand, grasping one end, letting it unroll and flap carelessly to the ground. Aquila winced, and for a second she looked up at him before returning her gaze to the scroll.

She stood there looking it over in stony silence while he watched, and now and again gave a delicate nod. Was she satisfied? Aquila stepped back, ready to carry on his journey home, when the nymph let out a quiet snort.

"Your ink betrays you, Egyptian. This is a copy, is it not?" She looked up at him, and this time he could see an inferno raging scarlet in her gaze.

"We house copies! I don't know where the original is."

The nymph watched him like a lioness, her gaze fixed on minute movements of his face and hands.

"The copy cannot exist either." She held the torch to the papyrus and it lit up in a ripple, giving way to a ribbon of flame that cascaded to the ground in front of her and coiled at her feet. Black letters appeared briefly in the radiance before being swallowed utterly by fire.

The nymph turned to walk away, trailing the still-burning scroll behind her like the train of a queen, and Aquila watched her recede into the darkness.

Before she vanished entirely from view, she lifted the end of the scroll still in her hands, and carelessly, with a flick of her slender wrist, threw it. It cut a brilliant arc through the air, an illuminated bridge that seared the sky above the rooftops.

Toward the Library.

When the cry of "fire" rose, the nymph was already gone. Aquila turned and ran back, his nose tormented again by the scent of lead and blood.

By the time he made it back to the library, he could already see flames through the windows. His legs gave up on him, and he fell to his knees and wept. Centuries of work, of knowledge, gone. His eyes burned and his throat stung and tears splashed into the dust in front of him and he could hardly breathe.

Some of the nations represented in that collection no longer existed. Some of the languages on those scrolls had no living speakers. The words of centuries, generations of long-dead minds vanished into smoke and ash while Aquila crumbled to nothing in the street.

"Get up, Phoenician!" A kick to his side jarred another sob out of him, and he looked up to see Festus, grim as ever, with an armload of scrolls. "Grab what you can!"

With a heave of his exhausted arms, Aquila shoved himself back into a standing position and wiped his face on his sleeve.

"Where will we go?"

"The Serapeum. Hurry!" With that, he turned on his heel just in time for a handful of Roman soldiers to arrive.

Aquila entered the library. Thanks to the tears, he hardly felt the smoke in his eyes.

He walked past Thoth to see which of the poets could be saved.

* * *

>>> *Little is known about the magic traditions of ancient Europe and the Mediterranean, in part because most magical orders kept their lore a tightly-guarded secret and forbade the creation of magical texts. Such a text could transmit sacred knowledge to the uninitiated–a deadly sin.*

What we know about the magic of the Mediterranean world comes from unearthed "curse tablets", like the one created in the story. Clay tablets praying to the gods to make a rival ugly, or enact some other revenge, have been found in Greek and Roman ruins. The ritual of their creation remains a mystery.

Cat McDonald

Cat McDonald is an Edmonton-based author, editor, and game designer who can see the whole city from here. Her short stories have appeared in *Tesseracts Fifteen*, and *Here Be Monsters*, and she co-edited *The Dame Was Trouble*, from Coffin Hop Press. You can listen to her playing Invisible Sun on the podcast *Truth Hidden Among Hearts* (www. hiddenamonghearts.com), and she sometimes tweets using @CatlingGun. She is, it's safe to assume, up to something.

The Guardian of Wisdom

Mary-Jean Harris

It was called the heart of wisdom. I had considered it little more than a legend, a fanciful tale told by those in the East to explain the great wisdom of the philosophers and priests of Egypt. I hadn't known then, on that day thirteen years ago in the garden of fig and myrtle trees at Mieza, that Alexander would take it to heart.

It was just after midday, and after a meal of barley bread and deer's meat — Alexander and his Companions had hunted early that morning — Alexander had been inclined to stroll with me on the shady pathways while the other boys rested to escape the summer heat. We had stopped next to a waterfall that twisted down to feed a stream flowing through the clearing. It originated from trickles of water leaking through cracks in the upper stones of the Nymphs' cave, about twenty feet above us, creating a gloss of moisture like sweat over the dark rocks. Down here, the trickles combined to form a greater flow that misted cool moisture upon my warm cheeks as it fell into a shallow pond next to the entrance of the cave.

Alexander, never bothered by any turn of the weather, removed his leather sandals and left the shade of the pathway to wade in the pool. The water, a mirror to the heavens, was bright cerulean, glossy like a jewel and flecked with glints of white from reflected sunlight. Alexander also shone with his golden curls of hair and polished gold leaf belt recently sent from his mother back in Pella.

He had asked me to tell him something about Egypt, so, after he'd returned to the path, I mentioned the heart of wisdom as we continued strolling next to the pool. The pathway was lined with small blue mountain flowers and twisted wild roses of cream white and pink.

"But what is it really?" the boy asked.

"What do you think?" I was preparing him to one day rule Macedon, when he would have to analyze the claims of others for himself.

"But, Aristotle, I don't know!"

"What would you guess?"

The boy frowned. He was used to getting what he wanted, from anyone and at any time, yet I had determined to break him out of it. I had no doubt then I would succeed, for he was a clever boy, honest, and devoted to his studies, but most of all, relentlessly determined. I had yet to appreciate just how far that determination could extend.

"Well," he relented. "It must be some sort of treasure, guarded by the priests."

"It is a legend, told by scholars and statesman regarding the wisdom held by the philosophers of Egypt. The heart of wisdom contains the secrets guarded by wise men throughout the ages. It is a curious legend, most likely nothing more. Those who believe in its existence speak of an object of great power hidden within the most sacred pyramid."

"Which is?"

"Oh, one of the ones at Giza, I would say. But I have never been there. Do not concern yourself with such details. It is an enlightening case to consider as an example of how a legend can arise from improper understanding, when one has glimpsed a grain of truth while the fuller wisdom is only grasped—"

"What about legends that have more truth than falsehood?"

"Certainly there are some."

"But this heart of wisdom, whoever has it would be the most powerful man in the world, wouldn't he?"

"Perhaps he would."

Alexander's steps became ponderous, his sandaled feet crunching the dry lichen between the stones of the pathway, slowly, as if he was creeping up on someone. "Who has seen it?" he eventually said.

Deciding to leave the discussion of metaphorical legends for another day, I humored him this once. "Assuming, that is, it is a real object, only the priests would have access to this power."

"And these priests... can anyone become a priest?"

"In theory, anyone can. Yet only those with the brightest of minds and the most intuitive of souls are able to pass the years of training and initiation required to join the higher priesthood. Of course, my teacher Plato was permitted to enter on account of his unparalleled wisdom."

"And you too? Would they let you in?"

I smiled. "I do not believe so."

"They must let the king in, if he wanted to."

"Yes, the Egyptian king functions as the conduit between the gods and men, so may enter." I glanced sidelong at him, catching what I took to be a dangerous glint in his blue eyes, like a wave rising from the depths of the ocean, and added, "The true king of Egypt, of the royal bloodline, may enter. Although the Persians have taken over the land, the priests will not bring Artaxerxes nor the present Egyptian governor, Mazaces, into the council of their inner priesthood."

"But if Mazaces knew about it, he could just force his way in!"

"I'm sure he could, but I do not believe he is aware of this legend." *Or,* I added to myself. *He doesn't take it seriously.*

Alexander let out a sharp breath. "To think the Persians could gain this great power over the world, could gain this magic—"

"I never spoke of magic, Alexander."

"And use it to conquer us all." His cheeks were flushed, though whether it was from the heat of the day or the notion of the Persians wielding a magical weapon against Macedon was not apparent. I now realize I should have dispelled his notion of a magical Egyptian artifact then and there, dissuaded him against any pursuit of the occult arts. I had glimpsed such a power long ago, when I was no older than Alexander himself, and had learned, through pinpricks of fear, that such powers were not meant for men to seek. Yet these powers were exceedingly rare, and I knew most such legends were no more than metaphors for wisdom which, to the unlearned, take on the mien of the supernatural when they are in truth entirely grounded in the world and the minds of men.

Yet I did not tell Alexander this. Whether it was due to the midday heat or my will for him to think it out for himself, I do not now recall. I only smiled and said, "With a great king like your father, I would not worry about any mischief the Persians might get up to in Egypt. Now, this afternoon, we will have a discussion of logic and formal debates. I will have you boys debating…"

I continued speaking about my plans for their afternoon studies, yet although Alexander gave occasional signs of affirmation, I could tell he had something else on his mind. Something else that would return to haunt me thirteen years later.

~ ~ ~

The soldier who handed me the letter scrutinized me. He was tall and well-built, his face centered with a snub nose burnt brown from long training in the sun. He wore the bronze-plated armor of Alexander's elite guard atop a white linen tunic and pleated kilt that reached to his knees, below which were polished bronze greaves. I knew him to be Alexander's man at once by his eyes: they had the same flame of decisive fervor that had caught in the minds and souls of his followers, growing brighter at every conquest Alexander accomplished.

I took the letter and unrolled it, taking a few steps back from two of my students who had been strolling with me outside the Lyceum. It was a warm spring morning, tempered by a sea breeze off the Athenian coast. I had been speaking about geometry, in particular, the mathematics found in nature, in everything from the arrangement of the heavenly bodies to the veins in the leaves of the trees whose boughs shaded the pathways we trod. I didn't know how much of my lessons Alexander had remembered from our time in Mieza, but his letter proved at least one of our discussions had not been forgotten. It read:

Alexander to Aristotle. Greetings. As you would have heard, I am now the Pharaoh of Egypt. It is legitimate, for the people know I am their liberator from the Persians and I was crowned by an Egyptian priest. Yet when I asked to see the heart of wisdom, they were elusive, and my men have been unable to find it. I require your assistance to seek it out and speak to the priests. You are to come to the palace at Memphis with my Companion, Mitron, whom I have entrusted with your well-being during your journey. I expect to see you soon.

The image of Alexander seated upon the ancient throne of the Egyptian kings, crowned in the red and white double crown while the Egyptian people worshipped him as a sun god, came unbidden to my mind. I shook my head. By being crowned Pharaoh, he had gone beyond the mark of a conqueror, and I couldn't help but feel it was my fault.

I returned to the solider, who was speaking to my students in excited tones about the great feast held in Egypt at Alexander's crowning. I cleared my throat, surprising them out of their contemplation of the gilt festival, replete with banners proclaiming Alexander's victory in both Macedonian and Egyptian scripts, and women wearing garlands of exotic flowers that were unknown to the Hellenic world, and told Mitron the only possible answer.

~ ~ ~

With the fair spring weather, the sea route to Egypt would have been pleasant had it not been for the ambiguous feeling of being something between a guest of honor and a prisoner. I suspected if I had shown any reluctance to leave Athens, Mitron was under orders to take me to Egypt by force, which I had no doubt he would succeed. We reached the coast of Egypt four days later in a city recently founded by Alexander, and rather pretentiously named for him. A felucca with a cramped inner cabin, filled with bags of grain and a chest of treasures, bore us down the Nile to Memphis. We were accompanied by three more of Alexander's soldiers who ignored me completely as they discussed their next campaign to Jerusalem, set to begin next month. I didn't mind. Having never been to Egypt, I was overcome with a wonder at the natural world, the spindly-legged egrets with their cloud-white plumage, the elegant spread of sand dunes beyond the fertile plains bordering the Nile, swept into rippling curves by the wind, mapping the turns of the seasons. The snap of the falucca's white sail in the breeze and the splosh of water against the hull of the boat faded into dimness, a calm palate in my mind from which thoughts of this land arose. I could, for a time, forget why I was here, forget the daunting task of convincing the most determined man in the world to abandon the mission to which he had devoted himself ever since he was thirteen years old. For now, I was calculating and storing facts of the natural world within my mind, interrupted only when Mitron brought me a skin of water and some dried perch halfway through our journey.

In accord with the superhuman efficiency of Alexander's army, we arrived at Memphis only five days after I had received Alexander's letter. Mud brick houses and fishers' huts lined the upper banks of the Nile, far enough from the shore to escape the seasonal inundations. Mitron obtained a camel for me, and so from the back of that curious beast, I surveyed the land as we passed into the city. At every turn we were met with Macedonian soldiers, who, although armed, were manifestly at ease after having succeeded in their conquest of this ancient land. The wide main road, bordered by fig and acacia trees and leading to the temple of Apis, was strewn with lotus flowers from the night's festivities. Yet after the troddings of merchants with pack mules and camels, the petals were crushed into the hard-packed earth in contorted patterns, no longer white, but wilted and rust-colored.

After speaking with another soldier, Mitron informed me Alexander had gone south to subdue a group of Persian mercenaries, and, as he put it, "liberate the people." So I did not receive much of a reception upon my arrival at the palace apart from a brief meeting with Cassander, who, as one of Alexander's Companions, had also studied under me in Mieza in his youth. I hardly recognized the lanky, mouse-eared boy in the tall, red-bearded man before me, clad in light, silver armor and a pale blue cloak. Cassander had remained here to see to the retrieval of the heart of wisdom and to arrange spies to watch over the priests of various temples. My presence here, he claimed as he led me through the vast courtroom of the palace, was a blessing from the gods, for he had been making no progress and was convinced that I would be able to solve the problem in a couple of days. I made no comment on this, and Cassander, apparently taking me to be brooding over a plan of action, led the way silently.

The vast stone pillars lining the hall bore hieroglyphic inscriptions from ages past, painted in orderly, yet at the same time, beautifully diverse rows ascending to the ceiling, their greens like crushed herbs, blues like patches of the early evening sky, and reds like dried, crusted blood. A lower door at the back of the hall, framed with more inscriptions and emanating an earthy scent, led us to the inner temple. We stopped before an opening curtained by a maroon silk cloth, which Cassander parted, gesturing for me to enter.

I realized at once my uneasiness about being a prisoner hadn't been ill-founded. Although I hadn't entered anything resembling a prison cell, the lavish room, equipped with everything to please even a man of luxury, spoke of confinement until I had achieved what Alexander desired.

Cassander, a trifle hesitantly, expounded on the collection of Egyptian scrolls, newly arranged amongst bronze statues of both Greek and Egyptian deities, from Heracles wrestling a lion to the cat-headed goddess Bastet, a few delicate wooden chests lined with gold, and some other curious artifacts of Egypt. The room was newly frescoed in bright colors, depicting a Macedonian valley on one wall, and on the opposite wall between two large windows, the image of an angelic boy remarkably similar to how Alexander had looked in his youth. I couldn't help but grin sardonically at the thought of Alexander arranging what had once been an Egyptian's chamber into an abode for a Macedonian scholar, complete with a low cot covered with linen sheets and a fine wooden desk laid out with fresh papyrus, reed pens, and ink. The surface of the desk was inlaid with brass, depicting an engraved map of the known world with the cities Alexander had conquered or founded labeled prominently in Greek script. A scent of myrrh and Kyphi incense still lingered in the air.

"The King left you a note," Cassander said, returning to the desk and gesturing to a scroll next to the blank papyrus. "If you need anything else, at any time, just inform the guard out the door."

"I have a guard, do I?"

"For your own protection, teacher, only for your protection."

"Did Alexander tell you that?"

Cassander looked taken aback. "Of course!" Something of that mousy boy returned to his features as he spoke.

"I see. Well, thank you for your hospitality, Cassander. I shall settle in and read Alexander's letter."

After Cassander departed, I peered around the curtain and saw that, indeed, a guard had followed us here and was standing about halfway down the hall, leaning on his spear. I retreated back into the room and sat behind the desk, taking up Alexander's note.

> *Alexander to Aristotle. I trust Mitron has delivered you to Memphis according to my orders. I apologize for not greeting you myself, yet when I had written my first letter, I had not known that I would need to address matters in the south myself. Nevertheless, I have outfitted this room for you so that you may begin your investigations: the scrolls on the shelf may be useful, but I cannot read hieroglyphs and the priests claim to be ignorant of the language. They are lying, of course, but I need to keep them under the pretense that they are highly respected so have not pressed the matter. I have also included a list of the priests within Memphis with whom you will have to speak as well as others in neighboring cities. I believe I shall return in no more than two weeks' time, and I am sure you'll have no trouble obtaining the heart of wisdom by then. You shall be rewarded greatly, my friend and teacher. Until then.*

I wasn't sure whether I should laugh or moan: as it was, I sat back in the chair and managed a pained chuckle. Crossing my hands across my chest, I thought back to Alexander's schooling days and realized that I had been mistaken in teaching him to so rigorously strive for excellence, to prove and perfect himself through noble deeds. Such teachings are, of course, highly beneficial to those with a more tepid drive to achieve honor through excellence, but for someone who was already so motivated, so driven to be the best in everything he set his mind to…. Yet it was too late now. As far as I could tell, Alexander would not be content until he had conquered the known world, and then striven beyond that to lands as yet untouched by the hands of men. He would either succeed, or die in the attempt.

Yet concerning the heart of wisdom: I had never determined whether it was a real object of power, or, if it were one, if I even wanted to obtain it for Alexander. A creeping dread still lingered within me from my glimpse of that great, yet at the same time, morbidly terrifying power I had witnessed in my youth. The truth was that I was not at all convinced that the heart of wisdom was merely a metaphor. It might be real, given the great feats the Egyptian kings of old and their priests had accomplished. Indeed, ever since I had entered the temple, I had felt the remnants of a flame of power creeping amongst the very particles of the air, a flame kindled in ages past and now sparking to life at the whispered words of the high priests.

I shook my head and stood, taking a spot at the window where the warm, dry air dispelled any lingering incense of Kyphi.

~ ~ ~

I studied the scrolls left to me that afternoon, though not with the intention of discovering the heart of wisdom. Cassander, enthused that I was apparently making progress, spoke to me of Alexander's recent campaigns over a dinner of roast quail, pearl barley with capers, and red Egyptian wine. It was decided that we would call upon the high priests of Memphis tomorrow so that I could question them, and, as I was equipped with knowledge from their secret scrolls, Cassander had no doubt I would succeed.

By the time I retired for the night, I was still unsure how to proceed. Shortly after nightfall, beneath a silvery shaft of moonlight that passed through a parting in the linen curtains, I fell into an uneasy slumber. I had never been one to dream about the fantastical, those flights of whimsy that capture the minds of youth and poets, yet that night my mind meandered through visions which might have arisen in a fevered delirium.

I was in a long, dimly-lit hallway ascending to some undefinable height. As I walked on, I could only perceive the next few paces before me, for at every step I beheld visions reflected in the polished dark stone beneath me, leaping up to manifest in a cloud of sand, glinting with a hue of tarnished gold. The first vision showed me a kilted Egyptian man standing on the top platform of a step pyramid at night, his eyes closed, and his arms raised to the starry heavens. The next vision, that same man holding a curiously shaped golden object about the size of a fist which, though inscribed with bands of pearly hieroglyphs, had a remarkably similar shape to a human's heart. The next vision after that, the same small object in the desert where, over an elapsed period of time, supple green foliage blossomed from the sand. That vision transformed to yet another: the heart in the hands of a pharaoh gazing out over a limestone quarry and causing hewn stones the size of small houses to raise into the air and proceed in a line across fifty miles of desert. They hovered with an eerie fluidity, like phantoms of ancient beasts, and were eventually received by a group of workers and priests to incorporate into a pyramid.

Dozens of other images like these blazed before me within the miasma of that golden desert sand, recounting great deeds performed with this heart and how it had remained within the secret care of the Egyptian priesthood. Until now, now...

I felt a cold hand, clawlike with protruding bones, grasp my neck. I awoke immediately, grasping my throat with clammy hands, but there was nothing there. The room was cooler with the night wind from the desert dancing sinuously through the curtain. I sat up, removing the sheet and using it to wipe my sweating brow.

Of course, there was nothing amiss, but I couldn't shake off the profound touch of that vision, continuing to swirl like a sandstorm through my mind. Had I been an incredulous man, I would have deemed what I had beheld to be a true history of the heart of wisdom, but I knew that being in this ancient temple could have certainly conjured up something that fanciful.

Yet as I got out of bed and headed to the desk to light a lantern, the visions still felt so real. None of my dreams in the past had been so vivid, never before.... I paused as I was leaning down toward the lantern. I felt something around my neck, a chain that hadn't been there when I had retired to sleep. It was cold against my warm skin, like the claw that had gripped me, and from it hung a large object, swinging before me as I leaned over the desk. I straightened, quickly lit the lantern, and with equal amounts of horror and wonder, beheld a strange golden object on the chain around my neck. The heart of wisdom. Its surface gleamed a dusky gold in the firelight, and the white inscriptions glowed in the bands around its surface. I raised it to my eyes, my heart pounding, yet this cool golden heart stirred not a beat.

"How—" I muttered, turning it over. The inscriptions were in hieroglyphs, so I had to concentrate to understand their meaning. When I began to read, another voice arose to speak them, a deep, passionless voice whose words seemed to drip like cold water into the crevices of my mind.

He who comes in possession of the Heart of Osiris is entrusted with its secrets, and must keep it concealed from the eyes of all those who are unworthy. Only he whose wisdom is unparalleled by all but the gods may wield it, and only he whose fortitude is likewise unparalleled may guard it.

When the voice ceased, I released the heart, and it thumped back onto my chest. It had been real — but how was that possible? How could I have it within my grasp? I did not want it, did not want anything of such a nature. And yet, there must have been a reason for this. Knowing that I was not at all *unparalleled by all but the gods* in wisdom, I figured I must instead be the one to guard it. But just to have it next to me, this mystic power, heavy against my chest, unsettled me deeply. Could I not return it to the priests? Or, I thought hesitantly, give it to Alexander? For he wouldn't stop looking until he found it. If I could not learn of its location from the priests, he would search all their temples, probe every member of their order....

"No," I whispered. I sat behind the desk, the heaviness of the golden heart making my neck droop. They had anticipated that. The priests must have known that, eventually, Alexander would discover it. They had needed to remove it, prevent this man who was no sage of wisdom from using it to conquer the world. There had to be a limit, and despite his noble aspirations, Alexander had no limits in his ambitions. The priests needed another guardian; they needed someone who was beyond Alexander's suspicions and wise enough to guard it and offer it only to one who was worthy enough to wield its powers. They had needed me.

I did not want this burden. But I was not fool enough to shirk the great task set before me, even if it had arisen from the misting sands of Egyptian magic. I took hold of the golden heart again and lifted the chain around my neck. I approached the shelves of artifacts until I felt a loose piece of wood. I carefully removed it, and, as I had expected in this place that had once been a sanctuary for the secret order of priests, there was a small compartment about half a foot into the wall. It was dusted with grains of sand, and for a moment light from the lantern on the desk behind me caught on the sand, giving it a dull golden gleam. There was, physically, nothing mysterious or unusual about it, yet it recalled to my mind the mist of sand that had swept the heart of wisdom's history into my dream. Somewhere between the laws of the natural world and the realm of thoughts, there existed another realm equally real yet hardly as tangible as the thoughts within our minds. It was here the powers of the priests lay, here that the powers of the golden heart worked to captivate and elude philosophers such as myself.

I carefully set the heart in the wall amid the sand and closed the opening, rearranging a scarab of milky pink agate that I had displaced in the process. I would keep the heart here while I remained in Egypt, yet I now knew that, although a part of me despised it, I could elude these mysteries no longer. The heart of wisdom would be, unless I discovered someone suitable to wield it, within my guardianship. Perhaps I was not wise enough to wield it and accomplish great feats. But I was wise enough *not* to use it. And that was enough.

~ ~ ~

When Cassander came to find me the next morning, I was already at work studying the scrolls that had been left for me, though for the sake of scholarship rather than to discover a mystery that had already, beyond reason, found me instead. A servant came in behind him carrying a tray, a young Egyptian man with a shaved head and cream white kilt. He set the tray on my desk and left Cassander and I to break our fast.

Cassander, after swallowing a warm, spiced date drink that was popular in Egypt, and making haste through some figs and honeyed flatbread, was ready to embark to the priests. I hastened my own meal and followed him to the priests' wing of the palace, the inner sanctuary behind the throne room where, lined with limestone columns that shone a polished white, a man was waiting for us.

He stood as still as the ageless fortifications around him, his hands clasped at his waist, and his dark eyes unblinking as we approached. He wore the long white sheath of the priesthood, adorned with a simple belt of gold around his narrow waist.

"Greetings, Nakht," Cassander spoke, a bit hesitantly.

The priest, however, only regarded me. His long fingers, pale for an Egyptian's, rose to stroke his slightly pointed chin. "Aristotle," he began, his voice deep and hollow, like a hidden tomb, "the great philosopher."

At first, I did not speak. I knew his voice, the voice that had spoken through the golden heart to read its inscription. I swallowed and said, "I am Aristotle."

There was a slight upturn of his thin lips, almost a grin, and he said, "I trust we will understand each other very well."

I returned the smile for what it was. "I believe we shall."

* * *

>>> *Aristotle (384–322 B.C.) is one of the most eminent philosophers of the Ancient World. Often known as "The Philosopher" or "The Father of Western Philosophy," Aristotle's philosophical inquiries covered disciplines from logic and politics, to physics and biology, to ethics and aesthetics. He founded a philosophical school and library at Athens' Lyceum, where he produced many of his hundreds of books. After his teacher Plato died, Aristotle left Athens to tutor Alexander the Great in Macedon, assisting in the upbringing of a ruler who would conquer a great portion of the known world.*

Mary-Jean Harris

The Guardian of Wisdom: Mary-Jean Harris writes historical and other-world fantasy stories. She is the owner of Fairytale Princess Parties in Ottawa, Ontario, and has a Masters degree in theoretical physics. Mary-Jean has published various short stories in anthologies and online such as the Tesseracts anthologies, *Polar Expressions, SciPhi Journal*, and *Allegory Ezine*. Mary-Jean is also the author of the series *The Soul Wanderers*.

www.thesoulwanderers.blogspot.ca/

By A Thread

Geoff Gander and Fiona Plunkett

Freydís

Freydís Eiriksdottir ran a finger along the short staff of wool batting. The red dye was even throughout; the resulting thread would have made a fine garment, were it destined for that purpose. She picked up her spindle and teased a strand of wool over the hook, wrapping it down the length and tying it beneath the round soapstone whorl at the base. "Gudrun, please tell everyone I am not to be disturbed," she said.

The stout, red-haired girl gathered up her sewing and stood. "As you wish, Lady," she said. The hem of her light brown dress swished as she made for the door. She turned at the threshold. "If word comes from our men…?" Her voice trailed off before the hopeful note became too apparent.

"I will tell you," said Freydís. She turned away from her servant and looked out the window, and waited for Gudrun to close the door. It was a cloudless day — rare for Vinland, as she had discovered. The maples and evergreens swayed gently in the ever-present breeze, which was uncharacteristically calm today — another fact of life here to which she had grown accustomed. A fenced vegetable garden lay outside the window. It was too early to tell if the turnips and cabbage would do better this year; were it not for the abundant fish, everyone would have starved by now. *None of this could matter, in the end.* She would know by day's end.

Freydís rolled the spindle against her thigh and let it drop. It wobbled in mid-air like the mast of a ship pitching in a storm as a thin red line thickened around its base. Her father had once told her that a wise woman had read the spindle before his first voyage west and predicted great wealth. Eirik the Red had found Greenland instead of gold — wealth in a different form — and left his children with good land. Freydís's grip tightened on the staff of batting. Eirik also passed on all his good fortune to her older brother, Leif, whose own adventures led him to Vinland. *Even here, on the edge of the world, I stand in others' shadows.*

She grimaced and pushed away those thoughts. Spinning fortunes required focused calm to not only see distant events and the flickering threads of possibility amid the tangled knots of the fabric of life, but also to gently nudge the weave of fate. Her husband, Thorvard, was leading a force of men against the Skraelings somewhere to the south. Fate was woven by a thread, and hers must hold. *Sif, Mother of Earth and Giver of Grain, give me clear sight so we can prosper in this new land.*

Freydís spun the spindle again and cast her senses outwards, this time imagining herself running along the thread like a spider on its web. Her mind reached out to her husband, rising through the sod roof of her hall and above the cluster of buildings that made up Leifsbuðir. Light forest bracketed the camp — that her brother had founded — on three sides, while the calm, dark blue waters of the shallow bay opened northwards to Greenland and her old life. The rocky arms of the bay encircled Leifsbuðir like a mother holding her babe. She rose higher and looked south, past lakes, rocky ridges, rivers, and bogs. *Let the tidings be good.*

~ ~ ~

They held the hill — for now.

"Will they return?" asked a young voice to Thorvard's right. However old the boy might be, he'd be a man — here or in Valhalla — before the day was over.

"I'd bet my life on it," said Thorvard. He glanced left and right at his companions — too few to hold the hill overlooking the cove where their boat was anchored. The Skraelings were no doubt hiding in the forest that encircled the hill's base, content to wait until lack of food forced his band to abandon their position. Had it been another few days, they could have built a palisade at the hill's crown and, with a bit of successful hunting and fishing, been able to play a waiting game of their own.

"We can't hide up here forever," said a man. "Better to meet them, come what may."

Thorvard glared. "What did you leave in Greenland that would make you want to give up the rich land we hold here?"

"A stead where no one was trying to kill me."

Thorvard frowned, but said nothing. Leif had shown him the fine timber he had found here, and the rich pelts he had acquired from the Skraelings in trade. He had known it would be a gamble to go beyond the lands his brother-in-law had visited to seek his own fortune. Yet he also saw how his wife seethed in her brother's shadow, living in a loaned — rather than given — camp. He would support Freydís as a husband must. The Skraelings here had wanted his men's swords and spears instead of the bolts of cloth and pieces of worked amber, and quickly grew hostile. Whether out of fear or anger, his brother Bjarni had struck — and fallen — first.

"They're back!"

A ring of stout spearmen emerged from the trees and encircled the base of the hill. They wore leather cloaks belted about the waist, and rigid leather bands protected their arms. One of them, wearing a tall leather cap decorated with shells that framed his gleaming, ochre-reddened face, stepped forward and shouted at them, shaking his spear and pointing it at them.

"Hold the line, and spears ready!" said Thorvard. Twenty round shields rose higher and clacked together into a ring of wooden scales, like the Midgard serpent eating his tail. Gleaming steel spearheads sprouted over the top, quivering in their readiness to strike. Thorvard hoped he would have time to draw his sword after his spear found its home.

A deep roar rose from the Skraelings, and they surged up the hill. A scattering of long shafts arced overhead and clattered against the shields or embedded themselves in the turf in the Norsemen's midst. Thorvard grunted in acknowledgment of the ploy to distract and unsettle an opponent. If he fell, it would be a valorous end.

~ ~ ~

The thread thrummed. Freydís's eyes snapped open. She blinked in the darkness of her chamber and took a slow breath to steady her pounding heart; coming down from riding the weave was always a shock. There would be bloodshed in the south — the question was whose, and how much. She cocked her head and listened past the muted hubbub of the household. For an instant, while she watched her husband fight, she thought she had sensed the pulse of another riding the weave. *Nothing.* She sighed with relief and stepped into the main hall, and acknowledged the anxious looks of the household. Gudrun briefly met her eyes and looked down, her skirt bunched in tight fists. Freydís gently squeezed her shoulder; she was not the only one with family or loved ones in the south. "I have consulted the Fates, and everything still hangs in balance," she said. "There will be fighting, but Leifsbuðir is safe for now."

Sighs of relief broke the tense silence. Freydís nodded and went out to stand by the shoreline. She breathed deeply and gazed northwards. A gentle summer breeze from the south caressed her, carrying the scents of ripened berries and fresh flowers. The ships bobbed lightly by the dock. She could understand why her brother had chosen this place for his stronghold.

Life would continue for the moment, but strong as her people were, they were outnumbered by folk who were defending their homes, and who knew the land far better. Her brother had warned her that nothing she built in Vinland would last. He may have refused to give her the camp he had built here, but she would not be the one to lose it. Her grip on her spindle tightened.

Pedthae

"Focus harder! The pattern will not make itself."

Pedthae nodded in acknowledgement to the older woman and bent closer over the small, hide-wrapped wooden hoop nestled in her lap. She grabbed the piece of sinew and yanked it towards her, threading it through a nub of polished bone and tying it to a perpendicular strand of sinew she had already tied, before bringing it the rest of the way. It was the fourth one she had made today, and Demasduit was just as exacting as she had been with the first one.

"Are you sure that is the right way?" asked Demasduit.

"I am, Mother," said Pedthae, fighting to keep irritation from her voice. Drawing a line through bone would protect the life of the one who used this talisman, and sectioning the ring into four quadrants would honor the four directions, the elements and the ancestors. The question was whether the Great Shaman would agree that the medicine wheel was good.

Demasduit ran a gnarled finger along the sinew and plucked it, nodding to herself as she heard the thrum, like bowstrings pulled taught. "This one shall also go to our warriors. Now that I know you can work hard and apply what I have taught you, I have a greater task for you."

Pedthae blinked. "What could be more important than protecting our warriors?"

"Protecting our people is meaningless if there is no land to support us. This land is a sacred gift and we must honor it as such," said Demasduit. "I have dreamt of these hairy white men from across the sea. They were sent by the bad spirits, and would pen us like they do their animals. They do not hunt, as we do. They capture, imprison, and slaughter at will. No life is sacred to them. Even if we make peace, as our chief wishes, they will always push for more. The further I dream, I see none of our people on these lands. This cannot come to pass. Our people cannot become a mere memory."

"But this is our land, Mother; we know it. Our ancestors have lived here from time immemorial. Can we force them to be peaceful?"

Demasduit smiled sadly. "We can win a battle, maybe a few. But there are many more of these men in their own lands, and they will keep coming to build their mamateeks of wood and stone. The Great Spirit spoke to me of this, and any who make peace with the white men cannot go to his island after they die. This would divide our people, and we would be no more." Her gaze shifted from Pedthae to the newly-crafted talisman.

"What must I do?"

"Great changes must come if we are to live, and so a great medicine wheel is needed. My hands are too old to weave it;

someone else must craft the wheel and follow its path among the spirits. I ask a lot of you, Pedthae, for if you walk this path — which some call the Spider Path — far more may yet be asked. You may not be the same again."

Pedthae looked from her mentor to her callused hands. Before her training she had thought that the medicine wheels were made to protect people, heal the sick, but one of Demasduit's first lessons was that the tools of the Spirit World came in many forms, some of them innocuous. Her stomach clenched at the thought of making sacrifices to unknown powers, but she saw the fear in people's eyes when they spoke of the white men from the sea. Her promise to protect the people outweighed her personal beliefs to harm none. *How can I do any less than what is needed of me?*

She just hoped that what was needed would not be more than she could give.

~ ~ ~

Pedthae jumped at every scream and shout erupting from the battle at the hill. Demasduit had dreamt that no harm would befall her that day if she remained hidden and silent, but she wrestled with the urge to watch the battle unfold, to know the threat the white men posed so that she could help her people. Despite their skill and courage, the Beothuk warriors seemed unable to do anything to stop the invaders. The white men had hair on their faces, their chests, and their arms. They wore leather, as her people did, but covered it with small pieces of flat metal that seemed to turn even the sharpest stone knives and spears. Their own weapons were also of metal, which she had seen before, and knew that her warriors were starting to learn how to make. Her stomach churned as she watched them slice through flesh and bone as easily as she might peel the bark off a tree. *Demasduit was right: There can be no peace.*

Pedthae's hands shook as she opened the pouch next to her and pulled out a large, hide-wrapped wooden hoop — Demasduit's last talisman. "The Spider Path will demand much of you, but you are ready," she had said on the eve of her journey to the hill where the invaders had been spotted.

Ready for what?

A loud cheer erupted from the invaders, who now surged down the hill, hacking at anyone who stood in their way. Pedthae's breath caught. *The talismans aren't working!* She could finish the great medicine wheel and use it to strengthen the protection over her people, and the tide of battle might turn. She frantically tied a fresh piece of sinew to the hoop and drew it down to anchor it between two other strands. She took a handful of polished stones from her pouch and threaded the sinew through them. It was rough, but the angle was correct.

But there are many more of these men in their own lands, said Demasduit in her mind.

Pedthae's hand froze. There had to be another way. Her mentor spoke again, and this time Pedthae wondered whether this was memory or dream: *The spider's web catches all that pass through it, because its strands go in all directions and touch all things.*

"Great Mother, are you there?" asked Pedthae softly. The din of battle was her only reply. *The Spider Path is the great web of life and all that happens in it. It touches past, present, and future. I can't tell the spider what to spin, but I can be like the wind and blow the silk strands in a certain direction, and follow it wherever it may lead.*

Pedthae studied the stones and bones enmeshed in the center of the great medicine wheel, shut out the screams and shouts that were drawing near, and dove into the web, willing herself to be part of it.

The pattern of the crossed sinews grew larger and became a crossroads, each path heading into the distance over a misty plain. She probed the paths with her senses — one of them would lead to a place where the white men would leave her people in peace.

She jerked suddenly and gasped for breath as a constricting sensation, as though someone was binding her with cords, clamped around her. No way was open now. A force began to push her upwards, out of the wheel and back into the living world. Pedthae forced down a rising wave of panic in her chest and pulled out her stone knife. Someone else was walking the Spider Path, someone who meant harm. The invisible bonds tightened, pinning her arms to her sides. The crossroads beneath her began to fade into the mists while the roar of battle grew clearer.

She tried to fight her — for it had to be a her — but the other walker was strong. She glanced up, as the sky turned dark. Stars twinkled to life; more stars emerged than she had ever seen. It was a sign. Her ancestors were returning, however fleetingly, giving her strength. *You can do this. You are strong enough. You carry us in the blood that runs through your veins. We are proud of you, and we have faith.*

She collapsed in a heap of exhaustion, as she felt the bonds snap and break.

Freydís

Freydís streaked south along the weave, shifting between strands of possibility to stay in the present. She had no way of knowing how far in the future her vision of battle had been, but the whole of the weave itself was as tense as a drum; possibilities were converging, and fate would soon take a new course. The time to act, to secure a place for herself, and her people, was now. *And then I will no longer stand in anyone's shadow, and even my brother will have to meet me as an equal.*

She was on the hill's crown with her husband and his men, hovering above it. Flickering half-images of the people present followed after them, as children or old men — or not at all for those fated for Valhalla. She turned away from Thorvard — she had promised herself, and him, never to peer at his fate — to gaze upwards at the shimmering strands of the weave that were now visibly touching everyone. Just a few nudges would be enough to shift the pattern ever so slightly, to ensure Vinland would be theirs.

A vibration, gentle at first, then rapidly growing in strength, rippled in the back of her head. Her limbs tingled with shock and her stomach tightened. *Another one rides the weave!*

Her thread snapped. Her possibilities collapsed.

Searing, jabbing pains — like hot needles boring through flesh — ran up Freydís's arms and down her spine as she slammed back into herself. Her legs spasmed and she collapsed to the ground. Her shaking hands felt like she had burned them in a cooking fire. She lay trembling on the ground and prayed that no one would enter and see her in such a state. *How could the thread break?* She had been careful; she had been riding the weave since she was a girl. The only way a thread could break was if the spinner put too much of her own will into the weave, unless there was another present.

Threads can also be broken by opposing magic.

Freydís had been taught to sense others' weaves and leave them alone, for interfering would be akin to dictating to the Fates their business. Whoever had broken Freydís's thread didn't know about Viking magic, or didn't care.

There was still a way; all was not yet lost. As with cloth, fate could be rewoven — at great cost. But Freydís was willing to pay it, for her honor, and her own legacy.

She shoved the spindle into her pouch and gathered together the snapped thread and wove it around her fingers like a cat's cradle. The threads could produce patterns, and patterns gave insights. She would divine the source of this magic and identify her opponent.

She peered at her hastily-made web and sent her essence into the weave, dodging among threads that grew to the size of tree trunks and became a root-like mass suspended over a misty abyss. She ran along the furrowed path of yarn that scratched like rough bark underfoot. A faint spike of warmth pulled at her heart. *Ahead.* She quickened her pace, leaping over knotted boulders and wavering gaps of nothingness. She let the growing sense of warmth guide her steps while trying to keep her footing amid the increasing strength of the pull. A sudden yank made Freydís stagger forward, and only her grip on a ropy limb kept her from falling to the rough ground or over the side into the mists. Freydís gritted her teeth at the roiling heat in her chest, and the pull that felt like someone was trying to yank out her heart through her ribcage.

A young woman, wearing a hide cloak fastened with shell buttons, emerged from behind a ropy stalk. She raised a wooden hoop bound with strips of leather above her head and brought it down slowly in front of her like a shield. Her face, covered with a red paste, was impassive as she drew a circle in the air with the talisman, all the while murmuring in a sibilant tongue punctuated by clipped tones. The hoop left a shimmering trail of sparks in its wake.

Freydís clenched her fists. "You bitch," she growled. "You were the one." She beat down the urge to leap forward and attack; her hands would pass through the other woman because only her shadow was here inside the magical flow. Her fingers brushed against her pouch, and the reassuring solidity of the spindle that lay within. Freydís smiled grimly. Here, it was as real as it would ever be.

Pedthae

Pedthae regarded the tall woman with wild yellow hair, forcing herself to remain calm. From what she had seen, the battle may already have been lost; everything would be decided here. *By me.* The pale woman growled in her guttural language and quivered with rage, but visibly held herself back from lunging at her. She yanked a short length of carved wood from her pouch. Strange she may be, but she knew how the Spider Path worked, which made her dangerous. The strange shaman pointed the wood at her and shouted something unintelligible.

A cold, damp wind blasted Pedthae, driving her backwards until her heels lost contact with what passed for solid ground here. Her hand darted to catch something to keep her balance, grasping a rough, ropy red vine. The strange woman raised her wand again. The giant web strand beneath her feet began to pulse; the Spider Path demanded a choice. *But is it more than I can bear?*

She had broken the white shaman's spell, but even Pedthae knew that what was broken could be remade. *Protect my people or the land?* She looked in the pale woman's eyes and saw anger, and behind that envy, jealousy, hope … and fear. Deep within she saw a tamed land, filled with stone mamateeks surrounded by fences, barriers, and plants growing in rows, bounded by a sea dotted with massive wooden canoes full of white men. Yet beneath that she also saw the familiar hills, cliffs, and rivers of home — all bounded and constrained by the new world built by the invaders. Above it all stood this woman.

Pedthae blinked away the vision and gave thanks to the Great Spirit. *Demasduit said that protecting our people is meaningless if there is no land to support us, but these people will never leave us alone as long as they covet it.* She would protect the land and share in the price that must be paid. She raised the great wheel before her as the white men on the hill had done.

The pale shaman faltered in her spell. Her wand lowered.

Pedthae cut the sinews with her knife, seized the ends, and rebound the wheel. The Spider Path trembled underfoot.

"It is done," said a soft voice in her mind. *"The land will be free, though it will be unkind to you."*

"I accept," said Pedthae, as she collapsed upon the ground.

The silence was broken by the crack of the white shaman's wand breaking. She looked at her stricken talisman and turned her gaze slowly to Pedthae. Tears streamed down her cheeks as she faded.

Freydís

Thorvard led his men through the wooden gates of Leifsbuðir, sighing contentedly. They had broken the Skraelings and it had been hard not to give chase, or track them to their camp and plunder it. Bjarni, at least, had been avenged and their enemy would be licking their wounds for a good while. But there was a bigger prize than any amount of loot; Vinland was theirs. His brother-in-law's warning had rung false. His spirits rose at the bustle in the camp — his wife's by right, certainly. *Let Eirik brood in Greenland.*

A man bearing a heavy sack burst from a hovel and shouldered him aside, without looking, on his way to the dock. Thorvard's hand darted to his sword, then stopped. *Not here, not after our victory.* He swallowed his anger and asked the man his business. The other man stopped and held Thorvard's gaze for a long moment, then shook his head and walked away. Thorvard continued, irritated and puzzled, into the hall, where servants briskly filled sacks and baskets and removed decorations from the walls and tables. He edged past them into the inner chambers and found Freydís by their bed, red-eyed with old tears, directing her maid to pack her things. "Why are people making as though to flee? We should be celebrating the defeat of the Skraelings, which you must surely have seen."

Freydís sniffed. "You beat their warriors, husband, not the people themselves."

"What does it matter? They won't move against us for a long time and our position here is now secure."

Freydís glared. "Secure, yes. But what value is that in a land that will no longer sustain us, faced with people who will oppose us at every turn?"

Thorvard frowned. "But our battle—"

Freydís shook her head. "Your battle wasn't the only one fought that day." She produced the snapped thread from her pocket. "Their roots run deeper here than ours, and they have chosen to make their land harsh to keep it safe. Our time here is done."

She brushed past her husband and strode unseeing down the dimly-lit corridor, past servants busily packing up the household, and outside into summer air that now held the crispness of autumn. She glanced back at the long wooden hall with its heavy sod roof, which had withstood the harsh seasons of Vinland since her brother had built it. *How long will it stand, once we are gone? Will anyone remember that we were ever here?*

Freydís faced the choppy, gray waters of the shallow bay, whose rocky arms seemed to strangle Leifsbuðir like a noose. A sudden gust from the south raked her with a stinging chill, bringing the musk of dead leaves and cold earth, and tossing the ships violently.

She hurled the broken spindle into the sea.

* * *

>>> Our story is an exploration of how Newfoundland — believed to be Vinland — transformed, through a battle of wills, from the lush place described in the Viking sagas into the harsher place it is today, while also exploring the

complicated character of Freydís and her possible role in the Viking colony's fate, intertwined with Pedthae, a Beothuk woman whose declining people inhabited the land from time immemorial. We saw parallels in the Aboriginal medicine wheel and the European spindle, which recalls the Norse mythology of the Fates weaving the destiny of the Universe. The story, as some may say, wrote itself.

Geoff Gander

Prior to writing fiction, Geoff Gander was heavily involved in the roleplaying community, and wrote many game products. He has been published by *ChiZine Publications, Metahuman Press, AE SciFi, Exile Editions, McGraw-Hill,* and *Expeditious Retreat Press*. He primarily writes horror, but is willing to give anything a whirl. In his spare time, he Steampunks, demolishes flooring, and wrangles two teenagers. Geoff lives in South Mountain with a lovely witch who carves soapstone and plays the bagpipes - not at the same time.

Twitter: @GeoffGander

Fiona Plunkett

Fiona Plunkett is a "mostly sane" freelance editor, researcher, and do-er of things. Born in England and transplanted to Canada's capital region by her Canadian parents, she now resides in the small town of South Mountain, Ontario with eight cats (full time), five skeletons (full time), and a "mostly sane" author (part time). She has a university degree in History, and a college diploma in Interactive Media Management. In her spare time, she plays the bagpipes, tenor drum, and bass drum (not all at the same time) for the Kemptville Legion, Branch 212, Pipes & Drums, carves soapstone, talks to cats, Steampunks, communes with nature in her backyard sanctuary, and terrorizes local children on Hallowe'en as The Witch of South Mountain.

Facebook: @fiona.plunkett.beyond.the.realm
Instagram: @fionaplunkett

Mirror of Alchemy

Katherine Cameron

1 January 1554/55

    In the begynnyng was that worde. In the gospel according to John, these are the first words. I remember reading my father's illustrated Tyndale Bible when I was ten. We read it secretly, my father and I, for it was illegal to own the book in 1536. That was the year Tyndale himself was burned for heresy, refusing to recant.

    Next to the illuminated letter *I*, in gold and blue, is an illustration of a young scholar in a crimson robe, holding an open book and looking towards the sky. When I was young, I would try to decipher the words on the book he was reading, but I could not read them, no matter how hard I strained my eyes. It seemed to me the book within the picture must contain all the mysteries of the universe. A world within a world.

    My father taught me to read. A wool trader and a reformer, he believed in the power of words. I practiced my writing by copying my mother's receipts so that I could preserve her knowledge. But I rarely have time to read or write now, for my husband's house requires many hours and many hands to run.

3 January 1554/55

    We have taken in a boarder, a young priest named John Dee. He tells me his name was originally *Ddu* in Welsh, which means *black*. The family claims to be descendants of Arthur, but I do not know how they could trace their lineage back into that distant time. My husband, Thomas, knew Dee's father, a churchwarden until he fell into disgrace several years ago for stealing gold plate from the parish of St. Dunstan's. Father Dee has returned to London, after studying abroad in Louvain and Paris for several years.

As she was brushing my hair last night, my maid, Nan, asked me if I thought Father Dee was not handsome.

"Hush, Nan. He is a priest and a scholar and far beyond you," I said. "His family is descended from King Arthur." I do not believe this, but Nan is only fourteen and impressionable. I do not want her climbing the stairs to Father Dee's room in the garret. I have troubles enough keeping her and the kitchen maid safe from my husband's apprentices.

Father Dee is about my age, perhaps a few years younger. Not yet thirty, yet so accomplished: a scholar from Cambridge and the University of Louvain, fluent in several languages, an accomplished astrologer. His hair is a mahogany brown below a black skullcap; he has a long beard, and his eyes are so dark they appear black. He wears a priest's black tunic, for he has only recently taken his vows. I think that his father's disgrace and death may have forced him to choose the church, for he does not seem particularly devout.

5 January 1554/55

We eat this night in the dining room, with the mullioned windows patterned with frost flowers. Over our supper of boiled eels, Master Dee tells us this year is inauspicious. "1555. So many fives. The number five signals violent changes, false beginnings."

He is right about the year being volatile, but this is true of every year since King Henry abandoned his first wife and married Anne Boleyn, changing our church so that he might do so. Now his older daughter, Mary, who rules over us, has reunited the church with the Holy See in Rome, back to Latin and idolatry, away from the words Tyndale and Wycliffe have given us. I write these words only for myself. Thomas tells me it is dangerous to say such things aloud.

Thomas changes the conversation to the cold weather. "I remember years ago, the year the Thames froze over. That summer that followed! Rain upon rain and the rye and wheat rotted in the fields. I hope we are not in for another year of bad harvests and the bloodie fluxe." He refuses to speak of politics, or at least he refuses to speak of them with me. He changes his religious opinions with the tides, as a merchant must.

Thomas does not say that the people blamed Henry and Queen Anne for the rain and the bad harvest, that the Maid of Kent prophesized the King's death.

After dinner, I bring fresh linen to Master Dee in his garret room. I could send Nan, but she pulls the bodice of her gown lower before she climbs the stairs and pinches her cheeks to make them red; she lingers in his room asking him of his experiences abroad. I am a sedate matron and can be alone in his chamber.

Master Dee is seated on a stool by the window, reading by the last light. He shows me his copy of Johann Stoeffler's *Ephemerides* with notations in the margins. "I note the weather to account for the influence of the planetary bodies. This year is ruled by Mercury, swiftly changing."

A numinous cloud of numbers surrounds him. He is not only a scholar and a rector; he is also an alchemist and an astrologer. He reads numbers as well as he reads Latin; he can foretell the future through the position of the planets. What would it be to have such knowledge? I see the world darkly, through a veil of ignorance.

1 February 1554/55

The rain continues. The Council repealed the Royal Supremacy on January 3 and the Pope reigns over us again. The Rood hangs in the sanctuary. I must take the Mass again.

8 February 1554/55

The Queen is burning heretics. I lie awake in the dark, terrified of dreams of scorching red flames. Four days ago, on February 4, John Rogers died at Smithfield. His crime? Preaching at Paul's Cross against the Papacy, idolatry, and superstition. I heard he died bravely, holding firmly to his beliefs.

Beside me, my husband snores into his feather pillow. No flames dance around his head. The damask curtains of the bed keep out the night air and the drafts, but they cannot keep out these evil visions.

After prayers, I climb the narrow stairs to Father Dee's room with clean linen, into the dark garret with its window looking out over the muddy brown of the Thames River. Spanning the Thames stands London Bridge with its crowded shops and houses. Our house is close to the wharf, where John trades in wool and spices. The tang of salt water from the tide swirling upriver mingles with the stench of piss and shit pooling in the gutters.

Books and manuscripts lie scattered around the room, in great stacks on the floor, in untidy piles on the desk. So many books in so many languages: English, German, Latin, and alphabets I do not even recognize. I pick up one written in English, thinking of how few books I own: my father's Tyndale, now carefully hidden under a floorboard in my bedroom, my sanctioned Book of Hours with its illustrations of the psalms in green and blue.

Father Dee finds me there, holding his manuscript translation of Bacon's *Mirror of Alchemy*. "Do you truly believe that angels live among us?" I ask.

He sits down on the stool and takes the book from my hand. "Spirits can manifest themselves in the world. See this crystal." He unwraps a square of yellow silk to reveal a clear multifaceted stone set in silver "If I hold it up to the light, the light refracts through it, breaking into a spectrum of color. I believe that these colors are the origins of the universe. If I use the Art of Sintrilla to reverse the process, I can capture angel spirits within the crystal's housing."

He has me sit on the small three-legged stool in the corner and places the crystal in a shallow pewter bowl on the desk. Into this bowl he pours oil from a flask and inscribes a symbol I cannot read in the pool of oil. "Look into the crystal and tell me what you see."

I stare into the bowl, feeling slightly foolish. It seems to me as superstitious as the love potions Nan obtained from a wysewoman in Charing Cross. I stare at the crystal, which catches a ray of light from the window. Then I see a shimmer of something. Leaning forward, I look closer.

Flames. Orange flames burning at the base of a wooden stake. A man burning. Not John Rogers, whom I've heard preach several times at St. Paul's. The place is not Smithfield. The man has his hands bound behind him. The flames smolder; wood crackles. The reek of fat drippings, like roasted pig, fills my nostrils. The man's face contorts, wretched in agony. Then an onlooker in the crowd strikes him on the side of his head with a halberd and the man sags against his chains. Dead, I pray.

Gasping, I sit back and put my head down against my knees, the soft wool of my kirtle brushing against my face, trying to escape from that place of horror. Roasting flesh sears my nostrils.

"What did you see?" Father Dee asks, his eyes bright with interest.

I describe the vision. "It was not John Rogers," I say, thinking Father Dee might think me a weak-headed woman who saw the burning last week and wishes to gain importance in his eyes by pretending to have visions. I do not know how I saw what I saw. I was there, and then I was back in the tiny garret with Father Dee leaning over me.

"Mistress Constable, you could be a powerful scryer."

I do not want this power. The world is a dangerous place for reformers and for women.

12 February 1554/55

It has been a week of martyrdom. First Rogers and Lawrence Saunders. Then, the day after I saw the vision in Father Dee's crystal, Rowland Taylor, the Archdeacon of Bury St. Edmunds, burned to death in Hadleigh. Did I truly see his death? On the same day, February 9th, Bishop Hooper was hung in chains and burned at Gloucester.

1 March 1554/55

I have avoided Father Dee since I saw that vision. All spring the fires have been burning. William Hunter in London, John Laurence, Robert Ferrar, the former bishop of St. David's. Many other men rot in prison or in the Tower. The world becomes more dangerous by the day for believers in the word. I do not wish to see these deaths in Father Dee's crystal.

This morning he stops by me as he is coming down the stairs. I try not to think of the Irish curse of ill luck for passing on the stairs.

"Mistress Constable, I am sorry if I have offended you." His dark eyes are contrite.

"I was not offended. I was frightened." I offer him nothing more than the truth.

"A true gift exacts a price," he says. "Perhaps you are right to avoid the cost. I will not ask you to scry again. Forgive me for showing you something you were not ready to see."

I curtsy to him and he bows and passes me. The thoughts of the flames burning in that crystal still haunt me. At night, I smell burning flesh. And I think of his words: *something you were not ready to see.* Would I ever be ready to see sights such as those again?

5 April 1555

Nothing changes. The burnings continue.

Father Dee has been summoned to Woodstock Palace to cast a horoscope for the Princess Elizabeth. This seems a precarious undertaking. The Princess is not in favor at the Court and now that her sister is married even the succession is not secure.

"Be careful, John," I say, as he is leaving. We have called each other by our first names since he apologized to me on the stairs.

"I am only going to say Mass," he says, his eyes laughing. This is the cover that the Princess is using. She is under close guard. I watch him walk away accompanied by two of her gorgeously dressed courtiers, a dark crow in his black tunic between these popinjays in red velvet doublets, the sleeves slashed with yellow silk.

That night, he shows me the horoscope, the circle split into the twelve houses with notations for the planets. I recognize the sun, a circle with a dot in the middle, and the crescent moon. "See," he says, pointing to the section near the top of the circle. "The Princess Elizabeth has Venus and the sun in Virgo the eighth house. Virgo, the Virgin. The moon in Taurus. Capricorn is the ascendant. Her mask is the father, the leader. One day she will be a great leader, greater even than her father."

This verges on treason. Queen Mary is alive, and if the rumors are to be believed, pregnant. If she births a son, all the reforms of the past twenty years will be lost. Already the Tyndale Bible has been burned, along with John Rogers and Bishop Hooper and other martyrs to the true Christian faith. Some members of the court support Prince Philip, others the Princess. The Queen is thirty-eight, old for childbirth. If she dies, I do not know which side will prevail. To be ruled by a Spanish Papist would mean the end of all church reforms.

I was only eight in 1533, the year the Princess was born, but I remember her mother, Queen Anne, dressed in white cloth of tissue and a mantle trimmed with ermine, her dark hair loose down her back, carried on a litter through the streets of London to her coronation. The crowds were silent, even though they had been paid to cheer. I heard a woman yell, "Whore." Three years later, the King had her beheaded.

28 May 1555

The Queen's Guards are pounding on the door. "Open in the name of the Queen!"

I meet John at the exit to the privy. "They've come for me," he says, his dark eyes anguished. "I heard this morning Thomas Prideaux has informed against me to the Queen. They will accuse me of treason, of plotting in the cause of the Princess Elizabeth, of performing a destinary horoscope to see her future." He reaches out and grabs my wrist. "Hide my crystal and my writings. You know what the horoscope predicts. It cannot be found. Please, I beg of you."

He is asking a great deal. I too could be charged with treason if they find the papers. I nod. "Go," I say, gesturing to the back door.

Leaving Nan to open the door to the guards, I gather up my skirts and run up the three flights of stairs to the garret. The pages of the horoscope are on the low desk with the crystal in its usual place, wrapped in silk. I grab both and turn back down the stairs. The front door bangs open. There is no time to leave the house by the back door, as I had originally planned. Instead, I walk quickly down a flight of stairs to my bedroom. In the corner is a loose floorboard; I pull it up and hide the papers with my Bible. The crystal I string onto a leather cord, tucking it under my bodice. Then I go downstairs to face the guards.

1 June 1555

John has been accused of conjuring and witchcraft. He is being questioned in the Tower. Maybe tortured. Rumors swirl in the city that he summoned demons, that he plotted the downfall of the Queen. His room has been sealed for Suspicion of Magic.

I have taken clean linen and also some money to the Keeper of the Tower. John has no family in London; his mother's house in Mortlake is over seven miles away. His friends at Court have forgotten him. At night I lie awake, listening to the wheeze of Thomas's breathing and the ringing of the church bells.

2 June 1555

More arrests, this time of the auditor of Princess Elizabeth's household and Christopher Carye, one of John's pupils. The net of treason is closing in. Thomas has told me not to return to the Tower. Our household cannot be seen to be associated with a traitor.

I would speak the word. I would look into the mysteries of the universe. I would see into the future.

I wait until my husband is out and the servants busy. In my closet, I set out a pewter bowl on the clothes press. I have no knowledge of arcane symbols, no scented oil, no rituals to follow. I pour a bit of fish oil into the bowl and place the crystal in it.

Opening my Book of Hours, I read aloud Psalm 120. *In my distress I cry to the Lord.* And then I stare into the crystal. And I wait.

The closet is dark, but the crystal shimmers. I look closer.

I see a room with many books, piled on shelves that bow beneath their weight. I see myself in this house, seated at the same dining table that sits downstairs, candles burning in my pewter candlesticks. I see John sitting opposite me, in the same dark scholar's robe, but his hair is graying. He is reading to me. The words seem to form in the air between us, sparkling with light like dust motes in a sunbeam. *In the begynnyng was that worde.*

The vision fades. I know now he will be safe. The treasonous horoscope is safely hidden beneath my floorboard. I will wait.

* * *

>>> *John Dee had several reflective or refractive objects he used for scrying, including a purple crystal he claimed was given to him by an angel, an obsidian mirror from Mexico, and a glass crystal ball. A scryer would look into the surface of the object and see visions or communicate with captured spirits. Like many alchemists of his time, Dee believed he could communicate with spirits, who would foresee events, find hidden treasure, or reveal a universal language. Dee's crystal is in the Science Museum in London; his crystal ball and obsidian mirror are held by the British Museum.*

Katherine Cameron

Katherine Cameron was born in Swift Current, Saskatchewan. Her debut collection of poetry, *Strange Labyrinth*, was published in 2015. Her short stories and poems have appeared over fifty literary journals and anthologies, including *The Antigonish Review, CV2, Descant, echolocation, The Fiddlehead, FreeFall, Grain, Queen's Quarterly, NonBinary Review, Room, Prairie Fire, PRISM international, Beyond Forgetting: Celebrating 100 Years of Al Purdy,* and *40 Below: Volume 2.* She saw John Dee's obsidian scrying mirror in the British Museum and his astrolabe in the Whipple Museum of the History of Science in Cambridge.

The Inland Beacon

Kate Heartfield

July 1588

As the day darkens, Susanna climbs. Dampness in the air slicks the ladder and makes her joints twinge. She scrambles onto the little wooden platform on the roof of her cottage, next to the chimney, and peers away toward the south.

"Mind you don't break a bone," comes her son's voice from below. He speaks carefully, does not slur. He is a very skilled sot.

"Whisht, Walter. I haven't broken anything in forty-five years of climbing this ladder every night, and I won't today. If you were that concerned about your old mother, you'd get your arse up here and save me the bother."

"I've better ways to waste my time."

She looks down at her son. "Waste? When Her Majesty has asked all the beacon-lighters to keep a close eye? When the Spanish Armada may be lying off our very shores as we speak?"

He makes a rude noise and points an unsteady arm toward the northwest. "There is a lovely beacon at the north coast at Codden." He pivots, points northeast. "There's another two off that way, at Bampfylde Hill and Barrow Hill." He turns again, like a weathercock in a storm. "And there's Chawleigh and Beacon Moor to the south. We are, in fact, surrounded by beacons, all of which can see each other perfectly well. I'm not sure what effect you expect our little fire to have, my dear mother."

"Our beacon will bring help," she snaps.

"What kind of help?"

"The worst kind," she mutters. It's more than she should say, out loud, but Walter says nothing. Not listening. He never has listened.

She stops looking down at her son and looks, instead, to every horizon. She stands at what has always been the center of her world, the little stone cottage in Devon where she was born. So old, it looks as if it's part of the hillside. And at the top of that hill, just a little higher than the roof where she stands, sits a great wooden box, filled with wood and pitch, awaiting the flame. Never in her lifetime has that flame been lit, and never in the lifetime of her father neither, nor his father before him. But they were ready, as she is ready.

The house is set into the south side of the hill, so she has a clear view of the coast to the north. Walter is right about one thing: Devon is dotted with beacons, of a more ordinary kind than her own. Devon juts out from the southwest corner of England, connecting Cornwall to the rest of the country, and it has the sea on two sides. Will the ships come from the north, sailing up the Bristol Channel? Or will they come to the south, straight across the English Channel? A fleet of one hundred and thirty Spanish ships, ready to convey a vast army across that little ribbon of seawater.

God save us. A splash of gold on the southern horizon. Is it a light? She squints. "I see something, Walter!"

"I'faith? Well, that must please you."

Why does she go to the trouble to even speak to the scoundrel? Why does he stay here with her, when he clearly hates her so? There was a time when he spoke to her gently.

There was a time when her eyes saw clearly, so clearly she could thread her needle on the first try and work the finest embroidery in southern Britain. Now she does not see well in twilight. Susanna sees a flame on the southern horizon — she is sure of that much — but it dances and flits like a will o'the wisp, and the more she blinks, the greater the halo around it grows. Is it one flame, or two?

She has seen the new beacon-house down at Chawleigh, a stone beehive, to keep the beacon-tender dry and warm. Much more comfortable than standing on the top of a hill tending a bonfire, she has often thought with some resentment, but her own beacon must not be set in iron. Her own beacon must heat the ground beneath it. At Chawleigh, a ladder-pole leads straight up through the middle of the roof, with two iron fire-baskets to be filled with gorse, broom and pitch.

The beacon-keeper at Chawleigh can light one of those baskets, or both.

One flame could be nothing more than a report from afar of one unknown ship.

Two fires, in an inland beacon such as Chawleigh, means the enemy has been spotted. Two fires means invasion. Two fires means she must light her beacon, come what may.

"I can't tell how many fires are lit," she says, out loud, although Walter is the only one there to hear.

"Come down then, and I'll have a look."

"You're half pickled, Walter, you'll kill yourself."

"Only half, Mother. Quickly now. If it's three, there's no time to lose, is there?"

He's probably mocking her, but he's right despite himself. She eases herself down the ladder and stands toe to toe with her son, who stands half a head taller than she. His breath stinks of sack, fruity and sharp.

He picks something out of her hair: a piece of thatch from the roof. Then he hands her the bottle he's been swilling: dark green, long-necked, globe-bottomed, half-empty. Slightly bemused, she takes it.

Walter climbs up the ladder, groaning a bit although he's just past twenty. He takes his time about it, and when he reaches the top, whole ages pass, cathedrals are raised and toppled, before he says, "Mmm."

"Hmm? What do you see, Walter? One fire, or two?"

"I see— hmm. I think it's only that we're seeing two different beacons, the one at Chawleigh and the one at Beacon Moor, and from this distance they seem close together. Sometimes it does look like two fires on one hill."

"And other times?"

Instead of answering, he lumbers down, rung by rung, plants himself back on the ground and takes the bottle back from her.

"I could light the beacon, to be safe," Walter says, and tips the bottle into his mouth.

"I light it, not you. And never but in the darkest need," she says, rubbing her hands.

"Heaven forfend that the farmers of Devon should drive their sheep into the hills or fortify their courage with an unnecessary dram."

She snatches the bottle out of his hand and throws it down. It lands on the earth with a heavy thud and does not break. "You lump of dough! How many times did I try to teach you, as a child? The Brogan Beacon is like no other. The future of Britain depends on us, though Britain has half-forgotten it! But I do not forget. I cannot forget. I tried to teach you, but you did not listen—"

"Oh, I listened. How could I forget? 'Always put out the household fires first before you light the beacon. No, Walter, we cannot use an iron pitch-pot; our beacon must be a bonfire of wood, and it must be set upon the earth. And you must never light it but in the darkest—"

"Don't ape me, boy. You may have set the words to heart, but you did not understand—"

"What? What could I understand? There is nothing to understand! It is all nonsense. Tell me, Mother, what is it that you think will happen if you light the beacon?"

Her teeth clamp as heavily as a portcullis, her gaze a ballista. She is fortified against him, against her own desire to speak, to say what she must never say, lest she upset the delicate bargain she did not make and barely understands.

Susanna's son shakes his head as though in grief, and the arm that was holding the bottle now drapes around her shoulders. He pulls her to him, pulls her forehead to his own. "Why would you never tell me what you know?" he whispers, his drunk breath filling her nostrils.

"We must not speak of it," she whispers back, desperately. "We know, but we must not speak."

He pushes himself away from her, and laughs, a short bark. "But the truth is, Mother, that I *don't* know. I don't know! And I am tired of being a servant to your fears."

"I dream of it, sometimes," she says, so lowly she can barely hear herself. This is something she has never said, not to anyone. Not to Walter's father, who was here and gone within a fortnight. Not to Walter. And certainly not to herself. "Haven't you dreamed of it? Haven't you seen it, in your dreams?"

He turns away from her. In the gloaming, he is nothing but darkness in the shape of her son. "I try not to dream. The wine helps."

Walter and his wine. She turns from him, stares toward the coast, but there are no answers there. She is alone, and Walter is no guide or help to her.

"I'll saddle Dobbin and be at Bithell Farm in a trice," she says. "They have many sets of young eyes there, and they're on high ground. They'll be able to tell me how many fires, for certain."

"That's four miles. Let me go. I'm a faster rider than you."

"Ha," she says, more harshly than she means to, but he's only hindering her, doesn't he see that? "Let you gallop off half-soused in the night?"

"What do you think will happen?" he scoffs. "Do you think I'll take the wrong road and end up in Faerie?"

She glowers at him. "Whisht, foolish boy! I think you won't come back to me, that's what I think. I'll go myself, and be sure of things."

Dobbin is a slow old horse, and there's not much galloping to be done, in the low light on the grassy roads rumpled by a summer's worth of floods and droughts. Susanna rides as quickly as she can, a small lamp in one hand.

The guardianship of this beacon is too much for one woman with failing eyesight. There used to be more like it, her father told her. Once upon a time, Britain had inland beacons from one side of the island to the other, ready to call for aid. Susanna remembers the day her father spoke to her about it as he carefully walked around the beacon, pouring whey in a steady stream upon the ground. It was a ritual he performed once a year, and he always wanted her to come with him, to learn the way of it.

It had been hundreds of years since the last beckoning, he told her. England fended off the Norse near York, but it lost a great deal more. So many young people.

"In the battle against the Normans at Hastings?" she'd asked him, so proud of her knowledge.

"Very near," he'd said, a strange answer, but then her whole life was composed of strange answers and missing questions and half-remembered dreams. Her father had taught her how to speak safely around the truth, but somehow she had failed to teach that to her son.

Once her father had spoken to her very plain, the day before he died. "You must be ready to give yourself in payment, Susanna," he'd said. "To light the beacon is to offer yourself. It is your task, now, and I hope you may never be called to perform it."

Someday, she will have to say the same to Walter. Someday it will be his duty to perform. And yet, she can't imagine he will believe her. When she is dead, he will wander away, to Bristol or London, and leave the beacon untended. She has failed, somehow, to keep the line unbroken from the past into the future. She has broken the chain, and she cannot even say when or how it happened. What was the year, the day, the moment, when she lost her son? He is still there, still in the cottage, and yet he is lost to her.

The path winds around a low hill; Dobbin steps around an outcrop and the sky lights up. She doesn't need to go any farther; she can see the beacons from here. Yes, there is Chawleigh's, and it is lit. There is Beacon Moor, and it is lit.

And they both have two fires. Two fires each.

She pulls on the reins and turns Dobbin around, her heart hammering. Two beacons, from the south, and no beacons yet to the north. The Armada, and from the south coast. One hundred and thirty ships, all packed with soldiers bent on invasion.

When Dobbin has trotted for a little while and comes to patch of high ground, she thinks the old horse has gone awry and circled back around, because there's a great gold flame in the sky before her. She blinks, and her eyes adjust. It's a bonfire on a hilltop.

It's her bonfire on her hilltop.

No, she thinks, knowing it is bootless to say the word, saying it out loud anyway. "No."

She slides down off Dobbin and leaves him, knowing he will find his way to his stable, knowing that they are home. Brogan Beacon has been lit.

And the man who lit it, her son, stands in front of it, a patch of blackness, walking toward her.

"In God's name, what possessed you, Walter?" Susanna cries.

"I looked again," he says. "There were two fires. I knew you would return, and light the fire. I knew that you must. I knew what would take you. Did you think I have not had the same dreams?"

His voice wavers strangely, but perhaps it is only the crackle of the fire, the heavy logs shifting. She runs to him and takes his face in her hands. The air stinks of heavy, pitch-laden smoke.

He smiles, and lifts her hands off his cheeks, brings them down, holds them. Looks her in the face, though it is so dark she can hardly see anything but the firelight in his eyes.

"You must go from here," she says. "Quickly now. Oh, my dear boy, I fear you will never be easy in your own skin again."

"Mother, did you think I ever was?"

The roar of the fire rises in the roar of the wind and the black smoke forms shapes against the sky, darkness on darkness, and her eyes can see only dimly. Still, she sees the hounds leaping out of the fire, and the horses, and a shape like a black goat trots past her. She smells not only smoke now but fur and sweat and far, far off, she hears a long, low horn.

Hoofbeats and a raucous laugh and something knocks her down. She falls to the still-cold earth and looks up, her arm shielding her, and sees her son lifted off his feet and into the sky before he becomes a swirl of bright embers, a trace of black smoke, a strand of night. She hears him cry out once more, not in fear and not entirely in grief, but with abandon.

The wild host rides up into the sky and on the scraps of fire-lit clouds it bears southwards, pulling the winds behind it. South toward the sea to scatter the ships of Spain.

~ ~ ~

April 1589

Susanna spends the winter alone in the cottage; it is January before the smell of burning finally subsides.

The English fleet engaged the Spanish Armada at Gravelines and people say it seemed as though the wind was on England's side; the English ships dodged the Spanish guns, darted in and out of the waves, and dealt Spain a blow.

So the Spanish sailed north, and the wind followed them. The wind chased them around the top of Scotland and dashed them on the rocks, wrecking the ships along the coast of Ireland. Some of the Spanish sailors have turned up in Scotland, in Ireland, even here and there in England. Queen Elizabeth orders that they be hanged on sight.

The harvest was bad that year; the weather has been strange.

But the danger has passed; Britain is saved again.

In the spring, Susanna begins to walk abroad, not seeking her son but mourning him. She walks the slopes of the hills, and one day she follows the trail of a rivulet that carves a narrow ravine, leading north toward the sea.

She smells smoke first, and then sees it: a black wisp against the pale sky. Susanna's breath catches and she follows it to a ramshackle shelter, barely more than a cave with logs set against its entrance. A man is squatting by a small fire, cooking a fish on a stick.

He stands, and looks at her, saying nothing, making no gesture. He is not her son. He is, though, someone's son. Someone far from here.

Susanna looks around this place where he has made his home, for a time at least, and sees a few broken wooden planks, a couple of pieces of cracked but brightly painted pottery, a few bottles, an iron chain.

They stare at each other for a moment, the woman and the shipwrecked sailor, and then she turns and walks away from him, slowly, calmly.

Susanna returns the following day, and every few days thereafter. She brings bread and cheese, and once, a few sausages. She has little to spare, but she can still see well enough to sew, and she has enough piece-work coming in to keep herself from starving.

They never speak to each other, but the third time she comes, he gives her a small, sad smile, not quite a greeting.

A few days later, she returns, and he is gone.

She walks farther, following the ravine, as the stream leads her to the shore of the River Taw. She looks to the north, where the river widens and leads into the sea. Did the sailor go back this way, or did he go further inland, or to the south? Is he trying to make his way home or is he happy to be somewhere else, somewhere new, even in this place where he can find no rest?

A glint catches her eye: a bit of dark glass, bobbing in the waves. She lifts her skirt and wades into the cold river.

It's a bottle, just like the one Walter was drinking from the last night she saw him. Heavy, dark glass, with a bulb at the bottom. And in the bulb of this one, a small roll of paper.

A message for someone. Not for her; if it were meant for her, there are easier ways to find her. A message for home, a message for family. A reassurance, perhaps, or a cry for help. Written, she has no doubt, in Spanish.

Susanna picks up the bottle, weighs it in her hand. Cold and heavy.

She lifts it high and throws it back into the river, downstream, toward the sea.

* * *

>>> *In 1588, Philip II of Spain sent a fleet to invade England under Queen Elizabeth I. The Armada was first sighted off Cornwall and a network of beacons spread the news as the Armada sailed east. The English managed to gain the upper hand by sending fireships into the Spanish fleet and using the wind to their advantage. Harsher winds would destroy many of the Spanish ships as they sailed around Scotland. This story also draws on traditions about ritual 'need-fires' that ward against disaster, and with stories about the Wild Hunt, which is sometimes associated with a fairy host.*

Kate Heartfield

Kate Heartfield writes fantasy, science fiction and non-fiction, including the historical fantasy novels *Armed in Her Fashion* (ChiZine Publications 2018) and *The Humours of Grub Street* (ChiZine Publications 2020), and the time-travel novellas *Alice Payne Arrives* (Tor.com Publishing 2018) and *Alice Payne Rides* (Tor.com Publishing 2019). Her novella *The Course of True Love* was published by Abaddon Books in 2016. Choice of Games released her interactive novel, *The Road to Canterbury*, in 2018. A former newspaper journalist, Kate now teaches journalism at Carleton University in Ottawa, Canada, and is a freelance editor and writer.

heartfieldfiction.com — Twitter: @kateheartfield

The Witch of Glencoe

Bev Geddes

It snows. The black sky brightens with the flutter of white. How easy it seems to be to make the world lighter with only frozen teardrops from the sky. I look down at my hands, splayed against the snow, watching red blood seep from beneath them and know there is nothing in this world or the next that will cover the stain.

The world was simple as dawn broke yesterday. One day. One breath past. One heartbeat away from what might have been. If only. Words echo through me, searing my heart and soul with regret.

This is not how it should be.

This is not how it needed to be.

I crouch beside the lapping borders of Loch Leven in the bruised silence of dawn. The February snows have left a crisp of ice across its dark surface. One quick rap and the water thickens on the surface, dissolving the ice shards beneath its chilly depths. Behind me the wind glides through the tree tops, down between the ridges and valleys of Glencoe.

Glencoe. The place I came to call my home and the people whom I came to call my family. The MacDonalds. The reivers of cattle. Thieves in the night. The unruly sept. Jacobites. Hated and feared by the Campbells. Loved by me.

Love. Such a strange word. Wielded in the name of God, a sword striking down, destroying. Used to justify so many things that make souls diminish and hide away, afraid of cutting edges. Love that thunders and vows and is everything that is not love on the inside.

This is not how I have known love. Before Glencoe, I knew only the love of the mountains and streams, of the small boggy places and their tender shoots, of the turning of the seasons, each with their own rowdy winds and scents and secrets. This love of place came as naturally to me as opening my eyes to the sweet crisp of each morning.

Then I came to Glencoe and the MacDonalds and my wandering spirit found a place that allowed all I am without diminishing me. I stumbled into Coire Gabhail, the Lost Valley, and felt the breath of spirit tickle my ear. *Home.* A clearer sign I could not want, and so I stayed.

They welcomed me, the MacDonalds. The whisper of *witch* was not fearsome to them. I tended to their sick, I birthed their babies, I bound their wounds after each cattle raid and I, in turn, never threw the word *reiver* back at them. We found a peace in that.

I am not a MacDonald. I do not belong to anyone. It has been so most of my life. I am wild, unfettered. A witch, as called by some, and shunned. But not by the MacDonalds. Perhaps they understood the wind that blew through my soul and lit my heart and kept me moving. Always moving. They knew *hate* as I did. *Hate* for being different, for living a life that others do not understand. It killed them in the end. *Hate.* Not all of them, to be true. But enough. Enough.

It is their blood that stains the shore of this lake. It traces behind me, running a ribbon of red between the tiny stone homes, the byres with their orphaned goats bleating, and to the Great House. There is blood on my hands, although I did not take the breath from any MacDonald.

Perhaps my sin was the greater one, for I could *See.* To catch a glimpse of the future before it unfolds is the one thing I do not cherish about *witch.* For all the herbs and cures in my bundle, I am glad. For my hands which can heal a child's fever, I am glad. For a heart that sees souls and allows, I am glad. But for the *Seeing,* I am not so glad.

For you must understand, Death prowls the shadows between the worlds, lonely and in need of company. I have sat in silence with its stalk-limbed presence, knowing I can never fill its need, never dissuade it from a course of action once decided upon. I can only turn back to the world of people and try to ease their passage through Death's door and on to the next world. People fear the Realm, the place-that-is-next. I mix possets and potions to ease their fear. There is nothing to fear in the Realm. It is only the way to the Realm that is fearful.

And the Clan MacDonald made that passage in the most fearful of ways — betrayed. Betrayed by those they housed as guests and gave haven when the snow drove hard against them and they were in fear of freezing as they walked. Soldiers. The Orange King's men, some merely boys. And of course, the Campbells.

When they staggered through my valley from Rannoch Moor in the snows just past Hogmanay, I knew. Death dusted their footsteps and hatred swirled around their heads. An old hatred, looking for the chance to rise from the depths like the Kelpies with sucking mouths and bog-weed hair, always hungry for a wayward traveler in the mist.

So it is with hatred. Old or new. It lies dormant, unspoken when the day is bright, and the sun dimples the forest floor with beams of warmth. But when the mist descends and the shadows grow long, it stirs. The black-hearted, bone-chattering scratch of it.

Other, they proclaim. *Not us. Evil. Dangerous.*

And then it becomes easy to justify killing or to avert their eyes and allow.

Did I do this? Did I avert my eyes when my heart knocked against my chest with the coming of the soldiers? I would like to think that I did not. I would like to think my words of warning saved some lives. That the herbs I cast into my pot along with whispered words of protection, wrapped some with spells that sent them out into the early feather-gray dawn before the bloodshed. Before the massacre.

My memory stirs. I wish it would not. I think that it will forever haunt me, those few weeks. I cannot make sense of what happened, but I must search for my truth in it.

~ ~ ~

The massacre crept up on us like a storm breaking in the night after a clear evening sky. It took its time and whispered nothing of the blackness that shrouded the thoughts of men who scuttled into our home with smiles and hungry bellies and thirsty mouths.

That first day, I was up on the ridge behind my hut, filling my wooden pail at the stream that poured down from the snowy peaks of Aonach Dubh as the soldiers marched past, their red coats shining against the purple-gray rocks and dead-crisp heather. The wind plucked at their hair restlessly, the storm already settling into the glen and the snow thickening as their breath steamed and feet crunched. I slipped down from my perch, dropping my bucket at my front door and followed quietly, keeping to the high places, out of sight.

Through the pass between the hills they moved, and I knew where they were heading. I had explored every inch of this land, down to where the water poured ice-cold from the peaks and up to the heights with its knuckles of rock and tufts of heather. I knew the ways of this place following the deer and rabbits and chasing the eagles as they soared.

These King's men made for Carnoch and the Great House of the Chief of the MacDonald Clan. The MacIain. A great bear of a man, with a mane of hair so white you would think it came from the top of the Pap of Glencoe itself. A proud man, a fighter all his life. More's the pity how he met his end. But I did not know that then. I knew only of the darkness that shrouded this company and that they moved relentlessly west toward the man who had granted me sanctuary on his lands.

I pushed through a thicket of birch and blackthorn bushes crossing over the peak, cutting the time in half so that I could reach Carnoch before William's men. The MacDonalds were known Jacobites, following the exiled Catholic James Stuart over the conquering Protestant King William. The arrival of William's regiment would never bode well for Jacobites, but the lingering specter of death drove me harder over the flint-sharp rocks and down the steep ridges.

Carnoch rested in a broad glen. A handful of homes and the biggest cluster of MacDonalds in Glencoe. The MacIain's home was a proper house, built mostly of stone but with glass in its windows and slate on its roof; so unlike my tiny hut with the turf roof and flaps of deerskin to keep the winter winds from blowing through the narrow windows and door. The River of Coe ran through a long meadow of sweeping grasses and towering pines. The smell of peat smoke hung in the air and tumbled through the huddled settlement, unable to dissipate beneath the damp snows that fell ceaselessly now.

I hurried to the back of the Great House and dragged a breath into my burning lungs. Pushing open the door, I slid into the kitchen to the warm smell of bannock and roasting meats. Beeswax candles guttered on the walls as I entered.

"Close ye tha' door."

A huge woman with enveloping breasts and rosy cheeks glanced up from the pot she was stirring above a roaring fire and frowned.

"Sorry, Mara. 'Tis frightful outside." I struggled to push the door closed, finally latching it with a sharp click.

Mara's frown evaporated. "Ah, 'tis only ye, Corrag. I thought 'twas that wee beastie of a lad, John, back in here for another nip at the heather ale. Tshh, girl, but ye're covered in snow. Shake off by the door and then come in, closer to the fire. There be some barley cakes fresh out of the oven that will warm ye inside and out."

"I canna, Mara. I need to see Himself. And right smartly."

"My, but are ye a wee piece this morning. The MacIain isna receiving this day. He's yet in his dressing room. He'll nae be ready for company afore midday."

I closed my eyes, searching for that place within myself that held my *Knowing*. It pressed back, and I felt the flush rise up within me, a sharp impatience that prickled and insisted *no*.

"I must, Mara. They are coming. The MacIain has to know."

Mara's brow crinkled with concern. "They? Who be they, child?"

"Redcoats, Mara. Up from Rannoch Moor. They came marching through my valley just now. The MacIain must know. They bring darkness."

Mara hesitated, her eyes bright and assessing, and then she turned to the linen-capped scullery girl. "Take her," she snapped.

We pressed through the house to the suite of private rooms on the second floor. The house was hushed in this early hour; only the murmur of the servants below disturbed the silence. A deathly silence. My guide knocked sharply on the door.

"Come," a deep voice rumbled from within.

I stumbled as I entered the receiving suite, my limbs watery with fear. Against one wall, a fire hissed in its hearth and snow pattered against the window. The MacIain stood by the fire, a silhouette in the thin light that drained into the room from outside. Pressed between his palms, a mug steamed with tea and a giant hound lay curled at his feet. The smell of peat, wet wool and leather hung in the room, layered by the honey-sweet smell of candles.

"Corrag," the girl beside me announced, dropping into a deep curtsy and backing out of the room. The door clicked shut behind her.

I pulled a breath into my lungs, smoothing my skirts with both hands. My hair clung in wet strands to the side of my face, but I did not push it back. There was no time. The words spilled out of my mouth as though afraid if I gave the moment thought, there would be no words left to say.

"Redcoats. Up Coire Gabhail. There is danger. Ye must prepare. Call the men."

The MacIain narrowed his eyes. He was not an unkind man to those of his clan, but not one easily swayed by a spit of a girl in a tattered cloak, half-covered with mud and dripping water on his rug. I could feel his disbelief collecting, anger following close behind.

"Corrag," he said steadily. "Welcome to my home. Ye look cold and uncomfortable. Please, sit by the fire and have a cup of tea to warm yourself."

I stomped my feet. The weight of *Knowing* slid up my body and tipped into the room. I had no time for the niceties of the Highland ways. Food and drink must always be offered. It was tradition. I hissed in frustration.

If the MacIain was offended by my lack of manners, it did not show on his face. He swept his arm wide in the direction of the hearth and smiled as he bent over to pick up the pot of tea where it steamed beside the fire, sloshing some of the hot liquid into a tin cup.

I made another noise of displeasure but joined him, accepting the cup and sipping obediently. There was no point in arguing with the MacIain on matters like this; he took great pride in his household and the welcome he could provide.

He smiled down at me, this mountain of a man.

"There now. Start ye, lass, at the beginning so that this old man may ken yer words. What has ye in such a tizzy? Redcoats, ye say. Surely ye must be mistaken."

"No, I am nae mistaken. I saw with my own eyes. I saw them marching. And more."

I tried to ignore his raised eyebrows and overly placid face. It bespoke disbelief and I needed him to believe my next words even more than the first.

"More?"

"Aye, there is a falseness that hangs o'er the company. 'Tis dark and fearsome. I know that no good follows these men here. Do not receive them, sir. Turn them back from your door and drive them from these lands. Ye must. Ye must believe me. A terrible thing awaits if ye do not do as I tell ye."

The MacIain turned from me and stared out the window at the snow that drove against the house, shaking it and moaning to be let in. When he finally spoke, his voice was so low that I had to lean forward to make out the words.

"I signed the Oath of Allegiance a moon past. I sold my soul to that devil, William, to protect my clan. There is nothing to worry about from his lackeys now."

"But ye signed late. Six days past Hogmanay."

"How do ye know that, Corrag?" the MacIain snapped, his words sharp and cutting as a blade.

He swung around to face me, his face dark. I did not shrink back from that fearsome figure but drew myself up as tall as I could muster and faced him, my heart thundering in my chest. He must believe my warning.

"All of us know this, and we ken why. No one blames ye for not wanting to swear the Oath in front of that Campbell at Inverary. But ye were forced to it, and now Campbells march with the Redcoats, up my valley and into yours. Do ye not see the devil's hand in this, sir? Have yer men ready. Do not let them in. I beg ye."

"Corrag, ye have been good to me and my kin. We have accepted your pagan ways. 'Twas not so long ago that all Highlanders followed the Old Ways and those times still whisper in our blood. These things are part of all we are."

The MacIain lowered his cup and ran his hand across the scatter of books and papers that covered the long table in front of the fire.

"I dinna mind ye doctoring and patching up me and mine, but I willna fall prey to your future-seeing. 'Tis the devil's work and not to be trusted. No, say nothing more. I am not being disrespectful, so do not cast the Evil Eye upon me. There is no way for me to turn these men away. Even if it was done tactfully, I would bring the wrath of William and that simpleton, Robert Campbell, upon my head. The Campbells will look for anything they might use to destroy us now they are in bed with that Protestant King, so we have all the more reason to stay clear of their lot. No, I'll not set my dogs against them until I am sure of their ill intent. I'm no fool, Corrag. Ye must trust that I'm chief of this clan for reasons that are good enough."

His face slipped into a half-smile and a sigh escaped his lips.

"Do not glower so. I have heard your warning and I will watch these men closely. They come because the garrison at Inverlochy is full and there are more soldiers to be quartered and fed. I canna deny them if they ask for lodging or help. If I do, that damnable Oath I swore will be forfeit and they will have the right to fall upon us, here and now, with drawn swords. Can ye not see that I have no recourse but this one?"

He leaned over, lay his huge hand upon my shoulder and squeezed gently. "Go home. Fit out your potions and spells to protect our clan. It is the best ye can do now. Leave to me the responsibility of protecting those I love. Be at peace."

"Send them to Appin," I rasped. "Send the women and children to Appin then."

I was light-headed with the ache that lay beneath my ribs and pressed into my heart. The inevitability. The understanding that nothing would change his mind. Destiny was in play. Choices had been made. I told myself there was nothing more I could do here and perhaps my possets were the only thing left to try. My words fell through the room without reaching purchase. To speak further was futile.

I pressed my lips around the bitter taste of failure. *No, no, no* echoed in my mind. The urge to retch was strong and my eyes felt scratchy in the smoky room. I needed to be outside, on the mountain, where the stars swept the night sky and the air is clean and fresh. Away from people and their complications.

"I will consider your words, Corrag," the MacIain sighed and turned back to the fire.

I slipped from the room and hurried through the halls. The sound of the approaching soldiers thrummed in my ears. I did not want to be here when the MacIain came down to greet his unwelcome guests. I knew what he would do. Food and drink would be offered. Each tiny home would take one or two of them in, offering simple fare from their limited winter provisions. Whiskey would flow. The guests would be entertained and welcomed. Perhaps such generosity of spirit would turn the hearts of these soldiers. Perhaps what I saw was only one possibility for the future.

I scurried home, the snow curling around my shoulders making a mantle and cap of white, only to melt and drip down my collar. I was soaking and shivering by the time I gained my hut, glad I had the foresight to bank the fire earlier. The peat still glowed as I stirred it to blazing once more. I stripped off my wet clothing and pulled my woolen plaid around me. A gift from the MacIain for helping with the birth of his grandson four moons ago. The MacDonald plaid.

Pulling down my iron pot, I busied myself plucking herbs from where they hung along the beams of the roof.

"Monkshood, hyssop, horehound, bay, foxglove."

I muttered to myself as I crushed the dried leaves and stems, waiting for the pot to boil.

"Heather can be dipped in the water of the creek and hung over the doorways and windows. 'Tis cold enough, and pure. Birch and bilberry bark can be boiled together, but the other herbs will need their own pots. Indigo weed for protection. Nettle to dispel darkness and fear. Bay leaf for strength, and monkshood to ward off the evil intents of strangers. What else? What more am I missing?"

Icy patches bloomed between my shoulder blades; tasks halted as the plants' properties tumbled loosely in my mind. I could not think with such fear driving me. I sucked air through my teeth to calm and ground my spirit. The spells needed to come from my heart, not my head, to be their most potent.

I forced myself to put down my grinding stone and place my wet clothes close to the fire where they would dry. Wrapping the plaid tightly about me, I lifted the deerskin that served as my door. The wind had ceased its endless searching and had taken itself off elsewhere to create mischief. But the snow still fell, fat and lazy, from the night sky, so thick it was hard to imagine that the stars still pricked above that white veil.

"Goddess, give me strength to stop what is coming. Help me weave the magic needed to keep my people safe, for I fear the MacIain trusts too much in the promises of men."

As if in response, a wolf howled in the distance. It was a lonely howl that made the hairs on my head stand to. I turned away from the doorway and busied myself with my potions, heart unquiet within me.

~ ~ ~

For ten nights the snows fell, sometimes thin, wisped by the wind and sometimes thick and heavy. I did not turn from my work and the eaves of my hut steamed from the boiling pot and the sweet scent of herbs.

Twice I ventured close to Carnoch in the dark of night during the empty hours that few inhabit. I peered in the windows and saw the Lowland soldiers laughing and eating the food of their Highland hosts. I watched their hosts smile meagre smiles and mutter to each other in Gaelic, nervous in their movements, careful with their words. It was an uneasy truce I witnessed through those glowing windows but there was nothing threatening I could pinpoint to take to the MacIain and press home my warnings. Still, as I turned away to retrace my steps through the snow, the silence left behind was unsettled and frayed on the edges.

I did try one more time to speak with the MacIain but he would not see me. There was no sign of his taking my warning and sending the women and children to Appin. Who could blame him? Who would harm women and children? It is unspeakable to even contemplate such evil. Still *Knowing* plucked at my mind and stole my sleep until I was unsure if day bled into night or night simply stayed for all the darkness that gathered behind my eyes.

As the moon rose on the thirteenth night since the arrival of William's men, I must have dozed off for I awoke with a start to my fire burning low and the pot boiled dry. Dread quickened within me. And guilt.

Now. It comes. Now. Now.

I rose hastily, wrapping my cloak about me and darted into the waning night. The moon painted the snow silver in the blue darkness and I ran as only those who know panic pounding in their veins can run. Straight to Carnoch. Straight into the nightmare that no one should ever know or see.

Muskets firing. Men yelling. Screams echoing off the black ridges and down through the valley. People running. Everywhere— running. Angry faces. Frightened eyes. Pleading mouths. I ran into the noise. Followed the Lowland voices. Manic, blood-frenzied, foreign to all that is human.

"Find the MacIain's cubs. Find them. Kill them all."

I made it to Carnoch, slipping through the gun-powder clouds, dodging the bayonets and knives, needing only to know that the MacIain had slipped through their fingers and lived. Fire roared through the back of the house, but it did not stop me from my quest.

I plaited the prayer, *Goddess help us*, into the air and hoped it would hold to keep me strong. I threw open the door to the MacIain's receiving room. It had been tossed. Raided. I stepped into the bedroom beyond, my heart thudding in my chest, knowing already what awaited.

On the floor, face down, still in his bedclothes, that mountain of a man lay. Shot in the back. Twice. Tears prickled my eyes and I knelt beside him, placing my hands on his head and whispering the Prayer of the Dead so that his soul might fly to the Realm, unencumbered and free.

A small sound like the coo of a bird rose from the other side of the room. I moved around the bed, nearly tripping on a pile of blankets bunched on the floor. The pile shifted slightly, another moan emanating from its depths. I yanked on the cover and it pulled free. Leaning over, I retched in the back of my throat.

It was Lady Glencoe. What was left of her. Her clothes had been torn from her and blood seeped from her mouth and the countless stab wounds that riddled her body, some in spots I cannot speak of nor wish I ever saw.

I pulled her head into my lap, stroking her hair.

"Tshh, tshh, my Lady," I whispered. "I will take ye to my hut. I have herbs to heal and mend."

She stared up at me with eyes that straddled this world and the next and raised a palm to my cheek.

"Do not fret, Corrag. I go where my soul will heal. I go to join my husband. Know ye, did my boys escape? The MacIain tried to send them off. Said ye warned him. Some left. Not all. Did my boys escape?"

I nodded, although I didn't know. Many lay in the snows that surrounded Carnoch. I had not stopped to count the dead. There were so many of them. I could not tell her that.

"Ye lie, Corrag. Your face has always been easy to read. Never mind. There is nothing either of us can do to change what has happened."

She moaned low in her throat. Blood dripped from her mouth. Quicker now.

"My time is short. There is one more thing I wish to do on this side of the Veil. Under the bed, strapped to the bedframe, the Sword of the MacDonald rests. Take it. Do not let those betrayers have it. Put it somewhere it cannot be found. Do ye promise me ye will do this, Corrag? Do ye promise with your soul?"

I nodded, tears flowing down my face mixing with the blood of this good and kind woman.

"Say it. Say the words."

"I promise I will take the sword. It will never fall into the hands of those that hate the MacDonald clan. I promise this."

"Good. That is good."

Those were the last words of the Lady Glencoe as her soul tipped over the edge of life into the Realm.

I did not hesitate. Covering her mauled body with the sheet once more, I pressed a kiss onto her forehead. Then I reached beneath the bed, my fingers searching for the blade. There, twisted within the ropes that held the mattress, I felt the cool shaft of metal. I tugged furiously until it loosened and came free. A claidheamh-mòr, blade heavy and cross-hilt gleaming.

By rights, I should not have been able to shift such weight, but it shivered with something beyond my meagre powers, beyond this world and into the next. It came into my hand as a glove might, as though fitted to my soul.

I ran, wielding the sword. It sang through the air of its own accord, cutting down those who stepped into my path. Wild with frenzy. Ripe with the promise I had made to the person who had given me *home*.

I cannot tell you how many Redcoats I cut down, but I prayed more than a few Campbells fell alongside them. I took my share of wounds, to be sure, but felt none of them.

My heart was shattered. There was nothing left to feel. Nothing left to do, but one thing.

~ ~ ~

Now I sit by the wintery shores of Loch Leven. Glencoe and its massacre behind me. The Sword of the MacDonald in my hands, washed with the blood of revenge. It is the gloaming, the time-betwixt-and-between. A potent time for spells. I have one more to cast. I failed to protect those I loved as they lived. I will not fail them in death. The sword sings once more as I fling it out over the still waters of the lake and whisper my final spell.

As dawn slips onto the horizon, I stand to leave this place of death. No MacDonald will die by the sword in war again, as long as the MacIain's claidheamh-mòr remains hidden below the black surface of Loch Leven.

It is all I have left to give.

~ ~ ~

The witch, Corrag, existed at the time of the Glencoe massacre. According to folklore, no local men died by the sword in battle for two centuries following Glencoe. Then, in 1916, a sword was dredged from the depths of Loch Leven and brought ashore.

The Battle of the Somme was the next day.

* * *

>>> *"The claidheamh-mor (claymore) is a double-edged, two-handed sword used by the Highland Scots between the 15th and 17th centuries. The Gaelic name is roughly translated as "great sword" and is thought to have been developed by Hebridean warriors.*

In mythology, the sword serves as a gateway from physical life to the spiritual realm. Swords are often believed to contain the soul essence of the owner or to possess a soul of their own, imbuing them with mystical powers and unearthly abilities."

Bev Geddes

Bev Geddes is a school-based speech/language pathologist, and author. Her short story, *Living in Oz*, appeared in the Aurora Award winning anthology, *Strangers Among Us: Tales of the Underdogs and Outcasts* (Laksa Media) and was also short-listed for the award, receiving an Honourable Mention in Gardner Dozois, *The Year's Best Science Fiction: Thirty-Fourth Annual Collection* for 2016. Her second story, The Gift, was published in the Aurora Award winning anthology, *The Sum of Us* (Laksa Media) in 2017. She has written non-fiction pieces for organizations such as Mood Disorders Association and Canadian Parks and Wilderness Society. Her speculative fiction novel, *Secrets of Shalott*, has recently been completed. When not reading, writing, or running away to her cabin on Lake Winnipeg, she enjoys playing the harp, aided and abetted by a menagerie of cats, dogs, children and chums.

Winged

Michal Wojcik

In his youth, many adults had warned Andrzej about the dangers of going to the lake, especially at night. He ignored them; and now teetering on the edge of manhood, he felt more secure in discarding their words.

Beyond the reeds, the water reflected the occasional shock of moon and starlight. But there was another light, and this was what he was meant to flee: the cold glow of pale translucent skin as a head gradually surfaced, revealing slick but tangled hair and empty eyes.

Yet this rusalka did not reach out her arms to grab him and pull him underwater. She only crawled up the bank and huddled her knees against her chest. Her skin looked dead for she was dead — so the stories went — but she would sometimes seem to try and speak, lips parting yet giving out no song as rusalkas were said to do — just a strained and raspy breath.

"I'm leaving tomorrow," Andrzej said, seated on the rocks just above the mud and muck at the lake's edge. The rusalka sat at his feet, her held tilted up to watch him. He could not tell if she stared, because there were no pupils in her eyes, no ring of color or tiny veins, just an occasional flicker of light like a firefly's. "Pan Jarema Kaszewski told my father this morning I will be the part of his retinue."

She bent her head closer to her knees. Andrzej didn't know if she understood Polish, or any language, though he'd spoken to her through countless summer nights for some five years. Her companionship was always one of silence.

"I'll fight alongside the winged hussars," he continued. "Maybe I'll become one, some day, and have my own retainers. I'll come back to you. If I come back. That's to say… goodbye. For now."

At the word *goodbye*, the rusalka suddenly crawled up the embankment. She was quick, but not graceful, her bony limbs trembling erratically at the effort of moving without water. He had no time to escape when her claws pierced through his shirt. This was what the elders told him to fear, and his heart quickened as the sharp points pressed cold and wet against his rib cage.

But all she did was hold him so their noses almost touched, and he saw the dancing flame within her skull. And then she let go, with slow and gradual reluctance, before slithering back into the lake.

Andrzej held his chest where the chill still lingered and would for hours more, then let out an uneasy laugh before heading back to the path where he'd tied his horse.

~ ~ ~

The two brothers did not appear alike. Jarema Kaszewski had a stocky build of compacted muscle, and tight-curled hair and mustache; Hieronim Kaszewski was lanky and his hair hung long and straight and unadorned. Jarema managed his estates and used the income to buy lances and horses and flintlocks of the finest make, traveling from battlefield to battlefield in service of the Polish crown. Hieronim almost never strayed from his small castle in the foothills of the Carpathians, where he carried out experiments in natural philosophy.

To Andrzej, it did not appear the two saw each other often or talked much at all. Jarema announced they would go to his brother before joining their hussar banner, "for there is some business we must attend to," but he otherwise said little about why, or the type of man Andrzej was to meet. This was odd, for Jarema was taken to talking and loved to rattle off on whatever topic came to his mind, be it the latest cheap book sold at market squares, or of the peoples found in the Americas, or the eating habits of Tatars. Just as often, he would sing the latest tune from the last inn or town, and force his new retainer to join.

For a man who rode with such a sense of ease, Jarema had become increasingly uncomfortable as they neared the hills and small castle built thereon. He shifted incessantly and made odd asides about the history of the place, until at last he settled into a near-quiet grumbling while they traversed the final path with their string of horses and baggage. As they came to a stone bridge, Jarema had halted and abruptly gripped Andrzej's arm with strength enough to crush the bone.

"Listen, Andrzej, what you will see, what you will hear… it may stir fear in you. It always stirred fear in me. But it must be done. You must endure. You hear?"

Bewildered, Andrzej had simply said, "I will if pan desires," and in turn endured Jarema's piercing stare. At last, Jarema gave a satisfied grunt and let him go, and they crossed the bridge together.

Hieronim lived with few servants and within the old, near-crumbling walls of the castle drafts blew in regular chills. Yet he did not live a sparse life. Everywhere throughout the tiny fortress were leather-bound volumes or maps or taxidermied beasts or vials of various shapes and colors and sizes. There were peacock feathers tucked between the bookshelves and barrels, and bundles of herbs hung in baskets from the rafters.

Hieronim had not come out to greet them, instead sending a woman of some forty years who seemed to hold more muscle beneath her smock than even Jarema, and she escorted them up the single tower to the highest study.

The embrace between brothers was short, perfunctory. The scholar hadn't even set his quill down to do it.

This room was even more cluttered than the others, yet Andrzej's gaze fell on something distinctly out of place among the astrolabes and star charts: a suit of hussar armor hung upon a frame. It came complete with two rows of wood-and-feather wings articulating from the back and tracing a graceful swoop conforming to the bend of the spine until they curved over the helm. It was what marked the winged hussars most on the battlefield, this strange device that rattled and whistled as they charged into the enemy. One of Jarema's cast-offs? Andrzej wondered, before becoming aware of Hieronim's keen attention.

"So, you've selected another retainer," said the younger of the brothers, setting off the inevitable string of introductions. Hieronim passed through these motions with slight disinterest, until he did at last put aside his quill on the desk beside a half-finished illustration. "I trust he fulfills all the criteria. One with *affinity*." Now he walked a circle around Andrzej with an air of appraisal.

"Aye," Jarema replied gruffly, "a boy born on the edge of the steppe, a boy who's seen speaking with spirits, who walks the unknown paths, and shows no fear of the dead."

Andrzej had never told the lord that, and he felt the sudden betrayal in realizing he'd been watched on his nightly escapades.

"Most excellent. You may go, brother, enjoy the dining hall. I should like to speak with your retainer alone."

Jarema turned to Andrzej and looked briefly into his eyes, face lined with worry and regret and a touch of anger, and then gave a nod before striding out the door without saying a word.

"We never did get along," Hieronim said with a sudden ease; his tenseness had been well-hidden until Jarema had gone, and was suddenly palpable in its absence. "My brother only ever visits me when he has business pertaining to his knightly duties. Andrzej, he said your name was?"

"Yes, pan is correct. Andrzej Zuchowski."

"Your family has some small renown in Zuchowa, I'm sure. And now you have the privilege of serving in Jarema's retinue and riding among the winged hussars."

"It is a great honor."

"But you will not just ride," Hieronim said, taking in Andrzej's puzzled look before smiling. It wasn't a pleasant smile, but not a threatening one either. Rather the grin of anticipation that came before someone shared a secret. "Do you know why my brother brought you here?"

"He said he had some matters to settle with pan before we would join the banner."

"He has little business with me," Hieronim replied. "I, however, have some business with you. Did he tell you what I do here, what I am?"

"He said pan was a scholar and a man of science. Like Copernicus, or John Dee."

"I aspire to their heights, yes. But I also have other duties. I am a member of a brotherhood, the Divine Order of Czarodzieje. Our order has ties to the Clan Ostoja, and we have worked with the winged hussars since the first horsemen banded together to ride across the steppe and the fight the Turks. If a man of certain qualities joins the hussars, he must be brought before one of us to test his worth and make him… more than he is."

Andrzej could not fill the expectant pause.

"Well," Hieronim said, with a tinge of disappointment, "I suppose he truly did keep you in the dark. Let me explain, as best I can."

He ambled to the suit of armor, running a hand along the close-packed ostrich feathers so that they made a soft hiss as he spoke. "You've been eyeing this since you came into the room. No other cavalry in the world wears such a thing on their backs, not the Tatars, nor the Berbers, nor the knights of China. And no cavalry in the world compares in might and renown. Victory after victory. Mercenaries demand in their contracts that they be permitted to leave the field if the winged hussars arrive.

"At the Battle of Kłuszyn, the Russians outnumbered the hussars six to one. Thirty thousand Russian soldiers, and the hussars only lost a hundred men while they slaughtered five thousand. Where else have we heard of such a thing outside the deeds of the Spartans or Alexander the Great? Those wings have come to strike fear in the hearts of any who challenge the Polish crown. But why?" He looked at Andrzej expectantly.

The young man answered with confidence, this time. "We breed the best horses in the world; the hussars take their pick from the greatest stock. I've never seen a beast as fine as Pan Jarema's horse. Hussar lances are hollow so they can be longer than any other; their fighting spirit is like nothing else, and when they do fight, it's as a group moving as one body together. Though I've never seen it, I've heard the stories."

And I will be with them, he thought, and his heart quickened.

Hieronim nodded all the way through Andrzej's list. "Yes, yes. That is all true. But," he chuckled, "it isn't enough. They aren't the first army to do any of those things. The Macedonians knew the value of a long lance, and the Persian cataphracts knew the worth of good horses and fine armor. There is another advantage, one lacking among other nations because the art is lost. These wings," he waved once more to the frame, "are not just for show. Look." From a nearby bookshelf, he drew a leather-bound tome and laid it open upon the desk, beckoning for Andrzej to come beside him.

The pages were scrawled with notes and diagrams, and while Andrzej recognized Polish and Latin, there were other scripts pushed into the margins, perhaps Arabic and another close-packed arrangement of pictographs. But nested between the various scraps of text was an unmistakable sketch of a man with wings fixed directly to his back in the arrangement and style that the winged hussars wore.

Andrzej couldn't help but touch the figure, skin pressed to vellum.

"We of the Divine Order of Czarodzieje took from the knowledge of alchemy and medicine passed down from Hermes Trismegistus and applied it to the human form," said Hieronim. "If we find a body receptive to the process, we change it. This is the secret we keep with the hussars, their true power in battle, how they seem to know the enemy's movements before the enemy even puts his plans into motion. For some among the winged hussars can fly."

Hieronim let the words hang as he too pressed his finger to the sketch, to the contours of muscle and wood and feathers twisting together, to the key parts of the arrangement labeled with strange symbols.

"Pardon?"

"Come now, you know such things are possible. You wouldn't be here if you did not," said Hieronim, now pressing those same long fingers to Andrzej's shoulders to steady him from a spell of dizziness. "You were raised on the borderland and see across it. You consort with uboze, zmorami and rusalkas. You have seen the preternatural and do not fear it, but what is important is that you have *seen* it. Your mind and body are receptive to it, and so we can infuse you with magical formulas. We have given the gifted among the hussars a chance not to just *bear* the eagle standard but to take on the qualities of an eagle. To see as an eagle or hawk would, or dive upon your prey with the same swiftness. And, in some cases, to take to the air. To have wings, true wings, so you may observe what others cannot.

"*This* is the secret of the hussars. And by standing here now, you are sworn to keep it."

"Then I must... become such a person? But surely there are others like *me*. It doesn't have to be me who does this."

"That is another secret I must share," said Hieronim, scratching at his neck and furrowing his brow as if carefully weighing his next words. "Even a hundred years ago there were not so many such as you, but there were far more than we can find now. As time passes, there are fewer among your number. It is a decline, the enchanted realm retreating just as we have gained some mastery over it. They cannot practice the same spells and curses in France or Spain as we do here, except in valleys high in the mountain regions, or villages forgotten in their forests. The Polish-Lithuanian Commonwealth is blessed that so many of our lands in the east were untamed and teeming with strange creatures. But they grow scant, and scanter are the people who can see them.

"It will be a terrible day, when we no longer have such folk. Our Commonwealth lies on a wide plain and rolling hills; to the east and the west we have no natural defenses, our fertile fields lie open to the eyes of the Czar and the Sultan and the Holy Roman Emperor alike. It is through our magicians, through our magic, we were able to prosper and hold our territories, that the Commonwealth became such as it is now. But already the enchantments grow more difficult to weave, and if that is all to fade, then the hussars will be no more, and the Commonwealth will disappear along with them."

Hieronim took a deep breath, and Andrzej could see the speech had taxed him; he seemed older then, less imposing, his whole body carrying a hint of mourning. The scholar brought the book to a close.

"You can become the hidden strength of the hussars. Will you?"

A different bearing, than before — Hieronim did not say it as an order, but as a plea. And because of this, Andrzej felt something stir within him, beneath the fear and confusion he had felt, and then above it.

"Yes, pan. I will."

~ ~ ~

Pan Jarema did not accompany them to the chamber in the castle cellar that evening. At the dinner table he had only asked if Andrzej had agreed and showed both relief and concern when his retainer said he had. Then his brother emerged saying the preparations were in place and escorted Andrzej to this cell lit only by wax candles. There was an operating table in the center, and a small desk on wheels housed a book, several pitchers, and a rack of sharp-edged implements usually unseen in the lifetime of a layman. On another board affixed to the wall were joints and segments cut from oak or steel and, strangest of all, a cage containing an eagle with hooded head. The eagle shrieked when it heard their footfalls.

Hieronim instructed Andrzej to drink a foul liquid from a mug, some concoction of minerals and oils the color of honey and the consistency of blood, then to remove his linen shirt as he coughed and heaved from the taste, and finally to lie face-down on the table. There Hieronim secured leather straps around Andrzej's prone arms and legs before cutting a new quill. Andrzej grimaced as the nib scratched along his back leaving cold ink in its wake.

The scholar explained as he worked, "I am inscribing on your flesh the Alphabet of the Magi, to ready your body for the changes to come. This is a variation on the original procedure, following the method of Michael Sendivogius, but I have made my own improvements. Before, the operation required the subject actually wear a frame of wings after the fact to be able to call forth their shape. This way, you should be able to summon them at will without the need for sympathetic magic to animate the frame. They should grow no matter what you wear. I will be taking notes. I hope you find that agreeable."

As if what I say would matter now, Andrzej thought.

Hieronim set aside the writing implements and exchanged them for something else; with his head to the side and in the flicker of the candlelight Andrzej could only see a shift in shadows.

"This will hurt. I will not lie. The infusion will dull some of the pain but not all. Rest assured, it will be over soon enough."

Then came some words in a language Andrzej could not place, and Hieronim fed him a dowel to keep teeth from tongue, and then Andrzej's mind swam through muffled screams.

Splinters were driven into his back, first low near the pelvis and then into his shoulders, then screwed in through muscle and meat and bone. Skin peeled back to accommodate sharp metal insertions clicking together or pulling other facets of Andrzej apart, long iron rods and wires strung along his spine. He was aware of these things, and unaware of them, still conscious when he should have fainted and then coming to the sickening realization that whatever Hieronim made him drink was meant to keep him awake through the pain, not take it away.

"Preparation of the flesh successful." The voice seemed so distant. "Now I will synchronize the eagle with your vital forces." The cage clicked open and talons pricked into Andrzej's scapula, but by now that intrusion seemed so much less than what came before. Hieronim yelled something in that same strange language. A brief scream from the eagle followed, this time, and then a writhing, flapping body pressed against him. Feathers brushed Andrzej's skin and shed to fall along the table and mix with the blood that poured from him.

There was something else, though, a sudden twinge that penetrated his body in a different way, and with the last thump of the convulsing eagle body against him he felt it *sink* into his core, pushing through where no incision had been made.

Hieronim wrenched out the structure he'd embedded into Andrzej's spine and carefully pressed the split halves of flesh together, pouring another foul-smelling liquid from a pitcher over Andrzej's mangled skin.

"This will seer the cuts and bind them. Better than stitching. Wait now.... Good, it's taking effect. The new form should be enclosed within you, it may take some time for the muscles to accommodate but I've set it as best I can." The scholar hastily loosened the straps that had held Andrzej's body tight as he'd arched and struggled against the bonds, and he helped Andrzej sit up as the bit rolled on the floor, tooth-marks visible in the soft wood. "The procedure is finished. It went most excellently, I might add. Now that wasn't so bad, was it?"

Andrzej was too busy dry-heaving to reply.

"Here, have some water. Now, it might be a bit early, but… can you try flexing them?"

Looking back over the operating table, there were spots of fresh blood and a few eagle feathers, but nothing else.

And only then, did Andrzej understand.

~ ~ ~

Long lines of winged hussars rode across the pontoon bridges that spanned the Danube, hoof-falls drumming against the wooden planks, the winged frames on their backs bristling in the breeze. Shouts crossed the water as men loaded cannon onto barges. Just beyond the sappers' tents, King Jan Sobieski observed the river crossing. The army of the Polish crown was far from Kraków, marching on the long road to Vienna, for the Ottoman Turks had laid siege to that city, and King Sobieski struck an alliance with the Emperor to come to its aid.

Andrzej was already on the far bank with Jarema's retinue and a small selection of their banner, taking shade under a copse of trees. From here the King should have appeared as a speck, but if Andrzej focused his sight he could clearly make out His Highness's bulk and the pennants flapping upon the lances of the royal guard. With a little more concentration, he would divine the pleased expression on Jan Sobieski's face, doubtless for reaching the river in time to ford it unopposed by the Ottoman army.

Outwardly, Andrzej's eyes were the surest sign that he had changed. The other marks were well-hidden by cloak and armor. He had larger pupils, a slight shift in shape and color of the iris, a keenness to his gaze that he once lacked. It would cause discomfort for folk to look in them, if they did not know what he was. He stared with the intensity of a wolf eyeing a reindeer, or a falcon observing a field mouse, deciding whether to descend from its perch.

That had taken some time to adjust to, this new gift of sight. There were many things, after that day, to which Andrzej had to adjust, and he wasn't sure if he would ever find complete ease with what had taken residence within him.

"Come nightfall, we have orders to send one of the gifted from each banner into the Janissaries' camp, to feel out their positions, and cause some chaos to weaken their resolve." Pan Waldemar Wisniowiecki, commander of Andrzej's banner, spoke pointedly to Jarema. "I trust your retainer is up to the task."

"You can depend on that."

"Will you be able to make it to the outskirts of Vienna by sundown? It's still a fair distance to the city, I know, but your kind have made further flights before in less time."

Andrzej bowed deeply before answering. "Pan, if I leave now, I believe I can."

"Good. Then please, do as you must." Waldemar made a show of turning away. Jarema only gave a nod of encouragement before also turning his back. Andrzej busied himself with securing supplies from his horse to his belt and making sure the straps on his helmet and breastplate were pulled tight.

He walked to the far side of the copse, out from the sight of most, and clear of the trees so he came into a fair view of the open sky. He dropped to his knees, loosening his sabre from his belt and leaning upon it, then crossed himself and said a prayer.

It was not the first time he had done this. Even during this march, he had scouted the terrain many times for his banner, doing his part to guide the army on the swiftest route to Austria. Yet he could not stop the churning in his stomach or the sudden stiffness that came to his limbs just before he embarked. So he asked God, once more, for forgiveness and guidance.

The small measure of comfort was enough to calm him for just a moment. He closed his eyes, and called upon the thing that now shared its body with him. At first it came as a slight drumbeat in his temples, a tightening of his muscles, a thickening in his veins.

He gripped the sword's hilt tighter as he heard and felt the scratching beneath his skin, of talons forcing their way out. The trick now, he reminded himself, was to concentrate on breathing deeply, and maybe then he would not moan or scream.

The wings erupted from his back, forcing their way up through the mail and plate as spectral forms of bone-like smoke that stretched to either side. Then solidifying, not into pure feathers and skin but rather sharp-edged steel. Feathers unfolding in a fan of knives.

Andrzej's breathing had gone ragged, he wheezed and coughed, but he was ready, it was done. Only a few drops of blood splashed the grass, this time, and he unsteadily rose to his feet using the sabre as a crutch. Twitching his wings experimentally, he affixed the sword again to his side.

He took one last deep breath, and leaped, and wheeled his way ever higher into the sky.

Come nightfall, he was swooping upon the Janissary encampment from above with his fellows, striking at the enemy with his sabre and leaving screams and blood and panicked horses in his wake. The soldiers weren't much older than he was, many far younger, and they fled before the demons who fell upon them from the darkness.

~ ~ ~

It was nearly a year later that Andrzej returned to Zuchowa bringing tales of the great winged hussar charge to the gates of Vienna that routed the Grand Vizier Kara Mustafa Pasha's army. It was far more than a year since he last came to the marshland by the lake.

Another still night, no wind rippling the waters, and a new moon so only the stars shimmered on its surface. Andrzej sat on a stone amidst the reeds and whistled a gentle tune, waiting.

She came eventually, the disturbance from her head emerging above the water lapping against the shore. The rusalka had not changed, but she was hesitant, as if wondering, *Is that truly you?*

She waded closer, awkwardly, but suddenly stopped. The expression of soft curiosity he remembered was gone then, replaced by confusion and apprehension and then — terror? Could a rusalka feel fear?

"Wait!" he called, standing up as she took one step back, then, two. "It's me! It's still me!" And he stepped forward as if to go after her, but the rusalka recoiled. Another step, and she dove back into the water with a splash.

He stood there, arm still outstretched towards her, and thought to dive in after her, but knew even as he was, *because* of what he was, he would never catch her.

The next few nights he again waited on the shore, but the rusalka would not appear, and some days later the winged hussars were called to muster. Andrzej rode off again from Zuchowa, not with head held high in pride as he had on the first occasion, but rather staring at the grass below while shedding tears. For while at first he held hope that she had simply avoided him at the lake, he knew now she was gone from the place, and would never return, and that it would happen thus throughout the eastern marches of Poland, because of people like him.

* * *

>>> *When studying the history of 17th century Europe, I sometimes feel like soldiers won battles based on how fancy their uniforms were. No horseman dressed quite the way the Polish hussars did, though. Along with their plate armor, they wore actual wings — wooden frames hung with feathers that they strapped to their backs. These made, by all accounts, a terrifying impression, and I've never shaken the image of their distinctive dress since I first learned about it at age 12.*

But maybe, just maybe, the hussars used those wings for more than scaring the bejesus out of their enemies?

Michal Wojcik

Michal Wojcik was born in Poland, raised in the Yukon Territory and educated in Edmonton and Montreal. He has a Master's Degree in History from McGill University, where he studied witchcraft trials, medieval priests who tried to summon demons and, occasionally, 17th century texts about giant wheels of enchanted cheese. His stories have appeared in *Those Who Make Us*, *Clockwork Canada*, *On Spec*, *The Book Smugglers* and *Pornokitsch*. He currently lives in Whitehorse.

Saddle and Snake

R. W. Hodgson

I want to shout it's not my fault, but as Delgado pulls me from my pony, twisting my foot from the stirrup before setting my feet flat on the dusty earth, I realize it doesn't matter. When you're a hundred feet down a cliff side from your cattle drive in the middle of the Sonoran Desert during a drought, suddenly 'a cow kicked a calf and spooked my pony' doesn't seem worth the bother to speak.

"Wait here," Delgado calls, running through the brush towards his screaming horse. My pony has run off into the canyon. Delgado's broke its leg when he brought it down the cliff after me.

Above the ridge, the brown tips of a line of cattle heads snakes along the edge. And there: the brim of a pale hat of one of the other vaqueros. I call up to them, my voice as loud as a boy's can be, but there's no sign they hear. As if to emphasize the point, Delgado lets out a great whoop and fires off his gun. The sound echoes around the canyon but the cattle drive does not stop.

Delgado clutches his leg; the horse must've kicked him. He's trying to put the horse out of its misery but it takes him three more bullets. Alfaro, the eldest vaquero, always said Delgado couldn't shoot. But seeing as he's so good at everything else a vaquero might do, I never quite believed it until now.

Delgado struggles with the body of his horse. When he is done I am unsurprised to see him lift his prized saddle in triumph before slinging it over his shoulder.

"Do you have any water?" he says. He's huffing from the exertion; the sweat is pouring down his face. It's only mid-morning, but down here in the valley the heat is near enough to cook a man.

I shake my head. "Everything was strapped to the pony."

Delgado checks himself. He has two canteens strapped to his hip and another four on the saddle, but out of them all only three still have water.

"We'll follow the trail as best we can." He squints against the sun. "Keep out of the worst heat of the day." Delgado smiles but he already looks strained. There is no *following the trail* here; we must walk around the steep cliffs through dry creosote bushes for miles and miles before we are near the path again.

We start out but don't get far before we have to sit huddled against the cliff in the only shadow left in the valley, and wait for the worst swelter to pass. We take cautious mouthfuls of water from one of the canteens, warmer than the air and laced with the taste of oiled leather.

"Why did you bring the saddle?" I ask, even though I mostly know the answer, anything to cut the scorching silence.

He takes it from its perch on his shoulder and lays it out in front of me, lets me run my hand over it. It's a tradition-al vaquero saddle, but exceptional with pointed, toe-shaped stirrups and wide fenders to protect the legs. The seat is ivory, the horn topped with silver. The rest, including an oversized skirt, is brown leather, nearly every inch of which is inlaid with rings and swirls of silver and gold. Nunez, back at the hacienda, says it's just tin and brass, but to me it looks real.

"See this?" He traces the inlay lovingly with a finger. "When Cortés defeated the natives in Tabasco, he commissioned this saddle to commemorate his victory. The gold was from the crown of the king of the Mayans and the silver from the bracelets of their high priest."

It changes each time; once it was the saddle of a vaquero who stumbled upon El Dorado; another time it was crafted by a *duende* spirit who lived in a vast hacienda and made it in thanks for a rescue from a fire. Once he even claimed it had been inlaid with metal from the Holy Lance and the

Holy Grail, brought back to Spain by a crusader and somehow hauled across the world to the deserts of Mexico.

I point wordlessly at the base of the horn, where carved crudely into the ivory it reads 1817.

"That is the year I was born. I was my father's first son. He presented it to me right away so my mother could lay me across it. He carved the year he passed it down, as every owner of the saddle before him. Can you see?"

I squint. It's hard to see in the shadows but I make out scratches beneath.

He rubs the ivory lovingly with the worn, tan sleeve of his jacket. "No saddle is more comfortable, no saddle gives you such control over your horse, no saddle protects you so. How could I leave such a saddle in the desert?"

"Is it heavy?" I ask.

Delgado heaves a long sigh. "Yes."

I sleep, clinging to the shade, hot and restless. We set out again once the sun begins to dip, but I feel no relief until it goes below the horizon. It's cooler after sunset, but so cool I shiver. Delgado wraps me in his saddle blanket; it smells like stale horse sweat but I am grateful for its warmth. Him, he keeps warm by slinging the saddle across his back and singing into the night.

The sky is clear, I can see every star in the heavens but I see other things too. Three times I almost call out to Delgado that I've found a pool of water only to find it's disappeared after a few steps. Sometimes, when I turn my head too quickly, the wall of the cliff changes for a moment into the smooth brown clay wall of the hacienda. There is no heat to trick my eyes so I can only think it's because of how tired I am.

The morning sun only makes it worse. When the heat of the day arrives, the world seems to melt and change around me with every step. It's like walking through a dream. We are down to the last few mouthfuls of water from Delgado's canteens, and the murky sips do nothing to calm my visions. Delgado struggles under the weight of the saddle on his shoulder. He was sweating before but now his skin is dry and taut; he's panting and struggling to keep his eyes open, as am I.

He takes me round the shoulder and leans me against him as we stagger on.

"What do you see?" he asks.

"I see the hacienda." I try to wet my dry lips. "I see the pond in the field where the cattle drink. I see the barrels of water waiting by the door with their long-handled ladles." I say this even though now, with my hat bent up crookedly against his shoulder, the visions are far away again, merely shadows out of the corner of my eye.

"I would like to see the hacienda," he says, "but at the moment I'm trying to see the snake that is following us. Can you hear the rattle? It's like nothing I've heard before."

I strain to listen. Even when the vision of the hacienda washes over me and I see a rattlesnake sunning itself on the rock by the back door, I hear nothing.

We sleep over midday again, using the saddle skirt for a pillow. I shake when I try to stand, but Delgado pulls me up. Our steps are slow, the radiant earth calls us.

Sometime later, Delgado lets go of me and I sink to my knees in the dust.

He looks around the canyon. "Stop the rattle! You must stop!" He throws the saddle to the ground. "What is the use of this if I am dead?"

I am at the hacienda. The air is warm, but pleasant like a mid-morning in spring, the last scent of night flowers hangs in the air. The calves low in the pen, the old mesquite tree invites me with its shade, but first I turn to the barrel, dip the ladle and pull out fresh water, no doubt drawn from the well by Senõra Mendez this morning. I put it to my lips and drink deep, though it doesn't quench my thirst.

Out of the corner of my eye I see something splayed on the ground. *Delgado's saddle.* But why? Why would it be in the middle of the yard? And wasn't I out in the desert?

I turn back to the ladle. Across the round, polished bowl, there's a sliver of movement. There, behind me, slithering across the ivory seat, as red as fire and blood with a diamond head, is the largest snake I have ever seen. There's a cold prickle at the back of my neck and suddenly I understand I am not at the hacienda, but dying in the desert.

"Delgado!" I can't see him in the layers of mirage. The snake's tail slides off the saddle with a hollow rattle like a coin in a tin bucket. Then the snake is gone again, covered by the false world.

I race for the saddle; it's the only thing that seems real. As soon as my fingers touch the horn, the hacienda dissolves and I am back in the Sonoran. I scrape my hand across my mouth and spit; it wasn't water but creosote leaves I'd been shoveling in.

Delgado is behind me drinking dust, and behind him, the snake. Its body is at least as thick around as I am. It's coiling itself up, preparing to strike him.

I leap to my feet; the snake's tail rattles. Within moments, the mirage appears again at the corners of my vision. I run back to the saddle and heave it over my shoulder. I stagger under its weight. *How has he carried it all these miles?*

"Delgado." I put my hand on his arm. He looks up at me, the glaze lifting from his eyes. He smacks his mouth as though he's just realized what he's been putting in it. The sensation of being watched creeps over me; the snake's rattle echoes through the canyon. I can't explain why I didn't hear it before.

I push Delgado down, just out of the way of the strike of the snake's fangs. Its body slaps hard against me.

Delgado is clutching at his head, but as he presses on my shoulder, his hand on the saddle, he focuses on the snake in front of us.

"My God!" he says, pulling us both up. We run through the sand, crunching the creosote beneath our boots, each with a hand in a stirrup. The creature moves like the crack of a whip, no longer needing to stalk us. Against the cliff face we turn and I pull out my knife. Delgado pulls out his revolver.

He shoots twice. Neither bullet lands near the snake. I'm not surprised. If he was a terrible shot before, two days of baking in the heat would help no man.

The jaws of the snake open wide as it strikes, its fangs spring out, longer and sharper than my knife. Delgado yanks the saddle from my hand just in time to block the creature from his face. It recoils. I stab with my knife but it seems to glance off the scales. It's difficult for me to tell as the hacienda is growing about me again.

A smack across my face. Delgado has thrown the saddle at me. He's down in the scrub trying to reload his revolver: he must put black powder and then a bullet into each chamber. I stand on my feet and peer about the canyon. Impossibly, the crimson snake has disappeared into the dust.

Delgado throws his bullets on the ground and drinks dirt again. Since he needs both his hands to load, I take off his hat and throw the stirrup fender on top of his head. In a moment, he's working at his revolver again.

The snake's rattle returns, but I can't determine where the sound is coming from.

"There, Delgado, do you see it?" I poke him with my boot.

"I'm almost ready."

The snake looks almost ready too, tightly wound, tail rattling, its snout just peeking over a coil.

Delgado throws his hat back on his head and gets to his feet, clutching the stirrup in his left hand and the revolver in his right. The snake strikes. Delgado fires off a shot, this time he hits it but the bullet doesn't penetrate the thick scale. Before he can cock back the revolver and pull the hammer, the snake changes direction and comes right at me. I raise the saddle as a shield, but the snake's weight knocks me to the ground. I stab at it around the saddle. Near the ground my knife glances off of it, but on my next swipe at the point where the creature touches the saddle, it sinks easily into the flesh.

I pull the knife back in surprise. The creature writhes, then slithers back and moves to strike me again. Delgado is aiming at it and, in consequence, at me.

I drop the saddle and run. Distantly, I hear the crack of the revolver and the snake's rattle, but they fade into the gentle buzz of a cicada. I look around the yard for the water barrel, the day is calm and not too warm. But behind me in front of the calves' pen, I see the strangest sight: Delgado's prized saddle hovering above the ground and pressed against it, an immense red snake.

I stare at it, the strangeness of the scene fighting against my desperate need to find the water barrel. Something small and hard hits my knee and I buckle to the ground. The object disappears before I can see what it is. Then something else lands in my lap. I find one of the stirrup guards in my hand, cut loose from the saddle. As the mirage fades, I find the pistol at my feet.

Delgado screams my name as he fights the snake. The creature's teeth swing open like a gate from its mouth, snapping over the edge of the saddle. I pick up the pistol and aim it. I'm no crack shot, but the vaqueros at the hacienda like to fight over who taught me best.

I aim for the tail at first, but remember my knife and point it up to where the snake's head touches the saddle. I fire one shot, hoping the bad aim is Delgado and not the revolver itself. I hit the creature. I expect a scream but it only flails in silence, twisting like a frayed rope in the wind. Delgado drops the saddle with the snake on top of it, and I tip up the revolver, cock the hammer and fire again. I make my mark a second time.

Delgado pulls his machete from his belt and hacks at the neck of the snake over the ivory seat until its head come free from its body. His eyes widen and I rush to his side. The creature has no innards: no muscles, guts or bones. It is hollow and empty. Instead of blood, a liquid, clear like pure, fresh water, rushes from the wound like a fountain. Delgado cups his hands beneath and drinks handful after handful.

"Come," he says. "Come and drink."

I take a step back, and then another. The thirst in me is great but so is the fear.

"You must drink!" he cries.

I turn and run through the dust. I only make it a few steps before Delgado throws himself on top of me and pushes me to the ground. He pries my mouth open and tips a few drops onto my tongue. The moment it touches, the thirst leaves me. And for the rest of my days, I never feel thirst again.

We take the skin of the strange creature and sling the saddle between our shoulders as we walk. On the edge of nightfall, we see a wasp and later a bat. By midnight the cacti are watching our steps in their tall silence and the coyote is howling from a distant ledge. By morning, we have found the hoof-trodden trail.

Somewhere along the way Delgado starts muttering. At first I think the desert heat has driven him mad; it is only when we are in view of the hacienda that I realize he's talking to the ants crossing the trail and the birds flitting above us. As a matter of fact, far at the edges of my hearing, I am sure I can hear them too.

Delgado never again drove cattle across the Sonoran. He remained a fixture on the porch of the hacienda into his old age, talking to the cattle and mice and cursing the blackbirds.

One evening, not long after our return, he paused conversation with a sparrow long enough to give his saddle to me. He'd scratched out the 1817 and wrote 1848. "The year it becomes yours."

I grew to be a vaquero the likes of which the Sonoran had never seen. It was said the animals listened when I talked, the wildest calf would calm in the yoke of my snake skin lasso and I saw every crevice of the desert as I perched on my inlaid saddle. I told a different story every time someone asked me its origin, but my favorite was of a vaquero who found it while wandering under the desert sun.

I feared nothing, except the days when I passed Delgado by the door and he would say, "There? Do you see it? There's a snake curled in the yard."

* * *

>>> *Most horses were owned by haciendas, but vaqueros provided their own equipment. Saddles were prized possessions which could make or break one's skill on a horse and were passed down from generation to generation. Vaqueros originated in 16th century Colonial Spain and still exist to this day. Emerging from indigenous horse riders hired to manage cattle by colonial landowners, many of their riding and cattle handling techniques were adopted by American cowboys.*

R.W. Hodgson

R.W. Hodgson lives with her husband and two children in Ottawa. She spent her childhood in Lawrencetown, Nova Scotia. Her short fiction has appeared in *Tesseracts Twenty-One: Nevertheless* and *Fire: Demons, Dragons, & Djinns*.

Joint-Eaters

Halli Lilburn

Fairies do not like potatoes. Tis cos of the eyes. If the eyes of a potato can see them they run a hide. A fairy won't chucker any shenanigans if the eyes are watching them.

When the blight came from America in '45 all the lumpers got the dry rot and every small plot o' land that grew spud crops were lost. True, we were starving but 'twas the fairies that turned all of Ireland to hell.

Father returned from a bout o' work in England where they fed him real meat all winter. I thought he'd be healthy looking at least, but he was weak, and his flesh hung off his bones like a naked, baby bird. His eyelashes were falling out and his teeth were loose in his mouth. He said 'twas from the water; that fairies went in his mouth when he drank and ate half the food down in his stomach. He called them joint-eaters. I suppose they were starving too with nothing to eat and without the eyes, nothing was putting fear in them. They could take whatever they wanted.

"There's no cure for joint-eaters just as much as there's no cure for the blight," he says to me.

"That is false, Da. We need eyes," I say.

He picks up a lumper lying dead on the ground and crushes it in his hand. "And where will ye find some?" He drops the remains and they float down like dust.

I stomp on the dirty rubbish left of our garden. "We'll make some, won't we."

"I'll try anything," he says.

Paint is easy to make if ye don't mind stirring bird droppings and lye and whatnot. That's for white colors. Black is easy too. Ye just burn some wood and scoop up the remains. Our cottage is made of stone. That's where I paint the eyes and some on the walls and on the path, all the way to the road. All Ireland's made of stone, so I find the closest looking to potatoes and build nice-sized piles round the door. I get a wee bit creative and put some character in them. I make them angry and penetrating, stacked up four or five pair at a time.

"No fairies will be cursing us now," I say.

"Siobhan Slack, what have ye done?" Father grabs his beard. "I cannot work nor sleep with all these eyes on me. Even on me cup and me plate? I cannot ate on this. Tis bird shite."

"Don't fret, Da, there be nothing to ate besides."

The yard is quiet. No birdsong, not even any wind. I lay awake waiting for me father to go snoring, but he don't start. He's awake too, listening to the nothing outside. We stay still in our beds half the night looking into the dark and waiting.

In the morning I pluck a dandelion root and make some tea. Father stays groaning in his scratcher.

"I'm so thirsty," he whines so I give him the tea.

"More, lassie." So I give him mine as well.

I realize even if no more joint-eaters invade our gaff, there is still one down in his belly that must come out.

"Come on, Da, git up. We got work to chucker."

"No, Siobhan, the life has left me. You must go on without me."

I've seen people starving. A load of people. They fall asleep and don't wake up. Father should not have reminded me.

"Why do men do so much whining?" I say. "You know, Mother never let out a peep when her time came."

"Oh, Siobhan, I'm so sorry. Bless your mother; her memory gives me strength to hold on." He wrestles with himself to sit up and swing his legs over the bed. "I'm so thirsty."

"Let's go down to the stream and fetch water for tea." I carry the bucket cos Father is too weak.

On the way I think of how to pull the blight outa his belly, but I can't scheme up anything. Why would the bugger want to leave? It's got a warm, cozy place that's safe and feeds himself.

"It's got to want to leave cos its living space is undesirable," I say to meself.

"I need a drink fiercely." Father sighs. He sees the creek and hobbles faster.

"No, Da." I catch him round the collar. "Ye cannot drink. Keep your wee belly dried up." I pull him back to the house.

"I'm dying of thirst." He gets desperate and strong.

"That's it." I find a rope to bind him to the post.

"Ye'll not restrain me," Father shouts and puts up his forks like an American boxer. His mustache quivers.

It might have terrified me when I was young, when his shirt fit properly, and he had muscles to go with those arms, but now his hollow cheeks and knackered eyes gobsmacked me. I notice how skeletal he's gotten; thin as a willow and ready to snap. Still, his eyes are lit with a strange fire. His need for a drink is driving him mad.

"Yer missing a full shilling. Don't fight me, Da." I hold the rope up ready to toss it round his middle.

He swings out and grabs it, but I tear it out of his poor hands, throwing him forward onto his hunkers. I wrap the rope round him and drag him to the post.

"Demon wane!" he screeches and kicks the back of me hunkers.

I fall into the post but keep my grip on the rope. I land hard on me shoulder and role away as his foot comes looking for me noggin. It slams into the dirt beside me head like he was an elephant crushing a peanut.

I imagine what my brain would look like smooshed into the dirt and I scream, "That's it!" and yank that rope so hard he knocks his noggin against the post and passes out.

I lash the rope round him as many times as it'll go. Me shoulder isn't working so I wrap it up in a sling. Eejit. Fool. I am trying to help, and his crazies will kill me. While the ol' lad sleeps I go and get meself a water bucket. Me cup is painted with eyes. As I'm drinking, I gawk into the liquid.

Would Father's belly get dried up enough to expel the joint-eater or would it kill him first? What if he's tied up for days? There must be a way to make it happen faster.

I look round the room trying to fen something to help. Me eyes land on a wee box of salt. I haul the box to Da who's leaning on the post with his gob wide open. I spoon it down until his throat is clogged and he starts choking. It wakes him up and he coughs up salt for donkey's years.

When he can talk he yells, "What the bleeding hell have ye done?" He struggles under the rope but gets nowhere.

"Tis for yer own good." Once his gob is empty I give him another dose of salt.

He spits most of it out. "I need a drink right nigh!" he howls.

"No, ya don't." I stomp me foot. "Ye can't give it what it wants. Ye need to starve it out."

"I'm gonna die," he cries.

"Think before you speak, Da."

He huffs and grumbles to himself for a donkey's years. Tears fall down his bake. "Tis everything happening round us. Tis more than I can handle. We gotta go."

"Go where?"

"To America. Before we land in our graves like yer Ma." He looks out the windy towards her plot under the garden.

"Well, we are not taking that fairy with us to America. He is staying right here. So, open yer gob and ate this." I shove the box in his bake.

"Tis bleeding dear." He pouts for a moment, shuddering, then spoon after spoon he forces it down.

I set the water bucket in front of himself.

"Ye torture me." He can't reach the bucket, but the fresh peggy dell floats under his nose.

"Not ye. The fairy." I make a soothing mud on the floor and smear it on his cheeks, trying to make the outside of him more happy than the inside.

Night falls. I light a fire to ward off the chill outside. The day has drained me soul and misery weighs on both us. I try laying down for a rest but the ol' man is sweating and gagging. His throat starts wobbling like the buggers are trying to crawl out. His whole body is heaving like he might explode, and it scares me.

"Da, what do I do?"

He can't answer me. His eyes roll back into his noggin. A blackness fills his gob and he coughs up a dark liquid. In his heaving, out squirms a salamander, quite unnatural in shape and size, its features slightly human-looking and down-right evil. The creature pulls its squishy body out from inside me father, leaving a trail of black slime running down his chin, mixing with the mud. I hold me hands over me gob to stop meself screaming. Then another wicked slug crawls out with a sloppy sound. Then another. Father pukes it out with a gush of slime. How he could survive, starving from the famine and having three joint-eaters, I'll never know. Bless me poor ol' man.

The black creatures slither over to the bucket in a hurry but that drink they were so desperate for doesn't come. A black and white eye painted on the bucket stops them short. The magic in the sigil starts working. The iris of the eye that I painted there looks straight ahead but suddenly it turns to focus down on the monsters. Anywhere they go the eye has them in its sight. They stumble over each other trying to back away from the staring eye, but, as they turn round, there is another eye glaring from the wall and another on the peg of the table. Each one has come alive to move and fen the salamanders wherever they run.

Writhing in agony, they squeak and scream, leaving trails of black goo as they scatter. I throw me cup at them. It bounces over and hits one, stamping a bird shite eye into its black skin, searing the mark into its flesh. They escape out the west door, but their panic rises even outside cos of the cairns and the wall and the path. All the rocks I painted were moving and tipping, chasing those blasted things away. Eyes stacked up upon eyes following them into the darkness of night.

When the eyes can no longer fen them wicked slugs the magic fades and their pupils hold still. The wind picks up, the crickets chirp and the land returns to normal.

Father slumps over and I pick his head up to rouse him. "Wake up, Da."

He comes round and he groans. "Water."

I untie his arms and give him the bucket. He plops his whole bake right in and drinks himself for donkey's years.

* * *

>>> *There is a half-acre site in Manhattan named the Irish Hunger Memorial to remember the one million Irish people who died during the Great Famine. One million more immigrated to America during the years 1845 to 1849. On this site grows grasses and vegetation native to Ireland. Rocks were brought over from every county with their names carved into each stone. A cottage was also transported from Carradoogan in County Mayo, donated by the Slack family. The roof is gone but the stone walls remain. On the door on the west-facing wall, under the lintel is painted the smudge of a symbol. The marking is made of charcoal and bird feces. It is in the shape of an eye.*

Halli Lilburn

Halli Lilburn was born in Edmonton, Alberta. Her first story at age nine was about unicorns and fairies. Over the years she has explored other genres including poetry, science fiction, paranormal and horror. She has works published with *Tesseracts 18: Wrestling with Gods, Spirited by Leap Books, Carte Blanche, Vine Leaves, Renaissance Press* and many others. She teaches workshops on creative writing and art journaling. She is a certified structural editor with essentialedits.ca and is an editor for *The Dame Was Trouble,* with Coffin Hop Press. She is a librarian, artist, and mother of three.

http://hallililburn.blogspot.com

Lady Jordan

Bianca Sayan

There is something amiss, to be sure. There is little in the dirt to tell me much, none of the lingering smell of high emotion. The bank of Cape Fear River is a pleasant enough place, always seemingly quiet, but always deceptively so. Now, there is no one hiding among the bushes. No one shivering elbow-deep in the reeds. Not one wretched soul for me to come upon.

Gods above and below, what I would do for a bounty right about now.

It is here that I usually make very good slave-catching. It isn't the best trod path in that railroad. One is just as like to find an escapee in town, hiding behind false papers and a well-heeled hat. But Fayetteville has more than its share of lazy slave-catchers in town, all jostling to seize upon any poor fool they can. Out here, one is more like to find the slave who looked north one day and just started walking. There is nothing but plantation north of Fayetteville. Bad for hiding, bad for sneaking along quietly come daytime. Only on the banks can a runaway make good time. For me, the best slave-catching is done here, along this stretch. It is a different kind of hunt than catching a well-dressed escapee. These fellows aren't necessarily well-prepared or able to find their way. Their bounties are more modest, but I do just fine and am happy to do without the bother of the townspeople. It has reliably made good income for me for several seasons. But, it's deadly quiet now. Deadly quiet. I've yet to run a bounty this spring, and I'm starting to feel the pinch.

In the fat years, it was a simple matter. I'd come into to town to examine the fresh bounties posted and reconsider older postings. I'd wager I'm a decent assessor of which of these fellows I'm likely to find. In the evening, I run down the bank of Cape Fear River till I come upon them. I follow emotion left along the trail: the anxiousness, the sorrow seeps into the soil and the river itself, rolls off them like sweat.

I've tracked it for much of three seasons, using and slowly sharpening my skill with Work. When I first started, I had barely an understanding of what I was doing; my Work bloomed memories of my mother's rough little backwoods spells. But I've come to understand, and, if I may be immodest, become quite skillful in my craft. It has afforded me a respectable clapboard house, a good horse, fine clothes, good living, and, one day, by God, a life of ease.

"It's no use, Dark." It's an affectation to talk to my horse, but I do it just so. "There ain't nothing to be found here."

But on the way home, with no witchcraft or like, just my hound sniffing away, that I find two white men with miserly bounties after them. I don't often go for criminal bounties. They are more dangerous, and I'd rather an easy bounty. Better to go after someone scared and poorly prepared, no gun or knife on them. But I'm feeling the pinch enough, so I go after them, make a show with my Colt. Nipping one on the ear quiets them real fast, and they become docile enough for me to truss them up and lead them into town. Tom, idle in his sheriff's hat, doesn't seem to mind the break in quiet. Jorge, a fellow slave-catcher, and his loyal bottle, keep him company. Jorge is not a very skillful slave-catcher, durn more lucky than skillful, but he makes do with his luck. Once the fellows are unhappily locked up, Tom digs around for the bounty, while I examine the bounties posted, only piling around each other.

"What's new?"

"See for yourself." He gestures at the hanging pages. "Not that you're like to find them."

"No." I acknowledge. "Not like, it seems." There are new bounties posted to the board, the amounts more favorable than I would expect. I suppose owners are becoming desperate as well.

"Well, Tom, what do you make of all this?"

Tom spits. "Damned buggers are getting wilier."

The comment is useless. That much is obvious. The question is how.

"You know it has been unbearably barren. Still as many bounties posted as before, yet every one of us has gross misfortune. Misfortune, yes." He trails off. "That's the only way to explain it." He shakes his head. "The only way to explain it."

For simple men, maybe. Unable to imagine, men like Tom use misfortune as their whipping horse, but that has never done me any good. My compatriots are quick to underestimate the slave, think of them simple. They are not simple. Moreover, they are desperate, which can make them quicker to think, quicker to run, and quicker to fight. These men are very happy when they are lucky, but many cannot make their luck.

Of course, I have an advantage over everyone else, a deeper power and knack for finding. Surely, I can root out the weevils of my fruit-bearing tree. I head for the town hexe, determined to help myself in this matter.

The hexe's name is Sarah Holden, and she appears to run a pocket millinery from her house. One enters the house to find a determined spinster among a pile of frills and notions. By some clever Work, whether a mirage or not, behind or amongst the millinery stuff is a sizeable collection spell work notions.

I find the shop as I found it last. She is wearing simple and severe clothing, as if all the frillery were scared off of her onto the walls. "Good day, Mizz Holden."

"Mister Caudle." She leaves some needlework be and looks to me expectantly.

"I need a few items, if you might have them." I read from my list. Most things I use are quite plain and I can find on my own, but often there is an intuition that something stranger is needed.

Mizz Holden purses her thin lips together. She never asks what for. I hazard that she is sensible enough to know the pernicious nature of her customers. She is a young thing, without seeming young. She is a woman, but powerfully unwomanly. It is the art of our kind, I guess, to obscure what one is and to make a vision one wants. She has made a vision of herself as a woman devoted to her craft and bound for spinsterhood.

She turns, huffing out a few choice words in some other language, something I haven't heard in these parts. She practices a Work foreign to me, but any practitioner, no matter their origin seems to find what they need in her shop. I don't know much about the Work of other languages. I hear in passing that Creole is particularly elaborate and expressive, that French is often unnecessarily flowery. I find German suits me, thoroughly spare and practical. The materials deviate similarly.

The air parts like window curtains, and she sticks her hands behind her mirage of frills and ribbons to pull out a few bundles. It's much like one would expect from the devil's work, grim things. It's best not to inquire how these things are got, but the human provenance is guaranteed with Sarah Holden.

As her hands draw from the mirage, the air flickers. For a moment I can see the shelves piled with uncomfortable things: English apothecary bottles, paper packets, bones in a jumble, vases of feathers and insects, pieces of paper with the mark of blood on them, coils of hair, apothecary jars, pieces of colorful rock. In the next moment I am again looking at cheerful cards of bone buttons, lace tatting, silk ribbons, jars of needles.

Sarah, too, flickers. In a moment quicker than my eye can understand there is another Sarah, darker, obvious features from an African mother or father.

She is still working away, packaging up my things as calmly as you please. My mind is slow to cotton on to it, and I am fumbling for an explanation. In any case, the poor woman is unaware that some Work of hers has failed dismally, if only for a moment. I am certainly not about to enlighten her, not yet. My own mind is still working away, deciding what to make of all this. I am nothing if not a careful card-player. I know to hold my hand until intuition tells me to play.

Out on her veranda, my purchases laid out discretely before me, I manage to fashion a little something for little Mizz Holden. I almost cannot bear the indignity of hiding the Work in a posie of fleabane and hawkbush, but it will make do.

She is back at her needlework, not even deigning to raise her gaze to meet me. Perfect. Before she even lays eyes on me, I blow through the posie; it but grazes her face, and a deep glaze sets in her. Her eyes are growing dull as the Work fills her up. I wait a moment or two, then I ask her. "Why has the slave-catching trade dried out in Fayetteville, Mizz Holden?"

I open her mouth and draw out a little bit of paper as the Work manifests itself. I swallow it and the answer sparks in my head, like an idea. *Lady Jordan.*

Blazes, with Work like this the answers are crooked, often no help at all. *Lady Jordan, Lady Jordan.* Maybe a woman? Maybe a ship? Maybe Work of some kind.

I am thinking, thinking, thinking. Well, it is apparent to me now. I have done what I have denounced others of doing, underestimating others. It is perhaps the first time that I have considered the underground railroad may be making use of its own Work. It has also occurred to me for the first time that this very sort of Work may be at the very center of the abolitionists and their mysterious new underground. This is a world all unknown to me, to bump up against other Work, to find it operating against me. It behooves another question, if Mizz Holden stays pliant.

"Well, Mizz Holden, pray tell, how does one banish a glamour like yours?"

Her lips press together, something at work behind them. They fold open like a bloom, revealing a little blood-red flower. I swallow that, too, and the sense of something, like a terrible opera, looms over me. I gather is it the intuition for the Work at hand. Why, thank you, Mizz Holden.

It never came a surprise to me there was Work in Sarah Holden's little nook. It is only sensible; we lie within a Christian nation and they may now not be susceptible to revisit witch-hunts, but I'm not inclined to invite the inquiry.

Also, one loses an advantage when spell work is recognized: the aspect of surprise. Of course, she would obscure her own Work from her customers. So few can comprehend what is operating against them. It's much like cleaving the head from a chicken; the body is still working to comprehend what has befallen it. And what a goddamned bunch of chickens, every one of them. I'm ashamed to say I've been one myself.

I tip my hat to her. "I assure you, Mizz, this won't weigh upon your pretty little brow. You won't remember a thing."

At home, I ponder the Work at hand. As a child, I never paid mind to my Work heritage, what my mother called *arbeit*. I have strong recollections of my ma speaking an unfamiliar sort of German that soothed landlords, found what was lost, made problems disappear. It is amazing what a man can do with a few memories. I resurrected from those memories the words for finding lost things, tried to use it to find runaways. It didn't work so well for people. I remembered how my mother twisted the words together with bits of grass to look like a little person, or carried a string of nightjar claws, or painted a little mark on the soles of shoe. It took me time to piece it together for myself. I took what I knew for finding things and changed the words, the movements, the physical things bit by bit, till I got what I wanted. It came by simple materials and simple methods: mixing kerosene, salt, rosemary in to the dirt and lighting a match, tuning it for finding fear. I kept testing it on townsfolk, writing something that sussed out secrets, fear. I tell you, I learned more about some townsfolk than I care to say. Lord, it took me all winter to put that spell together, but, come spring, it paid off in spades. Imagine my wonder when I first felt the pull, and was led to an escapee, hiding up in a tree and caught completely unawares. The next day, and I had a heavy twenty-five dollars in my pocket.

I didn't rightly understand *arbeit* until I cared to make use of it. I've come to learn it isn't the same for everyone. Never the same questions asked, nor the same bits offered up, nor the same effect. Everyone comes to it on their own, I suppose, and makes their own Work from things they see and feel and sense. A piece of Work has to be invented and discovered, found within the cracks of the real world, drawn out, shaped into something with intention.

I have two aims: to find these escapees as I did before, and to crack their glamors. The finding will be simple: as I was drawn to fear before, now I will be drawn to Work itself. By sundown, my intuition has lain out a rope soaked in a mixture of kerosene and dirt, the remnants of previous Work woven in. I light a match and wait for the fire to take its course.

Cracking the glamors are another matter. I pay heed to the horrible opera buzzing in the back of my head; a costly recipe if there ever was one.

I stand to gain quite a bit from revealing their true natures, but what I'll gain in gold I'll give in flesh. It is apparent this Work needs a sacrifice, and it is an uneasy matter of selecting a spot. I stare down at my body, trying to decide what may be spared. I am not a stout man. There is no generous material to take from. I pace the lean-to as the knife sits outside in the coals. When it is done, I'll take to myself. It will be a long night.

By sunrise, I already feel the pull. I pull my boots over the pink swaddling. It hurts something fierce, but I can't spare any Work for my own comfort. I'm too worn. There is a little bundle on the lean-to table. It is still fresh, but the longer I dawdle the less I'll be able to make of it.

I'm loath to go back to town, but the Work is fresh and I'm eager for an answer. My feet carry me past Tom's, past poor Mizz Holden, past Perry's gin mill and the respectable Searbook hotel, right to the town's train platform.

The train is in the station. My feet lead me to a knot of well-to-do folk: an aged grandmother and a young, handsome couple. The pull is insistent, but I can't help but doubt it. These folk look nothing if not terribly ordinary. The couple looks easy, smiling and laughing. They're making their goodbyes with the grandmother before they step on the train car, perhaps lovebirds on some sort of post-nuptial jaunt. I wager it isn't the couple I'm after, but I'd also wager that I'm not here for the grandmother, neither. If it's the couple, I'll miss my chance in a few moments. I take to the only thing I can think of, contriving to bump into the grandmother. I set my sights far beyond the station, her form just out of view, and affect a hurried pace. We almost collide; I brush past, but just enough to feel the fierce burn where we met and the pull back as I stride away from her. I don't need to look back to tell her eyes are following me.

If I were part of that damnable underground, I'd aim to look like a harmless old spinster, too, I say to myself.

Before leaving, I switch my lambskin coat inside out and put on my hat. She's not like to recognize me, but following her around town yields nothing. Finally, she sets off to the edge of town, a modest, but sizable lean-to awaiting her.

I think on my advantages and what I might find behind her door. While I can come and go now as I might please, the odds are in my favor and I don't care to take a chance on losing this trail.

Not for the first time, I think on the Work I have at my immediate disposal. This art is a long game, one of planning, acquisition, and strategy. It is not lithe and light on its feet. I've nothing in hand or at hip to aid me except my Colt, and I'm loath to use something as base and inelegant.

The spinster is in the back of the lean-to by the window, my entrance as easy as you please. I have to make myself known to her.

"Good day, ma'am."

She starts, but her manners get the better of her. "Good day, sir." Then, cautiously, "Is there something I can help you with?"

The gun makes my intentions known.

"Please—" the spinster calls out, discarding pretense. "You would attack a lady in her own home?" Her voice has a lovely empathic quaver, but I'm unmoved.

"Come now, witch, I've followed you about town all day on your little errands and I tire of this."

"Witch?" She affects a little gasp. I don't need any Work to see through it. I cannot stand another moment of her little game. I lob my bundle at her, a mess of gore and flora splatters over her chest, and, just like that her glamor is gone.

This woman has the rough look of a cotton-picker about her, baked in the sun for years, all the youth thrashed out of her. She is maybe four-score. Her skin is coal-colored and healthy, despite her years of hard living, but it bears many marks upon it. Either she once had a cruel master, or her personal Work often uses blood.

What only occurs to me now is there must be only a handful of people capable of doing the work. Perhaps she one of these, the proverbial Lady Jordan leading her charges to Jordan itself. I test my hypothesis.

"Well, well, it is Lady Jordan herself." She starts at the familiar name and gathers herself up, trying to conjure herself some dignity.

"My people will be coming for me shortly." She is haughty, arrogant in the face of my advantage.

I ignore her. "I suspect," I point at her chest, "if I were to follow that couple at the station and affect them similarly, I would see similar transformations and find two fat little bounties to match."

She is silent, confirming what I've only guessed.

"If I make good time, I might be able to cross paths with them, catch up with some of your travelers as far north as Baltimore. Hell, I imagine I would have very good luck finding your previous charges all over New York City. Halifax. Boston. I could keep myself busy for quite a while, even if your little stream dries up."

Her look is imperious. "You might, but we have God on our side."

I can't help but laugh. "Well, I can't say I've ever met a Christian witch before, but I can't imagine the Lord taking to that well." It is an odd match. Abolitionism is Christian-dominated, and it would be at best an uneasy friendship. Those that welcome spell work and practice it recognize the contradiction, naturally. There is no room in a man's heart for both God and spell work, and there is not a Christian among us. It follows that we are not dominated by Christian feelings, certainly not for the cause of a few wayward slaves.

She sniffs rudely, but we both know she is in no position to be contrarian. Anyway, I have what I want, and more. I could be taking bounties up and down the coastline right now, and there's no sense in dawdling here.

"I'm trying to think of any repercussions towards ending you."

"There are plenty." She is wary but not as afeared as I'd expect. It makes me inclined to believe she knows something I don't.

"Well, by all means, Mizz Jordan. Why don't you persuade me to preserve your breath."

She is looking at me with a depth of hate, a candor only a powerful person is capable of making. She spits out a few words, and I am quick to hit her hard in the mouth. I've drawn blood, which could make her Work worse, so I am quick to fumble out a few words, bind my fingers together around her bundle to seal up her lips tight. No barbed words from her tricky little mouth.

Of course, this is the opportune time for a knock at the door.

"Your people?" I ask. But, of course, she cannot speak, and her gaze is sullen. Her people, and they are not like to go away.

The knocking is insistent. Blast, I have what I want. If I could, I would just crawl through the window, and be leagues away by sunset, chasing after the pull of these little pouches.

"Lydia!" The call is from the other side of the door. "Careful as she flies?" But poor mute Lydia cannot render the phrases signifying safety or danger.

Their entrance is plum foolish, bursting right into the range of my Colt, but they're sensible enough to stop short at the sight of the gun. All are dressed plain and respectable, just the sort that doesn't get noticed.

"Lydia!" One of them squawks. There's five of them, a few more than is comfortable. It's just a matter of getting out alive, though, and I have more than one advantage.

"Come one step closer and I'll break the spell for the lot of you, everywhere from Savannah to Boston." There's a change in their eyes and I know I have them. How I might do that, I'm not terribly sure, but they certainly don't know that.

There's a terrible hushed silence, terrible for all of us.

"What do you want?" The girl in front is careful, eyes appraising.

"You'd be pleased to know my needs are modest. I've simply made a wrong turn and would like to be on my way." I can't help but smile, but their sense of propriety will preserve me.

There's an awful cry behind me, Lydia has pulled her lips apart against my little trick. Her face is a horror, blood leaking down her chin.

She lunges at me. "Sleep," she spits. Blood. Potent, powerful blood. I'm like a rag doll, the floor meeting me with a terrible thud.

"Bully for you, Lydia! He dropped like a stone!" They are tending to Lydia tenderly, dabbing at her lips. My limbs hold fast to the ground. Lydia looks at me dispassionately.

"He is inside a glamour of sleep, but it won't last for long. We must," she purses her lips together distastefully, "dispose of him. He told me he would take down the railroad from here to Halifax, and he has the means to do it. Look what he has done to my own glamour. It would behoove us to be cautious."

"String 'em up," a tall fellow mumbles, but the girl in front stamps her foot at him.

"I won't stand for it and neither will our God, Jonathan."

"You're a fool if you think he won't take every one of us in and dismantle the railroad itself, bit by bit. There is more at stake than one man's life."

"I think...." Lydia's uncertainty is my salvation, I can see it in her eyes. She's clever with glamors certainly, but this is another matter, one that requires blood. It's their moral compass that holds them back and plays to my advantage. I really have so little fear from a lamb of God. "I can silence him, but ... it will not be our finest hour. I'll need his tongue."

My tongue.

"No." I don't know why I say it out loud. Then, more carefully. "Lydia, I would think again. If you do this, I will find you. I might not talk, but I will have other means at my disposal."

"No, I imagine your flesh will be sufficient to make this particular Work very powerful. You won't be able to write, neither." She has the audacity to sound sympathetic. "I think it will extend so far to greatly limit the kind of Work you do. It will certainly keep you silent on the matter."

"Lydia—" Not this. I'd have nothing, hobbled, with no means to make my way and make my advantage, all possible Work still there, but just beyond me. Banished back to a world of crude fumbling, plain things with no secret means.

But the boys have me by the head and jaw and the rest are circling.

"I'm so sorry. God forgive us," Prudence whispers.

Lydia stands over me, her eyes a pool of empathy. Damn these treacherous bleeding hearts. "I'll do what little I can for you. I'll make a little illusion to send you somewhere nice, serene. You won't feel much. When you wake up, it will all be over, as civilized as we can make it." The compassion in her voice only makes it worse.

* * *

>>> *It is terrifying to read first-person accounts of human beings escaping US slavery pre-abolition, setting out alone by foot in the backwoods or through cities and railcars. People that made the decision to go were hunted while racing toward some intangible threshold for freedom. The current understanding of the US Underground Railroad and escaping up north generally is that it was a varied, improvised, and largely one was on one's own. These accounts also reveal so much agency, cleverness, bravery, and integrity, but also the horror of human beings when they have 'othered' and dehumanized another human. In this story, the Railroad is more talked about at the time, more structured and organized, with formidable magical element on its side.*

Bianca Sayan

Bianca works and hibernates in Toronto. During the day, she fiddles with code and spins yarns about a brave new world of data transparency. By night, she is losing the battle against her closet of hobbies. She spends a lot of time thinking how to make things better and is pretty antsy for the future to arrive.

Things Better Left Buried

Chris Patrick Carolan

Halifax, 1880

The dinosaur had no more business in the Halifax Public Gardens than a halibut has behind the steering wheel of a steamcarriage, but there it stood regardless, indolently chewing huge mouthfuls of ferns and flowers. A few yards away, Isaac Barrow stood scratching his chin.

"It's a stegosaurus," he declared, pointing to the twinned rows of bony plates running the length of the creature's spine. "Othniel Charles Marsh identified the species a few years ago, though he thought those plates laid flat along the creature's back like a tortoise's shell." He chuckled. "I'd like to see the look on his face when he hears about this!"

"None of which explains what the damnable thing is doing strolling about the Public Gardens," Inspector Jonathon Eddings said impatiently, puffing one of his thick cigars. "I thought dinosaurs were all supposed to be extinct. You're the spellmaker, Barrow. No one knows more about this kind of nonsense than you."

The constables had formed a rough perimeter around the scene, doing their best to hold back throngs of curious onlookers. A half-dozen men among the crowd were armed with hunting rifles. At the head of their group stood a scrawny fellow in a garish yellow and black checkered suit, a petulant expression on his face. He made no move toward the stegosaurus but eyed the constables with haughty contempt.

The uniformed men, in turn, eyed the creature warily. It had shown no hint of violence, lazily munching on the greenery, but the men held batons at the ready, weapons which would be all but useless if the dinosaur swiped at them with its spiked tail.

Some of the constables, Barrow noticed, cast glances in his direction which were nearly as apprehensive as those they gave the dinosaur. He had assisted the Halifax Constabulary with several investigations over the last few years — most often those involving the occult — but they remained cautious of him all the same. Prejudice against spellcasters still ran deep.

He sighed, setting that aside for now. "Of course they're extinct, Jonathon. I'm glad you sent for me, though. Seeing a living dinosaur with my own eyes is beyond magnificent. But I couldn't begin to speculate where the beast came from."

The inspector shook his head, resigned to the unending parade of peculiar occurrences that passed through Halifax. "So what's your best guess, then? Could it've been magicked up?"

"I suppose it could, but one would need a sample of the animal's blood, which in itself would be a near impossibility. Even with that, recreating an entire living creature from such a small sample would be an unfathomably complex application of the laws of similarity." He frowned as he thought it over. It was far from the sort of magic he had studied at the Technomancers' Collegium. "Frankly, I don't know of any spellcaster on this side of the Atlantic who would be skilled enough to work such a feat."

Eddings said nothing, but gestured for Barrow to go on.

"Therefore, its presence must be explicable by purely physical means. Some have speculated there are vast caverns where dinosaurs have survived for millennia, and of course there are the even more implausible legends of Hyperborea and—"

Eddings cut off any further guesswork with a brusque wave of his hand. "So we don't know where the thing came from. Fine. We can sort that out later. Tell me this, though — is it dangerous?"

"It's herbivorous," Barrow answered, watching the stegosaurus placidly work its way through enormous clumps of foliage. Noting the piqued expression on the inspector's face, he added, "It eats plants."

"I don't care if it lives on sunshine and the bedtime wishes of children," Eddings blustered. "What do you suggest we do about it? As much as I might like to, I can't just lock the garden gates and walk away."

"It can't stay here," Barrow agreed, looking to the restless crowd of spectators, particularly those who carried firearms. "If anything, the creature is probably in more danger from these gawkers than any threat it might pose to the public."

He thought it over for a moment. "Laudanum," he offered, drawing another baffled look. "Sedate the beast, and have your constables haul it somewhere safe. The Citadel courtyard, perhaps."

Eddings puffed his cigar and eyed the stegosaurus. Like a cow chewing cud, it returned his gaze with bland indifference.

"We're going to need a bloody lot of laudanum."

~ ~ ~

The pterosaur was sighted over George Island three days later.

Standing at the quay, Barrow and Eddings watched the creature swoop and spiral through the air. With a wingspan wider than an albatross, it flew with a relaxed grace Barrow never would have expected from something so vicious-looking. Gulls squawked angrily and fled from its path. It dove to skim the surface, artfully picking a large cod from the water with its needle like beak.

"A farmer from up past North End came to us babbling about a flying monster snatching up lambs," Eddings said. "I thought he was fit for the asylum at first, but with that other monster we've got penned up—"

"It seems to be nesting on the lighthouse," Barrow observed, pointing across the harbor.

"Looks like it," Eddings nodded. "The lighthouse keeper fled for his life when it came along. Thankfully, the fellow had the presence of mind to leave the lamp lit, but if it burns out before we get rid of the beastie we'll be in a right mess."

The inspector was right, of course; George Island sat right in the middle of the busy Halifax Harbor. With ships coming and going at all hours, a darkened lighthouse would be disastrous.

"We were able to get the big one to take the laudanum easily enough. All we had to do was put down buckets of the stuff in front of him and he lapped it up like a kitten at a saucer of cream." Eddings jabbed a finger skyward. "How are we supposed to dose *that* monster up there?"

Barrow had no answer. Instead, he raised another point. "The appearance of one primordial beast in the present day might well be called a miracle, Jonathon. Two such creatures, though? That suggests something deliberate."

Eddings scowled at the notion. "Bloody hell."

~ ~ ~

That evening, Barrow sat alone at the table he regularly shared with Eddings at the Carleton House Men's Social Club. They had arranged to meet for dinner, but the inspector had sent word he was running late. Not one to seek out idle conversation in the interim, Barrow scanned the pages of the evening newspaper while he sipped a steaming cup of bergamot tea.

The front page, as it had for the last three days, featured another piece about the prehistoric creatures. The article was accompanied by a fairly accurate engraving of the pterosaur over the harbor. Barrow knew the paper would have little new to say about the case, but he read the article regardless.

Like the papers, the Carleton's busy lounge was abuzz with chatter about the fantastic beasts. The appearance of the first had been a curiosity, but with the second the situation was quickly becoming a sensation. Speculation and wild theories were running rampant. Barrow did his best not to eavesdrop, but it was hard to ignore some of the more outlandish statements that reached his ears.

"I think they're just a pair of overgrown clockwork automatons," one man said. "Someone built them as a lark."

"Perhaps it's some sort of advertisement?"

"Servants of the devil, they are, sent here to bring about the end of days," declared another.

At the next table over, though, sat a pair Barrow found impossible to ignore. The two men were an exercise in stark contrast; the older gentleman had at least two decades on his companion. Paunchy and gray, he had the disciplined carriage of a man who had been a peak specimen in his youth. Despite his age, he still seemed formidable. *Former military*, Barrow surmised.

He recognized the younger fellow by the garish checkered suit he wore. Here was the man who had stood sneering with a rifle in his hand at the Public Gardens. Up close, he looked as though he had held the expression for too long as a child, leaving his face permanently stuck that way.

"That idiot Halliday was supposed to release the brute over in Ferguson's Cove," he said tersely. "How were we supposed to hunt the damned thing in the Public Gardens?"

"Hardly very sporting, Mister Winston," his older friend agreed. "Though from what I hear, the monster had no savagery or cunning to it whatsoever."

Barrow didn't catch what was said next, as Eddings arrived just then and dropped himself into his seat across the table, red-faced and rather out of breath. "Sorry about the holdup," he said, waving to catch the attention of a passing waiter. "I've got the constables trying to snare that flying monster on George Island with fishing nets." He pulled out a cigar and set it between his teeth while he searched his pockets for a match. "Those who aren't standing guard over the big one at the Citadel, that is."

Distracted by what he had overheard, Barrow scarcely noted the inspector's greeting. He rose and walked over to the table where the mismatched pair sat, leaving a confused Eddings gawping at his back.

"Pardon the interruption, gentlemen," he said, "and forgive me for eavesdropping, but by any chance were you talking about Nigel Halliday just now?"

"That's right," the older man answered.

"Does he have something to do with the dinosaur in the Public Gardens?"

"I should say so! If you were to take Halliday's word for it, he's the one who set it loose in the first place."

"Our club was organizing a hunt to take down the beast, until the constabulary got involved," Winston put in. He reminded Barrow of a petulant child who had been denied a sweetmeat before his dinner.

Barrow turned a withering glare on the wiry fellow. "That animal's very existence is a wonder unlike any other, and your first impulse is to slaughter it?"

"We're big game hunters," he answered, as if it explained everything. His friend nodded vigorously.

"Overgrown adolescents proving their manhood to each other by killing things from a safe distance with their rifles, more like," Barrow retorted.

"Now see here!" the older man blustered, rising to his feet. "I'll be damned if I'll let some sniveling—"

He was cut off as Eddings stepped up and put his body between them. "I suggest you retake your seat, friend," he said in a voice that brooked no debate.

"And who are you to get in the middle of things?"

"Inspector Jonathon Eddings, Halifax Constabulary." He pulled back the lapel of his jacket to show the badge pinned to his waistcoat.

With that, the fight went out of the older man. He sat down, but his glare remained stony.

"That's better," Eddings said, turning to the younger man. "Now, you were about to tell us about this Nigel Halliday?"

Winston looked to his friend, then to his plate. Anywhere to avoid the inspector's gaze. "He told us he could offer game no one else in the world could match," he said with an affected sigh. "Our club raised a fund and paid him a great deal of money."

Barrow opened his mouth to say something acidic, but Eddings waved him to silence. "Have you any idea where we might find Mister Halliday?"

"We wouldn't know," the older man shrugged. "Halliday came to us."

Winston nodded agreement.

"Very well, gentlemen, we'll let you get on with your dinner," Eddings said with a congenial smile, "after you give me your names and addresses, that is, just in case I need to speak with you again."

Barrow looked down his long nose at the two men. "Hunting for sustenance is one thing, gentlemen, and all well and good," he said, "but it's a savage and disgraceful thing to slaughter an unwitting beast for the sport of it. There's enough destruction in the world without adding to it for the sake of amusement."

While Eddings took their information, Barrow retrieved their coats and hats from the checkroom. "I'm afraid dinner will have to wait," he said, handing the inspector his long wool overcoat. "Nigel Halliday. It *has* to be him!"

"Who is Nigel Halliday?"

"He was a colleague at the Technomancers' Collegium," Barrow answered as he popped his bowler onto his head. "Well, he was a year ahead of me, but you get the idea. His thesis proposed employing ley energy to improve the accuracy of clocks and watches, but he was never able to prove his ideas actually worked."

"Ley what, now?"

"A form of magic energy," Barrow answered as he headed for the street. "I've a task for your constables. We need to find Nigel Halliday."

~ ~ ~

As it turned out, Nigel Halliday held a job as a machinist at one of the North End canneries, operating the contraption that cut, rolled, and soldered sheets of tin into cans to be filled with cod, lobster, and anything else to be preserved for shipping to distant markets. At the far end of the factory from the gutting floor, the machine shop was as clean and efficient a facility as Barrow had seen. Even still, the place reeked of fish and brine.

"Naw, ain't seen Nigel for near on two weeks now," said the foreman, a stocky fellow named Herman Scott. He spoke with a Newfoundland accent. "You finds 'im, though, you make sure you sends 'im my way. Bugger owes me two dollars, he does."

"I'll see what I can do," Eddings promised. "Do you know where we might be able find Mister Halliday?"

Scott rubbed at his shorn scalp. "We sent one of the lads 'round his place when he didn't show up for work three days runnin', but he weren't there. What's this all about, anyway?"

"We just a have a few questions we'd like to ask him, is all."

"Had Mister Halliday been acting oddly at all lately?" Barrow asked.

"Only since his first day on the job," Scott replied with a chuckle. "Never did fit in none too well. Pretty much kept to 'imself, y'see. I was about the only one he talked to, and even then it weren't often much more than a *how-d'you-do*. Kind of a twitchy, nervous sorta fellow. The lads figured he was touched in the head, if you take my meaning, but I figured he just wanted to be left alone. Good machinist, though."

Barrow nodded.

Eddings handed Scott one of his calling cards. "If you think of anything else, come see me at Constabulary Headquarters."

"Y'know, there was one other t'ing. Nigel once told me his family owned a bit of farmland, up along Campbell Road way on past Africville."

"Thank you for your time, Mister Scott," Eddings said, scribbling the detail in his notebook.

"That farm would be worth looking into," Barrow said as they made for the exit, drawing a nod from the inspector.

"You read my mind. There has to be a land title on file somewhere. I'll have Constable O'Hara pull some records and see if we can't track down the address."

~ ~ ~

The Dalhousie College library didn't have much in the way of paleontological reference, but there was enough to keep Barrow occupied while Eddings worked on locating the Halliday farm. He spent the day reviewing Othniel Charles Marsh's papers, wryly amused at how different the *Stegosaurus* had been from the naturalist's renderings. He couldn't fault Marsh, though — working from incomplete fossil specimens was bound to invite error.

The librarian almost had to forcibly remove him at closing time; he had been so deep in study he hadn't heard her announcements. With a sheepish apology, he handed her the book and headed out into the night. Checking his pocket watch, he swore under his breath. He would have to hustle several blocks over to catch the last streetcar home.

Had his thoughts been more in the here and now, he might have noticed the massive carnivore before he was almost on top of it. The beast's muzzle buried in a hog's carcass, it didn't take notice of anything else as it noisily fed, blood and entrails splayed across the cobblestones. With each bite, massive jaws crunched through bone and tore away chunks of porcine flesh, swallowed without much chewing. Blood tracked from its maw down its neck and was smeared along the beast's forearms. Barrow wondered briefly where in the college district the dinosaur had managed to snatch a pig, but quickly decided such details didn't really matter.

It's an allosaurus, he realized.

Taking care to move as quietly as he could, Barrow took a slow, backward step. He wasn't one to carry a firearm, but even if he had been armed, he wouldn't have tried to engage the towering carnivore. Quiet retreat struck him as the sensible option.

A carelessly discarded tin can underfoot gave him away, clattering across the cobblestones. The noise wasn't loud, but in the otherwise silent street it may as well have been an alarm bell. The allosaurus looked up from its meal and fixed its eyes on Barrow. It cocked its head to one side, regarding him with mild interest, as though weighing whether he were a distraction worth pursuing.

In a moment of sickening awareness, Barrow realized the question in the monster's mind came down to simple math — which had more meat on its bones... him, or what was left of the hog?

He must've come out on the short end of the equation. With a savage roar clearly meant to paralyze prey with fear, the beast turned from the carcass and started towards him.

Barrow did the only thing he could: he turned on his heel and ran.

He darted around the corner and was halfway up the next block before he chanced a look over his shoulder. The allosaurus was faster than anything that size had any right to be, but it took the corner awkwardly.

There aren't many right angles in nature, Barrow realized as he redoubled his sprint.

A loose cobble tripped him up and brought him to the ground. The fall knocked the wind from his lungs, giving the predator the seconds it needed to catch up. Barrow scrabbled at the sidewalk and kicked his feet, panicking as he found himself unable to move.

The allosaurus had him by the tail of his coat.

He squirmed, trying to strip off the garment, and kicked the beast in the jaw. If it even noticed, it gave no sign. The grip of its dagger-like teeth held fast to the fabric. The carrion reek of the dinosaur's steaming breath filled his nostrils like an odiferous punch.

He closed his eyes, waiting for those teeth to rend his flesh.

Salvation arrived, dressed in red. A dozen British soldiers from the Citadel garrison hustled down the street, Eddings alongside their captain at the head of the march. Their heavy boots and jangling kit raised a racket, to say nothing of the captain's bellowed orders. He called them to a halt less than twenty yards away.

The allosaurus forgot about Barrow, releasing its grip on his coat as it turned its attention on the interlopers to unleash a ferocious roar in their direction. Distracted from one meal and now cheated of another, it knew only anger for the red-coated men as they spread out to form a firing line.

"Riflemen, ready!" came the command. As one, the soldiers raised their rifles and set their sights on the advancing beast.

"*Fire!*"

Gunshots pealed like thunder, echoing off the buildings on either side of the narrow street and filling the air with smoke.

Well-trained riflemen at such close range didn't miss a target this size. Every round struck the carnivore, its own blood a torrent mingling with that of the hog down its front. It staggered and roared in pain and rage, but kept its feet.

"Reload!"

The second round forced the creature to the cobbles. It collapsed to its knees, then slumped onto its side, chest heaving as it struggled for breath. Instead of another roar it gave a wheezing, bloody cough. Several bullets must've torn through its lungs.

Barrow gave the dying allosaurus a wide berth as he walked over to Eddings and the soldiers. It writhed and kicked feebly in its death throes. Even with the animal's strength ebbing away, its savage claws were nothing to underestimate.

"I might've known you'd be here already," Eddings commented. The soldiers had reloaded their rifles once more. They held them in firing position as they made a measured advance toward the dying creature. "Thankfully, the boys were at the ready, standing guard over the other one. When I got word this monster was on the loose, I ran up to the Citadel to call them to action."

"I suppose it's just as well that you did," Barrow said. As much as he hated seeing the animal slain, he knew there would have been no way to capture and contain the powerful predator. He was about to say as much, but was cut off as the riflemen unloaded a final barrage into the allosaurus. When the smoke cleared, the beast lay still.

~ ~ ~

Fusing the essence of a ley wisp to a nautical compass was a simple feat of technomancy, but the device clipped to his bicycle's handlebars had still taken most of the night to complete. It was sloppy work, Barrow knew, but there was no help for it; Halliday had to be found, and quickly. He had no way of knowing if the modified compass would detect ley energy, but it was the only idea he had. As he sped past Africville, the needle started to point to the northeast. He followed its lead down a winding dirt track, the needle spinning in circles as he skidded to a stop by a gate with a faded wooden sign.

Halliday.

It was an abandoned-looking place, eerie in the predawn light. The grounds were choked with brambles and overgrown clematis, the house and outbuildings boarded up and sagging. If not for the massive boiler beside the barn belching coal smoke and steam into the air, Barrow would have turned and headed back to the city.

He had come alone, reasoning that Nigel Halliday might be more inclined to speak with him as a fellow spellcaster without Inspector Eddings at his side. Passing the house, he headed for the barn. The big door was closed, though the rutted dirt track leading to it looked like it had been recently disturbed. A smaller side door hung off rusted hinges, and he shouldered his way through it.

Bright lighting assaulted his eyes, but they soon adjusted. A series of electric dynamos powered by the boiler outside were spinning, easily generating more than enough to power the lights. He knocked loudly on the door behind him, doubting he'd be heard over the din.

"Nigel Halliday?"

"Over here," came the reply. Looking past the row of dynamos, Barrow spotted a raised platform near the rear of the barn. Approaching it, he saw a wondrous assembly sat atop the dais, a series of polished brass, copper, and silver plates arrayed in three concentric circles.

Nigel Halliday stood there, looking much as Barrow remembered him from their time at the Collegeum — tall and lanky, wild-eyed with dark features. His movements were quick and birdlike; Barrow remembered now how just watching Halliday at work could be exhausting. Only the gray starting to frost his temples indicated any time had passed.

He wore heavy leather gloves that came to the elbow, fastened with a large buckle. Each had a length of cloth-wrapped wire attached at the wrist, but Barrow couldn't see where they led. Oversized goggles hung around his neck.

"Why, Isaac Barrow," he said in greeting, waving to invite Barrow to join him on the platform. "Really, it has been too long!"

Halliday's salutation struck Barrow as genuine. "Hello, Nigel," he said as he climbed the steps. There was a large control console to Halliday's left. It easily had fifty buttons and half as many brass levers. "What is all this?"

"Chronometric displacement," Halliday explained, gesturing to his machine. "I've finally done it! One of the core concepts eluded me for years, until a realization came to me in an opium fugue. If objects can be moved from one place to another, why not from one time to another?"

"How do you mean?"

"Don't you see? Just like a thing's mass, *duration* is a measure of its existence, and I've devised a way to manipulate it."

"This machine… lets you travel through time?"

Halliday shook his head. "Perhaps one day I'll make such a breakthrough, but I can no more travel through time than I could walk through the wall," he said. "I can, however, reach into the past and move existing things from their native time into the present. But there's no way to reverse it, so once something is brought here, it's here to stay."

The implications set Barrow's mind reeling. "You could do so much to benefit mankind with technology like this! You could recover Shakespeare's lost plays, or salvage countless lost works of art."

"I don't care about lost plays or works of art," Halliday said dismissively. "I want to resurrect the dinosaurs."

"Your benefactors want to slaughter the dinosaurs," Barrow pointed out.

"A pity, that," Halliday admitted. "But none of what I've accomplished would be possible without their investment."

"Bollocks to your accomplishments," came a voice from behind.

A handful of men strode across the barn, rifles in his hand. Winston in his checkered suit led the march. "You promised us good hunting, and we'll have it right now, or take it out of your hide."

A look of alarm flashed across Halliday's taut features. "I don't think so," he said, grabbing the goggles and pulling them over his eyes. "I've too much important work yet to do here."

Halliday took a step toward the control console as Winston scrambled up the steps, his fellows close behind. He shouldered past Barrow and grabbed Halliday by the collar with his free hand. Two of Winston's friends grabbed Barrow by the shoulders. He smelled whiskey on their breath.

"Your work be damned!" Winston said. "We paid you good money, you huckster!"

The two men grappled. Neither struck Barrow as much of a pugilist, but Winston had some advantage of strength on his side. The awkward gloves and goggles that connected Halliday to his machine also got in his way, the wires getting tangled as he struggled to free himself of the game hunter's grip. Winston rapped him on the side of the head with the butt of his rifle, sending him sprawling.

Halliday fell onto the control panel, mashing buttons and forcing levers as he landed. The machinery above started to move, the metal plates rotating in different directions as electricity arced between them.

"You fool!" Halliday cried as he tried to get to his feet. "I haven't set any control coordinates! The machine could—"

He didn't get the chance to say what the machine might do. His shirtsleeve had become caught between a lever and the console's steel faceplate. He tugged desperately, but the fabric would not come free.

With the men holding him distracted, Barrow broke free and clambered over to Halliday. He grabbed at the fabric, pulling with all the strength he could muster. When it didn't budge, he threw his weight against the lever. The cloth caught in the mechanism held it fast. "Do any of you have a knife?"

The wide-eyed men looked to each other, each of them shaking their head.

The machine's pace quickened, the electrical arcs between the rotating plates now scattering like lightning. "It's no use," Halliday shouted. "Get out while you still have the chance!"

Barrow opened his mouth to protest, but was cut off by an explosion from one of the dynamos. The metal plates overhead spun at a maddening pace, raining down sparks. The dais rattled and swayed, acrid smoke billowing out from underneath. Winston and his cohort fled.

With a resigned nod, Barrow made for the stairs. Winston looked past him toward Halliday, a sour look on his face. They had barely reached the bottom of the steps when the electricity issuing from the machine surrounded the platform like a mad cyclone of lightning, swirling and crackling.

They sprinted for the exit. A bolt arced over their heads, striking the wall and leaving a smoking scorch mark on the gray wood.

"Get down!" Barrow shouted, catching Winston by the shoulder and diving to the floor as another streaked past.

The explosion filled the room with white light and a deafening rumble, but surprisingly little debris. As the light faded, Barrow looked back at what was left of the smoldering dais.

The machine, and Nigel Halliday with it, was gone.

~ ~ ~

Eddings shut the file folder and handed it off to a constable who left the small office quickly. He didn't even give Barrow a sideways glance.

"Well, that's that," Eddings said. "We've taken Winston and his club into custody, though I don't know what we can charge them with. I'm sure I'll hear from the mayor later, once he's read the report." He pulled a bottle of scotch and two glasses from his desk drawer and poured himself a drink. He nodded to the second glass, knowing full well Barrow would decline the offer.

"Could you rebuild it?" he asked after taking a sip. "Halliday's machine, I mean."

"I wouldn't know where to begin. The machine was utterly destroyed in the explosion, and Halliday's notes — if he had any — were incinerated along with it."

"Pity, that."

Barrow nodded agreement. "What will you do with the dinosaurs that are still here? We can't send them back where they came from, and you can't simply slaughter them."

Eddings swirled his scotch as he mulled it over. "We'll put the beasts on a steamship and send 'em off to England," he announced. "The London Zoo claims to be the best in the world. Let them figure it out, I say."

"That's as good a solution as anyone could've come up with," Barrow said approvingly. "I do have to wonder, though, if there were any other prehistoric creatures Nigel Halliday loosed on the world before we caught up with him."

"Bloody hell, Barrow," Eddings said. "You do have a way of looking at a storm cloud and finding a darker lining."

"Can you blame me, Jonathon? Look closely and you'll usually discover a third, even darker lining behind that one," he laughed.

A moment later, Eddings joined him.

* * *

>>> *Between 1864 and 1892, some 136 species of dinosaur were unearthed through the work of Charles Othniel Marsh and Edward Drinker Cope. A fierce rivalry developed between the two scientists during this period of discovery, known today as the Bone Wars. Their race to identify new species led to some sloppy science and all but bankrupted both men, but fueled intense public interest in these long-dead beasts. To the Victorians, dinosaurs must have seemed akin to creatures of myth. These living artifacts walk the streets of 1880s Halifax, Nova Scotia in 'Things Better Left Buried.'*

Chris Patrick Carolan

Chris Patrick Carolan is an author, editor, and hovercraft enthusiast whose stories have appeared in the *Enigma Front* anthology series (Analemma Books, ExitZero Books), *49th Parallels: Alternative Canadian Histories and Futures* (Bundoran Press), and *Baby, It's Cold Outside* (Coffin Hop Press). He is Managing Editor of ExitZero Books and is currently working on revisions to his first novel, a paranormal mystery set in 1880s Halifax, Nova Scotia. You can find him on Twitter as @cpcwrites but, consider this fair warning, it's mostly just nonsense and *Simpsons* memes.

Phlogiston's Rainbow

Erik Jon Spigel

1882: *la fonction essentielle de l'universe, qui est une machine
à faire des dieux*

When heaven disbanded in 1882 there were tears, hugs, well-wishes and the like, before all the angels went their separate ways, ages, genders, and desires. Uriel, whose very name meant *The Light of the Divine*, but who the Book of Enoch had associated with upheaval and destruction — *change!* It was *change!* — decided that he could best serve as shepherd and guardian to the new age of science.

He opened a delicatessen emporium in San Francisco, *Lightman's*, in the Western Addition at the odd diagonal corner where Montgomery Avenue meets Broadway.

To all appearances he was a tall, gaunt, hunchbacked Jewish man with a neatly trimmed beard and mustache, and long, graying hair braided at the back. He was given to wearing, night or day, silver wire-framed glasses with amethyst lenses.

John Dee, Elizabeth I's astrologer, had called him, what? The *Master of Wind* or some such. Kinder and perhaps more poetic than Enoch, an invisible mover of things after all, but still, Uriel felt, missing the point, somehow. Yet he was oddly grateful for it, and gave the astrologer a small gift of crystal, the same as his own eyeglass lenses were now made. In the right light, one could see a little of the *now*, the *then*, and a little of the *will be* all at once. It allowed angels, who knew no time, to order eternity as past, present, and future.

1888: *Mr.* Chao not playing the lute

Every day at 2:30 — except on the Sabbath — as was his habit, Uriel turned over the running of his shop to a young man from Chinatown, a Mr. Everett Quong, and, making a package of some smoked meats and pickles, as well as some sundries such as tobacco and talcum, walked the short walk down Pacific past the cigar factories and up the short flight of stairs above a hardware store to the practice of Mr. Chao, his acupuncturist.

Mr. Chao had been surprisingly phlegmatic when he first saw Uriel's wings.

"Binding them up like that," was all he had said, referring to Mr. Lightman's hunchback, "it must be very uncomfortable."

Mr. Chao thereby began a long study into the *chi* of angel wings. It was the only procedure that brought Uriel any relief.

This day, as always, he presented Mr. Chao with the parcels of smoked meats, pickles, and sundries.

"If you gave me money, I would only end up buying these things from you anyway," Mr. Chao had once said. Now, closing the blinds, dousing the lanterns, Mr. Chao motioned Uriel to unfasten his wings and lay down on the table. Uriel removed his glasses last and his halo flared into luminescence, bathing the room in light. He lay down on his stomach and relaxed. Mr. Chao applied a needle to the base of Uriel's left wing, the one that was always bound beneath the right when he went out.

Through the window there were scraps of a melody played on *erhu* mingled with the tintinnabulation of a child practicing piano. A breeze in the air was redolent with spices, stale beer, and the odors from the brothels.

Mr. Chao placed a moxibustion stick between Uriel's shoulder blades.

A shift in the wind and the faint tang of sea salt, fish, horse manure. Sometimes the smell of human waste mingled with the flowery scent of opium.

Uriel could hear Mr. Chao not playing the lute.

He often reminisced on his childhood in Kowloon, how badly his family had been treated in America, and how they still called them names and worse, and wondered out loud as he had many times before, why his family had come to America in the first place.

At the end of every session, Uriel stands and stretches, suddenly in a human moment and striking a human pose. He puts on his glasses.

Mr. Chao said he was always relieved to be able to talk about these things with Uriel.

"Your memories," Uriel nodded. "Your wings."

Afterwards, Uriel continued on his day, taking the streetcar to the city hall and the public library on the second floor there. He liked to read the newspapers and journals, and on this day, it was the November number of *The American Journal of Science*, an article by Albert Michelson and Edward Morley. On page 341 he read:

It appears, from all that precedes, reasonably certain that if there be any relative motion between the earth and the luminiferous ether, it must be small; quite small enough entirely to refute Fresnel's explanation of aberration.

The implication, lying there, was that there no ether at all.

"Now when," Uriel thought, "did *that* happen?"

1898: *Dreyfusisme*

Two parcels awaited Mina Macgregor Mathers, née Bergson, daughter of Polish -Irish-Jewish stock, and wife of the occultist Samuel Liddel Macgregor Mathers — she just called him Mac — when they arrived at their rooms in the Hotel du Brésil in Paris. The larger, from London, was not a mystery. The other, from her brother Henri in Auvergne, delighted her more. She eagerly opened it first. There was another small package within, as well as a letter:

My dear sister,

I hope you have safely returned to Paris. It is, perhaps, not the best of times for us. I have forebodings of a Dreyfusism eroding the polite veneer of the civil society to which we have become used. For myself, this has yet to reach Auvergne, and I am happy in my teaching, and make steady progress in my own researches...

She and Mac had overstayed in Ireland.

Yeats had summoned them there having located the demon, Hephesimireth, responsible for the tragic cholera that had taken such toll in Europe for more than a half century. The poet had trapped it in the ruins of a small *dún* in County Sligo, surrounding it in a mote of oil and salt. But the creature was still unbound, and the mote a stopgap, not a banishment; presently, others of its order would come and set it free.

...I have begun of late to speculate on memory and time, and I wonder if that which is 'I' is no more than a reflective moment ... this 'I' is made of time itself...

Yeats had known her Mac for ten years, since the very founding of the Golden Dawn Society in 1887. Happier days then, spent in the exploration of the elder and lost races ... the first communications, and later establishment of diplomatic relations with the Faerie Folk and the Aesir.

...of this duration, *this time that one differentiates from the time of the physicist but is the time that is me...*

"Lombard. I think I would have my tea now."

She called out for the Synthetic Man — that product of *The Ada Company (Lovelace, Soeurs et Filles)* that was ubiquitous among the European middle classes, who could not meet the price of human servants. It had been a wedding gift from her parents.

But Lombard was severely damaged in Ireland in contest with the host of Hephesimireth, and when they arrived again in England en route to France, they were met by a Company representative; Mina had expected Lombard would be returned to the factory for a speedy repair. Instead, they were told:

"We regret that we will be unable to reactivate your Synthetic Man product at this time. All our Synthetic Man products have stopped. It appears that the ... galvanic principle Miss Mary Wollstonecraft discovered and bequeathed to her sister has ceased to be efficacious. We must retire that arm of our business for the foreseeable future."

She had come to take the Synthetic Man's labors for granted, and still felt its loss. She still called its name by reflex.

...I had opportunity to discuss these thoughts with an agent of The Ada Company, and they devised the most wondrous mechanism which I have sent to you...

Mina unwrapped the smaller parcel and found wrapped in a soft violet chamois, a palm-sized, many-faceted egg of gold. A seam joined what she concluded were a top and a bottom. On one half was an inscribed emblem surrounded by the words, *Exister consiste à changer, changer à se mûrir, se mûrir à se créer indéfiniment soi-même.*

She recognized the emblem as the symbol Ouroboros.

...You see that I do not disregard your own researches, my sister. And you will find amusement in this point: The Ada Company tells me the gem which underlies the mechanism within is a piece of the crystal the English mystic, John Dee, claimed he had received from an angel, and through which he could see the future!

She twisted the two halves of the device. They opened with a soft pneumatic hiss until they made the ends of a shaft of silver laminae inside a helical gold spring. The tiniest purple gem was set at the bottom of one end.

...They have devised to call it The Emautochron. *It keeps one's own self-time, one's duration. Gently twist to open it, then press the halves together and release them as you would a concertina. The helix will start to spin...*

Mina obeyed the instructions, fascinated at first by the mechanism alone, then—

1896: *You shapeless fires, that were the souls of men*

They had almost been too late. Already, a murder of lesser demons gathered like smoke above their master. They threw themselves in clumps into the mote, dissolving into a thick black tar.

Yeats had enlisted the son of a local, a theater critic and novelist who, though now an expatriate in London, remembered the stories his father told. He also had some passing familiarity with occult practices, and claimed to possess one of the authentic iron *styli* of St. Cassian of Imola. In the ninth book of Prudentius' *Peristephanon Liber*, it was recorded that, for refusing to worship the Roman gods,

Cassian was pricked to death by his own students with their writing instruments.

Mac began drawing a Magick Circle almost immediately, chanting in Latin, the Preparation of the Soul:

"In the Name of the Father, and of the Son and of the Holy Ghost...."

The smoke and stench of boiling tar was overpowering. Mina heaved with each breath. Mac was losing his strength and concentration. Yeats had closed his eyes and mumbled a benediction while supporting the writer, who looked soon to faint. More, the ululations of the demonic host were literally maddening, and stirred in them dark impulses long suppressed by habits of manner and class.

Mac froze. He need inscribe, now, the Hebrew Tetragrammaton, but could not remember it. Instead, he wondered not for the first time, how Bill Yeats had known Mina before he had. What had they shared, what confidences, what intimacies.... He began to contemplate another use for the pick he had been using to draw the Magick Circle. He tested its heft in his hand. It felt like an extension of his arm. One swing and it could crack a skull... yes it could....

Yeats hated the writer, Stoker. Rather, he envied him. On the one hand, he thought Stoker a traitor for leaving Ireland for English society. But he craved the writer's access to London's artistic elite. And yes, when he thought of it, he envied the writer's wealth and resented the flippant way he displayed it. He could feel Stoker's wallet beneath his fingertips as he held the writer steady on his feet.

The Magick Circle Mac had drawn in the ground vanished as footprints in the tide. Hephesimireth took its first clawed steps out of the *dún*.

Mina watched in horror. The creature should at least have been slowed down. But it was that foolish book of Mac's, *Armadel*! A *systematic, scientific analysis of Dee,* he had declared it; a working of the latter's opaque visions and writings. Three years lost to the damn thing. Useless! The system destroyed the magic. Three years! Three years without intimacy, and she already late to become a mother... all the while Mac claiming he was following the ways of the Hindus and channeling his potency into the text....

"I have it!" Mina cried out suddenly. "Stoker — give me the St. Cassian stylus, and pray it is indeed authentic. Seat yourself over there, beneath that oak. Write! Begin a tale...."

Stoker shook his head and freed himself from Yeats's support. Still in a daze, he did as he was told, sitting down at the base of the oak, his back against the trunk. He opened his lap desk and set out a succession of fountain pens within easy reach of his right hand. He carefully untied the ribbon from a ream of paper he carried in his bag. Placing two sheets on the lap desk and taking up the first pen, he poised to write—

"But what shall it be?" he demanded.

"A tale," Mina repeated. "Any tale. Whatever your writer's wit best tells you is allegory for that thing!"

Stoker nodded, bewildered, and began, *Jonathan Harker's Journal....*

Mina, meanwhile, plunged the iron stylus into her left palm, mingling her blood with the dried scale of Cassian. She bent to the ground and began to draw a Magick Circle around the writer.

Each stroke cost her more blood, but also elicited a scream of pain from Hephesimireth. It smashed through the mote, oblivious to the remaining salt and oil that singed it. It reared on its three hind legs and roared. Mac vomited. Yeats cowered and began reciting a rosary. But the creature's shriek was more of frustration than of defiance.

Within the ring, Stoker was writing at supernatural speed.

"...for certainly if I had been fully awake I must have noticed the approach of such a remarkable place..."

"Once more have I seen the Count go out in his lizard fashion..."

"Strange and sudden change in Renfield last night..."

Hephesimireth raged. It threw itself in the mote and rolled itself in the tar. It clawed at the ruins of the *dún*, trying to anchor itself in the old stone.

But all this to no avail. At first in tiny, atomic pieces, as almost invisible embers of coal, it began to dissolve into the air. Larger pieces now, like letters of movable type, falling from this plane into Stoker's narrative through the lens of the Magick Circle.

Mina, faint from loss of blood, at last drew the final stroke closing the circle, just as Stoker wrote:

"*...later on he will understand how some men so loved her, that they did dare much for her sake.*"

There was a final rush of air filling the absence of the demon. Then silence.

Yeats was still sobbing. Mac stood up unsteadily, and could not bring himself to look at any of the others.

Stoker lay down his pen, the last in the sequence he had prepared before, and flexed and rubbed his aching wrist. Mina, depleted, simply sat back and sighed.

The stylus suddenly became searing hot in her hand and now glowed like a filament. She dropped it. It flared once as it touched the Magick Circle. Then both blazed into illegibility in the ground.

Awhile later, Stoker asked, "Now what? Do we burn the manuscript?"

"No!" Mina replied. "Hephesimireth thrives in contagion, but even it cannot support more than one such at a time. Make a copy of your manuscript; the original should be forever hidden in a secret place. By all means publish your story. It is certain it will be read widely and well, for age after age, and each reader will diminish the demon's power, as each prick of his students' styli took away the lifeblood of Cassian."

They returned to Yeats's lodging in Sligo. No words were spoken among them for several days. Life was a mechanical affair of food, toilet, and sleep. On one day, she found Mac's *Book of Armadel* in the kitchen waste bin. Dully, she removed it, cleaned it as best she could of stains, and brought it back to her room. She didn't know why.

Soon, Stoker had gone, returned to London.

Then they were in Cork, she and Mac. They kept to separate rooms, Mac briefly informing her of the schedule of their ticket to France.

Mina snapped the halves of the Emautochron closed again. Eyes closed, breathing slowly. The sounds of crowds and pedestrians. The smells of bread, human sweat, stale milk and spilled wine. Then a remnant of the bells of Notre Dame, an *eli, eli* shibboleth that lingered, unperturbed by its passage over the Seine.

She sighed, certain of the contents of the other parcel even as she opened it. And there it was — a dedicated edition of Stoker's *Dracula*, the work in which the demon Hephesimireth was bound. Mina had already read the original manuscript in Ireland during those long, empty days in Sligo after the creature had been defeated.

Stoker pledged to her then, "Madame, for what you did this day, I promise you have a place most prominent in the tale!" But it did not matter. The nature of the incantation was such that she would forever be bleeding into stories. She had not had her *end of the month* in the nearly a year since… and she strongly suspected she would not be able to conceive a child. Which facts she kept from her husband, fearful of his reaction.

And the writer had indeed been true to his word. There was a character in the manuscript that did bear her name, although 'Mina Harker' was merely the most prominent victim, for all Mina *Bergson's* part in the defeat of the real demon.

"Ah, that wonderful Madam Mina! She has man's brain — a brain that a man should have were he much gifted — and a woman's heart. The good God fashioned her for a purpose, believe me, when He made that so good combination."

She tossed the volume the writer had sent her into the fireplace, and quickly composed a letter to Yeats that she would no more be working with the amateurs he sought to press into service.

1900: *We are so grateful to you for having killed the wicked Witch of the East, and for setting our people free from bondage.*

On a table outside a room at St. Ignatius College were arranged stacks of pamphlets advertising local events of public interest. There was one for the American chapter of the Guido von List Society:

ATTENTION all good *Austrian, German* and
SELECT *English* men!
(White men *ONLY. No! Italians or Irish*)
LEARN the ancient secrets of Wotanism and the
Aryan race!

Meanwhile Mr. Lightman and Mr. Chao at the back of the room, listening to a presentation:

On the rectification of the races with special attention given to the photographic sciences

Father Sherrod, Jesuit brother and amateur natural philosopher, went on, "We are of course indebted to the Englishman, Mr. Francis Galton of the Royal Society, for his most excellent technique of composite portraiture, through which we may elucidate the races of man....

"We collect as many photographs as we may, from varied exemplars of each race. We then pin them one in front of the other, as a deck of cards, so that the eyes of all the portraits shall be as nearly as possible superimposed. The remainder of the features will also be superimposed nearly enough. We then direct a photographic camera upon them. We expose the plate to the first portrait, then replace the cap and remove the face just recorded. The second face will now be revealed, aligned with the first. We expose the photographic plate once again to record it and replace the cap. And so on, until all the portraits have been so exposed on a single plate."

He removed the cap from a magic lantern, throwing a sudden pane of light on the blank wall behind him.

"These were made from Mr. Galton's own," he said, projecting slides one by one, extemporizing on the characteristics of each of the faces on them. Strange portraits, with intense charcoal features, like the drawings of the mad.

Father Sherrod expounded on "The Hebrew race... the Negroid... the Mongoloid..." and as each of them was itemized, both Uriel and Mr. Chao flinched as if struck.

Later that year, there was national remorse when at a mine in Lattimer, Pennsylvania, a sheriff's posse opened fire and murdered twenty-one unarmed East European immigrants in response to their strike action and desire to unionize. And Uriel wondered what portrait would emerge if all the victims' faces were superimposed. Could we then elucidate the salient features of the Unionist? The Victim? Or the Poor?

The next day, at 2:30 P.M., as was his custom, Uriel turned over the running of his shop to Mr. Everett Quong and, with the customary packages of smoked meats, pickles, and sundries, walked the short walk down Pacific past the cigar factories to the practice of Mr. Chao. He tried the door, always left unlocked, but it would not budge. Confused, Uriel took a few steps into the street and looked up.

Little to be told from there.

He could see the windows of the second floor where Mr. Chao lived and worked, but they were closed, and the blinds drawn. It was a chilly, gray December day, so it was not out of the question that the windows be shut, but he would not expect the blinds to be drawn, and would, if so, at least expect to see a light from candle, lantern, or lamp, cast against them.

He approached the door again and hesitantly knocked — he had never done that before.

There was no answer. Uriel backed into the street again, looking up, then around.

He tried at the hardware store on the main floor of the building, but the man there just shrugged.

He tried the basket maker next door. He went as far as the laundry and the undertaker at the end of the block and behind the hardware store. No one knew of Mr. Chao.

His shoulders were sore. His wings were chafing, and he thought they might bleed, though he was not altogether certain they or he could do that.

Dejected, he returned to his shop.

"Mr. Lightman, this letter was left for you," Everett Quong said.

Uriel accepted it. It was from Mr. Chao. With as much surprise to himself as any other, he wrote, he had decided to return to China and join the *Yihetuan*; to fight with the Boxers against the British and the Americans.

Uriel felt lost. Not knowing why, he composed a message to be sent to one distant in his line:

Cousin. Something plunges us into chaos. Come to San Francisco. Urgent.

Was it one of the hosts? Andras? Naberius, Beleth, or Halphas? Or Buer. Yes, Buer. Buer, who the sorcerers claim teaches moral and natural philosophy. It must be. It must be.

But Mina could help, yes. She had dealt with such before. He would have to send his message by Ada Company Aerophone to reach her in time.

On Christmas Day, he was sitting in the back room of his shop, wings gratefully unbound, glasses removed and halo filling the room, examining a small package from an unknown source, stamped merely with the logo of The Ada Company. In it, a soft violet chamois that wrapped a palm-sized, many faceted egg of gold.

There was a small scrap of paper, *Instructions for use of the Emautochron.* He twisted the halves of the egg apart as described, and pumped them together like a concertina. The helix began to spin.

The duration of an Angel is both forever and but a moment: his body flashed and vanished into ash in an instant, his remains falling to the floor as fine salt and arranging in a circle of symbols and ancient letters. From the center of the circle a horror emerged. It slouched from the store and out into the street, reared on two of its five spiderlike limbs tipped in silver cloven hooves, and stretched two more to the arc lamp wires overhead. In a shower of sparks and with a shriek that was not a sound but an odor, the scent of powder after a gun has fired, Buer launched itself into the night.

San Francisco shook with an earthquake that took six lives.

1901: *Many have done excellently, but you exceed them all.*

She almost didn't make it to New York.

An airship of Her Majesty's Service, the *Artegal*, had been commandeered to take her to America. With less than a day to landing in New York, the craft was losing speed and altitude. The Maxwell's Demons that kept the Carnot engines functioning were spontaneously turning to dust.

Mina requested a copy of the Engineer's Grimoire, quickly absorbing the mechanisms involved and memorizing the appropriate sigils. In the engine room, she expected the moonlight glow of the Maxwells, but it was instead lit with lanterns and candles. The demon scuttles hung idle on the walls, their Hebrew inscriptions capturing the candlelight and reminding Mina of a synagogue. The floor of the room was coated in a gray residue that had a flat, musty odor, like dry earth. The demons' remains.

"They're gone," she said quietly. "Not banished or exorcised. Just… gone. Like the dead."

She could summon more. Enough to reach landfall, perhaps. And that may be all that there are. Her Majesty's Airships would fly no more.

In theory, it was always easier to bring the demons in than cast them out. Yet it was still strange, she thought, after so many years of keeping the host at bay, that she should now find herself tasked with the opposite. And it was more difficult in the end than she could have guessed. A single summoning should have filled all the chambers, yet only a few of the demons came through. She was forced to make cast after cast after cast, bringing a trickle in each time.

When they finally reached New York, Mina was spent from the effort.

From New York, it had been arranged she meet Nellie Bly, who would take her to San Francisco by conventional airship. And again, near calamity as over every city and town that had been wired for arc lighting, lightning attacked them from the ground. Bly's airship soon became a smoking wreck, and they all but crashed in Reno. Mina opted for the Overland to take her the rest of the way.

Even then the train was sluggish, as if fighting its way through molasses. All clocks and watches had seized and stopped. In the dining car, even the cutlery seemed heavy and found the floor at the slightest provocation. Mina recognized the phenomenon as a powerful magnetism. The rails themselves sought to hold the train in place.

Well, magnetism was the hidden twin of electricity, as Maxwell hypothesized, joined by light.

She understood what was impeding her progress, and she knew Uriel was as gone as Maxwell's Demons.

This would be the last one, she realized. *It is the last one, this one in San Francisco.*

And it found her, shortly after she arrived. Down Pinckney Place, a small alley across from *Lightman's*, she saw a scattered, moving glow.

Buer had mounted some poor denizen of the street. It sat at the back of the man's neck, one of its legs buried in his spine, two more still overhead, cloven hooves fitting the arc wires like locomotive wheels on train tracks.

It spoke to her… in a voice like the modulated scatter and rasp of the telegraph. Words of temptation, of longing, of threat. It promised her deepest desires would be fulfilled. It promised violence and vengeance; it promised answers to all questions of matter, earth, and sky.

Each staccato word lit the man's eyes from within — an awful orange streaked with red — and Mina gasped when she understood that the man was still alive, being slowly cooked and devoured by the demon.

Yet it saw in her no fear or temptation. Merely weariness. And then compassion. It recoiled from her empathy.

"I know what you seek," she told it. "I know you are not whole."

It shrieked again; the odor of singed hair.

Unafraid, she withdrew a simple Shelby Electric Company bulb she had obtained at a hardware store. Her only preparation was a binding invocation in Hebrew that she carefully inscribed around the base.

"In here," she told the demon, "You can be forever with the light and with your invisible twin."

Tentatively, Buer released the body of the man who was its host, and let go of the arc wires overhead, while Mina recited aloud and from memory, part III of *A Dynamical Theory of the Electromagnetic Field.*

She tossed the bulb and the demon caught it with three of its five legs. It touched the base of the bulb and there was the briefest flash. The demon was taken within.

She turned the glowing bulb over to The Ada Company, who gave it to a trusted associate, one Dennis Bernal, of the Livermore Power and Water Company. When told what it was, Bernal knew exactly what to do with it, and donated it as an *interesting curiosity* to a local fire station. For where else would the Earth be safe from a being of the kingdom of fire than in the presence of firemen?

It became known as the Livermore Bulb. It would burn for more than a century and generated no small commerce for the town. Along the way, a young patent clerk in Bern would snap shut his Emautochron and wonder, if there is no firmament to serve as a frame of reference, then perhaps it is *between* all things that nature lay?

Meanwhile, Mina Bergson returned to London by rail and steam.

* * *

>>> This story unfolds in a tension of ideas at the end of the 19th century. On the one hand is the notion that underlying everything is a reality indifferent to human perception, which manifests itself most heinously in nationalism and race (whence the vignette in the middle of the story). Yet there is also an understanding that existence and meaning live in the space amongst things, not necessarily the things themselves. The story begins at what is today City Lights Books in San Francisco, near where the artifact is. The artifact: nothing less than a symbol of ideas themselves.

Erik Jon Spigel

Erik Jon Spigel is a professor of the Humanities specializing in Japan, who also has a background in pure and applied mathematics. He has lived in the United States, Japan, and Canada working as a language teacher, a translator, an academic, and currently as a software engineer. He learned math in German, literary and cultural theory in French, Modern Japanese in English, Classical Japanese in Modern Japanese, and Classical Chinese in Classical Japanese. Rarely in his adult life has he been where he is in his own head. He currently lives in Toronto with his wife, Rui.

The Horn of Winter

Jason Lane

It was in the wind moaning over the steppes. It was in the howls of the wolves echoing through the woods. Singing through the Siberian night. Clear. Pure.

The Horn.

Anya heard it. Felt it. A tremble through her. A song calling to her. Calling to her as she was forced out of the cabin with her father, her mother, her sisters and brother, and into the fresh fallen snow.

The scream of the train's whistle wrenched her from her dreams. She sat up sharply, blinking. The world closed around her and took the shape of the cramped rail car. Peasants swaddled in heavy clothes filled the seats, a number clustered around the stove in the corner.

Captain Berlitz looked at her from the seat opposite. Broad, with a drooping mustache and bristling salt and pepper beard, he wore a heavy winter overcoat with a wolf fur collar.

"Something the matter?"

She shook her head. "Nothing."

He maintained his stare. She looked away. It was so beastly hot in the train. All the bodies crammed together. The smell of them was near overpowering. And dark. So dark with the winter night outside, the wind howling. The train swaying and beating the tracks with a *shakka shakka* sound.

She reached up and touched the locket around her neck. She popped it open and looked at the people within. A man with a swooping mustache in a fine red military coat and a blue sash. A woman, stiff and proud but with eyes of deepest compassion and pain. Children gathered before them. Girls and a boy all smiling up at the camera.

"Put it away," Captain Berlitz said. He was glancing about the car. Some of the peasants had raised their heads.

She scowled at them, but snapped it shut with a sound like a steel trap and tucked it under her heavy coat. A few looked over, but at the sight of Berlitz in his military jacket they wisely turned away.

"You should not bring that out," Berlitz said.

"Why not? I don't care if they see. They should see what they did."

"Anya—"

"Don't call me that."

She looked out the window. She had seen the other name on his lips. She huddled into her thick woolen coat, the fabric itching and rough. She remembered the softness of silk and the smoothness of a carriage ride, bells tinkling along the sledge.

"Why should I help them?" she said again.

"They are our people."

"Are they? I wonder who forgot that."

Berlitz's dark eyes glinted. She turned away from him. He had his opinions. She had hers.

She watched the barren landscape swoop by as the train rattled on. A light winter buried the deep forests and fields. Weeks they'd ridden the trains. Weeks of hiding, ducking from soldiers, fleeing the west, always heading east. East, into the lands the Cossacks claimed inch by bloody inch in years gone by.

Russia.

Her Russia.

She leaned her forehead against the cool glass, watching it all pass by. She dozed, soothed by the swaying of the train. Its whistle screaming in her dreams.

A different scream woke her.

Anya sat up. Ice crawled down her spine at the shriek piercing through the air. The other passengers were awake, milling in confusion. Berlitz grabbed her. "Down!" he shouted and pulled her beneath the seat. The scream roared over the train. Bullets pierced the ceiling, stitching through the aisle and seats, sending splinters flying. A man fell by her hand, his eyes staring and glassy. And blood, red blood, spilled across the floor.

Anya stared, fascinated. The scream grew fainter. Fell away. She scrambled away from the body and rose to the window, peered out into the white of the day. A shape like a bird swung through the sky. Soaring back towards the train. It began to dive, screaming like a banshee.

She winced, covering her ears. The winter wind gave a great howl. A sheet of white washed through the window. The scream of the plane fell away. Coughing in the dark.

Faded.

Somewhere, she heard a muffled whoomph.

Anya cracked open her eyes, peering through the storm. A figure flickered just at the edge of sight, standing on a snowy mound. 'A man in black, a soldier's coat whipping about him..

She blinked. He was gone.

The train moved on, winter bleeding into the car through the bullet holes. People sobbed and shuffled about. Later, they passed by the tail of a plane stamped with the iron cross, sticking out of the snow like an arm raised in stiff salute.

~ ~ ~

They rolled into the station hours later. Anya stepped off with Berlitz and stood aside as soldiers carried out the bodies, stacking them like cordwood on the station platform. Anya turned away from the men in red, pulling her hood lower.

Berlitz's heavy hand landed on her shoulder. "Come, Anya. We must go."

She nodded stiffly and turned. They walked slowly down the street of the former peasant village.

"We will meet guides," he said. "They will take us on."

"They know the way?"

"It is the old country."

It was all the old country, she thought. Yet new buildings rose about them. Heavy, brutal things of cement and brick. Far more numerous were the old, wooden buildings that slumped beneath the snow and their years, blending into the background of the encroaching forest and drifts of white piled against their sides.

They reminded her of the monk. The one with those powerful, intense eyes. The one who gazed into the face of her brother and calmed him and stopped his weeping wounds. She grew a little warm at the memory of him, speaking in a soft, deep voice to her and her sisters. She remembered him passing them pausing before each, smiling, speaking. She remembered when he reached her, how he'd placed his hand on her shoulder, staring deep into her eyes.

"You," he had said.

Later he had spoken in murmured conference with her father.

But that had been before. Another life. Another name.

Berlitz brought Anya to one of the slumping buildings and pushed open the door. A samovar simmered in the corner and icons were gathered on the wall. Two men were within. One, his feet propped up on a stool, was big as a bull and his head was slumped forward, a heavy fur hat resting on the back of his chair. Not far, a bony man was meticulously writing on a bunch of papers, his hair slick and black, tongue sticking out the corner of his mouth.

The thin man looked up as they entered. His gaze flicked to Berlitz.

"Berlitz?" he said.

"Rogozhin," Berlitz said, then to the large man. "Boris."

Boris grunted. Stirred and raised his head.

Rogozhin rose, his legs creaking faintly. He stalked forward and peered at them. "So, this is her, is it? The one who will blow the horn and save our Mother Russia?"

"Yes," Berlitz said. His heavy hand rested protectively on her shoulder. "You'll take us on?"

Rogozhin peered closer, ignoring the tall soldier for the moment. "I saw a portrait of you. Very long time ago now. In the papers before the Revolution. And such comics! Is it true what they said about the monk?"

Anya shied away from the man. His intent gaze and thin-boned face reminded her too strongly of another man from a life before. He grinned.

"Rogozhin!" Berlitz barked.

Rogozhin jerked upright. He waved his hands errantly. "Yes. Yes. All prepared. Not uncommon for men to make the trip along the mountain. Bourgeois used to do it all the time. I sometimes took generals along it before the war. But these days you need papers. Used to be just a few bribes but these new men are all about papers. Fine with me!" Rogozhin chuckled and swept a hand back towards the desk. "Cheaper than it, I say! Always new men too. Very keen. Hard to get a good word in."

Berlitz moved over to the papers and looked them over. Left alone, Anya's attention trailed over to the samovar, the fireplace, the chairs and desk. Anywhere not at the leering Rogozhin.

"Yes! All ready. Boris!" Rogozhin barked, kicking the bigger man. "Get up! We're going now."

Boris rumbled, yawned and sat up. He crouched down and picked up a pair of massive boots, jamming his feet into them one at a time. He stood slowly and grabbed the fur hat, pulling it over his ear. "Yes," he said, fetching a rifle.

"Not many go there now," she heard Rogozhin continue. "Wolves very aggressive. Soldiers have been warning people away. We think they are too hungry."

"Do you?" Berlitz said.

"Oh yes," Rogozhin said, delighted. "But we will make it. I know all the short cuts to the mountain. So long as you know what you are looking for."

"We do."

"We should not bring the girl," Boris rumbled.

"We must," Berlitz said.

"Then we best go soon," Rogozhin said. "There may be shooting. I hear one of the German's planes shot up your train. They do not usually fly out so far. Very far from the front. Do you think they know?"

"They may," Berlitz said. "I expect there will be trouble."

"Good," Rogozhin piped, patting his pistol. "I could use some new boots."

~ ~ ~

Winter winds sliced across the barren steppes. A Cossack village, ruined, tumbled upon itself, clawed out of the snow like bones of timber, nail and beam. They walked through it, single file. Heavy furs against the cold, rifles slung over backs.

Anya alone carried none. She trudged, the rough cloth scratching her skin. Exhaustion plagued her.

"Only a little further, Anya," Berlitz said. "Only a little further."

"I'm coming," she gasped. "I'm coming."

She lifted her face, and in the distance saw the peak. It rose out of the landscape, bald and terrible. The nearer to the mountain they drew the harsher the wind cut and the snows stirred.

They went on. Captain Berlitz led the way, his drooping mustache and beard speckled with ice. Boris followed, the heavy man's trudge breaking a path through the choking snow, his stolid face red from the biting wind. Behind them came Rogozhin, wasted and thin, but of the hardy peasant stock.

"My father took me hunting this way," Boris puffed as he forged ahead. "He was big man. Knew every trail. He hunted with rifle. Good rifle. Still used old flintlock in those days. I remember sound when it fired." He made a popping sound with his mouth that made Anya wince. "It was good rifle."

They rested in what had been an old tavern. Rogozhin grumbled as he searched the basement for a drop of vodka or beer. Boris collapsed on a chair, and Anya bundled down in a chair near the hearth, flinching as Berlitz broke a table and started a fire. A glow began, filling the room, light flickering on corners and edges of dust covered barrels and old cracked steins.

The warmth pushed away the cold, but the darkness of the abandoned place lingered just beyond. Crouched in corners like the *domovoy* her *nyanya* had once spoken of, describing the little house spirits that the peasants still had faith in. An altar stood in the corner, the once fine gilding worn down to the wood beneath.

"Driven out," Rogozhin said, stomping upstairs. "Long gone I'd say. The Reds came through."

"Could have been the Whites," Berlitz said.

"Doesn't matter. Soldiers! That's all I know. Only soldiers take all the liquor and burn everything else." He spat into a corner and slumped into a seat. "Left the icons. Probably the Reds. We'll stay here tonight. Take the mountain tomorrow."

"Is it far?" Berlitz asked.

Rogozhin laughed. A sharp, biting sound Anya hated. "Noooo. Not far. Just near the foot of the mountain. People around here don't like it, though. Probably why no one else took up residence. No one ever goes near the mountain. They fear a curse. Peasant stories talk of the cold and that winter never leaves it. That it gathers in the valley even during summer. Hah! High time we got rid of all that."

"My babushka talked of the valley," Boris said. "She said we must never go. That it is too cold and always cold. Not a place for people. But wolves. Many wolves."

Anya left them to their conversation. She went to the smoke-stained window and looked out into the snow. Winter hung thick over the remains of the village. The forests grew wild on the outskirts of town.

She squinted, staring, spotting a dark figure against the treeline.

"Something's happening."

Instantly all three men were moving. Boris went to the door, rifle in hand. Rogozhin drew his own and dashed up the stairs, peeking out a hole in the wall. Berlitz joined her, peering out into the twilight.

"What did you see?" the old soldier asked.

"A man. I… think."

"You think?"

"I saw him before. At the train. After the plane attacked."

His mouth tightened. "We're leaving."

"Now?"

"Now."

Boris grunted and threw his pack back on. Rogozhin came running back down the rotting stairs with a sound that sent Anya's spine rattling. Berlitz grabbed her and pulled her to the back of the old inn.

The kitchen was caked with dust, and pots and pans clattered under their feet as they moved to the back door.

The way through was open, the door smashed in by some boot in years past. Through it they re-entered the snow choked village. The ruins rose around them in ragged shapes. The sun was setting, the slate-gray sky for a moment stitched with a blaze of colors.

"Move. We must move!" Berlitz grunted.

There was a crack. Anya barely heard it. Then Rogozhin reeled about, clutching his chest. He fell into the snow with a thump, and in moments the snow was filling in the hole his body had made.

"Run!" Berlitz shouted.

And they were running.

Anya looked back and saw other figures chasing. Men in storm gray coats and helmets that swept down to cover their ears raced from the treeline. Near a dozen of them. Berlitz turned, firing with his pistol. One of the gray men went down, feet flying from under him like he slipped while skating on the Saint Petersburg canals, but he never got up. The others came on. Grim, purposeful men with guns like those who had taken her and her family out behind the cabin.

"The trees!" Berlitz bellowed. "The trees!"

The soldiers in gray came on. Firing wildly now. The snow puffed with every missed round.

Over the gunshots, she heard the howls.

The wolves streamed past the trees. Ragged, mangy, starving things. The men in gray shouted in surprise. One swung about but the wolf was already on him. Teeth fastened on the man's throat. Both went down, struggling in the snow. The others fired again. One's weapon jammed in the frigid winter air, and he went down screaming under a mass of fang and claw and bristling fur.

Boris bellowed as a wolf tackled him into the snow.

"Run, Anya!" Berlitz roared as more wolves raced for him. He fired, drew his saber from his belt and hacked the first one down. Blood spilled. Blood red and so warm it steamed when it hit the snow. She heard the sobs of her sisters. Her mother and father's painful dignity as they stared down the men in red. The maids whimpering and crying. And a voice echoed through time, shouting at her the same word from that dark night.

"Run!"

Anya clamped her hands over her ears to silence the screams, the howls, and ran into the woods.

~ ~ ~

The winds roared down through the trees.

Every step was a fight through snow so hard the crust broke with a crack under her feet, leaving solid pits in the white that swiftly filled. Her breath steamed in the air. Her lungs burned with effort and her face tingled with that cold. That terrible, terrible cold.

Berlitz was dead.

She shuddered and buried her face in her collar.

Father was dead.

Mother. Olga. Tatiana. Maria. Alexei. All dead. All gone.

She was alone.

And in the distance she heard the howls.

Closer.

Closer.

She fought on. Fought forward. There wasn't anything else to do. If she stopped she'd freeze, perhaps even before the wolves got to her. She almost laughed at the thought of the animals breaking their teeth on her blackened, frozen face. But that thought was too near hysterics, and instead she choked on the sound.

A root, hidden under the snow, caught her foot. With a cry she went down. For a moment lay in the snow, gasping, sobbing.

The wind died to a whisper.

She raised her head.

The man stood before her. His booted feet only just touched the snow. His dark, soldier's cloak was wrapped about him and a sloping helmet not in fashion for a hundred years or more was on his head. A saber was sheathed at his side. His beard was a thick white thing, mustache sweeping in a style popular when Frenchmen marched across Europe under their emperor.

But his eyes were older. Far, far older than mere centuries. Not even the monk's eyes had held such power. The casual ease to carry death. The utter absence of any warmth. A thousand could die at that man's boots. A hundred thousand could claw at his cloak and he wouldn't even look down at them as they blackened with frost and stilled. He could pass through fields and leave whole villages to starve without an ounce of interest. He didn't mean to. He simply did. He simple was.

He simply didn't care.

Anya had faced death before. Looked down the barrels of rifles as she stood, soaked in the blood of her mother and sisters in the cold snow behind the cabin.

She saw something worse than death in those eyes.

The fur of her collar was stiff like porcupine spines around her head as she stood. Her tears froze on her cheeks, burning with numbing pain. She looked him in those eyes.

"Where?"

He moved his head. An acknowledgement? A greeting? She wasn't sure. But he stepped aside, and like a white curtain to the stage, the blizzard parted.

A cave lay before her, cut into the mountain's face. Stone worked with strange designs flanked it in a pair of heavy pillars. Shapes without form she could recall spiraling across the two *bautasteiner*. They reminded her starkly of the writing in the illuminated manuscripts the patriarch had shown her before that dark night at the palace. But this was rawer. More unevenly cut, like the winds had carved the stones.

He said nothing. Merely stood aside. Waiting. She glanced his way, then ventured through the cavern mouth and into darkness.

Her footsteps echoed hollowly within. Chimed off icicles hanging from the ceiling. She breathed in. Out. Her breath no longer puffed in the air.

A blue light shone ahead. She forged on until the light became a doorway, and she stepped through, and into a memory.

The walls were made of clearest ice as though she walked into a room of crystal. Elegant filigree curled in corners and arched above. Pale light glowed from a chandelier hanging above, its every candle lit with a blue flame. It was a room she knew. The palace at Saint Petersburg.

In the middle of the room stood a throne. And on it sat a woman of striking beauty. She was still, her skin like marble. Her hair was white as snow, and her gown as blue as the water from the freshest spring. Her throne was worked from the trunk of single great tree, its branches rising into the air to spread out and clasp the roof of the palatial chamber.

On her lap, in her hands, was a horn carved from antler.

Anya stared at the woman. Slowly, she approached, her footsteps chiming in the stillness of the chamber. She climbed the cut steps to the throne and looked down at the horn.

She reached out and grasped it. It was stuck. With a scowl she yanked.

The woman shattered like glass. Anya gasped, stepping back as the woman's flesh fell to pieces on the throne. The shards dissolved, melting on the ground.

The throne was empty.

Anya held the horn.

She ran her fingers over the ancient thing and traced designs like those on the stones outside. She felt the heft of it.

So this was it. This was what would save her country? Yet, even as she held it, she knew there was more to it. She turned slowly, and he was there.

He stood in the middle of the room, his black soldier's cloak rustling in a wind that wasn't there. Around him, wolves made of the rotting, black ice of spring crowded around his feet. The old man stared at her. Not accusing. Not eager. He simply waited. The wolves sat on their haunches, expectant.

She stood before the throne beneath the mountain and put the horn to her lips.

And blew.

The sound boomed through the cavernous palace. Rang off the icicles in the passage beyond like a chiming band of the Moscow Concert Hall. The wolves sat up straighter. The rotting ice of their forms grew more solid. Clearer until they shone like the finest diamonds, the bared fangs, quivering with eagerness. Anya drew back her lips, gasped, her throat raw with cold as though she'd swallowed razor blades.

She blew it again.

The sound boomed past the mountain and into the valley. She saw it reach out, swirling the snow and wind. She saw more men in thick gray coats and helmets fighting through the snow stop and listen. The wind picked up, rustling their thick winter clothing, biting them with the bitterest cold. They screamed, shielding themselves, hunkering down as the buffeting winds ripped through them.

Anya gasped, her mouth hot with a bloody iron taste. She blew again.

The long note rang deep. The wolves of ice lifted their muzzles and howled with it. The old man touched his sword and drew it. He turned and left the space beneath the mountain. The wolves carried past him, running with the wind that raced out before them, carrying them beyond the frozen shapes of the men in gray, flesh blackened, frost crusting them and arms raised like statues in torment. The wolves surged past, rising into the air. The wind in the valley churned with them, ripping the snow from the trees into a column of ice.

Anya took her lips from the horn. Breathed in.

And blew once more.

The Russian Winter surged from the valley, spreading across the country. Rivers cracked as they froze. Men and women hunched in their homes and huddled nearer stoves. She saw them all. Saw the stormy winter clouds race in every direction. North and south and east and west. The winds howled with the voice of wolves. And above them all came the thundering roar of the horn.

Winter swept down, deepening. To the west it blanketed the landscapes in drifts of white. Aircraft painted with the Iron Cross sputtered and struggled. Tanks creaked as they fought to advance, their engines freezing. Trucks ground to a halt. Men died huddled for warmth and were buried in the snow.

The winds swept through broken buildings, attacking men in red and gray without distinction. Freezing hands and feet and faces. The ground hardened like cement in the terrible cold. She could hear the earth tighten in the grip of true winter. As though viewing a map, she saw the dark advance from the west stall and halt across her homeland. She saw the men who ordered the deaths of her family sit back and order preparations as the winter rattled the windows of their snug, brutal buildings. She saw forges billow smoke and factories rumble to life with industry, turning white snow black with ash and smog.

The note died. Her thoughts receded from the country and back into the valley, down the passage and into the palace beneath the earth. She lowered the horn and touched her numb, blue lips. She exhaled, and the thin puff of warmth died in the air.

Slowly she sat down on the throne at the root of the mountain. She sighed, a sound that whispered through the room of ice and stone and crystal. She set the horn in her lap and closed her eyes, and dreamed her winter dreams of palaces and czars, and a Russia that had once been.

* * *

>>> *The Horn of Winter is itself a piece of fiction, though such items are common in lore and histories. So for my story, it's more the Russian winter that struck during WW2 and halted the Nazi advance that was the artifact in the story. Russia itself has a very rich lore and history, and I was glad to get the chance to plunder it a little here.*

Jason Lane

Jason Lane has lived in Whitehorse, Yukon, all his life except for occasional visits to the southern climes, always to gravitate back towards the pole when winter calls. Weird tales and fantasy are his lifelong loves but science fiction always has a special place in his heart. He is a huge fan of Ray Bradbury and Terry Pratchett, and when not writing, can be found perusing the local used bookshop or libraries. His works have appeared in several publications including *Tesseracts 21*.

Uki Dreams

Colleen Anderson

The clear sky tantalized, even though the brooding ship marred the flat snowy horizon. A breeze tickled Uki's nose with the stinging scent of melting sea ice. The delicate fragrance of green plants pushing through the thawing permafrost added to the bouquet. Uki closed her eyes, smiling. The great bowl of the sky embraced the sun that would continue through the long months ahead, each day warming more.

She swallowed saliva, anticipating the range of food they would gather; bright purple saxifrage, cloudberry, ptarmigan eggs, fish and so many abundant meals to come. Shrugging the heavy caribou atiqi lower on her shoulders, Uki pulled off the outer layer, leaving only the inner furs snuggled against her flesh. How she wanted to bask in the sun forever. Like all Inuit, she hunted, walked, slept and lived in the cold every long winter, but the summer. Oh, the summer! So many colors and things to see; so many flavors and scents and new horizons. Snow and ice presented a relentless tableau. And even the foreigners' umiak was a welcome interruption to that white plain.

Uki shivered, keeping her eyes closed, remembering Pavvik and great grandmother's tales about previous generations where they hunted and lived on the white snow plains, of summers bright but the tundra still frozen, of living in igloos the whole year round, not the pit houses or skin tents they used now in the warm months. Uki want to skip about, because soon there might be no snow. She loved the color and change from the boring flat landscape.

Arnaluuk ran toward her, the woman's braided and looped black hair bouncing on either side of her head. "There you are, Uki. What are you doing? We have to gather the saxifrage now, and then we have to practice singing the animals to us."

Uki refused to open her eyes and dispel the mood. For just one moment she wanted to savor the warmth, to not worry about the melting ice, and the strange men who had come from across the ocean in their dark umiak the size of a whale. She wanted only to feel the heat and not think of the freezing dark nights that would follow the long summer of constant sunshine. Uki dreamed of a summer that would last forever.

"Uki!"

"Arnaluuk!" Her eyes snapped open. "Can't you ever just enjoy the day without worrying about what has to be done?" Uki walked back to the tents that whispered and rustled as the wind ran fingers across the brown skins.

She passed Kanaak and Nattiq, the two men talking and gesturing toward the inlet. Beyond the patches of white ice, tinged with soft blue of melting pools, and visible over the yellowish plants, the wooden umiak sat alien in the water, much taller and larger than the largest Inuit umiak. Kanaak stumbled over the foreigner's name; they had no sounds similar in Inuktituk. "Ruggutur is promising more singing metal."

Nattiq stabbed at the softening snow with his whalebone spear. "He is also saying we have taken his men."

Uki stopped and listened while rebraiding her hair. Then she dropped the outer parka in the tent and grabbed a gray sealskin bag. She looked south where the men from Frobisher's ship had gone. With only hand signals and a few words being taught between the two groups, interpretation had been difficult, but she'd been there when the five qallunaat paddled up in their small all-wood umiak. They had looked angry and tired when they came into the Inuit encampment from the umiak. Pointing south, away from the increasing sunlight, the one man had motioned, making walking symbols. Away from the ship.

They had traded their smaller umiak for some food, weapons and warm caribou atiqis, then the Inuit had directed them south toward land without snow and rumors of other people living on grass plains.

Uki had never been to the treeline. All the tales passed down told of the dangers, and the more terrifying ones involved men willing to kill for food or women or land. The Inuit stayed safe, living in the cold, working with the animals who provided them with food and clothing.

A sweet sound rang clear across the tundra. Everyone halted — Arnaluuk chewing purple saxifrage, the children chasing each other in circles, Nattiq and Kanaak arguing, and Uki, her hand over her heart. The call came again, making her shiver. If the spirit of the tiny, plain wheatear's song could be captured, this would be it, and somehow Frobisher had found a way to put a bird's soul into metal. Metal was so magical; hard and strong and it could be sharper — sharper than a whalebone spear or knife made of seal ribs. The qallunaat chief had traded several small *bells*, plus other items before his men left him. Then, stranded on his large wooden umiak, he accused the Inuit of having stolen his men and his other umiak.

Kanaak said, "I will go to his umiak and see what he wants."

The air vibrated again and Kanaak slid into his yellow sealskin qajaq and paddled toward the ship. Uki and several other men and women followed along on land, avoiding the softening ice. Kanaak floated alongside Frobisher's umiak. Uki cringed. Their metal was a wonder but the men who came ashore carried long weapons of the same shining material.

Arnaluuk's shadow momentarily shaded Uki, but she didn't turn to look.

"What is he doing?" Arnaluuk moaned. She gripped Uki's arm.

"He is going to talk to the aquti of the umiak." Uki admired Kanaak's courage. These people brought change and new things. She wanted to follow as well, but what could she exchange for a bell? Maybe one of her caribou atiqis, but how would she get to them?

Kanaak reached toward the large golden bell Frobisher's men hung over the side of the ship.

Uki gasped. "What are they doing!" She ran toward the water. "Kanaak! No!"

As Kanaak grabbed for the bell, a smile creasing his eyes, two of men with great moss-thick beards reached down and grasped his wrist. He yelled, but they lifted him into the ship, qajaq and all, his paddle falling into the water.

People ran forward yelling, grabbing spears and harpoons, splashing through the puddles of ice water. Two men threw harpoons, but they dropped harmlessly into the water, sinking out of sight. No one dared paddle out after the sturdy all-wood umiak that loomed above the horizon.

"No!" Uki squeezed her fists. They were ruining everything.

Pavvik yelled, signaling, stopping anyone else from wasting weapons or pursuing Kanaak.

That night they all gathered in Pavvik's tent, some people standing outside. A soapstone qulliq filled with whale blubber had been lit, adding light and heat to the chill within the tent. Pavvik shook his head, his shoulder-length hair shifting on his shoulders. "Aquti and his men, they have taken without asking."

"Can we get Kanaak back?" Nattiq asked, twirling his spear into the packed ice flooring. Already, Uki noticed the softening. Soon even the most shadowed ice would be gone. "He is headstrong, but a good hunter and my friend."

Kannarjuraq, stooped over with the burden of her years, her teeth worn to nubs with the many skins she had chewed, coughed and moved into the center. "They have metal that can hurt us. We must ask the spirits of those who protect us."

Uki and Arnaluuk looked at each other, then stood up and grasped each other's elbows. Uki's fingers moved over the slightly stubbled surface of Arnaluuk's atiqi. "Which spirits shall we call, Kannarjuraq?"

"The most powerful — polar bear and walrus."

Two men moved toward the back of the tent where the qulliq's flickering light danced amber against the skin walls. One man brought out two walrus tusks and the other the skull of a polar bear.

Uki said, "I'll call Nanuq, you call the sea brother."

Humming deep in her throat, Uki let the rhythm choose itself and uttered a series of buzzes and grunts in repetition.

Standing close in front and swaying side to side, Arnaluuk punctuated Uki's chant with her own rhythm. They continued back and forth, their mouths close, pulling air from between, setting a resonance that wove around them and flowed out to touch the people.

At the same time, other people droned or hummed in the background as the men moved up and down imitating the swaying gait of the polar bear and the undulations of the walrus.

The world flickered around Uki as their back and forth rhythm quieted everything else. Time froze, and Uki dreamed. *Nanuq lumbers across the snowy land chasing a fox, her baby running behind her. The silvery fox turns into a mist of smoke and disappears. Nanuq's baby falls through the ice and Nanuq follows her child, never resurfacing. Then the ice melts away and only the sun remains.*

Uki stopped, wailing. Arnaluuk's chant halted a breath after hers and the two women hugged each other. Then Uki relayed her dream.

Arnaluuk, wringing her hands through Uki's words, hiccupped. "Aiviq, old tusker, swam beneath the ice. He chased a fish. He grabbed the fish, but a harpoon speared him. Aiviq died."

The silence was only interrupted by the sides of the skin tent crackling as people shifted.

Kannarjuraq's voice cut like an icy wind. "To pursue aquti and his men will be the death of us. Kanaak must find his own way home."

Nattiq shook his head. "I cannot abandon a friend. I will go out tomorrow to Aquti's umiak and ask for his return. I will not get too close and hope the qallunaat will listen to reason."

Uki's thoughts whirled. Too much was happening too fast. Why couldn't Frobisher and his ship just leave, but after returning Kanaak? She wanted only sun and warmth and to explore. She did not want a polar bear in man's skin to hunt her. That thought made her stomach tighten.

"That is not the worst. Uki and Arnaluuk dreamed more than of Aquti."

Every person looked at Pavvik. "Uki's dream speaks to greater problems. Our land is changing. With the melting snow, we will lose everything."

"No," Uki cried, "that cannot be true. We've survived in the tundra forever. Why can't we adapt to a warmer world, to Nunavut in summer forever?"

As the discussion continued Uki left, running through the spring's twilight evening and into her tent. She nestled deep under the furs, hiding her head. Why did they all fear change? That was not what the dream meant. It was only about Aquti's challenge, only about the umiak from beyond. Only that.

Uki dreamed fretfully, tangled in her furs. Aqsarniit, the great lights of the sky flickered in her dream world. Umiaks made of wood that was so scarce in snow-blanketed lands, strong and towering like a shadow polar bear, these *ships* from strange lands converged on the Inuit, where bushy-faced men stole the people and took their food. The great white bears perished. Snow fell and coated the land. The foreign umiaks froze in the ice, men turning to pillars shimmering blue and white with the darker core of death inside each one. The cold moved on, relentless.

When she awoke, Uki felt so chilled by the dream that she donned her outer parka as well. The dream coated her vision, darker than she had seen while throat singing. Busying herself was the best way to not think about it.

Nattiq had already taken his qajaq out toward the ship, the sky seeming to have paled against the events. He floated far enough to avoid capture, his hair tied back with sinew, his paddle across this boat. He waved a halloo to the men aboard. Frobisher showed, standing with his arms crossed, looking down and scowling. Nattiq indicated himself and his qajaq and motioned for the return of Kanaak.

Frobisher, dressed in a thin coat of black fur that looked as if it would not warm him when the snows returned, shook his head, then held up his hand, pointing to each finger. He then motioned at his men and toward the tundra.

Nattiq tried to indicate that they had helped the men who had traveled south but Uki knew Frobisher didn't understand. Anger and horror washed over the man's face. What did he think they had done to his men?

Nattiq returned empty handed.

~ ~ ~

Arnaluuk ran up to Uki as she pulled up long strands of translucent seaweed and aligned it on the shore for drying.

"Uki. Uki! What are we going to do?"

"About what?"

"About Kanaak. About… about those men." Arnaluuk's eyes were rimmed in dark, speaking of her sleepless nights. She twisted the dark brown cord of her ilupaaq, open to let the sun touch her flesh.

The dreams weighed them like a whale carcass.

Uki sighed. Kanaak had been held on the ship for ninety-eight days now. "There is nothing we can do, sister. We cannot reach them, and it seems they cannot reach us, unless they use Kanaak's qajaq. I think the umiak their men brought ashore was their only one."

The air cracked as if a crevasse had open. A black ball hurled past them, smashing into the tundra, spraying water and mud into the sky. Women shrieked, and men yelled. Instinctively, they moved as one, women scooping up children and picking up bows, men grabbing spears and harpoons. They ran as fast as they could away from the dark ship. Dogs howled and yapped after them.

Two more balls hurled at them from Frobisher's umiak but they fell short of the fleeing Inuit.

Pavvik beyond the reach of the metal balls, stabbed his spear into the ground and waited for the people to gather. The younger men had each picked up a grandmother or grandfather and run with those too slow to escape over their shoulders.

Several people began to mourn, wailing low in their throats.

Pavvik looked at his people. Uki wiped tears from her eyes. She loved everyone. They were her family and community but surely there must be another way?

Their camp of ten tents had been set up in the best place for summer harvest. "We can always rebuild, and the long summer affords us enough light to do so," said Pavvik to his people. "But Aquti's weapons are not so well aimed as a harpoon or a spear. If only two people go at one time, we can bring our camp to us. I doubt he can hit us. Move as if Nanuq pursued you."

Even Uki and Arnaluuk did their part to gather items, moving swiftly and low to the ground. Not one person was injured and no more balls of metal came from Aquti's umiak. Later they would gather those metal spheres and see if they could use them.

Uki stood alone, staring out at the dark umiak. Frobisher had ruined everything. Without him and his men the sun would have come as always, the plants and flowers would have grown and the year would turn, bring warmer days around. The Inuit would have reveled in the sun and would have adapted. But now... the sun meant men could come on land.

Uki hated the cold, so tired of it that she never wanted to leave her furs. The treeline would be interesting, warmer, a landscape that wasn't merely ice and snow and ocean. But Frobisher threatened them and if he could, would kill them all.

Uki paced until she had worn the softening snow away and trudged the underlying earth into mud. To keep quiet meant abandoning her people, and she could not do that.

She approached Pavvik as he sliced off a piece of seal meat and handed it to Kannarjuraq who sat upon a flat, brown stone sunning herself, her creased face tilted up to catch the sun's smile.

"I...I have dreamed...." She told them of aqsarniit flickering in the sky and of Nanug. Kneeling beside Kannarjuraq, she wept. "I wanted the land to warm, for summer to always be here but this can't be without us dying, without Aquti's men showing up again and taking all of us as they did with Kanaak."

That evening, though night did not descend in the months of summer, the community talked about Uki's dream.

Reluctantly, she spoke up. "If Arnaluuk agrees, we can try to sing in the cold. I know we often sing for guidance or for bringing the hunt to us, but I feel that if I sing in the arqsaniit and Arnaluuk sings in the cold, we can bring it back. We...." Her heart felt like an anchor stone. "If we do this, Aquti and his men will leave."

Kannarjuraq coughed. She waved a withered hand toward Uki. He eyes shone like black stones. "You are brave, Uki. Only once before do I remember singing in the weather. It can be done but it is difficult. I once dreamed as you do and this, we must do. Aquti will be back, at least twice. The only way to keep them at bay is to make Nunavut uncomfortable and to camouflage what we have."

~ ~ ~

The Inuit had hunted and prepped and as the summer sun waned, they prepared. After a good sleep, Uki and Arnaluuk walked together, talking, warming their throats and voices for what was to come. They were given extra seal meat and whale blubber that they ate, even when full. Neither worked through the day as they strengthened their throats and souls.

"Uki?"

"Hmm?" Uki rolled over from staring into the fathomless blue sky, for once not thinking of the terrible dreams. She focused on Arnaluuk's high brows and full cheeks.

"Can we do this? Can we save everyone?"

"I don't know, sister. But I think we can link to the power if we remember we do this for our people, our family. I was so tired of this life; I wanted summer to be always."

Arnaluuk sighed, rolling onto her back. "Me too. It is so nice to feel the sun's warmth on our skin."

"The price is too high," Uki said, finally realizing it.

~ ~ ~

Uki and Arnaluuk wore only the inner caribou atiki, the light skin glowing against their own brown flesh. They grasped each other's elbows and began to sway side to side. Around them stood the community, ready to catch them or help if needed. The sky continued relentlessly, but the blue had darkened over the weeks to dusk.

They began, their mouths only a handspan from each other. Uki hummed a low resonant tone, longer than normal for throat singing. She punctuated it with a short crescendo, dropping again to the hum. Arnaluuk gave short sharp barks with an undertone of a vibrating growl. Starting softly, they built in volume, then leveled out, the tones alternating, blending into one rhythm. Often, when they were singing for fun, one would run out of breath, or laugh from the sounds. They kept their concentration firm, droning on.

Time lost meaning. Uki floated, knowing her body continued singing. She searched for the threads that wove the lights, calling on them, pulling them to her. *We need you, aqsarniit. Only you see all the land, only you can protect us from the outlanders.* She reached up to pull down bright green, a pink that flowers could not imitate, a soft blue, yellow. The power frizzled along her fingertips, tingling her spine.

Still, she continued singing, feeling and hearing Arnaluuk's counterpoint. Could they call the aurora to bring about the change, to add the saving cold into their lives?

Uki did not know how long they sang, but it was longer than ever before. Yet, she knew it wasn't long enough and squeezed Arnaluuk's elbow. Arnaluuk squeezed back, for a moment their eyes focusing on each other, an understanding passing between them that they were not there yet.

At that point they both changed pitch simultaneously and Arnaluuk's eyes grew round. Uki squeezed harder, keeping Arnaluuk focused. They must not break the rhythm.

The sky shaded darker in Uki's peripheral vision. Thin twigs of light speared down. Uki's body vibrated and she felt a resonation through Arnaluuk as well.

They stopped when the first snowflakes dusted their eyelashes, collapsing against each other.

~ ~ ~

Every day, upon waking, someone paddled out toward the ship and tried to negotiate. Unexpectedly, a week later, Frobisher released Kanaak, looking gaunt but whole. The umiak raised its sails and moved away.

Two weeks later, the five qallunaat who had traveled south returned to the Inuit camp. One man grasped his broken arm close to his body. All looked like they hadn't eaten in a long time. The Inuit gave them food, though the qallunaat insisted on eating their flesh cooked.

Uki helped tend, slowly trading words of two languages. With signing, she learned of the land from which the qallunaat came. It sounded exciting and disturbing. Places where people sang, or storytellers told foreign tales, and an array of strange meats and bright vegetables abounded. But they spoke of cities crowded with people as if it were a joy, of murder and crime as just part of the day to day.

As the snow fell thicker, the men started to build an umiak. The Inuit watched, supplying material or tools but letting the qallunaat work on their own design.

The umiak stood finished in the bay, sturdy and big enough to hold eight men. The ice grew thicker every day and in a few weeks no boats would be able to move in the ocean. Pavvik and Uki tried to tell the men to wait until the days lengthened again, but they said they could not eat that much seal. Outfitted in caribou qulittag sturdy enough for the coming snows, food and tools, the men stepped into their umiak. The Inuit sang them farewell.

When the qallunaat appeared only a week later, their umiak battered and sails ripped, Uki was not surprised. The song she and Arnaluuk had chanted, that had brought the magic, would not let many enter or leave. Though they nursed the five men, they perished, one after another until none were left by the time total night arrived.

Uki looked up at the strands of green and pink and yellow rippling through the sky, a soft chiming reminding her of Frobisher's *bells*. This sounded purer and made of nature's song. Tears trickled down her cheeks. To explore beyond the treeline had been a dream and she could not fulfill it without abandoning her people.

She breathed deeply, the crisp air filling her lungs. Millions of stars laced the black sea of night. Each year, she and Anarluuk would sing back the winter, keeping the invaders at bay. She would have children and they would have children and they would dream of keeping their people safe and would sing in the cold.

* * *

>>> *The Inuit survived against invasions by white people because, for a time, they lived in a climate inhospitable to others. Frobisher came to the Arctic looking for the NW Passage and thought he had found gold, but his men didn't know how to survive what was alien to them. The alchemy here is the Inuit throat singing with the power to call animals for the hunt and to alter the weather. We face climate change now and the threat of losing the Arctic way of life for people and the animals.*

Colleen Anderson

Colleen Anderson's 200 plus works have appeared in such venues as *nEvermore!, Beauty of Death, Heroic Fantasy Quarterly, OnSpec, Amazing* and *Cemetery Dance*. She is a three-time Aurora nominee and has received honorable mentions for poetry and fiction. Her past includes book buyer, book rep, Chizine poetry editor, Vancouver ChiSeries host, *Tesseracts 17* and *Playground of Lost Toys* co-editor, as well as freelance copyediting. She recently received a Canada Council grant for writing. In 2018 she edited *Alice Unbound: Beyond Wonderland* through Exile Publishing, and Black Shuck Books, UK published her dark fiction collection A *Body of Work*.

www.colleenanderson.wordpress.com

Intentions

Lara Apps

Tutting, Mother brushed bread crumbs from the front page of the evening *Times*.

"Those suffragettes are a scandal, Ida, a scandal. It says here they planted a bomb at St. Paul's! Trying to blow up the chancery!"

She took another bite of toast, necessitating more crumb removal.

"They should let them rot in prison. None of this feeding them when they go on hunger strike. Let them die, if that's what they want. I don't know what this world is coming to, I don't. You're well out of it, Ida, you are."

"Yes, Mother."

Ida set her spoon down in her empty bowl too sharply, but Mother was absorbed in the news, her lips moving slightly as she read. Ida rose from the table and began the washing-up, earning an absent "Good girl," and assent to her retreat once she was finished.

She locked the door to her room before reaching under her thin mattress for the other news: the *Suffragette* newsletter. Ida's own lips moved when she read, but only sometimes, when she had to sound out the longer words. She had attended school until she was twelve, the compulsory minimum, but since then she had worked in the dye factory alongside Mother until Mother's health broke down. Father had died so long ago that Ida had only the vaguest memories of him as an exhausted, broken presence at dinner.

She received the *Suffragette* in secret. Mother thought she had quit the Women's Social and Political Union after Black Friday. But for three years Ida had paid her nominal membership dues, read the newsletters, and silently cheered for the suffragettes who bombed mailboxes, smashed windows, and went to prison. She just wasn't as brave as them, that's all. And what would happen to Mother if she got herself arrested? It had been a close thing on Black Friday, in 1910.

She found Edith in an alley, crumpled on the cobble stones, curled around herself. Her coat and hat were gone, her dress torn and muddy. She didn't respond to her name. A bruise darkened one side of her face, and blood from her nose and split lip had dried on her skin. Her naked breasts were shockingly white, but tinted purple where they, too, were bruised.

Ida roused Edith, covered her with her buttoned-up coat, and took her home. She staggered under Edith's weight and the pain of her own ribs, which she thought must be cracked. Mother pursed her lips and said barely a word while she helped get Edith undressed, bathed, and into Ida's bed.

The suffragettes had tried to enter the House of Parliament, to protest their veto of the bill that would have given at least some women — not the likes of Ida and Edith, but proper ladies — the vote. Churchill sent in the police, who spent the next six hours manhandling the women. Ida stood before the small mirror in the bathroom and peeled away the cardboard wrapped around her ribs. It hadn't done quite enough to protect her, but she hadn't expected a kicking from a policeman while she was on the ground. Her ribs were bruised and sore, and it was hard to breathe. Her left eye was blackened and swollen shut from the punch that had knocked her down. She thought of poor, brutalized Edith, coaxed to sleep by a drop of Mother's laudanum, and of the violence and hatred the protesters had all suffered. Her shoulders began to shake, and she wept quietly into her hands.

"Do you see now, Ida," Mother said when she came out. "Do you see now that this fight is all wrong? Look at what's happened to you, to poor Edith. Can you say it's worth it, all this for the silly vote? I've never had the vote, and I've never

wanted it. And you and Edith suffered today for what? To protest that rich women didn't get the vote? Do you think those women are then going to vote for the likes of you and me and Edith to have it? They're using you. You're nothing but cannon fodder to them. Enough of this foolishness, Ida. Enough."

With some effort, for she was tired from a long day on her feet at the factory, Ida focused on the front page of the newsletter. She wished Gran were there. Gran might have been a wicked old baggage, as Mother once called her in a moment of bitter recollection, but Ida had loved her. Gran would have been there at the protests. Gran would have happily smashed shop windows and taken a horse whip to Mr. Churchill. Gran had other ways, too. Secret methods that Mother couldn't know about, that she taught to Ida while Mother was at the factory and they were alone in the house.

Her thoughts had drifted to the past again. She frowned and turned back to the paper, gasping when she read the main article. Emily Wilding Davison was being released from prison! She had been incarcerated several times at Strangeways in Manchester and Holloway in London. The WSPU *and* the regular newspapers had reported on her arrests and hunger strikes. Davison was perhaps the most militant, the most daring of the suffragettes, completely willing to sacrifice herself for the cause. Ida soaked up every word of everything written by and about her. Davison was going to spend a few days recuperating in London before going home next Saturday to the town of Morpeth in Northumberland, where a welcome was planned.

Ida laid the newsletter on her lap. She mentally counted how much money she had hidden in the box under her bed. It was enough, just, for a train to Morpeth and back. It would take her a full day, but she could swap a factory shift with one of the other girls. She checked the date and time of the welcome and wrote it carefully in the diary where she kept her appointments, such as they were. She put the newsletter back under the mattress and felt for the other object she was hiding from her mother's too-keen eyes: a partly-finished, embroidered tricolored silk sash in the white, green and purple of the WSPU. She checked the lock on her door, fetched her sewing kit, and prepared to get to work on the lettering. She was only partway through the word *Votes*. She had begun the sash in January, after reading Emmeline Pankhurst's letter about militancy.

To be militant in some way or other is a moral obligation. It is a duty which every woman will owe to her own conscience and self-respect, to other women who are less fortunate than she herself is, and to all those who are to come after her.

She wanted so much to do more, but for now, all she could do was embroider a sash to wear when she felt brave enough to attend a WSPU meeting again. It was nearly June, and she hadn't finished the sash or done anything besides read the newsletter and silently pray for the suffragettes' success. She felt like a fraud.

She fingered the smooth material, tracing where she had sketched in the rest of the letters. The sensation of the cloth on her skin called Gran to mind again. Gran had taught her something one day, something that she had forgotten but was now pushing its way into her memory like a snowdrop coming up through the soil in springtime. Gran had shown her certain knots... and said certain words... spells to help you get what you wanted, she'd said. Gran used to slip such spells into the caps and scarves she knitted for Ida. She gave Ida an embroidered handkerchief the day she started work at the factory, pressing it on her with the instruction to always keep it with her while she was at work. Ida had never thought about it, but she obeyed the instruction, and she was the only girl Mr. Pritchett hadn't called in for a special meeting with him. She'd never thought about it, because he still pinched her backside when he passed by and tried to peer down her dress. But she'd seen girls come out of those meetings pale, or red and weeping. Gran must have known what a factory foreman would be like.

Perhaps there was, after all, something she could do besides reading and praying.

She took up her needles and thread and got to work, thinking ahead to where the knots should go. She would work hard and finish the sash for Saturday, and give it to Miss Davison. It would bring Miss Davison luck and success in her work for the suffragette cause. As she began the stitching, Ida thought, too, she should include a spell for bravery. Miss Davison was already courageous, but who knew what her next challenges might be? A little help wouldn't hurt.

Votes For Women... Ida twisted her tiny colored knots into the letters, saying the words her Gran had taught her, stitching magic into the sash for Emily Davison. She was bent too close to her work to notice the faint glow emanating from the new stitches.

~ ~ ~

It was a fine morning, almost noon, as the train crossed the River Wansbeck toward the Morpeth station. Emily knew there would be a crowd — by Morpeth standards, that is — when she arrived. She would have liked to slip home quietly, without a fuss, but this was too good an opportunity for the WSPU to pass up. She did not, she thought, feel much like a returning hero.

She dreaded the thought of returning to prison. Yet she knew she would; indeed, there was no question in her mind on this point. She would do whatever it took to bring attention to the cause, and if that meant prison, so be it. She would go on hunger strike again, and again, and again, if necessary, until the government treated the suffragettes like political prisoners instead of common criminals.

She shuddered at the memory of the hunger strikes and forced feedings she and so many other women had endured. Of the matrons that held one down, of the steel gag that forced one's jaws open and cut one's lips, of the doctor pushing the rubber feeding tube down one's throat, of the terrible sense of suffocation. Of the gagging, of the vomit that rose up through an esophagus that was already stretched and made raw by the tube. Of the degradation, the violation, the rage. She had always resisted with all her power, even to the point of throwing herself down a set of prison stairs, but it had done no good. Still, it gave her a renewed sense of purpose, this ritual of violence. What could more clearly demonstrate the justice of the suffragettes' fight? But would it not be better to turn public opinion, and to make the government take them seriously, with one daring public coup?

The crowd, when she reached it, was larger than she had expected, but cheerful and friendly, buoying her spirits. This was, after all, her home. She smiled at the banner over the road, waved at the people who had come to support her.

Her attention was drawn to a young woman at the front of the crowd. She was dressed neatly, in a simple brown skirt and white blouse, both several years out of fashion. She had removed her hat in the spring heat, and her light brown hair had started to come loose from its bun. Something in her plain face made Emily move toward her, and the smile that transformed the young woman made Emily go and take her hand.

"My dear, thank you for coming to greet me," Emily said.

The girl stammered a hello and bobbed a half-curtsy, clearly overwhelmed. She pressed a small package wrapped in tissue paper into Emily's hands.

"Please, Miss Davison, I made it specially for you," the girl said. "It don't look like much, I know, but it'll bring you luck."

Emily unwrapped the gift then and there, revealing a silk sash in the WSPU colors. She had seen and worn many of them, but she unfurled it to admire the words and the way the silk shone in the sunlight.

"It's lovely, my dear. You can be sure I shall wear it," she said. "What is your name?"

The girl's face shone. "It's Ida, Miss. Ida Miller."

"Well, Ida, thank you very kindly for your support and for the sash."

Emily kissed the girl's cheek, making the young woman beam even more, and slipped the sash over her shoulder and across her chest. For a moment, Emily felt as if she were glowing herself, but from within. It was merely the power of adulation, she scolded herself, and moved on.

~ ~ ~

Derby Day was glorious. Emily held her hat to her head and looked up at the bright blue June sky with a smile. It was always a shame when race day was spoiled by rain. This fine weather meant the grandstand and infield would be packed full with racegoers, and that no one's view would be obstructed by an umbrella.

The sash felt warm inside the sleeve of her black coat. It had seemed almost to have a life of its own over the last few days, making her skin tingle and her mind fill with light whenever she touched it. In her innermost thoughts, she wondered if it was a gift or sign from Heaven. There had been no question of which item to bring with her for today's demonstration.

She kept away from the police and plainclothes men who were on watch. They might know her face and throw her out of the grounds if they spotted her, ruining her plan. Others might also know her, of course. Several times she caught a flash of recognition or a puzzled look from a man or woman as she moved through the crowd, but no one raised a hue and cry. Perhaps the girl Ida had been right: the sash was bringing her luck. Now if only she could get to the paddock, where the horses would be saddled. Pinning a sash that proclaimed *Votes For Women* on Anmer, the King's Derby horse, with the newsreel cameras on the scene, would gain more worldwide attention for the cause than any hunger strike.

But Emily could not get close enough. Past the elaborate hats of the women and the craning necks of the men, she caught glimpses of shining horses and jockeys' silks. There were too many policemen; she could not enter the paddock.

Not to worry, she thought to the sash. *You'll have your moment.*

As she made her way to the infield, and then to Tattenham Corner, she allowed herself to smile fiercely. The paddock plan had always seemed too weak to her. *This* would be a true spectacle.

Deeds not words, she thought. *Deeds not words*.

She made it to the Corner just in time. The race was on! She looked across the track. Yes, more cameras were there, ready to catch the dramatic sweep of the downhill turn toward the home stretch.

The crowd was loud around her, but she could hear the thunder of the horses' hooves on the turf as they approached the corner. The sash beat against the veins of her wrist, both pulses racing faster as the horses surged closer. She leaned out over the rail to see around the other people. The runners were bunched together; there was no hope of getting near one of them. But there were a few stragglers behind the main field, and could it be? She thought one horse, a bright chestnut with a wide white blaze, bore the Royal colors. It *was* Anmer. The sash stopped pulsing and simply filled her with a sense of lightness and focus, as if the rest of the world, gravity even, had disappeared.

Deeds not words.

There was no time to think about it. Emily pulled the sash from her sleeve and ducked under the rail. The first horses flashed past her, nearly knocking her down with the turbulence of their speed. The drumming of hooves was deafening. She stepped out further onto the track after the main field passed. And there was the King's horse, huge and fast, so much faster than she had expected, his head so much higher.

The colt's ears pricked at the sight of her.

She reached out with the sash, reached for the bridle.

In the moment before the horse struck her, she saw the sash glow.

~ ~ ~

Watching from the outside rail, where she had squeezed in along the Corner, Ida felt the impact as if it was she who had been knocked to the ground. A betting ticket fluttered from her numb fingers. Anmer flipped over the woman's body, throwing his jockey and kicking the woman as he thrashed. Horseshoes flashed silver in the sunlight. The colt got to his feet and galloped away. The jockey and the woman lay still on the track. Before their bodies were obscured by the rush of men running to help, Ida saw a column of green, white and purple light shoot into the sky from something on the turf. It burst like a firework above the race grounds, but no one else seemed to notice it.

It was Miss Davison on the track. It was the sash she had made.

"Watch out!"

Someone caught her as she pitched forward in a faint. They lowered her to the ground.

"What's she saying?"

Her eyelids fluttering as she slumped in a stranger's arms, Ida muttered, over and over, "That's not what I meant, not what I meant...."

* * *

>>> *Emily Wilding Davison, a militant suffragette, died on June 8, 1913, four days after being knocked down by the King's horse during the Derby. Historians continue to debate Davison's intentions that day — her death has often been described as a suicide — and contemporary reactions were mixed. I have taken some artistic liberties in creating a moment for Ida and Emily to meet; other aspects of the story, such as the force feeding of suffragette prisoners — including Davison — Black Friday, and violent acts committed by suffragettes, are historical. Emmeline Pankhurst's January 10, 1913 letter to the WSPU members is available through the UK's online National Archives. Women were granted the vote in England in 1918, after WWI.*

Lara Apps

Lara Apps has a PhD in History from the University of Alberta. She is the co-author, with Andrew Gow, of *Male Witches in Early Modern Europe* (Manchester University Press, 2003), and has also published scholarly articles on eighteenth-century witchcraft and atheism. She works for the Alberta Human Rights Commission and for Athabasca University. Her fiction has appeared in *Bewildering Stories*, *SNAPLine*, and *Stories of the Nature of Cities* (forthcoming).

Darkness Peering

Kurt Kirchmeier

Québec, 1914

I knew something was wrong with Jarvis even before we left Valcartier for England. It started with little things, like the way he would pause while out on a march, cocking his head as if someone had called him, even though no one had, or the times he occasionally chose to stand apart from the rest of us, staring off into the trees beyond the rifle range as if he sensed that something was out there, watching.

And then there was the sleepwalking. Twice, I woke to find him wandering around our dark barracks like a blind mouse lost in a maze. On its own, this wouldn't have struck me as particularly odd, but Jarvis was doing things while he was sleeping that just didn't make sense, like staring in wonder at his own reflection in a handheld mirror, and stopping to stand over other soldiers' bunks, his chest rising and falling as if he were trying to breathe the other men in, and not just the scent of them, but their whole essence. Afterwards, he'd return to his bed — right next to mine — and lay there shivering as though from a fever.

In light of the friendship I shared with Jarvis — we had both grown up on the prairies, and both shared a love of poetry that we often took razzing for — I felt it was almost my duty to get up and check that he was okay, and yet I couldn't. It was as if all my muscles had seized. Instead I watched him, and wondered what his favorite writer — Edgar Allen Poe — might have to say about these curious happenings in the night.

I wondered, but I didn't truly start worrying until the night Jarvis sleepwalked right out the door and didn't return for a full three hours. I'll never know for certain where exactly he went, or what he might have seen while out there, where a forest stretched off to the north, and a moonlit river raced beside it, but what I do know is that when he came back, all traces of the Jarvis I knew had been stripped away — along with his clothes. My friend was naked except for his boots, his breaths coming fast and uneven as he laid himself down on his bed, his penis fully erect.

I watched him through slitted eyes, my heart pounding as I feigned sleep. There was something dark on Jarvis's chin and around his mouth. I somehow sensed it must be blood. There was a smell in the air as well, wild and animalistic. It reminded me of hunting trips with my dad, which I'd always hated, and would later become a source of resentment.

As if sensing I watched, Jarvis slowly turned his head sideways and looked right at me. His eyes were like those of a doll or a corpse, dark and empty yet somehow gleaming all the same. Then he licked his lips and began to touch himself.

I clenched my eyes shut as an icy chill suffused my whole body, my flesh breaking out into goosebumps as I waited for Jarvis's breathing to return to normal, and for that death smell to finally lift, which it did, though I swear it wasn't for hours.

In the morning, all was normal again, or at least it seemed that way. On two occasions, Jarvis quoted Poe and asked me to guess, and although both times I did so correctly, it wasn't without hesitation, for I could see now something had changed inside my friend. When he smiled at me, I thought I saw two smiles, one from a fresh-faced recruit with the soul of a poet, and another from something darker lurking within.

I tried my best to keep up appearances, but each night was now an exercise in anxiety as I waited and wondered if something similar would happen again. It never did, but even so, when a few weeks later we left Québec by way of the Gulf of St. Lawrence, and began our eleven-day journey across the ocean to England, I was relieved to discover Jarvis and I would be traveling on different ships.

It was September 30th. We were bound for Southampton, but ended up detouring to Plymouth when reports came in of German submarine activity in the English Channel. We made port without incident, and from Plymouth, embarked on a seven-hour train ride, followed by a ten-hour march to the Salisbury Plain.

By the time we finally reached camp, and unpacked our gear inside the small tents that would serve as home until our deployment to the front line, Jarvis's cold dark eyes and his pale white cock had all but dropped right out of my mind. But that's not to say I would no longer think of him at all. Even though circumstances had separated us, and even though our duties were different now, and our interactions brief, I still found if I awoke in the dead of the night, I couldn't bring myself to look at anything other than the canvas ceiling above me. I had nightmares as well, brief ones that jolted me awake with the force of a lightning bolt.

But the past was the past, and since my energy was much better spent on trying to prepare for surviving the future, I resolved to put that night behind me. I focused instead on settling in, but Mother Nature wasn't making it easy. The Salisbury Plain was a mud-soaked hole that never once dried up the entire time we were there. A layer of underground chalk prevented the moisture from completely draining away from the soil, so that even when we did have consecutive days without any rain — which was rare — conditions barely improved. Our standard-issue boots were a joke, offering little in the way of protection from the harsh conditions. It wasn't long before the British took pity on us, and outfitted every last one of us with a brand new pair. To say that we were grateful would be an understatement.

Slowly but surely, we were transformed from a rowdy and ramshackle bunch of adventure-seeking, borderline delinquents into a force that could march and maneuver with the absolute best of them. What we lacked in refinement, we made up for in courage and character, or so we liked to tell ourselves.

We left Salisbury Plain in early February, most of us in the cold dark cargo holds of small boats, in raging seas that left us sick and almost nostalgic for the mud we'd just left behind. Still, we had it better than our horses, which stood on the steel deck above us, absorbing the full brunt of the westerly gale. Many of them were knocked right off their feet. Some were injured so badly they had to be shot and tossed overboard.

When we finally docked at St. Nazaire, France, two days later, I felt as if I'd spent a week inside a barrel at the bottom of Niagara Falls, and we still had more than six hundred kilometers to go to reach the front, on the Belgian border. We traveled by train, with men packed into boxcars like sardines into tins. Driven near mad with claustrophobia, some of the men made the fatal mistake of climbing out of the carriages and up onto the roofs, apparently never considering what would happen once our train reached a tunnel. We were all so green and naïve, so young and stupidly reckless. I myself was only eighteen.

At last, we reached Armentieres, where each of us was paired with a British counterpart for trench warfare training along the front line. I wish I could say I was prepared for my first night of being bombarded by the Germans, but I would be lying. The scream of the incoming shells was like something demonic unleashed from above, and the craterous impacts rattled my eardrums so bad I thought they would surely burst. For hours, my skull rang like a tuning fork, every movement bringing on vertigo, which then triggered nausea. It was embarrassing, how much time I spent on my knees trying not to throw up, this while being laughed at by the veteran Brits.

By day four, I felt somewhat normalized to my new reality. I was still scared stupid, and still felt my cursed hands shake through the full thirty minutes of every morning and evening stand-to, but at least now I could endure a shelling without pissing my pants.

After a week of trench training, the Brits deemed us ready and sent us along to defend the line at Fleurbaix. It was here I started hearing rumors that reignited my unease about Jarvis. There were reports of him wandering off into no-man's-land during the night, and then returning just before dawn with ghastly souvenirs, like German fingers, or ears. There were some who said they hadn't seen Jarvis asleep in more than four days, but deep down I had to wonder if it was actually the opposite that was true, and that they hadn't seen Jarvis *awake*.

All my instincts told me to keep my distance, and so I did, at least during our stay in Fleurbaix. This would all change in early April, as orders came down to prepare for a move to Ypres, where we would be tasked with holding the area known as the Salient, our own soldiers slotting in between the French and Algerians, surrounded by the Germans on three sides.

The trenches we were assigned were abysmal. Dug shallow on account of the high water table, they barely provided protection to any soldier who dared to stand fully upright. We were forced to add more sandbags to the breastworks, which were neither high enough nor deep enough for our liking.

But worse than the shallowness of the trenches or the weakness of the breastworks was the problem of human refuse and waste. There was excrement everywhere, pools of it emitting a stench that defied all description. Rats and lice thrived, and although the former were sometimes as large as small dogs, it was the latter that all but drove us to the brink of madness. Some of the men took to running a flame along the seams of their garments in order to singe all the freshly laid eggs there, while others — myself included — experimented with thoroughly washing ourselves in oil. But nothing really helped. The itching was almost unbearable.

Jarvis and I were soon reunited as two members of a six-man unit charged with repairing some of the barbed-wire entanglements out beyond the trench lines. These were a guard against a full-on assault, and couldn't be left in shambles without possible repercussions the following morning. We set out at dark, all of us keenly aware there was just enough moon to make us vulnerable to German snipers.

I wondered what my dad would think of me now, a soldier on a mission in no-man's-land with death just a bullet away. Maybe this would finally mold his *soft* son into something harder, something that more closely reminded him of himself than my mother, who died of tuberculosis when I was just eight.

I still remembered her well, her smile and the way she danced. I remembered books and stories and sunshine through stained glass suncatchers, which my mom hung in every window, and my dad would later take down when the light and color became too painful to have to look at. One of the suncatchers broke as he put it away, and unbeknownst to him, I kept a small square of the glass as a permanent reminder of when home was *home* and not just the place I lived. I had that square of glass now, down in my pocket. I touched it whenever the darkness became too much.

We worked swiftly to complete our repairs, and soon enough were ready to scurry back to our mud-filled holes. But just as we gathered to leave, there was a *pop* and a *thwip* and then Charlie dropped beside me, a nice clean hole right between his eyes.

"Get down!" said Corporal O'Neill, and down we went on our bellies, just as another *pop* sounded in the darkness, only this time the sniper missed.

If there's one good thing to be said about mud, it's that you can squirm in order to bury yourself down into it, minimizing how much of your body remains a target. I made sure to cover my face with mud as well, and the others all followed suit. That is, except for Jarvis, who I suddenly realized had only dropped to one knee.

"Jarvis!" I hissed at him. He appeared to be scrutinizing the general area from which our sniper was most likely shooting, perhaps waiting for a flash so that he'd know exactly where to concentrate his fire.

"Down, soldier!" growled Corporal O'Neill. "That's an order!"

But Jarvis ignored him, even as the next *pop* got him right in the shoulder. He barely grunted, and the next thing I knew he was up and running, straight at the German line.

The private next to me, a kid named Jack Holloway, immediately got up to follow, but I managed to reach out and grab his ankle to trip him up. I then held on tight and wouldn't let go as he swore at me and tried to kick free.

"Goddammit, Holloway!" said O'Neill. "Hold your position!"

Jack swore again, but relented, his rifle pointed at the darkness into which Jarvis had disappeared.

We waited.

Now that I was no longer moving, the chill in the air began to find its way into my bones.

"What in the fucking hell was he thinking?" Whatley finally whispered, breaking our silence.

What in the fucking hell, indeed? I wondered as I stared out into the night.

Of the four of us left, Corporal O'Neill had the most acute night vision, so it was no surprise when he was the first to distinguish movement off in the distance.

With a whisper-soft *psst* and a pointed finger, he clued us in.

My heart was up in my throat now, my finger vibrating against the curve of my cold steel trigger. I watched as three figures materialized from the darkness, two of them walking ahead and one behind.

"Hold fire," whispered O'Neill, and it was a good thing, too; my nerves were so jangled I damn near let off a round.

As the figures drew closer, I saw that the first two were, in fact, Germans, but they were unarmed, their hands laced behind their heads in surrender. Prisoners.

Jarvis had somehow infiltrated the German trenches and taken hostages without ever being detected. It shouldn't have been possible, and yet here was the proof.

"Jesus Christ, Jarvis!" said Pete Cavanagh. "You're an animal!"

I didn't say anything, just stared at the faces of the two young Germans. Their eyes were huge and full of fear, and as Jarvis herded them towards me, I saw that their cheeks and foreheads were spattered with blood. There was blood on Jarvis as well, mostly around his mouth and chin and up over the bridge of his nose, a look reminiscent of a wolf that had buried its muzzle in an open carcass, and a look that instantly took me back to that night in the barracks.

Maybe Cavanagh was right; maybe Jarvis really was an animal, and the reason we hadn't heard a scream was because

Jarvis had torn out the vocal chords of the sentries before the men could even raise an alarm.

As if sensing these crazy thoughts of mine, Jarvis smiled right at me, revealing teeth which, just for a fraction of a second, I could have sworn were pointed and sharp. He passed me and kept on going, the other men falling into line behind him, like rats behind the Pied Piper.

Jarvis was later reprimanded for going rogue, but in the trenches, his legend grew. I kept to myself the fact that, although Jarvis had been hit in the shoulder, there was now no wound there.

A few days later, word came down the line the British had won back an important position known as Hill 60. They'd used sappers to tunnel beneath the hill, and then detonated a shitload of explosives, literally vaporizing the ground beneath the Germans' feet. The British then advanced on the dazed and confused survivors.

The Germans tried to win back the hill just shortly thereafter, only to be held off with bayonets. The fighting continued, with the 1st Canadian Brigade being placed at the disposal of the 5th Division, with orders to be ready to march on Hill 60 should the need arise. As it happened, the 1st Brigade ended up in action elsewhere, as the Germans set about bombarding the old medieval city of Ypres. I wasn't close enough to see it myself, but I heard it was a civilian bloodbath.

Our division, along with two others, continued repairing barbed-wire entanglements and filling sandbags for shoring-up the breastworks. We traded fire but sustained few casualties. Lice continued to be our greatest enemy. But it wouldn't stay that way for long.

April 22nd dawned bright and beautiful, with just a whisper of wind blowing in from the German lines. Morale was high, with some of the men kicking a ball around Mouse Trap Farm just behind our position. If you hadn't known any better, you might not have even realized there was a war going on.

The Germans sent a sharp reminder just around lunchtime, pounding the remains of Ypres and other nearby towns. It all went silent again in the early afternoon, and remained that way until shortly before 5:00 p.m., when another furious bombardment hit the French line first, and then our own. My ears were ringing, and my brain felt bruised by the time the shelling finally stopped. I was still in one piece, though, and I figured that after two heavy bursts, the Germans were probably done for the day. As it turned out, I could not have been any more wrong.

Just minutes after the shelling gave way to silence, a commotion began to work its way down the line.

"What in God's name is that?" said Private Burkhart from atop the trench ladder.

I joined a few others in climbing up to look over the sandbags, and there in the distance was a strange greenish cloud, drifting slowly over no-man's-land toward the Algerian line. At first, I thought it must be residual smoke from the last bombardment, but the coloration was just too weird, and it was also hugging the ground instead of dispersing up into the air — more like heavy fog than smoke.

In silence, we watched it enshroud all the forward trenches. That's when the choking and screaming started.

The next thing I knew, the entire Algerian line broke and retreated towards us, hundreds of them staggering as if they were drunk while clutching at their throats and gasping for air. Foam spewed from their lips as they struggled across the battlefield. We watched in horror as most of them collapsed and continued to writhe in the mud. A few of them managed to keep on going right past us, their eyes insane with panic and agony.

The panic was inside me, too, accompanied by a bone-chilling sweat. I had no idea what was happening, or whether a similar fate would soon be upon the rest of us, once the edge of the poisoned gas cloud — for surely that's what this was — expanded to reach our position. I wondered if maybe we should be falling back, too, and to hell with leaving a gap that the Germans might surge through. I looked to my fellow Canadians for an answer, but instead saw the very same question reflected back at me.

The French line broke as well. In pain and unable to retreat any further, a few of the fleeing soldiers dropped down into the trench right beside me, vomiting up foam and mucus and blood as their decimated lungs tried and failed to process air. I thought of a deer I had seen my dad shoot when I was a kid, and the look in its eyes as he held onto me and forced me to watch it die. I remembered wishing I would die first so I wouldn't have to see the poor animal suffer.

I felt no such mortal desires now. I wanted to live, if for no other reason than just to prove to my dad I could and show him one needn't be hard to be a good soldier, or, for that matter, a good son. Not every man need be a hunter or a grim provider. There was room in the world for dreamers and poets as well. But if I hoped to show my father anything, I would first have to survive the approaching fog.

As if in answer to an unspoken prayer, an officer appeared in our midst, yelling at us to quickly take out our pocket handkerchiefs and urinate on them.

I could make no sense of what I was hearing, but since it was clearly an order and I a soldier, I simply did as I had been told. I was then instructed to close my eyes and tie the urine-soaked fabric over my nose and mouth so I could breathe through it. This would later all make sense as I learned the ammonia present in urine could partially neutralize chlorine gas, but at the time, it all just seemed crazy.

I can't deny it saved my life. Sure, my eyes still burned, and my lungs still hurt, but as a merciful wind pushed the worst of the gas cloud past us, with a host of Germans advancing in its wake, I still had the strength in body and purpose to stand with my brothers and do my job.

Afraid of advancing too quickly into the gap the chlorine had opened for them — even with gas masks they were still scared — the Germans failed to fully exploit their brief advantage. They also failed to note a British Field battery stood in their way. When the artillery men who were manning the battery noticed the Germans advancing, they quickly swung their four 18-pounders ninety degrees to the left and let the Krauts have it.

Buoyed by fresh reinforcements, the rest of us continued fighting into the night.

By some twist of fate, I ended up right beside Jarvis in the trenches. His eyes gleamed with an eerie intensity, and I noticed his handkerchief was still tucked inside his pocket. I stared down at it in wonder and confusion, and when I looked up again, Jarvis was smiling.

At approximately 11:00 p.m., a number of us received new orders to form up and join the Canadian Scottish Battalion — along with a small party of French troops — in a counter-attack on nearby Kitcheners' Wood. I could have easily used this as a way of separating myself from Jarvis, but instead I chose to stay right beside him. In fact, I was suddenly loathe to be out of his shadow. After the rumors I'd heard and the things I had seen with my own eyes, Jarvis seemed somehow invincible to me. I guess I figured if I attached myself to his hip, some of that invincibility might transfer to me.

Fully formed up and ready, we were given the order to charge at precisely 11:46 p.m. There hadn't been time for proper reconnaissance before our advance, so those of us in the lead wave ended up running straight into a hedge interlaced with wire. We were forced to beat our way through it with the butts of our rifles while the Germans tore into us with machine guns from two hundred yards away. For several long minutes, men fell like dominoes on either side of me. But then finally we were through and moving, free to exact some revenge.

In the shadows and the chaos under the oak trees, it was impossible to tell friend from enemy until you were close enough to make out the whites of another man's eyes, and so it was that few shots were fired. Instead we fought hand-to-hand, our bayonets dripping with blood.

Jarvis was an absolute whirlwind, cutting down Germans as if he were built for exactly that purpose. I held my own beside him, fueled by a combination of fear and adrenaline. In all the fighting and confusion, we somehow managed to get ourselves separated from the rest of our battalion, so that suddenly we were alone in facing an onslaught at the edge of the wood. There were Germans everywhere, spilling out of the shadows as if from some void of endless supply. For every one we took down, two more seemed to appear. It was hopeless, and retreat was no longer an option. Jarvis and I were surrounded.

For a moment, I was convinced my death was imminent, but then the Germans apparently decided it might be better to take us both prisoner, perhaps as potential bargaining chips for a trade. Jarvis, after all, had already taken two of theirs. But the Germans didn't know what I did: that Jarvis was no longer quite human, and that hesitating to kill him might be a mistake.

No sooner did this thought cross my mind than the Germans began to fall back, their eyes wide and disbelieving. I turned to look at my former friend, only to find in his place something else, something cloven-hooved and antlered, with long clawed fingers and a big thick mane. Its snout was that of a wolf, and its eyes were orbs of shiny obsidian. A carrion stench hung thick in the air, and clogged my throat as I shrank in terror, my bladder releasing as my legs gave out beneath me.

The creature was inhumanly fast. Paralyzed with fear, I watched as it ripped limbs from bodies and carved away flesh, which it then consumed with an awful hunger, its razor teeth sawing. I was suddenly reminded of a night at a campfire when I was still just a kid, and of a legend that my mother shared with me just shortly before she died. It was an Algonquin legend, of a cannibal spirit that could creep inside a man's soul and slowly possess him, taking him over from the inside out.

It might seem strange a mother would share such tales with a son who was prone to nightmares — and perhaps it was — but I know she did it only to light a fire in my young imagination, and to set me on a path that would ultimately lead me to seek out stories of my own, which I fully intended to, just as soon as this war was done with me.

The cannibal spirit she spoke of that night was said to reside in the eastern woods, in forests not unlike those all around Valcartier. One need only follow a whisper and venture too near to find himself vulnerable.

"Wendigo," I whispered, my hand in my pocket now, touching glass.

The creature stopped, its antlered head swiveling, spraying me with gore and saliva. Its nostrils flared, and I swear I could feel the heat of its breath even from twelve feet away. The carrion stench became a taste in the air now, adding to the chlorine burn at the back of my throat. Perhaps in naming it, I stole some of its power, for all of a sudden its ravenous hunger seemed to abate. It cocked its head just a fraction, considering, and as I looked at its awful teeth and its bear-like claws, and the haunting depths in those obsidian eyes, I sensed I had only a moment in which to act, in which to attempt to bring Jarvis back to the fore. But how? I thought of Poe again, and of eleven little words from *The Raven* that fit so closely with my current predicament it was almost uncanny.

Deep into that darkness peering, long I stood there, wondering, fearing....

I spoke the words first in my mind and then with my mouth, expecting nothing, but hoping that this small reminder might serve as a trigger.

The Wendigo reared back and roared, then thrashed at a tree with its antlers, bringing down branches as thick as my arm. But within that roar was a human sound, tortured and angry, wailing into the night, but still possessed of a will.

Confident now in the power of Poe's immortal words, I recited the next few stanzas, finally concluding with those two little words Poe would forever be known for: *Never more. Never more.*

With one last roar that seemed to split the whole forest in half, the Wendigo turned and ran, becoming one with the impenetrable shadows beneath the oak trees, never to be seen again.

The battle for Ypres, however, raged on, not only through that night in Kitcheners' Wood, where I somehow lifted myself from the carnage and kept on going, but for weeks thereafter.

Although Jarvis was no longer with us, in the trenches his legend lived on, inspiring the sort of courage and valor that even a second cloud of chlorine couldn't hope to asphyxiate. For every ten of us, seven would die, but by god we held that line.

* * *

>>> *While Darkness Peering doesn't contain a physical artifact, it does contain a legend — of a supernatural creature known as the wendigo — that serves as a sort of artifact in that it exists as a possessive force and is representative of a time and a belief system whose origins can only be traced through the oral traditions of the Algonquin people of the northern forest areas of the Atlantic Coast and the Great Lakes regions of both Canada and the US. The earliest written reference to wendigo possession dates back to 1661.*

Kurt Kirchmeier

Kurt Kirchmeier lives and writes in Saskatoon, Saskatchewan. His stories and poems have appeared in *Abyss & Apex, Shimmer, Tesseracts 15, Weird Tales*, and elsewhere. His debut novel *The Absence of Sparrows* will be hitting bookshelves in May, 2019, courtesy of Little, Brown Books for Young Readers. When he isn't reading or writing, Kurt can often be found outside, photographing nature. He has a particular fondness for birds.

www.kurtkirchmeier.net
https://twitter.com/saskwriter

The First Pillar of Wisdom

Mike Rimar

The Arab boy lay huddled in a tight ball, filthy *thobe* the only defense against the overseer's vicious caning, his punishment for seeking shade behind a broken stone wall.

Lawrence looked on as if in a fugue state, hands clutched before him, fingers interlaced. *Act* his mind screamed and with a start he roused himself. "You there!" The dry heat of the Carchemish excavation site parched his throat. His voice, normally soft and delicate, cracked, robbing him of any authority. "Stop that right now."

The Turkish overseer continued slashing away, shouting in Arabic, "Get back to work, you dog!"

Lawrence spat out the desert. "I said stop that!"

"He is a lazy dog." The overseer glared defiance, chest heaving from exertion.

"I don't care." Lawrence's Arabic was halting, imperfect, the language still new to him. He marched up to the Turk who raised his chin to make himself appear even taller, more menacing. Lawrence was unimpressed. He'd spent a lifetime dealing with people taller and far more intimidating. "I told you to stop. The boy did nothing wrong."

The Turk tapped the wooden cane with dirty fingernails. "You do not give me orders."

"Are you so sure about that?" Lawrence stepped in close, held his breath against the stink of garlic and tobacco.

After a pregnant moment the overseer threw back his head and laughed, not a pleasant sound. "Have your little puppy. Pet him, feed him, do whatever you wish. I'm sure he will please you." Before Lawrence could answer, the Turk strode away on sandaled feet, stuffing the cane into his thick leather belt.

Lawrence remained fixated on the cane. What would it feel like to have welts rise across his fair skin? Only when the overseer melded into a throng of workers did Lawrence turn to the boy, but he'd also disappeared, likely rejoining his fellow Arabs with the dig.

"What a brutish display," said a very British voice.

Yes, dammit. Lawrence's cheeks burned with shame. *I should've acted more quickly.* He spun on his heel ready to apologize but the words faded at the two figures strolling across the broken ground. The first, dressed in the standard khaki uniform of a British Army officer he didn't recognize, but the second...

"Gertrude?" Dressed in a short-sleeved shirt, long skirt, and leather hobnailed boots, her fair curls poked from beneath a tan pith helmet. Although nearly the same height, he peered from beneath his brow, lips stretched into a cherubic smile. "Gertrude Bell! Have you joined our dig here in Carchemish?"

Gertrude reached out a tanned hand which Lawrence shook warmly. "Not exactly," she said, then stepped aside. "Thomas Edward Lawrence, may I introduce General Sir Margrave Fenway."

"Lawrence." Fenway spoke in a low register as if his vocal chords were strained from too much shouting.

"Sir Margrave," Lawrence responded with a frown. "Forgive me, but I'm unfamiliar with your name."

Fenway dabbed sweat from his upper lip with a plain handkerchief. "Understandable. But I'm familiar with yours. What do you know of the Staff of Moses, Mr. Lawrence?"

"Excuse me?" The blunt question caught Lawrence off guard.

Gertrude placed a warm hand on his arm. "Please answer, Ned. It's important."

Lawrence stiffened. He preferred the shortened, Ned, but found Gertrude's familiarity discomfiting. "I know as much as anyone who has read the Bible," he answered carefully. "Moses used the Staff to convince the Egyptian Pharaoh, likely Thutmose III, to free the Israelite slaves."

Fenway made a low disapproving grunting sound.

"Ned," Gertrude leaned close. "Tell him your theory on the Staff."

Lawrence shoved his hands deep into the pockets of short pants. A rare breeze rustled the canvas of a nearby tent. Distant Arabs sang a worker's chant as they cleared Carchemish's ruins. For a moment he wished to be with them. He'd grown comfortable among the Arabs, learning their histories and traditions, their woes under the Ottoman yoke. In contrast, his unexpected guests made him very uncomfortable. The imposing Margrave Fenway more so than Gertrude Bell.

He'd first met Gertrude while studying archeology in Oxford, discovering a shared passion for antiquities and the Middle East. Her views had been enlightening and he'd shared his own thoughts on certain aspects of history, but — His eyes opened wide when he realized to what she'd been referring. "That was a lark, Gertrude. The wild imaginings of a young mind."

"Ned, it's important."

He looked from Gertrude to Fenway and shrugged. If she wanted to impress the officer, what harm would it do to help? "The Bible states the Hebrew god Yahweh gave Moses the Staff. You probably know there was another Staff involved in the freeing of the slaves called Aaron's Rod — Aaron being Moses' brother. Two Staffs, each with differing properties. Tell me, General Fenway, do you know what a caduceus is?"

"It is the symbol of the medical profession," said Fenway with a low growl.

"Forgive me, General, but no. The Staff of Asclepius is the symbol for medicine, a single serpent entwining the shaft. A caduceus has two serpents topped with wings and was used by the Greek god Hermes. Gods of every sort have been integral to the history of mankind. One is very much like the other, perhaps even one in the same. I theorize that the serpents are symbolic and that the Staffs given to Moses and Aaron are two parts of a whole. Two serpents. Two Staffs. A caduceus." Lawrence paused for the usual scoffing or shouts of indignation at sullying religious deities. His mother had beaten him often for such crimes.

"Let's walk a bit, shall we?" Fenway placed a broad hand upon his back. "Do you think the two Staffs might be connected? That one might require the other?"

Lawrence ran fingers through hair bleached light by the sun. "The symbology suggests this may be true. The two serpents intertwine along the shaft until they face each other at the head of the Staff, indicative of a symbiotic relationship … but this is all conjecture. I've no proof. Both Staffs were kept in the Hebrew First Temple and subsequently destroyed when the Temple was sacked by the Babylonians. The Turks claim they have Moses' Staff in the Hagia Sophia, the cathedral in Istanbul, but I doubt its authenticity."

"You were right, Gertrude," said Fenway. "He may be the one."

"The one for what?" Lawrence looked enquiringly at Gertrude.

Fenway stared, expressionless. "The Staff in Istanbul is real."

Lawrence's abrupt stop kicked up dust. Chin lowered, he offered an impish smile. "You're having me on."

"Ned," Gertrude huffed. "Do you think I'd bring a British general all the way to Syria for a practical joke? Sir Fenway's question is in earnest."

"Mr. Lawrence," said Fenway, calm as a metronome. "I'm more than an officer in His Majesty's Army. I'm also head of the MOA."

"Oh? Is that some sort of club?"

"It stands for The Ministry of the Arcanum," said Fenway without a trace of humor. "We thought MOA sounded more dashing in our contemporary times."

"The Ministry of the… now you really are having me on."

"No, Ned," said Gertrude. "We most certainly are not. The Ministry of the Arcanum has been part of English history since Merlin."

"Merlin? King Arthur's Merlin?" He drummed fingertips upon his cheek in a struggle to keep his composure. "And what does this ministry do?"

"We track magic, and those who use it," said Fenway. "We call the ability *Talent*. Everyone has some *Talent*, although very few realize it. Fewer still master their gifts. Those we call wizards."

"Like Merlin," said Lawrence.

"Yes, like Merlin," Fenway continued unperturbed by his acerbic tone. "And Isaac Newton. And Florence Nightingale. There are others, less famous or completely unknown. Some use their *Talent* in service to their respective countries, others are more self-serving. Some are artisans and alchemists. We fight each other on occasion. Sometimes we win, sometimes not. It is a shadow war in a shadowy world."

Lawrence nodded. "So, why haven't I ever heard of this MOA?"

"Traditionally only royalty and top-ranking military officers have been made aware," said Fenway, "although our existence has been known to filter down to the common folk. We're mostly dismissed as irrelevant or mythical which is the way we like it. We're not some secret society, but we all try to keep a low profile."

"All?"

"Every empire and country of any strength has a version of the MOA," said Fenway. "The French, Germans, Russians, the Asian Peoples…. In peace we co-exist in an uneasy truce, but in the end we all serve our respective masters."

Lawrence addressed Gertrude. "And you're part of this MOA? Can you pull a rabbit from a hat?"

Gertrude's copper eyes flashed gold. "I don't like your mocking tone, Ned. And it's not like that. *Talent* is, well, it can be anything from uncommon luck at games of chance to drawing water from stone. It's not something learned. *Talent* is innate."

"Forgive my manners, Gertrude. It's just that, well…." Lawrence clasped his hands before him. "So, what is your *Talent*, then?"

"Magical artifacts, I sense them if I'm near enough, even learn their properties if I can take hold of them."

"Which brings us to our purpose," interjected Fenway. "I want you and Gertrude to look for the second staff of the caduceus. You've already explored some of the desert. You know this land and you're both familiar with its people. Your cover story is mapping of the Wilderness of Zin for the Palestine Exploration Fund.

"Tensions are rising in the world, Mr. Lawrence. Treaties have been signed, alliances made. The Ottomans have sided against us. Should the Turks or any of her allies discover Aaron's Rod and bring the two pieces together… well, you would do England a great service if you prevented such a thing."

Lawrence's eyebrows knotted in thought. In the distance Arab laborers toiled with pick and shovel, supervised by Turkish overseers, some armed with rifles.

"You're a man of science, an explorer, an adventurer," the general continued. "Whatever your thoughts of the MOA, Mr. Lawrence, this is a chance to prove your theory. Will you help?"

The Turks claimed the weapons were for protection against wild animals. Lawrence knew better. The Turks wanted to remind the Arabs they were only vassals in the Ottoman Empire.

For now. Chin lowered, Lawrence smiled. "Of course."

~ ~ ~

"We're being followed." Gertrude turned in her camel's saddle.

"Oh?" Lawrence, astride his own camel, looked up from his copy of the *Torah*. For the hundredth time he reread the *Shemot* and the *Bemidbar*, comparing the information to their Christian counterparts of Exodus and Numbers. They were into the second week of their *faux* mapping expedition without any luck and he hoped to glean some obscure clue that might help them with their quest. "Ah, yes. They've been following since we began." With an imperious sniff he returned to his studies. Evidently each Staff had its own unique properties. Moses' Staff appeared to focus on political goals and the means to achieve them; Aaron's Rod dealt more with ecology and the balances of nature, even sprouting fruit and nuts such as almonds.

"Truly?" Gertrude squinted at their pursuers. "I only noticed them today."

"I noticed them almost immediately."

This was followed by a childish laugh. "I am the one who told Lawrence."

Lawrence bit back a harsh retort, but seeing the grinning brown-skinned boy riding the supply camel, his attitude soon softened. Before leaving, he'd searched for the Arab boy the Turk had beaten. Lawrence had humiliated the overseer. Once he left Carchemish, the Turk would punish the boy further, perhaps even killing him. Salem Ahmed was the boy's full name, but he insisted on Dahoum. For his safety Lawrence invited Dahoum on the expedition ostensibly to tend to the camels and serve as their steward. He also taught Lawrence and Gertrude Arabic since the pair had decided to speak only the one language to practice their skills. Dahoum took excessive pleasure in correcting mispronounced words and errors in grammar.

"I noticed before you told me, Dahoum," said Lawrence straight-faced.

Dahoum waggled his finger at the obvious lie, showing a full set of remarkably white teeth.

Such a beautiful boy. Guilt burned Lawrence like the desert sun. He'd watched the boy's beating and done nothing … because he'd no longer been there. The agony and torment etched on Dahoum's face had transported Lawrence to his own youth and the beatings he'd received from his mother, punishment for questioning God and Christianity. From those doubts came his passion for archeology, and hope he might discover a reason for faith in the present from rediscovering the past.

He could've lied to prevent his mother's abuses, pretended to worship, to have faith. Instead, he'd deliberately continued to irk her, knowing her resolution would only serve to increase the duration and voracity of her beatings. The punishments had been a grand private experiment. Something happened to him when his mother left bruises on his arms, back, and buttocks, something he couldn't understand. When he'd witnessed Dahoum's caning, the tumultuous emotions had returned. And there was another he hadn't expected.

Longing.

Lawrence's fingertips brushed his cheek, hot with the fire of embarrassment. He dipped his head so that he might retreat into the protection of the loose white linen of his *keffiyeh*.

"Who do you think they might be?" Gertrude's *keffiyeh,* a light crimson, loosely masked her lower face.

"I would think one of your MOA counterparts," Lawrence answered, grateful for the distraction of his troubling thoughts.

"Probably the *Deutsche Zauberschule*." Contempt accented each syllable. "The German School of Magic. The Kaiser and the Ottomans are allies. We should do something about them."

Lawrence shoved the *Torah* into a saddle bag. "I think we should be more concerned about them." He motioned toward a group of robed riders approaching on horseback. "Didn't see them coming, did you, Dahoum?"

The boy shrugged. "I was waiting for you to point them out."

Lawrence shook his head and smiled, making sure to keep is hands visible. "Bedouins," he said.

"I can see that," snapped Gertrude.

Lawrence appreciated her tension. On the whole, Bedouins were cordial enough, but they had a strict code of honor and customs. The first meeting was always the most difficult. He counted four riders, a woman and three men, likely her escorts. When they were close enough, he smiled and raised his voice in greeting. "*As-salamu alaykum.*" Peace be upon you.

The woman, dressed in a voluminous blue *thobe,* replied. "*Wa-Alaikum-Salaam.*" And unto you peace. "I am Faizah. What are you doing here?"

Direct, thought Lawrence, likely the wife of a merchant, or perhaps the merchant herself. "My name is Thomas Lawrence. With me are Gertrude Bell and our servant, Dahoum. We are creating maps for my government. We have permission from the Ottomans, but if these are your lands,

I respectfully ask your permission also. If not given, we will humbly take our leave."

Faizah tilted her head, considering his words. He tried to appear nonchalant, but his stomach was in turmoil should she refuse. They'd never survive a fight with the nomads and so he'd spoken the truth; these were her lands and he'd respect her decision.

"Very well," Faizah finally said. "You may continue. Is there anything we can offer you? Water perhaps, or food?"

"Thank you for your generosity." Lawrence disguised his relief with a quick bow of his head. "We are well-supplied for our journey. However, there is one thing." He tapped his chin as though in deep thought. "We've heard tales of a staff such as a goatherd might use, only this staff was used long ago by the Hebrew prophets to journey through the desert. Perhaps you've heard such tales, or your elders, or your elder's elders." A long shot, Lawrence knew, but he needed all the help he could get.

Faizah shrugged indifference but one of her escorts leaned close to her, whispering in her ear. Dark brown eyes opened wide with astonishment. "Mustafa says he has heard such a tale. Go on, tell them. I, too, would like to hear."

Mustafa, a giant whose dark *thobe* and *keffiyeh* matched his beard, looked embarrassed by the sudden attention. "A tale told by my great grandfather when I was a child. An oasis where none should be, with no well, no source of water. An oasis that only appears to those in need of sustenance and deserving of its gifts. All surrounding a staff as you describe. Grandfather called it the Staff of the Hebrew prophet."

Lawrence clutched his hands before him to hide their shaking "Did your grandfather say where this oasis might be?"

The Bedouin pointed to the south. "Beyond the Seven Pillars of Wisdom."

Lawrence ground his teeth knowing the rock formation was weeks of travel to the south. Still, they now had a direction and a location. "I thank you, Mustafa, and I thank you also, Faizah." He turned dramatically in his saddle, looked behind him and sighed.

"Is something wrong, friend Lawrence?" asked Faizah.

Lawrence waved as if irritated by a gnat. "Behind us, some hours away, there is a party that has been following for many days. We fear they might be bandits or slavers, but dare not confront them."

Faizah grew very still and she gripped hard to her horse's reins. Lawrence suspected he'd made a mistake. "Probably just bandits," he amended.

The Bedouin nodded slowly, unconvinced. "As long as you travel my lands, you will be safe. We will question this party … of probable bandits."

"We thank you for your kindness and your protection." Lawrence touched his right palm to his chest. "May Allah smile upon you."

Faizah did the same. The Bedouins then clucked their horses into motion.

"Well done, Lawrence," said Gertrude. "That should slow down the Kaiser's wizards. What do you make of this oasis?"

"It's the best clue we've had so far," said Lawrence. "We've a long road ahead of us. We should get moving." Silently, he prayed Faizah would not act rashly.

~ ~ ~

Lawrence stirred from his sunbaked stupor and looked in the direction Gertrude pointed.

"Over there," she repeated.

"No." He waved her away. "The Pillars are further on."

"Ned, go over there. I… I feel it."

"You mean this *Talent* of yours?" His coarse throat made the question sound more like a rebuke. He drank from his canteen, swirled the water round his mouth then spat it out. Regarding her, he frowned, suddenly overcome with curiosity. "What does it feel like?"

"A tingling. A chill. A yearning." Gertrude swayed in the saddle like a drunkard. "A *need*. Please, Ned, we must go. It's there. I know it is."

A need. Something he understood. Nodding to Dahoum, Lawrence pulled on the reins and followed her lead. They traveled without conversation, Gertrude in a kind of trance, Dahoum looking on with undisguised concern. They'd grown fond of each other, a relationship that made Lawrence envious.

He was equally envious of her *Talent* and choked back the question he'd been yearning to ask since learning of the MOA.

If everyone has some Talent, *do I?*

Gertrude rode on, hunched forward, eyes open but he wondered what she truly saw. They traveled at a camel's normal gait, seemingly at random long after the setting sun stretched shadows across the hard, uneven rock.

Lawrence and Dahoum remained alert, silvery illumination from the moon and stars turning the desert into a nightmarish landscape. He contemplated calling a halt, but recognized the strength of Gertrude's *need* and kept his peace. Again, she yanked on her reins, redirecting the party onto a plain of stunted grass. A stand of trees arose before them like sentinels in the velvet night. Plump ripe fruit weighed down nearly every branch.

The camels bayed their hunger. Knowing the beasts as he did, Lawrence gave the command to kneel so that he might dismount. Once free of its human burden the camel ambled into the grove and chewed on lush green grass.

He forced Gertrude's camel to do the same, helping her to dismount as she seemed trapped within her stupor. Once on her feet Gertrude walked unerringly between the trees. Lawrence followed, leaving the camels to Dahoum's care.

The air chilled and gooseflesh pimpled his skin; he wished he'd had his own *thobe* instead of his standard European-style shirt and trousers.

Gertrude continued, unaffected. She walked with purpose, but unhurried as if knowing exactly where she needed to go. The air was a heady mixture of fruits and nuts. His stomach grumbled, and unable to stave off his hunger he plucked an orange. Half-peeled, Lawrence bit into the flesh. Sweet juice ran down his chin. To his right he saw a tree of unusual shape. Tossing away the orange, he stepped forward when Gertrude's coo of delight drew his attention.

In her hands was a long, carved shaft of wood. Her smile was broad and winning, then suddenly turned to alarm.

"Ned," she called out, but he sensed it was already too late. He half-turned in time to see his attacker before his head exploded in a flurry of bright lights — then black.

A thick German accent pulled him back from unconsciousness. Arms tingling, he tried to move, but was unable. He was tied to the trunk of an orange tree.

A pinched face topped with blonde hair shaved close at the sides wavered into focus. "Ah, you are awake. *Gut.*"

Lawrence shook his head, trying to clear his vision. "Where...." He battled nausea, then began again. "Where are my companions?"

His captor grasped a handful of Lawrence's hair and twisted his head. "There," he said.

Gertrude and Dahoum sat nearby, bound and gagged but otherwise unharmed. More Germans stood a short distance away. One held the staff Gertrude had discovered.

"Don't worry. I'll let them live. Think of it as a professional courtesy among the *Talented*. But you..." The German released Lawrence's hair. Utter disdain filled eyes so blue as to be opaque. His open hand swept across Lawrence's face. Pain electrified skin already burned red by the Syrian sun and he bit back the urge to cry out.

The German slowly donned leather gloves. "*Ja.* Very amusing, telling those tribal peasants we were slavers." He struck again, this time with a closed fist. "Slavers! Do you know how insulting that is? How distasteful it is to me?"

Lawrence tasted blood. The world was a fuzzy blur. Each passing second numbed the pain. Sensations twisted, morphing into something he considered... pleasant. But the pain of the initial strike, that's when he was most vulnerable. What had the German said? Yes, telling Faizah their pursuers were slavers *was* funny. Bracing himself, Lawrence chuckled.

"You laugh?" His captor straightened. "You think your joke is amusing, *ja*? Well, Herr *Komiker*. I. Do. Not." He punctuated each word with a vicious kick to Lawrence's stomach, ribs, a punch to the head ... another kick to the groin. Blows alternated between boots and fists, precision applications of torturous vengeance.

And in between came waves of delightful warmth, an erotic sensation he only began to understand. Eyes swelled leaving only sound; stifled cries from Gertrude and Dahoum; grunts of exertion from his assailant. Every nerve was on fire. The hair on his body felt like tiny stilettos jabbing his skin. He tried to speak but all that came was a muffled ruin of words.

"*Was?*" The German grabbed a fistful of hair. Hot stale breath brushed his cheek. "What do you want to say?"

Lawrence strained against his bonds. He had to keep the German from the truth, distract him from the oddly shaped tree not ten feet away. He knew of only one path. Shivering with anticipation and terror, his tongue wetted thickened lips. Struggling to form a single word, he forced it out into the world like defiance.

"More," he whispered.

"*Schweinehund!*" The German spat on him, renewing his assault with gleeful vigor. Lawrence thought he laughed before he was beaten into oblivion.

~ ~ ~

No dreams. No visions of family and friends. Brilliant white brought Lawrence back from the dead. He creaked opened his right eye to blinding sunlight and groaned. Labored breathing suggested broken ribs. Running his tongue around his mouth was a pleasant surprise; he still had his teeth. Other than that, he was only bruised.

Hundreds of bruises.

Everything hurt. Not the delicious pain he'd felt earlier, but true misery. Still, he'd survived. With a start he remembered Gertrude and Dahoum. He turned his head and relaxed.

Gertrude, free of her bonds sat nearby, watching him with a peculiar expression.

"Hello," he croaked, then tensed again. "Dahoum?"

"He is tending the camels," she answered. "Klaus, that bastard, left us to rot, but we managed to cut our bonds on a jagged rock."

Good, Lawrence wanted to say, but the set of her jaw, the tilt of her head alarmed him. "What?" he managed with great effort.

"How is your neck?" she asked carefully.

He tried to shrug, regretted the decision. "It's fine. Why?"

She paused, crossed her arms. "Klaus… I've never seen such a beating. You should have died, but you still breathed. You breathed… and you…. We freed you and you lay where you are now, moaning…. Aroused. I could tell because you lay on your back. I ask because I know that is a symptom of neck injuries. Are you sure your neck is fine?"

Lawrence considered for a moment. "It does feel… painful. Perhaps he did some injury, but as you can see my head turns." To assure her, and him, he forced himself into a sitting position. "Are you sure about my…." Memories of the beating flooded back, and he shifted position, crossing his legs. "I am sorry," he said.

"Don't be." Gertrude gave a worldly wave. "Nothing I haven't seen before. The important thing is that you're alive." Like a switch, her expression became one of anguish. "Dammit, Ned. We had it. I had the staff in my hands and that bastard took it. All that work for nothing."

Dim relief eased his inner turmoil. Through it all he hadn't revealed the truth. Klaus' intention had been punishment, not interrogation. "How did he find us?"

"His *Talent*," she said. "He can track like a bloodhound. That's why he stayed so far from us. He had no need to come closer. Sending the Bedouins only angered him." She knelt beside him. "But you know that."

"Yes." He touched his lips. They were thick as sausages. "But don't worry about the Staff. I don't know what you found, but it wasn't Aaron's Rod."

Gertrude pushed away as if insulted. "What are you saying? I felt its magic."

"Oh, I'm sure whatever you found was magical. It just wasn't *our* Staff."

"How do you know?"

With her help Lawrence gained unstable footing. "And it came to pass, that on the morrow Moses went into the tabernacle of witness." He quoted the Book of Numbers. Leaning heavily on Gertrude, he limped towards the curiously-shaped tree. "And, behold, the rod of Aaron for the house of Levi was budded, and brought forth buds, and bloomed blossoms, and yielded *almonds*." Lawrence reached out and plucked a ripe almond pod from a tree unnaturally straight. "I'd seen this just as you found your stick, but before I could say anything, what did you say his name was, Klaus? Yes, Klaus von Bastard attacked me. Lucky he did, too. Otherwise, he might have found this." He grasped the trunk and tugged. The tree lifted easily from the earth, rootless, blossoms retreating in heartbeats.

Gertrude gasped as if struck. "I feel it." She grinned, reached out to take it. "Before there was nothing, but now… now I *feel* it."

"Perhaps it needs to be held," Lawrence speculated.

"My God!" Gertrude looked to the north where Klaus had escaped. "If not for that other staff we may never have found this."

"Oh, I don't know," Lawrence mused. "Remember Mustafa's tale? The oasis only appears to those in need of sustenance … and those deserving of its gifts."

"What now?" She held the Staff with reverence. "Fenway will want to destroy it."

"I don't think anyone can destroy something created by gods."

"Distance!" Gertrude's eyes opened wide. Lawrence suspected she'd gleaned something from her *Talent*. "Ned, the farther we separate this from its companion, both will weaken."

Lawrence considered this. "Yes, that does make sense. The strength of the caduceus is in its unity."

"Then my people will be free?" Lawrence turned at Dahoum's voice in time to receive his warm embrace. "It is good to see you are not dead, Lawrence."

"I feel the same," said Lawrence with equal affection. "But merely weakening the Istanbul Staff won't free your people. Arabs must rise up and free themselves."

"An Arab revolt," said Gertrude, caught up in Lawrence's fervor.

"Led by you, Lawrence," said Dahoum.

"Yes." Gertrude, holding Aaron's Rod, struck a heroic pose. "Ned of Arabia."

Lawrence lowered his chin. "Let's not get ahead of ourselves," he said with his impish smile. "You overestimate me. I'm no superman, but quite ordinary."

But he wasn't ordinary, a matter to discuss with Sir Margrave Fenway.

* * *

>>> Before he became Lawrence of Arabia, T.E Lawrence was an archeologist specializing in the Middle East. He had a strong affinity for the Arab Peoples and viewed the Ottoman Empire as their oppressors. While there is no evidence the Staff of Moses and the Rod of Aaron were ever combined, in a world of magic the power of these two artifacts would be substantial. Lawrence and Gertrude's success served to weaken the Ottoman's hold over the Arabs and led to Lawrence's assistance in the Arab Revolt during the First World War.

Mike Rimar

Mike Rimar has matured. He no longer writes witty bios with clever puns. He has stopped comparing his two daughters to pets, especially after the cease and desist order. He sees nothing funny about writing science fiction, fantasy, and some horror, although many of his stories might be considered humorous, and purposefully humorous, not this-is-so-bad-it's-funny kind of humorous. As proof, his story, *A Bunny Hug for Karl*, was nominated for the 2014 Prix Aurora for the best in Canadian Science Fiction and Fantasy. He is also an associate publisher of Bundoran Press (www.bundoranpress.com) and co-editor of the anthologies, *Second Contacts*, for which he won the 2016 Aurora award and *Lazurus Risen*, for which he was nominated for the 2017 Aurora. He has been published in *OSC's InterGalactic Medicine Show, Writers of the Future XXI, On Spec*, and *Tesseracts 15*, all serious publications despite having the occasional humorous story.

www.mikerimar.com

The Berlin Golem

Geoffrey Hart

My first memories are of bitter cold, and of floating in a void. I hear nothing, see nothing, and smell nothing. There is only me. I have some sense of a torso, but it feels as if my limbs have been severed. In time, the cold fades, and I begin to feel my limbs, but they aren't talking to me and don't respond when I urge them to move. I can feel eyes, ears, and a nose, but they don't respond to my urgings either. I should be terrified, but other than that ghost-limb discomfort, there is no fear. Also no curiosity, anger, or any other emotion one might expect upon waking in a strange place, cut off from one's body and senses. I have waited before, and I will wait again, so I do that.

Time passes, and now I can hear a rich voice, speaking unintelligible words. It takes me more time to realize that the words are incomprehensible because they're in at least three languages (German, Hebrew, and Yiddish). Once I understand this, their meaning gradually becomes clear. I recognize the Hebrew, at least; it is from the Pentateuch, though how I know this I cannot say. Thinking back, it is clear most of those early words were from Genesis — appropriate enough for a newborn soul such as mine — but the voice has long since moved on to other books of the Pentateuch that feel less relevant.

Knowing there are words, I suddenly feel my tongue, and my mouth fills with the taste of dirt. It's not unpleasant, not really. It's… earthy. And the words bring me comfort, for they mean that I'm not alone — and that someone considers me worthy of their time and attention. My tongue twitches along with the spoken words, and I savor that feeling and the sense of shared purpose. If I felt fear, this would eliminate it. I don't fear, but the knowledge of my value brings a warmth that eases the chill. I feel an urge to smile, but my lips have not yet returned to me, and I must wait.

But *inside*, I smile.

~ ~ ~

I feel my eyelids twitch, and all at once, the voice ceases. Then it switches to German. "Ah, good. You're awake."

I try to speak, but all that emerges is a moan and wet, sloppy sounds, as if I were Demosthenes practicing oration with a mouthful of gravel. *How do I know about Demosthenes?*

"Don't worry that you can't move yet. I expect that it's perfectly normal after awakening."

I moan again. My tongue feels more nimble, but meaningful words elude it.

"Don't try to talk just yet."

I feel a hand on my forehead, and my eyes open. It takes a moment before I realize I am looking up at the ceiling. Then I see a seamed face leaning over, surrounded by white hair below and a grizzled beard above. Inverted, I abruptly realize, because he stands at my head, but even inverted, I can see the twist in his spine.

"I'm Igor Berliner, but please just call me *Igor*. I've been your *shomer*, sort of. It's my pleasure to meet you and welcome you to the world."

I think, *Are you my creator?* but only a moan emerges from my lips. I feel my heavy brows furrow in frustration.

"Rest. Relax. I will read to you, and in time things will come clear." The voice switches back to Hebrew. Deuteronomy this time. He speaks of entry to the holy land, the need to honor the customs of one's people, and of the promise of salvation through repentance. But it is not clear why this is relevant to me: Have I entered the holy land, do I have a people whose customs I must learn, is there some deed for which I must repent, and do I have any hope of salvation? I sigh. All will become clear in time. The voice drones on, and I go with it, tongue twitching in harmony with the speaker's enunciations.

After a time, the feeling of gravel in my mouth abates and I can move air through my mouth and nose without sounding like a drowning man. "Who am I?" I croak.

"Well done! Not so well *asked*, unfortunately. As of yet, you have no name. But if it were up to me, I'd name you Yossi."

"Why Yossi?"

"Your ancestor, the Golem of Prague, was named Josef, but nicknamed Yossele. Hence, Yossi. A proud name for you to reincarnate."

No other name suggests itself. I manage to nod, and Igor goes back to reading his book to me.

~ ~ ~

Upstairs, the door slams and I hear heavy steps moving across the ceiling. Igor puts down his book.

"The master has returned."

"Master?"

Igor chuckles. "Judah Halevi, my employer. His father named him after the Spanish physician philosopher, but he's no physician and only an indifferent philosopher. Still, he pays well, and who else would employ a crippled *alterkacker* like me?"

The door to the basement opens, and the *master* flings himself down the stairs. He's a younger man, his thick beard still black and his face unlined, save for a deep furrow between his eyes that seems permanently engraved there. He wears richly woven robes, stained with something thick and black.

"Is it still lying there? Get it moving. We have need of it."

"What happened, Judah?"

"The *Gott verdammt Hitlerjugend*. They cast pig's blood upon me. Now I'll have to burn these robes." He crosses the room and seizes my arm, lifting it from my slab and letting it fall heavily back with a dull slapping noise.

"We're making progress, Judah. His eyes are open, and his tongue has grown sufficiently nimble he can pronounce a few words. Give him time. In a day, he'll be up and about, skipping like a young goat."

The younger man snorts. "See that he is." He storms up the stairs once more, slamming the door behind him.

I find my voice for the first time. "Is *he* my creator? My *god*?"

"Yes to the first, but no to the second. You were created from the same dust and clay as Adam, the first of us. So yes, he *created* you. But not even Judah is so arrogant as to believe he gave you the spark of life. That would be an act of hubris for the ages. Not that this has stopped others from believing in their own genius."

"Then where *did* I come from?"

Igor chuckles. "A question that has obsessed countless sages throughout the millennia since we were first cast from the Garden. Should you happen to learn the answer, please feel free to tell me."

His words are not comfortable, but the humor behind them is. "I surely shall do so, Igor."

"Good. In the meantime, let's see if we can get you on your feet." He forces his thin arms under my shoulders and, groaning, tries to lever me from my slab. I don't move so much as a centimeter.

"If it wouldn't kill you, could you perhaps help?" Igor cocks an eyebrow at me.

"For you, my only friend, I shall do my best." I have no idea what passes for muscles beneath my smooth and heavy skin, but whatever they are, they obey me, however slowly. I sit up.

"Bravo! We have, however briefly, achieved verticality."

"I'm glad to help you, Igor."

"Can you stand?"

I ease my legs over the edge of the slab. Igor nods approvingly, but nonetheless takes a judicious step to the side. "So far, so good." But when I attempt to slide from the slab to the floor, I fall on my face, the flat *slap!* of clay on stone echoing in the basement. When I rise, shaky but stable, Igor's hands go to my face. "Here, let me." There's a feeling of tension, and my nose returns to its former position. "Still a face only a mother could love, but at least a mother would recognize it once more."

"Thank you, Igor."

"Thank me by walking, so Judah will have one less thing about which to *kvetch*."

I comply, slowly but gaining in confidence, until at last I am comfortable and stable on my feet. Skipping like a young goat will be a challenge for another day, but at least Igor is beaming at my progress.

~ ~ ~

I wake to a small but not inconsiderable weight upon my chest, accompanied by a rumbling vibration like that of the traffic on the street that must lie outside our home. The word *cat* comes to mind, and I reach out instinctively to run my hand through its fur. With a screech, it flees the room like a hand-warmer flung from a catapult. I feel a distinct sadness, followed by a wave of relief. I'm still working on fine motor skills, and might have crushed it. Like all the other knowledge in my head, I wonder where this knowledge came from. No answer is apparent. But now I have another reason to improve my dexterity. I rise cautiously and begin practicing the mobility exercises Igor has prescribed for me.

Some time later, the light comes on and I hear Igor's steps on the stairs. They are distinctive; he is both lighter than Judah and slower. He always seems less rushed for time, but also his bad back must slow him terribly. I tell him of the cat, and he smiles and pats my shoulder, standing on tiptoes to reach. "Good for you: you've reinvented the Hippocratic oath."

I pause a moment, then the memory floods back. "*First, do no harm.*"

"Precisely. It's an ancient Greek thing, though Hippocrates undoubtedly learned it from my people. One of our key ethical points is that we must guide our behavior by the desire to avoid harm, before even the desire to do good."

His words evoke a sudden poignancy in my breast. "Am I not one of your people?"

Igor's eyes widen, and his mouth drops open. "Forgive me, Yossi. I do not know the answer to that question."

I feel a sudden need to belong to something. "If not, then what could I do to become one?"

Igor is clearly seeking a delaying tactic. "Hmm... from your lack of clothes, it is easy to see that circumcision would not be an option. Nor are you female. A wiser man than me would be required to answer your question."

"Is Judah that wiser man?"

Igor bites his lip, struggling again for a diplomatic answer. "You must be a Jew. Only a Jew would ask such vexing questions." He sighs. "No, Yossi. Judah has an impressive body of knowledge — enough to create you, for instance, which is not a trivial feat. But knowledge is not wisdom."

"What is the difference?"

Igor laughs. "A *knowledgeable* man would open a dictionary and tell you the answer. A *wise* man would know the difference without such aids, and could explain it in terms you would understand." He sees something on my face, and his mirth disappears as he puts a hand on my hand. "I'm sorry, my friend; I did not mean to mock you. Laughter is how I survive in this sometimes horrible world." He takes a long breath. "I would say that wisdom is the ability to apply knowledge to accomplish good in this world."

"So is Judah wise?"

Igor shakes his head, sadness in his eyes. "Before he created you, I would have said yes. Now? Now we must wait to see what use he makes of you."

"You say that as if I am nothing more than a tool."

The sadness returns to Igor's eyes. "You are certainly a tool that was shaped to fit his hand, and in his eyes, that is all you'll ever be. But even a sledgehammer can be used to build, not destroy. It all comes down to how one uses the tool. More importantly, we Jews believe that although it is not inherently morally wrong to own a slave, we must treat them with the same care and respect that we would treat ourselves."

"Am I a slave then, rather than a tool?"

Igor forces a laugh. "*Definitely* a Jew." He pauses a moment, gaze gone distant. "My friend, I cannot say. Judah may perhaps think of you as such. I suppose the question of freedom comes down to whether you can disobey his request, and willingly suffer the consequences of that disobedience.

There are undoubtedly more sophisticated tests, but that one may suffice for the moment."

I pause a moment myself, then ask the difficult question. "Are *you* a slave, Igor?"

He laughs and pats my arm. "Always with the awkward questions. I would say no — and yes. No, because I can leave right now and never return if I am willing to accept the consequences. Yes, because with my bad back and age, I am unsuited for manual labor. Moreover, I lack any skills such as silvercraft that would gain me other employment. Last, not being a rabbi, there is little I can teach that others would pay me to learn."

I pat him on the shoulder, offering comfort, and he winces. Evidently I still have a way to go before I can pet the cat. I sigh. "Why is everything so complicated?"

Igor smiles, this time without pain. "Presumably because *Hashem* would soon grow bored with a simple world. I know *I* would." He straightens his back as much as he can, winces, then smiles up at me. "Enough philosophy for now. Let us work on your fine motor skills."

So we do.

~ ~ ~

I wake again to the cat upon my chest. This time, I am more cautious: I lift my arm slowly, and hold my extended fingers up for inspection. The cat sniffs them, each in turn, and then, rumble growing in its chest, butts its head against my fingers. With exquisite care, I move my hand above it and stroke its fur. The cat tolerates this for a moment, then slashes at my hand. There is no pain, but clear score marks appear in the damp clay of my skin. The cat jumps down and walks away, leaving me to smooth away the signs of his disapproval.

I finish and am sitting up by the time someone comes to me. From the weight and pace of the steps, it is Judah rather than Igor. He descends the stairs in his usual hurry, then stands before me, critically assessing his creation.

"Good morning, Judah."

He startles. "Don't call me that."

"What shall I call you then?"

"*Master*. You are my creation, and mine to command."

I let that statement pass uncritically, my conversation with Igor yesterday still fresh in my mind. "Yes, Master."

"Good. Now I need you to do something." He turns and goes rummaging under the stairs. He returns with an iron horseshoe. "Bend this into a straight bar."

I take it gently from his hands, and without any noticeable effort, bend it into a straight length of metal. His eyes widen.

"Excellent." He looks around, then his eyes come to rest on the edge of the thick table that is my bed. "Now strike the corner of this table as if you mean to tear it off."

I carefully judge the table and length of my arm, then reposition myself. Then with a controlled swing, I strike the corner of the table. There is a loud *clang*, and the thick metal bends downwards at a sharp angle.

Judah steps back, eyes gone wider. He is breathing faster than normal. "*Excellent*! Now hand me the horseshoe."

I comply, and he steps back, takes a deep breath, and swings the bar hard towards my arm. There is a hollow slapping noise as it embeds itself in the clay. I feel the impact, but there is no pain. Judah, in contrast, is rubbing his hand and frowning.

"Ow!"

"I'm sorry, Master."

"It's not your fault, golem. I should have been more careful."

I hesitate. "My name is Yossi, not *golem*."

"Is it now? And who told you that?"

"Igor. He says it was the name of the Prague golem, and thus a suitable name for me."

"Did he, now? I shall have words with him when he returns. But in the meantime, *golem* shall be your name. You are a creation, not a man, and should aspire no higher than to be my willing tool."

"Igor tells me I am no tool, and that Jews no longer keep slaves."

"Igor thinks too highly of himself. He will need to be reminded of his place."

I feel a wave of regret at having caused trouble for my friend. "Please do not discipline him. It is my fault for aspiring to more."

Judah frowns at me. "Yes, it is. But would you have done so without his encouragement?"

"I think… yes. He is always telling me I have too many questions."

"He's right in that. One thing we learn in this life: accept your lot."

"And what is my lot, Master?"

"To serve me as is your duty to your creator."

The thought passes through my mind that though Judah is the creator of my physical shell, he is not the creator of *me*. That skill lies beyond him. But Judah has inadvertently taught me one aspect of wisdom: that sometimes it is best not to say what one thinks and to hold one's own counsel. Judah turns on his heel and leaves, and I spend a few moments smoothing over the damaged clay where he struck me with the horseshoe.

~ ~ ~

Igor is holding the straightened horseshoe. "Remind me never to anger you, Yossi."

"You could never anger me, my friend."

His eyes smile at me. "My wife would beg to differ." I hold my counsel. "Well, then, what shall we do with our day today?"

I change the subject. "Did Judah discipline you for what you have taught me? He threatened to do so."

Igor's smile widens. "Judah is sometimes like the quacking of ducks. Much fuss, and little meaning. One learns to bow one's head and nod acceptance until his quacking runs down and he changes topics."

"I'm glad." The image of quacking ducks amuses me. "When I asked him whether I was a slave, he avoided the issue. He reminded me of my place: as a tool shaped to his hand."

Igor shakes his head. "No. You are unquestionably a man like me." He smirks. "Well perhaps not *quite* like me. I'm more handsome. But a man nonetheless."

"How can you know this?"

Igor laughs outright. "We Talmudic scholars have a saying: *if it quacks like a duck, it is probably a duck.*"

"Then Judah is a duck?"

Igor opens his mouth to reply, then his eyes narrow a moment. *"You*, my friend, turn my words on me as if you were a Talmudic scholar yourself. I half suspect you of having a sense of humor."

"If it laughs like a duck..." I say.

Igor erupts in laughter, slapping his knee and hooting. After a time, his mirth runs down, and he hauls himself up to sit upon the edge of the table, gasping. Then he notices the bent corner. "What happened here?"

"Judah asked me to demonstrate my strength."

Igor passes his hand over the bent metal. "Can you restore this to its original condition?"

I comply, effortlessly.

Igor's eyes widen. *"Ir zent a groys aun shtark mentsh."*

It takes me a moment to translate. "Yes: big and strong, as I was designed to be."

"Let's see what else you can do." And we spend the day testing and improving my mobility.

~ ~ ~

The next morning, Judah comes to get me. "Get up. I need you to accompany me in the streets."

"Yes, Master." I rise and follow him up the stairs, the risers groaning under my weight. He holds the door open, and I pass through, stopping a moment to gaze at the street around me. A phrase comes to mind: *das Getto*. When he steps out onto the landing, I notice that he has placed a white armband with a blue star of David on it around his bicep.

"Stop sightseeing and follow me."

He brushes past me, and I follow, slowly and ponderously. Around me, other citizens — also wearing the white and blue armband — see me and recoil, eyes going wide. They are many, densely packed, but within moments we are walking in a great bubble, the crowds flowing around us, nobody coming within meters of us. Some retreat so quickly, they push others into the heaps of trash that have accumulated on the sidewalks, and are spilling into the street. I assume my appearance must be fearsome, and resolve to ask Igor for a mirror at first opportunity.

"Master?"

"Yes, golem?"

"Why is there so much trash?"

He snorts. "Because the *verdammt* Germans like it that the trash of their society drowns in its own trash."

I reflect on this for a moment. "But are we not also Germans?"

He snorts again. "*You* are a lump of mud into which I have breathed life. You are nothing. *I* am a German by birth, but denied that status by faith. Think on that, and be silent."

I obey, for there is nothing to be gained by fighting with him in public, and much to lose if he suspects I have the power to disobey.

We come to an intersection in the road, where the streets suddenly open up and become simultaneously less populated and scrupulously clean. Looking back, I see a prominent sign on the post that bears the street names: *Jüdischer Wohnbezirk*. It means *Jewish quarter*. We continue walking, and the few people on the street see us and run. All but a group of youths, clad in light brown shirts and black shorts. As we approach them, they exchange nervous glances. Then they gather their courage and move to block our path.

The leader accosts Judah. "Hey, *Juden*! You're not wanted here. Go back to your ghetto."

We walk amidst them and stop, surrounded. Judah clears his throat. "I am German, like you, and have the same right to walk these streets as you do."

"You are *Juden*, and have no rights," the leader notes, spitting on the ground at our feet. Something flung strikes me in the back of my head, then slides down my back. I ignore it.

Judah straightens and stiffens his spine. I had not noticed before how he had unconsciously hunched over once we entered these new streets. I can see him tremble. "Get out of my path immediately, or my servant here will move you for me."

Despite himself, the leader looks up and meets my eyes. He takes an involuntary step backwards, even though I haven't moved. *"Gott in himmel!"* Then he too stiffens his spine.

"Go back!" he shouts, sweat beading on his brow.

"Golem? Move them from my path."

Remembering the cat, I try to be gentle, but the first one is too slow, prevented from moving fast enough by the boys at his back. When I try to push him gently, something in his arm breaks, and he shrieks and falls at my feet. The others turn and flee in all directions. The wounded one follows them, scrabbling along the pavement, then rising and clutching his broken arm.

Judah takes a shaky breath. "Golem, we must flee too. Back to our home at once." Then he turns on his heel without waiting for any response and half walks, half runs back into the ghetto. I watch the fleeing boys for a moment, then turn and follow him. When we are home, he banishes me to the cellar. I lie down on my table and try to fall asleep, but it is hard. Despite feeling good that I was able to protect Judah, I feel a measure of guilt at not having been more careful.

~ ~ ~

The next day, when I awake, the cat is again upon my chest. But I have learned when to stop petting him, and he leaves without scratching me. Igor arrives at his usual time. When he reaches the bottom of the stairs, he stops and sniffs, then his face wrinkles in disgust. "What is that horrible smell?"

Belatedly, I remember what was thrown at me the previous day. "I'm sorry, Igor, it's probably me. Some children flung something at me in the street, and Judah was so upset, I didn't stop to clean it off. Then I was too upset to do so."

Igor is clearly shaken. "He took you into the streets? What, was he *meshuginah*? Here, let me see your back."

He turns me gently, then curses under his breath. "Something rotten and unbelievably foul. Let me get something to deal with it." He leaves, and soon returns bearing a bucket and mop. He scrubs at my back, mutters something unintelligible but clearly disgusted, then turns to dispose of the mess. Before he can leave, I put a hand on his shoulder.

"Igor, friend: bring me a mirror?"

"A mirror? Have you suddenly become vain?"

"No. I just want to see what I look like so that I may know why everyone reacted to me with such horror."

He returns some time later with a thin sheet of glass, unframed and scarred, with many gaps in the silver. But I can at least see myself. In the mirror, I see a flat, broad face with a broad nose and thin lips — not unattractive — framed by long hair cut into an angular inverted V-shape, falling well below my ears but stopping short of my shoulders. I look at myself, and see nothing overtly to fear.

"Igor, why did everyone fear me?"

"Because you are large and powerful. Did you perhaps note that you were twice the size of most of them?"

"I had not noticed, but now that you mention it...."

He purses his lips. "First, tell me more of these children." I describe them as best I can, and when I'm done, he spits on the floor. "*Hitlerjugend*. Like some hell-spawned version of the Boy Scouts. Bullies, every last one of them, and like all bullies, they are driven more by fear than by courage."

Something else has attracted my attention. "What are these letters on my forehead?"

"Aleph, mem, and tav: *emet*, which means *truth*."

I belatedly realize the letters are backwards, and that quickly, can read and understand them. "Why are they there? You have no such letters, and was I not created in your image?"

He snorts. "Not in *my* image. If you were, you'd be hunched over and ugly enough to scare children." He sees the look on my face, and holds up a hand to forestall me. "Peace. They are there because of the Jewish mysticism behind the magic that created you. I suspect it has something to do with *tefilin*. He pauses a moment in thought, then recites a quotation: "*And it shall be for a sign for you upon your hand, and for a memorial between your eyes, that the law of the Lord may be in your mouth; for with a strong hand did the Lord bring you out of Egypt.* That's from Exodus, one of the texts I read you after you woke. But as I've told you, I'm no rabbi. Should you happen upon one, ask *him*."

I hear familiar footsteps, and Judah descends the stairs to join us. "Golem, prepare yourself. We will soon have need of you."

Igor frowns. "What's wrong?"

Judah draws a deep, quavering breath. "He broke the arm of one of those vicious children yesterday. They have summoned the police. They are on their way as we speak." He takes my arm. "You must come with me now."

Igor begins a protest, then sees the look on Judah's face and bites his lip.

I follow meekly, and he leads me outside and down the steps. "Stand here, and wait for my command." I wait, alone, as he climbs back to the top of the steps and takes cover behind the door. When the police arrive, half a dozen uniformed men bearing weapons

, they bark commands at me, but as they are not Judah or Igor, I feel no need to obey. Then all at once, the leader raises his pistol and shoots me. I feel the impact of the bullet in my chest, but there is no pain and it in no way impairs my functioning. The leader swears, turns to his men and issues a command. They all raise their weapons and begin firing. I stand, unperturbed, as my flesh absorbs the bullets. When they have emptied their weapons, they turn and look at each other and there is considerable debate over what they should do next.

Judah calls down to me. "Disperse them."

"Master, I cannot. I might hurt them."

"They have no such qualms over you. Go! Run at them. They will flee before you have any chance to do them harm."

I sigh. It seems a sensible suggestion, so I raise my arms menacingly and begin moving towards them, slowly gathering speed. One of them notices my motion, shrieks, and flees. The others are so close on his heels that one trips another, and three of them fall in a heap, scrabbling frantically at the ground until they can regain their feet and continue running. When it is clear they are in full flight, I stop and return to my home.

Judah congratulates me. "Well done. Even better than I had hoped! Now come inside."

I follow him once more to the basement, where Igor is waiting. "And?"

"And it worked as I hoped, skeptical one. The bullets did him no harm, and he put terror in their hearts. They shall not return."

Igor shakes his head. "On the contrary. They will return with heavier weapons, and next time, it will not go so well."

"Next time, I will order it to kill them."

Igor draws in a sharp breath. "That would be most unwise. At best, they will send in tanks. At worst, they will bomb us into dust from the air."

I clear my throat, where a bullet has lodged. "Also, I will not kill for you."

Judah glares coldly at me. "Of course you will. You are a tool, nothing more. You have no free will."

Igor nods approvingly. "Try him. You'll see how wrong you are."

Judah turns his glare on Igor, then back on me. "Golem: pick up Igor, carry him upstairs, and deposit him on the street."

"Igor? Do you wish to leave that way?"

"Not just yet, Yossi. But thank you for asking."

Judah has gone pale. "How can you defy me?"

Igor shakes his head. "Perhaps controlling one's creation is harder than creating it in the first place."

"But it must defend us against the Nazis! That is its purpose in life."

"Perhaps if you asked nicely? Yossi, would you help Judah by defending us against those people who tried to shoot you today?"

"Yes, Igor, so long as I am not asked to kill them."

Judah reaches for me, then slowly pulls his arm back. "And what if I were to change the word on your forehead by deleting the aleph, leaving only *met*: death? Then will you do as I command?"

Igor clears his throat. "It may also mean the death of Yossi. The *kabbalah* is unclear about this."

As they debate, I ponder what Igor has read me. "Is not the sixth commandment *Thou shalt not kill*?"

Igor answers. "That depends on how one chooses to translate it. Some authorities believe that the correct translation is *commit murder*, which is not quite the same as *kill*. That interpretation would perhaps justify killing in self-defense. At the same time, we are taught that it is better to die than to shed innocent blood. But what, then, is *innocent*?"

Judah screams at the sky, or at least the cellar ceiling, in frustration. "You discuss sophistry when the Nazis plan to kill us for what this golem has done?"

Igor shakes his head. "Strictly speaking, for what *you* have done. You have tweaked the noses of these Germans instead of leaving well enough alone. They would have left us in peace without such a provocation."

Judah is almost weeping with frustration. "That is so naïve I hardly know where to begin. We need its protection desperately. And if it works once, we can build an army of golems to defend us. Perhaps even to earn us the place we deserve in this society we have helped to build."

"If we claimed that role by force, we would be no better than they are. And we must be better, to serve as an example before all the peoples of the world."

Outside, there comes a *crash* that shakes the building. Dust falls from the beams, pattering on my upturned face. I hear shouting voices, and the sound of breaking glass.

"You see?" shouts Judah. "They are coming for us. Golem, you must defend us."

I look to Igor. He shakes his head. "It is not mine to tell you what you must do. You must do what you believe is right, Yossi."

I look back and forth between their faces, and now there is a new noise, as if the guns of the police were all combined into a single large gun, all its barrels firing simultaneously. The sound of breaking glass intensifies. And then I decide. "I shall defend us. But to *my* death, not theirs."

Igor is nodding his head as I begin climbing the stairs, and I am encouraged. And yet, as I emerge into the street and see the armed men and tanks, I remember the ashen-faced child I harmed earlier in the day, and a fear seizes upon me. As the bullets pound into my flesh, not slowing me at all, I rush down the street and crush the barrel of the large gun in my hand. The heat of it bakes my flesh, creating a thin, crisp skin that is harder to move. As the barrel of the nearest small tank turns towards me, I rush forward and grab it by the lip of the muzzle, which I bend upwards, just as they fire at me. The barrel explodes both outwards and inwards, and a second later, the entire turret of the tank follows, strewing metal fragments everywhere. One of those scraps of metal strikes my forehead, and some of the clay falls into my hand. I turn it over, and see the letter aleph.

And then I hear voices shouting in German behind me, and as I turn toward them, the clay scrap falls from my hand.

* * *

>>> *This story was inspired by the intersection of the 200th anniversary of Mary Shelley's Frankenstein with a rising tide of antisemitism around the world. I chose an alternate history that let me explore those issues through the fascinating tension that exists between creation and destruction. As ethical beings, we face moral choices, whatever our origin, and those choices have consequences. We shouldn't leave those choices to our creator.*

Geoffrey Hart

Startled by an aggressive dictionary during the 9th month of her pregnancy, Geoffrey Hart's mother was shortly delivered of a child who showed a precocious antipathy towards the users of words. Over time, he was able to transform this antipathy into a more functional, if equally passive-aggressive, career as an editor. After nearly 30 years, the verbal flame burns as intensely as ever, leading to an errant, semi-evangelical career ranting against the evils of words from pulpits at any editing or technical writing conference that will have him, tirelessly seeking new recruits for his cause. In his spare time, he roams the globe, entertaining and enlightening locals with his creative and unrestrained interpretations of their linguistic conventions. He also commits occasional fictions.

www.geoff-hart.com

Khrushchev's Shoes

Liz Westbrook-Trenholm

Greusaiche found it easy to feel aloof, up high among the spot lights that edged the soaring dome over the UN General Assembly. Below, humans slouched or twitched, foreshortened blobs like badly stuffed hassocks, except that the creatures' hides were too frail to sew up into a nice footrest. Their skin was just thick enough to hold in all that water and fat and bone, and that blob of gelatinous mush within their skulls that drove them to breed and fight and kill.

Greusaiche could not be aloof, like it or not. The great Council of Folk had met in their shrinking, shattering world, that shared Aether where they hid their names, displayed their power, decided rewards and punishments and consulted on important doings. Humans had unleashed a destructive force, fire and wind under a mushroom cloud, that split apart the very foundations of existence. So powerful was it, that it smashed from the human world into the Aether, striking Faerie itself. The Yosei had disappeared from the magic lands linked to Hiroshima and Nagasaki. The songs of water nymphs were heard no more off the Pacific atoll testing grounds. The Khazakstan genies had been wiped out. Without their magic inhabitants, their Aether homes shrivelled and fell away into the Void. Unusual unity drew the Folk to one conclusion. Great and small, sprite or elf or warlock, must go out into the cold world of iron and salt to interfere. Not for fun, tricks or teasing, nor for love, affection or their children, but for the very, very survival of the magic folk.

Greusaiche's mark was moving. A short, stocky human, the leader of the huge lands of the north-east, strode back to his desk, his jerky stride speaking of anger and badly fitting shoes. The Assembly President had just expelled him from the podium, after he had denounced the head of the Filipino delegation as a "jerk, a stooge and a lackey" for accusing the Soviet Union of depriving the peoples of Eastern Europe of free exercise of their civil and political rights. What noise they made, as if such unnatural laws meant a thing. Nikita Khrushchev — how casually they tossed their true names about — flung himself into his seat, started and felt under his posterior. He'd found the Gift.

Wriggling uncomfortably, the First Secretary of the Communist Party of the Soviet Union drew out the shoes he'd just sat on, the ensorcelment causing them to appear as a fine pair of tooled leather lace-ups with cleverly cut insets designed to perfectly fit the little man's pudgy feet. Thanks to the compulsions Greusaiche had worked into every stitch, silver tack and nail, the man would glow with contentment and good will. He would stop stirring things up with they who'd invaded the western lands of the totem and raven and coyote folk and who called themselves Americans. He just had to put the shoes on.

The famous bristled brow and thick lips turned down in a scowl. Khrushchev carelessly thumped the shoes on top of the desk. Power flared at the impact, twisting and distorting into ugly shards. Impotently, Greusaiche cringed as irritation flashed across the face of the officials crowded beside the First Secretary.

To Greusaiche's relief, the First Secretary squirmed in a way that showed he was kicking off his own shoes under the desk. The official beside him flicked her gaze sideways but continued to face stolidly forward. At the podium, the Filipino head delegate continued his anti-Soviet rant. Khrushchev paused to thump his fist angrily on the desk, but dropped one of Greusaiche's shoes on the ground and attempted to bend.

There was insufficient room under the desk, given the rotundity of the man's belly. He stuck his foot out to one side and tried to don the shoe one-handed. No go.

The Rumanian Foreign Vice-Minister, a loyal member of the Eastern Bloc, called for a point of order against the Filipino delegate. Denied, he shouted abuse until the Assembly President ordered his microphone silenced. Incensed, Khrushchev jeered and banged the remaining shoe on his desk. Magic flared, wasted.

Greusaiche tore at his knuckles with his teeth.

Khrushchev thumped the shoe, again and again. The President of the Assembly demanded he cease, but Khrushchev thumped, laughed and shouted. Greusaiche's beautifully cobbled magic skittered chaotically throughout the chamber, ricocheting off delegates and dissipating into the lofty space above their heads. As the last sparks of magic flew, the red-faced Assembly President adjourned the meeting with a smash of his gavel that sent its head flying.

~ ~ ~

Greusaiche's son had left the entrances to their tree hut wide open, again.

"Mo-mhac! The wards!" No reply. Well, then, Greusaiche would ward, and ward well, and let the ingrate beg for entrance when the rain began. Exhausted already from his futile attempt to bring Khrushchev to heel, he delved deep within his well to draw up the sigils, bronzed and brown, the color of polished saddles. The split-level cottage in the shape of a boot shimmered out of sight, leaving the appearance of a giant, misshapen oak, to human eyes, at least. Greusaiche reached to wind a little confusion spell round the wards, but he was drained. Spent, spent. He staggered into his parlor, aiming for his couch. Where his son lay encushioned, cigarette smoke wreathing his dishevelled dark curls.

"Cat! You look zonked."

"Mo mhac! You left the place unprotected, and in the middle of Central Park."

"Don't blow your jets, Big Daddy. Only cats come this deep are, like, dixie-fried or way out on thrill pills."

Greusaiche collapsed onto a hard chair by the cold fireplace.

"I've no idea what you just said, but I suspect it was feckless and disrespectful."

"You are a square pair of handcuffs, man."

"Enough of that. How many pairs did you get cut out?"
Silence.

"The shoes. I left you the patterns and true leather."

"No time, man. I been swingin' on the syllables, chillin' on cool, cool waves of jive. Dig?"

"You did nothing all day, while I endured watching that Khrushchev buffoon lay waste to the precious shoe magic, shouting and laughing like a drunken ogre."

The mhac's smirk curled around a fresh cigarette. "Way out. That cat is one cool actor."

"So now you're a Soviet sympathizer?"

The mhac dropped a pair of sunglasses over his eyes, shrugged. "I make out with the muse, man."

"What's the matter with you, boy! I need to ensorcel those shoes tomorrow!"

"I'm no good with the shoe thing."

"And you'll get no better if you don't work at it."

"Not shoes. It's the mouth music moves me."

"Forget music. It's not your gift, boy. Become one with the leather and it'll walk you on the right path."

"You're not digging me, Big Daddy! I make the magic with words."

"Ah, listen to you. I'm half minded to let you fend for yourself among the meat bags and see how you get on then."

"Cease with the meat bag pejorative, man. It's grungy. Humans are cool cats."

"You're not mixing with those murderous creatures, tell me that at least."

"Their jive speaks to my soul."

"Soul! What's this talk of souls? Next, you'll be flinging your true name about, placing yourself in the power of one of those wretched, vicious creatures."

"Reverso, man. I make magic with their cool vibes."

"*You* make magic with nothing. All you have comes from me. Borrowed, boy! You're useless on your own! Now get cutting that leather. Those shoes are all that'll guide your meat bag friends off the path to their annihilation and ours!"

His son, white-faced with fury, slammed out of the room. Greusaiche allowed himself a small smile of satisfaction at the sound of his mhac's curse from the workshop. Any door he took now would lead only there. It was the simplest of magic, but it took his last energy.

~ ~ ~

Greusaiche rose lethargically into consciousness. He'd been so tired, he didn't even recall laying down his head but now he was physically rested and full of magic. Amazing what a good night's sleep could do. And it was still early, dawn a mere twilight creeping through the lattices. He closed his eyes, just for a moment's more doze.

He had no lattices on the windows. Greusaiche's eyes popped wide. He raised his head. Cobwebs festooned the window and every corner of his parlor.

Bolting upright, he caught sight of a scrap of parchment on his couch-side commode scratched with words in the human language. His son had slipped him a magic mickey.

Greusaiche tore through the house, seeking the mhac but found only scraps of parchment, paper or leather, all inscribed with the strange words. His limiting spell was broken. The wards forbidding his son's departure were down. The place was a mess. With mounting rage and dread, he flew toward the work room, but stopped dead as the mhac stepped through the front portal. His eyes were dark-ringed. A knapsack hung off one shoulder, he wore baggy fatigues and a patchy beard straggled off the bottom of his face.

"You woke up."

"Where have you been?"

The lad shrugged.

"With meat bags?"

The boy said nothing, but his eyes flared blue fire, so like his mother's. For a moment Greusaiche was cast back. Such a beauty she was, pale skin and hair black as a thundercloud. He'd wound it round his throat, drowning in it and her as they'd made their boy. She was gone, gone deep into the Aether to follow her musical magic, leaving him to raise this child alone.

"Who aided you in the spell?"

The lad blew a disgusted raspberry and shoved by him. "I'm tired." He paused, snickered, and added, "I could sleep for a year, like you did."

A year. A year when he should have been guarding the sector. So many words pressed on his chest he couldn't find the right ones. "I told you to cut out that leather."

"Be proud. I did it, like a perfect lackey of the establishment."

Greusaiche ran to the workshop. The boy leaned in the workshop doorway, smirking around a ridiculously large cigar as Greusaiche examined the pieces, cut out and glowing with the natural magic potential that needed only the sewing ensorcelment to give them the power.

A froth of pride and disappointment bubbled up in Greusaiche's chest.

"All well and good, but it's a year gone of their time and the shoes not made. You know how fast they fly to their destruction. A year, wasted, a year for them to destroy all our lands and people while you conspired to ensorcel your own faither!"

The mhac had the grace to look uncomfortable. "I didn't conspire—" He yanked the beret off his thick dark locks and threw it down. "What's the use?" He heaved an offended sigh. "All right." His son bent, dug in the knapsack he'd dropped by his feet and tossed a pair of shoes on the work bench. "There."

There indeed. The shoes Khrushchev had wasted, exhausted of the original spell, still glowed with the latent magic of the true leather, like an inheld breath awaiting release.

"Mo mhac!" Greusaiche cupped his hands around them, as if warming them at their magical fire. "How did you come by them?"

His son affected nonchalance. "UN Lost and Found."

Greusaiche hung there a moment, gazing — up — into his son's face and it was sweet, and pure and reminded him of bluebell glades Inside before they began blackening and falling away, poisoned by the infernal fallout.

"So, Khrushchev left them behind." He shook his head.

"Yeah. Well. You slept through that."

Greusaiche glared and drew breath.

"And before you start screaming at me again about conspiracies, the CIA and a bunch of Batista-loyalist thugs are heading to Cuba to steal it back from the legitimate revolution. The capitalist toady, Kennedy, is backing them. Did you want to do something about that at all or are you down with the neo-imperialist repression of the peripheral economies and the oppression of the people?"

"Nuclear bombs?"

The mhac rolled his eyes. "Work it through. You think Kennedy won't go in if they fail? If Kennedy goes in, you think Khrushchev will let that go? So, no. No nuclear bombs. Yet!" He thrust Greusaiche's silver hammer at him.

"Mo mhac." Greusaiche gestured to the waiting last. "Help me."

"Faither. Truly, I'm no good at cobbling." He gestured at the Khrushchev shoes. "Why don't you use these ones again?"

Greusaiche bristled. "First things first, mo mhac! We need more than a single pair to influence all those we must. There's Castro, there's Kennedy and there's that cretin, Khrushchev." He didn't say that the shoes worried him. They didn't behave how they ought.

The lad closed his eyes and opened them. "I'll help how I can."

They worked the day through, the boy accomplishing little. The fact was, the boy couldn't cobble, couldn't call the shoe magic. His one attempt at stitching was clumsy, and Greusaiche had to re-do the work. He set him to other tasks not requiring skill, but he was of little use. Rather, he apparently fancied himself some kind of poet. He stopped constantly to scribble his peculiar English hieroglyphs, which he left scattered over the work table. Greusaiche forced back his impatience at the waste of time, surreptitiously sweeping them out of his way as he worked.

At last, four shining pairs of shoes glowed on the bench, three new ones, and the recovered pair.

"I'll deliver them," his son said.

"Ah, you've no glamour, mo mhac."

"Can I borrow yours?" The lad sounded so young, Greusaiche waved the needed magic over. He watched sadly as the J.F. Kennedy's dignified negro valet stepped into the Aether to cross to D.C.

Only after he was long gone did Greusaiche realize the lad had taken the used shoes as well as the others. He knew it when those shoes called to him with magic stronger than anything he'd ever made, rippling and rocking through the world Outside with such power it ripped him from his workshop, tumbling him through the midst of a tragic circus.

Kennedy paced in the shining shoes, used once but not worn. Of all the ones the mhac delivered, did it have to be those he gave Kennedy?

The President swore as each CIA lie, each staggering failure in intelligence and every military blunder was revealed.

A plane painted with revolutionary markings feathered into Florida, bullet holes strafed across its cowling, yet the men within claiming to be defectors were CIA-planted Cuban exiles, the paint and bullet holes a ruse to raise America's ire.

Waves in the Caribbean rocked a flotilla of CIA-purchased cargo ships loaded with CIA-trained, Cuban exile fighters — Brigade 2506. Grim, gray American battleships loitered in the rear, pretending they weren't really involved.

Castro's bombs smashed through hulls. Medical supplies and ammunition sank or floated away into the darkness.

The Brigade 2506 invaders pushed on, full of conviction their fellow Cubans would rise to fight with them against Castro.

They did rise, but not with the invaders. Thin, dark-haired militia, green and untried, died in droves opposing them. Che's well-trained farmers, clerks and teachers defended their isle against the return of the corruption, crime and excesses of Batista, Cardona and their cronies. Castro, in new boots, inspired them as never before.

The CIA called for bombers, troop support, help, help, help.

But Kennedy in his oval office saw the reports of condemnations from his people and the world. He hesitated, and the invaders fell before Castro supporters' bullets, staggered dejectedly under guard, joined hundreds of arrested counter-revolutionaries in prison.

Pundits labeled the Bay of Pigs an unmitigated disaster for the U.S.A.

Greusaiche tumbled at last into his workshop, a timeless, silent twilight of comfort after the noise and drama of that world without. He sat, gazing at the bits of paper, parchment and leather scattered among the litter of leather scraps and silver tacks. Did the bits glow with magic, or was that the leather some were written on? How had Castro become so honey-tongued? There was a touch of unfamiliar magic in that, but whose? And to what end? The invasion had been defeated, but it had humiliated the great nation of America. That could not bode well for the future, surely.

He thought of his son, his clothes, beard and silly cigar, a replica of Che Guevara and Castro himself.

Greusaiche slept at last, but warded himself within his parlor, a-guard against his mhac.

The lad did not return that night, nor next day.

The days grew into weeks and amassed into months, and, discretely, he spied out for the mhac, warding himself at night, and on watch in the day for any interference of word or speech with the shoe magic he spread through his sector.

Nothing had the power of the shoes that kept Kennedy from sending his troops into the Bay of Pigs, but the footwear Greusaiche did seed into Kennedy's wardrobe helped the human to a wariness of war and strengthened his resistance to the braid and medal-spangled hawks at his council table.

Greusaiche retrieved the powerful Khrushchev shoes from Kennedy's closet to try them on one of those generals, beautifully ensorcelled to seem identical to the general's own and laced with gentling magic. The general kissed his wife more tenderly the day he wore them and went on to urge annihilation on the enemy so that peace would reign at last, under the eye of these United States of America, of course. Greusaiche did not risk shoes on generals after that. He was finding meat bags willful. His magic could channel human tendency, sometimes frustrate it, but the creatures' own base natures would assert themselves, despite his best efforts.

He found no help from the Council. They ignored him as less harmful than most of their foot soldiers in the Outside. Magic folk simply couldn't abandon their eons-long traditions of playing tricks, misleading and causing mischief for the bi-legged creatures who'd overrun the pretty blue and green playground that had once been theirs. Everything they did had to turn into a joke, or it wasn't elegant. And so, rather than a cessation of nuclear proliferation, more and more unlikely countries found the nuclear option within their grasp.

Silos sprang up in absurd locations. The Outside world was wound 'round thrice with a net of targeted sites down to the smallest leafy town.

A Soviet eye in the sky spat in that of the great, humorless America, and the Folk laughed in delight at the name, Sputnik, so gloriously amusing compared to the dull, lumbering American satellites, Vanguard and Juno, that came after. The buffoonery of the Cold War entertained the magic folk immensely, despite the darkness of the ultimate punch line. Even annihilation had a kind of elegant absurdity, a last chuckle before the destruction consumed them.

Greusaiche had never been much for tricks and laughter. He despaired of his fellow Folk. As a result, perhaps, he grew to hate the humans even more, trapped by them into this lonely eternity of vigilance against their flirtation with their own destruction and the Folks'. Forced to mingle with them, their smell, grinding voices and gracelessness grated on him, making him feel soiled and tarnished.

The mhac returned. He spoke little, went out often and made no effort to help in the work room, which was fine enough with Greusaiche, sure now that his son had somehow perverted the power of his shoes to some other end.

Greusaiche sent avatars under glamour to spy on him, justifying to himself that he was looking out for the welfare of the young one out in the dangerous lands of humans. What the avatars brought back to him confirmed his fears and suspicions. The lad spent ever more time in the company of the humans, not aloof or secret from them, but wide open to them, vulnerable.

One evening, as Greusaiche rested on his couch, he immersed himself in an avatar and followed the mhac to a place full of smoke, noisy music and earnest babble around small tables chock-a-block with bottles and glasses. His son was at the very center of it, mouthing the same mantras of peaceful protest, anti-establishment and the irrelevance of moral commands and prohibitions as the rest of them. Yet the creatures around him fell into rapt silence when he spoke, be-spelled by his rhetoric.

What was the mhac thinking? Did he suppose for an instant that the large, stinking men who held all the power would slink away because of a rabble of youngsters? He who said he so loved humans was about to lead them to destruction, and his own self with them.

It burst out of him and so his avatar, in a wash of fear and anger for his only born.

"Mo mhac!"

His son's blue gaze shot to him, and *saw* him, as if no glamour or avatar stood between them. The mhac drew from the air a beautiful fountain pen. When had he come by such skill? The dark head bent, the slender fingers spread a napkin, the pen wrote.

Greusaiche crashed onto his couch, the shreds of his avatar dissipating on a hurricane of power, raw, direct and full of anger. He lay in a shock of disbelief and denial until day came with the first scent of autumn, creeping through the shoe-house in a glow of turning leaves. Greusaiche stumbled to his workshop but cobbled nothing, the heart out of him, fingering leather but not knowing what to do with it. How to stop the cold war Outside when another raged within his own home?

A woman sighed, unmistakably the tone of love-making.

"Ar-gceann." His son's name. The name he and his dark-haired beloved had gifted upon him, *our one,* full of the love and power they felt for the magical fruit of their love before she drifted away from them into the Aether. The idiot child had given it away? To a human female?

He seized a length of leather from the workbench, rushing through the house with it, striking at anything that belonged to his son, or bore his imprint. He reached the room where his son most often retreated, slashed through the careless wards on the door and burst upon the two of them, his son's pale-skinned legs tangled up with the ebony limbs of a high-breasted woman, her head bent back, bared teeth white against her glowing dark skin as she cried his name again.

Greusaiche brought the leather strip down on the two of them, once, twice and thrice. The woman cried out in agony and his son leapt to his feet, arms spread, chin lowered and eyes blazing rage. He spat words and Greusaiche flung up wards, but they crumpled before Argceann's power. His son bore down on him, driving him backward.

"Mo mhac!" he cried. "You bring one of them in to this place? You give one of them your sacred name? What are you? What have you become?" His voice choked in his throat. "You have betrayed everything that we are." He dropped the piece of leather on the floor and fled Inside.

He stepped Out again at once, behind his son. He seized the girl's arm and pulled her into the Aether. He hid her in a bluebell glade, sleeping peacefully. There the marks of the magic leather would fade, and so would her memory of his son.

He evaded his son's attempts to follow, diving In and Out, warding and dodging as the mhac hurled sorcery after him. The Aether shook with raw magic as they tore Inside and Out.

They met at last, panting, in the parlor. Ar-Gceann raised hands and opened his mouth, but with a gesture, Greusaiche cast chains around his wrists and a sigil across his lips.

"Don't be throwing that raw power at me, you young fool. I haven't lived for hundreds of years to be bested by a stripling. Can't you feel what you've done, tossing all that magic about? You've mixed the two worlds! Khrushchev has planted the Deadly Threat on Cuba. Kennedy has called a war council. And you are fighting me over a female *human*?"

His son tossed his head and chains and seal crumbled from his wrists and lips.

"Give her back to me!"

Greusaiche raised his hands to ward, but his son heaved in a deep breath, stilled himself and said more quietly, "Give her back to me. And I'll fix this thing, so it stays fixed."

"And you'll do that how, all on your own? Words?"

"All *you* do is throw shoes at things. It's never enough."

Greusaiche, stung, retorted, "They're so full of hatred and darkness, it's all I can do to steer them a little away from the worst. At least I try. All *you* do is fling words at humans, stirring them up. You encourage their love of war."

"Humans aren't things to be moved about. Haven't you figured that out by now? They're as full of love as of hate, of longing for peace and tranquility as for dominance and power. They're magnificent beings, complex and lovely, giving all they can for the brief time they have. And all you see is... meat bags!"

"These lovely creatures are out to kill us all."

"And they're out *not* to. Both impulses are there, Faither. They burn hot, and fast, unlike the long-lived folk of Inside, but that just makes them all the brighter and more beautiful."

"Ar-gceann. Danger streams toward us." Greusaiche collapsed onto his couch, weariness weighing him down. "And I don't know what to do about it."

A silence fell, so profound that the murmur of a breeze without could be heard stirring the oak leaves of their home.

"You spied on me," said Ar-Gceann.

"You ensorcelled me, all the while pretending you'd no magic."

"That was the first I knew of it." Ar-Gceann chuckled. "Just needed the motivation, I suppose."

Greusaiche heaved a huge, lung-clearing sigh. "Put some clothes on, Ar-Gceann."

As the lad pulled on jeans and a shirt, (no black beatnik clothes or fatigues, Greusaiche noted) he talked.

"I'll work a letter," he said. "Carried by one they'll all believe, if not trust. A Soviet spy."

More words, deviousness and convoluted cleverness, but Greusaiche kept the thought to himself.

"He'll wear your magic shoes to give him courage and resolution."

Greusaiche started.

"My shoes."

"The Khrushchev shoes. Best you ever made. They *drink* up magic." He grinned. "How do you think I honeyed Castro's tongue and put poor Kennedy in a dither? Your shoes *reach*, Dad, I mean, Faither. It's like the other ones you make pick up on them and... resonate." His son finished buttoning his shirt and glanced at him. "What?"

Greusaiche cleared his throat and blinked away the prick in his eyes. "I, uh. This Soviet spy. You sound as if you know of one."

The Mhac nodded. "When I was flirting with communism I came within the sphere of such a one: Fontin, maker of spies, whisperer in the halls of power. He crouches in the Soviet Embassy in D.C. and weaves."

"Yet you have his name," Greusaiche smiled, but his son shook his head.

"He is so secretive he hides his true name even from his thoughts. The ensorcelment on the shoes must be as subtle and devious as him. Can you listen to my words while you re-work them?"

Greusaiche said, "You were truly about to accept communism?"

Ar-Gceann rolled his eyes. "A loving, lovely woman like Angela is preferable, don't you agree?"

Angel? His elven son with a human named… Angel? He spread his fingers on his knees and squeezed. Well, then.

"Yes, mo mhac, I'll listen. You've learned more of this world than I can ever know."

Thirteen days later, they collapsed in the parlor, warming themselves before a cheerful fire. Gifts poured from Inside to them, nectar from the shara flower good for the best dreams, butterfly powder for the Angel's lovely face, silver and gold filigreed jewels imbued with joy and laughter. The three of them sat in the midst of the charmed glitter, drinking human beer and reliving the best moments, the unexpected second letter Khrushchev sent the day after theirs — how that had sent them scrambling! The shoes and message that deafened the Soviet submarine captain and his crew to the order to fire their nuclear warheads, an order later rescinded and denied. The delicious, slow turn of the Soviet ships away from Cuba, taking their deadly load of missiles back east with them. The delicately managed delivery of promises and agreements helped on by the leaders' fresh willingness in the wash of relief and reaction felt by all but the most foolish hawks at the world's bare escape from death.

"Red telephones, one at each end," Angela said. "So they'll always talk to each other, no matter how mad they get."

Ar-Gceann glanced at Greusaiche (not his true name but do you think he'd let that be known) and saw a gleam of approval in his faither's eye.

~ ~ ~

A gift from a loving citizen, that what it must be. They made him want to dance. And such a delightful touch, the *sijo* tucked in among the laces, its three lines filling his chest with happiness. The pudgy man in the bowl haircut strode alone toward the border between North and South Korea, black shoes shining in the sun. Smiling with happy sincerity, Kim Jong Un stretched his hand toward his once-enemy.

* * *

>>> *Nuclear proliferation during the Cold War between Soviet Russia and the U.S. was terrifyingly definitive for my generation. We were on the lip of annihilation, caught in a game of political chicken between the Soviets and Americans. What artifact could epitomize that unreal era? Credit where it's due, my husband Hayden suggested Krushchev's shoe, which the colorful Soviet leader banged on his desk at the UN in order to disrupt debate on nuclear warhead positioning in Europe. Of course! And there'd have to be a fairy shoemaker. And a disaffected youth. The rest is history. Or my story, anyway.*

Liz Westbrook

Liz Westbrook-Trenholm has published or aired mainstream and speculative short fiction in Prix Aurora-winning or nominated anthologies, *The Sum of Us*, (Laksa Media), *49th Parallels* (Bundoran Press) and *Shades Within Us* (Laksa Media) and, most recently, in *Over the Rainbow* (Exile Press), with another tale coming in the August 2019 issue of Amazing Stories. Her story, *Gone Flying*, was long-listed for the Sunburst Award and won the Prix Aurora for best short form in 2018. She is a long-distance member of Calgary-based Imaginative Fiction Writers Association, and an at-home member of the East Block Irregulars writers' group. She lives in Ottawa with her husband, writer and publisher, Hayden Trenholm.

If There's A Goal

Michael Skeet

*In loving tribute to the Silk Hat Toppers hockey
team of Calgary, Alberta, circa 1950*

The thing is, it should never have come down to a single
goal. Shouldn't have come down to the final game, much less
the final minute of the final period. Al's demon promised us.

Of course, what Al's demon knew about hockey could be
engraved on the point of a pin. After the pin had been stuck
up his ass.

~ ~ ~

Friday night, the first of September 1972. Our last
weekend before the start of grade eleven at Dr. E. P. Fleeber
High School, Calgary, Alberta, Canada, Earth. The three of us
were in Al's basement, the way we were pretty much every
weekend. Two of us were staring at the symbolic circle on
the rec room floor. One of us was horrified — that would be
me. The other was trying hard not to laugh.

"Do you really think, Alan," asked Lionel between
suppressed snorts, "that a pentangle in a magic circle works
if it's made of masking tape stuck onto orange shag carpet?"

"Of course it'll work," Al said. "And my name's not Alan,
it's Alister." Al had got strongly interested in magic over the
last half of grade ten, though his interest in proper spelling
remained as weak as it ever was.

"Then why hasn't it worked?" That was me, being a pain
as usual.

"I'm still fiddling with it," Al said.

"You've been fiddling with it all summer and it's never worked. And that was when you used chalk on the floor of your furnace room, which I think is the acceptable way of making a magic circle. Better than masking tape, anyway."

"Maybe it doesn't work because you don't know what you want," Lionel said. He stuck a hand into the back pocket of his jeans. "Every time we come over here, you're thinking about a new thing to demand." He pulled his hand out of the pocket and held it out to Al. "So I've got it worked out for you."

We were all pretty serious about hockey. Well, Lionel and I were: Al was still looking for something to be pretty serious about. We'd known each other since we were eight, playing on a community-league team coached by Lionel's dad. Al stopped playing after a couple of years; I lasted until I was thirteen and couldn't keep up with the competition.

Lionel was the hockey genius; he'd gone on to star in Bantam, but then he'd hurt his knee. He was still trying to get himself back into playing condition that fall. Which was great as far as I was concerned: we spent more time with Lionel in 1972 than we had in a couple of years — or than we would once he started playing again. As for me, I was the information guy: you came to me if you wanted to know how many goals Dave Keon scored in the Leafs' last Cup-winning season — 19 — or the original name of the Philadelphia WHA team — Miami Screaming Eagles. These days, of course, any fool who can spell *Google* can find this stuff in an eye-blink; in 1972 it was pretty impressive.

Well, it was impressive to the sorts of people I hung around with.

Lionel dropped the puck into the center of the pentangle. "Face-off," he said. "Let the game begin."

"What did you do?" Al's voice went up an octave.

"There has to be an object the power lives in, right?" Lionel said. "So here's our object, and I know what we're gonna wish for."

Al got pissy and said, "We do not have to have a damned puck. Who's the expert here anyway?" He was mad enough that he made his desk-lamp wobble. As this was the only source of light in the basement it made the walls shimmer, and that made me a bit queasy.

"If reading a book makes you an expert, then you're the expert, buddy," said Lionel. "Hermetic Order of the Golden My Ass."

Al's eyes narrowed, and he opened his mouth. But it was a different voice that said, "No I don't think an object is required."

"Holy *shit!*" I think we all shouted at the same time, maybe in harmony. And I only just managed to stop from pissing myself. Judging from the smell, somebody else hadn't acted fast enough.

The fourth person in the basement looked like some sort of beaver-toothed upper-class twit out of Monty Python. Or at least he would have if his skin hadn't been the sort of green that glows. That green against the rusty orange of the shag carpet looked like one of my aunt's Jello salads. Now I was *really* queasy.

"Avaunt, Chokmah!" Al yelled, waving at the green guy as if he was swatting mosquitoes. "As I have summoned you, so shall you do my—"

"Sorry, old chap — well, young chap. The name's—" he kept speaking but whatever came out of his mouth wasn't in either official language— "but I suppose you can call me Woodman. That was my name when I was mortal." Mortal? I decided to look up who *Chokmah* was.

Al kept his head. "You're here to do my bidding."

"Oh, absolutely. Well, to the best of my ability, anyway."

"The best of your what?" Al's voice went up into that angry squeak again.

"The truth is, young chap, we're rather busy at the moment. The really top-goers are all in Washington just now. Something about causing an election landslide. Though I gather the biggest problem is this Nixon fellow who did the summoning — his own worst enemy, I hear. Still, you shouldn't give me too much trouble. You'll be after the usual things, I assume."

"No," I said. I hadn't really believed Al knew what he was talking about, but I'd thought about it anyway.

"No?" Al and Woodman said. "But it's tradition," Woodman said. "The love of the most beautiful woman, unlimited riches, immortality."

"Those all sound good to me," said Al.

"What the hell?" I asked, punching his shoulder. Hard. "Didn't you ever watch 'The Twilight Zone?' Or 'Alfred Hitchcock'?" Al's face showed me he knew the episodes I was talking about. "The wishes never pan out the way you want them to."

"Not precisely true, that," said Woodman. "Though all wishes do have consequences. The bigger the wish, the bigger — well, you know."

"So, then what do I want?" Al asked.

"What *we* want," Lionel said, "is to walk all over the Russians, starting tomorrow night."

"Beg your pardon?" Woodman asked. "The Russians?"

"The Summit Series," Lionel told him, the way he'd tell my little sister. "Canucks versus Commies. You know — world supremacy in hockey."

"Hockey?" Woodman asked. "Are you sure?" His greenish face wrinkled up in concern — made him look like a disgruntled cabbage. "In my experience, hockey is played on grass by girls. Homicidal girls. A free piece of advice: if anyone ever offers you a friendly match against a school called St. Trinian's, run away."

"We're Canadians," Lionel said. "Hockey is what we're about. On ice. Even if September is too early."

"It's just," said Woodman, "well, this is most unusual. Are you really sure about this?"

I gave Woodman the stink-eye. "How stupid do you think we are? Do we really care if Evelyn Kirby swoons over us? And you're going to give us an unlimited amount of lunch money? Or we'll be trapped in grade eleven forever? No to all of that."

"So let's just make it simple," Lionel said. "Canada wins. The Russians don't win a single game. Now let's send out for Chinese." He crossed his arms, defying anyone to question him. Woodman disappeared, leaving only a fart-smell behind. The only question I had wanted to ask was, *Why bother? Everyone says we'll win eight straight anyway.* But then again, I never really believed in that hocus-pocus stuff.

~ ~ ~

It didn't even take twenty-four hours for the wish to go wrong. I watched Game One with my family, and it was as if we were trapped in our seats: it was midsummer hot in the Forum that night, and Team Canada played like they were all still up at the cottage, waiting for the next beer to show up. The final score was 7-3 for the bad guys, and next day it was like Premier Lougheed had died or something.

Things did not get better after that. Yeah, we won the next game, in Toronto on Labor Day, but only by pounding the crap out of the commies, which might be part of hockey but isn't the game I like, not really. The win cost me a couple of days, in a way, because on Sunday morning I'd started wondering how we could have screwed up such a simple wish, but after the win in Toronto I stopped thinking about it. And the tie in Winnipeg I could ignore because the ice was so horrible it screwed up both teams. Lionel was right: September really was too early in the year for hockey.

Then came Game Four. We were in Al's basement again 'cause it was Friday night, and they played in Vancouver so the game started late. We moved our Saturday Chinese take-out to Friday for the occasion. But we didn't eat much. Nobody had an appetite.

"Jeez," Lionel said at one point. "Why are they booing their own guys?"

"Maybe because," I suggested, "our guys suck out there?"

Al giggled at the dirty language. Then he frowned. "I have to get that Woodman guy back here," he said. "He's doing it all wrong. He's screwing up everything."

"Not Woodman," I said, stabbing a deep-fried chicken ball and smearing it in the movie-blood sauce, then pushing my plate away. "It's us."

"Us?" Al asked in his offended-chipmunk voice. "We haven't done anything. You saw it, Ted: I got Woodman here! I bounded him to my command!"

"Bounded?"

"But why us?" Lionel asked. He took a vicious bite out of an eggroll. "Much as it pains me to agree with Al."

"Because that's always the way it works. We made the wish; somehow we screwed it up. Woodman's giving us the worst possible interpretation of what we asked for. I just can't remember what we said that night. Can either of you?"

Silence.

~ ~ ~

The series shut down for a couple of weeks while everybody went to Moscow (Team Canada by way of Sweden). So for a while things were normal — no, *seemed* normal. I didn't realize that they were still screwed up until the Friday night before the first of the exhibition games in Stockholm. The student council sponsored a Welcome Back Dance in the gym, and for some reason I went. I didn't normally go to dances; instead I hung out with Lionel and sometimes Al, and we played Avalon Hill wargames or something so we could stay awake long enough to watch the softcore pornos on the local access cable channel.

I'd been leaning against a wall for maybe ten records when I realized: Evelyn Kirby was standing against the opposite wall, and had been there as long as I'd been at the dance. She hadn't gone onto the floor with anybody. Not once. I looked closer; she had a strange sort of look in her eyes. I couldn't figure out what it was.

Of *course* I couldn't figure out what it was. I was a sixteen-year-old male, for chrissake.

And then, before I knew what I was doing, I was circling around the gym. Hugging the walls. Walking up to her. Asking her to dance. I'm not kidding, this really did happen before I knew what I was doing, because if I'd been aware for even a second I'd have stopped. I don't think I had ever asked a girl to dance before then.

She said yes. And it was very nice, and she was every bit as pretty close up as she'd ever been from a distance. Not gorgeous or exotic the way beautiful girls are in the movies, just — pretty. Soft curls in her hair, soft curves pretty much everywhere. Soft, full lips that smiled wonderfully. Easily the most beautiful girl in school. The song was "Long Cool Woman" by the Hollies. I thought that was appropriate. It was also fast enough that I didn't have to worry about touching her.

When the song ended, I didn't know what to do next. So I just said "Thanks. Gotta go." And I practically sprinted back to the opposite wall, grateful that I wasn't dancing to Al Greene's "I'm Still in Love", which is on the slow side however gorgeous a record it is.

When I got back to my spot against the wall, I realized I was feeling pretty pleased with myself. My heart-rate was in triple digits, but I thought that maybe I might have learned something here. Maybe girls were easier than I'd thought. Maybe there was more to life than two professional hockey leagues in North America. I was thinking about possibly trying again with some girl who wasn't quite as out of my league when I saw Evelyn Kirby moving. In my direction. In fact, to me. *Yikes*.

Didn't have a chance to think anything else, because she stopped about a foot away from me, hauled off and smacked the side of my face. With enough force to drive the zits off my chin and splatter them against the wall. "*That's* for what you said about me," she said in a voice so quiet it guaranteed nobody else would know what I'd done to deserve the smack. She turned around and stomped right across the middle of the floor; I closed my eyes and tried very hard to become invisible. "The Five Man Electrical Band informed me that not only was she right, she always had been."

~ ~ ~

It was after second period the next Wednesday that I figured out what was going on. At Fleeber they played music over the PA for the time between periods, making a school-wide version of musical chairs: the idea was that if you were still in the halls when the music stopped, you were Out. The office owned the grand total of three 8-track tapes, so for three solid years we were either confused by the Moody Blues, *irritated by Tom Jones, or appalled to the* point of vomiting by Lawren*ce Welk*.

So I was jog-trotting from English to the jaunty sounds of "Lovely to See You" — Moody Blues, *On the Threshold of a Dream* — because I needed to hit the can before Math, when a hand grabbed my upper right arm. Hard. Next thing I knew I was in the boy's room, but being there was no longer my idea.

"Guess what? It turns out I'm out of cash for lunch today," said a guy who looked like an inflated Steve Reeves and sounded like Truman Capote on Day Eight of a week-long bender. "And you're going to help me, right?"

It was Pebbles Posluszny. Well, he was *Rock* to his friends; we called him Pebbles when we were very, very sure he wasn't listening. Pebbles played Front Four on the Senior football team. Really. Not only could he play all four positions, he was wide enough he could play them all at the same time. How a guy the approximate size of the Columbia Glacier had a voice like Bruno Gerussi's baby sister was a constant amusing mystery to us. Just now, though, he wasn't being all that funny. Nor all that gentle. I suppose in his own way he was being nice: he could have just held me upside-down by my ankles and shaken me until all my money had fallen out. Instead he just held me by the throat with one hand while he rifled my pockets with the other.

I'd never been robbed before. I had just started to think, *I've had too many firsts this month* when it hit me.

I never did get to Math. That was a first, as well.

~ ~ ~

"You have got to get that demon back," I told Al at lunch. I'd spent math class in the library, researching. "Tonight. It's even worse than I thought."

"He's not a demon," Al said. "He's an angel."

"No," I said. "That Chokmah guy you thought you were getting, he's supposed to be an angel." I'd looked it up. "Wood-man plays for the other team." Al had been reading Aleister Crowley; I'd done my research in Marlowe and Goethe.

"Well, whatever he is, I can't get him back. I was trying last night," he said. "Nothing worked."

I thought about belting him in the chops, because clearly he wasn't taking this seriously enough. Then Lionel slumped into the chair beside me and said, "Why in the world would Evelyn Kirby start yelling at me in the parking lot this morning?"

"I have an idea about that," I said. But then Pebbles showed up and sat with his pals at the next table. By the time the earth had finished shaking Pebbles was smiling at me with such malign force that my voice emigrated to Dullard, Saskatchewan and I didn't regain the ability to speak until halfway through Social Studies.

Thursday afternoon Evelyn Kirby ambushed Al in the back alley near his place and kicked him in the balls while hissing at him like a demented goose. Thursday night Pebbles Posluszny slammed Lionel against a streetlight and stole the twenty bucks Lionel's dad had given him to buy a new stick and pair of gloves with.

Friday night was Game Five, the first of the four Moscow games.

~ ~ ~

"What the hell, Al? What were you thinking?" Al looked up at me from where he knelt on the rec-room carpet.

"What?" he asked.

"That!" I told him, pointing to what was — almost literally — right in front of his face. He had drawn a new circle-pentangle thing around center ice of a tabletop hockey game. From the rubble beside him it was clear to me Al had first tried using the boxing ring from a Rock 'Em Sock 'Em Robots set.

"It wasn't working with the summoning circle on the carpet anymore!" He pointed to the abandoned circle, its tape floating atop the straggling carpet fibers like the raft of the *Medusa* on the storm-tossed whatsit.

"What did you do with the puck?"

"Huh?" Al looked from me to Lionel.

"My puck, you moron. Where's my puck?" Lionel pointed at the center of the new pentangle, where the puck clearly wasn't.

"Woodman said we didn't need a focus object."

"Woodman," I said very slowly, "is a demon, you complete fugging idiot! The whole reason you got kicked in the balls is that he's a demon and he's screwing us around! When he says you don't need something — you need it."

"I'm beginning to get the idea," Lionel said, "that Alan isn't very good at this."

"Alister," Al whined absently. His heart clearly wasn't in it. "And it's not as if either of you bothered trying to do this."

"That's because this is stupid," Lionel told him.

"Or it was, anyway, until you called up a demon who is now going to kill us."

"What?" Al stared at me.

"Find the damned puck, you guys. Find the puck and then I'll tell you what I think is going on."

We eventually found the puck on top of the rec-room TV. Hiding in plain sight, really, because we'd been pausing in our searching every few seconds to watch the game. Team Canada was ahead 4-1 a quarter of the way through the third period, but I knew better. And sure enough, the Russians scored three goals in a little over two minutes to tie the game, then won it with five minutes to go.

"Who put this here?" Lionel asked, palming the puck.

"Who knows?" Al said.

"Who cares?" I said. "It's pretty much too late to do anything about the hockey now anyway. But— I don't know about you guys, but I'd like to keep living."

"What are you talking about?" Lionel asked. "You're kinda scaring me, man."

"I can't remember what exactly we wished for three weeks ago," I told them, "but I do remember one thing I said. I remember saying that I *didn't* want Evelyn Kirby to fall in love with me, or to have unlimited lunch money, or to live forever in grade eleven. And guess what's happening?"

"Evelyn Kirby hates all three of us," Al said, casually covering his crotch with both hands.

"Ted got robbed by Pebbles and then I got robbed by Pebbles," Lionel said. He looked at Al. "Monday's going to be interesting for you, pal."

"Okay, okay," Al said. "I get it."

"I don't think you guys do," I told them. "Think about that last thing I said."

"I told you, I get it," Al said, his voice going up into whiny chipmunk territory again. "Evelyn Kirby doesn't love us, we aren't rich, we aren't going to live forever in grade eleven."

"You *aren't* getting it. It's not that Evelyn Kirby doesn't love us — she actively hates us. It's not that we aren't rich — we're being robbed of what we already have. And it's not that we're not going to live forever in grade eleven — we're going to—"

"Holy *shit,*" said Lionel, dragging out the s-word until practically Saturday. He dropped the puck into the center of the original pentangle on the carpet. "Get that Woodman guy back, Al. Get him back *now.*"

Maybe it was the puck, maybe it was just the terror, but as soon as Al had finished his incantation or chant or whatever it was, Woodman was in the basement. Smiling with those giant glowing horse-teeth. "Enjoying the series, gentlemen?"

"It's time to stop this," I said.

"I don't think you're in a position to wish for that," he said.

"Says who?" I wondered what would happen to my fist if I punched him in the nose. "You never told us how many wishes we had."

"Oh, don't be silly," Woodman said. "Of course I did. It's always the first thing any of us—" I could smell something foul and bitter in the basement. Like sulphur after it had been burned and then shat on by an elephant. "Ah," he said. "Evidently I am incorrect." He blushed. A green-faced guy blushing is not something you want to look at while eating Chinese takeout. "Very well, you have one more wish."

Before either of the guys could say anything, I said, "We want you to undo everything you've done since Al summoned you."

Woodman laughed. "Oh, I don't think so. I can't grant you a negative wish. You have to wish for something positive, not its negation."

"Nice try, shithead." I picked up the puck from the pentangular center. "You've negated pretty much everything we wished for, or worse. As I understand it, you have to give us exactly what we ask for. And what we're asking for is that you undo what you've already done." I grabbed the back of his collar with one hand — it felt a little like getting a mild electrical shock — and gripped the puck in my other fist. "Or would you rather find out why so many hockey players are missing their front teeth?"

The foul smell got much more noticeable, but in a way that sort of went up and down — the way your voice goes up and down when you talk. I've always wondered if that was brimstone. And I try very hard not to wonder who — or what — was fart-speaking to Woodman.

"Oh, all right," he said, sticking out his lower lip to the point where I thought Lionel was going to step on it. "It's done."

And he vanished.

"Dammit," Al said. "Why did you do that, Ted? I had a great wish worked out. Completely foolproof."

"And you're just the fool to think that," Lionel said.

I just shook my head. *If you're so confident,* I thought, *you can always call him back.* I was very careful about not saying it out loud. "Any more almond chicken left?" I asked instead.

~ ~ ~

Thursday morning, the twenty-eighth of September. The final game in the series, and yeah, the goal everyone remembers. After we got rid of Woodman, Team Canada won the next two games, tying the series. The historians say that Team Canada finally gelled in Sweden and the coaching staff figured out how to counter the Soviet playing style. But I know what I know.

It was weird watching Game Eight in the cafeteria with hundreds of other kids. Weirder watching it with the teachers; I remember Mr. Phosgene sweating like Esposito, and Mr. Throatwobbler in a leisure suit whose jacket lapels were big enough they each had their own postal code. I was sitting by myself: Al and Lionel were watching the game in Al's rec room.

I have to be honest: I don't remember the game itself all that well. Oh, I do remember watching Alan Eagleson being rescued by the players after a bunch of soldiers grabbed him. I'm pretty sure that's the first time I ever saw somebody giving people The Finger on TV, which was cool. I also remember the way the transmission kept cutting out, and the teachers assuring us that the problem was being caused by Moscow, the dirty bastards.

Mostly, though, what I remember was when Evelyn Kirby sat down beside me. I had to work especially hard not to clap my hands over my crotch to protect my balls when I saw her standing at the end of my row; the stress was practically vibrating off her. And then suddenly she was sitting beside me and whispering an apology. "I don't know why I believed those guys and what they said about you," she said. "Especially 'cause you had been so nice to me at that dance. I'm really sorry."

And I was really embarrassed. "It's okay," I told her. I really meant it, too, and she could tell, I think, that I meant it. And when she smiled a nervous sort of smile at me, I suddenly understood something I hadn't figured out the night of the dance. The strange look on her face that night was because she knew what I had just figured out.

We were terrified of her. Not just me and Lionel and Al. *All* of the guys in school were terrified of her — and none of us knew why. She didn't know why either. Nearly half a century on I'm still guessing, but it seems to me we were — and are — so afraid of rejection that beauty of any sort turns us into nervous rookies, absolute beginners. No matter who we are, we're convinced they're out of our league.

The better ones of us learn not to resent this so much.

I'm pretty sure, though, that demons don't have anything to do with it.

Evelyn Kirby slipped away while I was trying to think of something friendly to say to her. And then the second period ended, and Lionel and Al showed up, sneaking into the cafeteria. They both looked embarrassed, a bit. Lionel said, "It didn't seem right not to watch it together. Whether we beat the Russians or not, we should watch as a team."

I said, "We should stop calling them Russians, you know" — and then I knew where we had gone wrong.

It was a nomenclature issue: Lionel and I had both referred to *Russians* — Lionel had said "Russians don't win a game," and that's exactly what that bastard Woodman held us to. They never called themselves *Russians*, at least not to us. They were *Soviets* — or *the Soviet*, to Foster Hewitt, who couldn't even pronounce *Cournoyer,* much less *Kharlamov.*

Speaking of whom, I found out much later that Kharlamov was half-Spanish. Tretiak (*Trekyat* to Mr. Hewitt) was born in Ukraine. So following the strict letter of the law, whatever the law was, Woodman was granting our wish. The Russians didn't win those three games because they weren't Russians, not all of them anyway.

When I'd figured that bit out I realized Woodman probably would have given us the hockey part of our wish, because the first part of what Lionel demanded was that Canada win the series. A basic wish, hard for even a demon to screw us on — though he tried.

And in the end, we did win — by the skin of Paul Henderson's teeth.

After the cheering stopped the PA came on and the principal told us classes were canceled for the rest of the day. More cheering. I wasn't cheering — well, not much. I was thinking, about hockey and girls. Mostly about girls. And I realized that hockey can only take you so far.

I took the long way home. I had a lot to think about. I knew I didn't want to spend the rest of my life hiding out in a basement with no friends other than Lionel and Al. But I also knew that whatever I was going to do for myself, I had to do by myself. Look at where counting on Woodman had got us.

Lionel once said something that was maybe more than he knew. He was talking about a game he'd played a couple of years earlier, but I remembered it again, walking home by myself. In the end, Lionel had said, we're all going in on goal alone, with nobody back. It's how we play the breakaway that counts.

* * *

>>> There are two artifacts in "If There's a Goal," one within the story and the other a sort of metadata. The latter's the song that inspired me to write this; an online search of the story title should direct the reader to the lyrics. The object within the story occupies the same ritualistic category as the so-called 'lucky loonie' buried beneath center ice during the 2002 Winter Olympics. As magical objects go a puck is sort of benign (most magical objects seem to be swords of one sort or

another), though anybody who's been hit by a slap-shot might disagree.

Michael Skeet

Michael Skeet is an award-winning Canadian writer and broadcaster. Born in Calgary, Alberta, he began writing for radio before finishing college. He has published two novels, (*A Poisoned Prayer; A Tangled Weave*) with Five Rivers Publishing, and short stories in the science fiction, dark fantasy and horror fields in addition to having extensive publishing credits as a film and music critic. A two-time winner of Canada's Aurora Award for excellence in Science Fiction and Fantasy, Skeet lives in Toronto with his wife, Lorna Toolis.

https://michaelskeet.blogspot.com

Holding Our Own

Holly Schofield

What I remember most about those years is the tiredness. Three, four hours a night we were at it, several times a month, in the wind and cold down on the docks, the weight of the handcart pulling at my lower back, already worn out after a day of mothering toddlers and an evening of bed-lifting old folks.

Me and the girls came from all over Duluth those nights — nurses' aides like me, waitresses, high society gold diggers, spinster librarians, mothers, all of us pulling away from our personal responsibilities for the greater good. We had a system to coordinate us — no cell phones or internet back in 1975, you know — just clever code words on land lines and such. We'd wrap scarves over our hair and run for the last of the buses heading down to the Port Authority, trying to hide our faces from the driver.

To maybe half of you who read this, I know it'll be foreign territory — what we were loading wasn't heavy, not in poundage. A gray wisp, most of 'em insubstantial as nightmares. *Banes* we called 'em then, least ways we did in Minnesota. The *Fitz's* cook, a big burly man called Glen, once told me some Canadian women call 'em *caches* — as if you'd ever want to go back for 'em later. Different names in different places, but all us women know what they do to us, those feather-light, soul-heavy parcels of hell.

"Wish we could burn 'em instead," my best friend, Elsie, said that night as the unheated bus barreled down icy November streets. "Like back in history."

Some women just kept 'em, but that was bad, of course. They build up a force of their own, an evil power, if you let 'em.

"Yeah," I answered. "I read a library book once, it said the Iroquois mighta set fires to clean out the forest around all the Great Lakes way back when. Get rid of all the brush and such, can you dig it?"

"Yeah?"

"I bet the women would throw in a few banes before they lit a match." I pictured a woman, all deerskin and grit, heedless of the heat, risking the flames, tossing away her stillborn hopes and her beaten-up dreams.

"No matches back then, fool."

I elbowed her good. "Smartie pants."

Elsie never held her tongue, even when there were consequences. She wore her cigarette-burned arms and lopsided jawline proudly.

We both stared out the grimy window at the crowded buildings and narrow streets speeding by. "No fireplaces or bonfires much these days, not like our ol' grannies had," I added. "And Ronald hates camping."

Burning is best, but women dump 'em in construction pits, in quarries, you name it. The ocean, too, o' course. For those who can see it, the high tide mark on most shores isn't just kelp and sewage scum and plastic, it's dune after dune of those faint grim tangles.

My sister, down in Vegas, always made sure her family's summer vacation included the Hoover Dam. She'd send her husband and kids off on a trail ride then throw her year's accumulations over the edge. She'd even bought binoculars so she could see 'em drift all the way down. If you aren't careful, see, banes weigh you down, turn your hair gray and rough up your dreams.

For me and Elsie and the rest, the ore freighters were our forest fires, our oceans, our canyons. The *Edmund Fitzgerald*, the *Arthur M. Anderson,* and other ships that crisscrossed Lake Superior helped ease our way. The dockworkers, the crew — except Glen — and the other men who worked in the area never caught on. We would have been surprised if they had.

That bone-chilling day in late fall, Elsie's call had come through as I'd cooked breakfast. I'd immediately asked for the night shift at the nursing home — easier to slip out from that than the worn wool blankets I shared with Ronald. Another aide would cover the most necessary of my duties as best she could, and the head nurse would turn a blind eye as usual.

For once, the buses ran on time, and we clattered out at the Port Authority curb just as good ol' Carol careened down West Michigan toward us, drab trails of gray wafting out the station wagon's rear windows. A solitary streetwalker avoided the faint cloud without a thought. The fedora-sporting man following a short distance behind looked puzzled as to why she'd detoured a few steps.

It's a rare man that can sense 'em. I only ever met a few in my time, Glen the cook being one.

A pinprick, then a stab, is what a bane feels like, if you're foolish enough to let one touch your skin. Every girl learns that real quick, usually before they even hit puberty. One Sunday morning after Elsie's man came home drunk, she'd sat in my kitchen while I taped up her broken jaw. A bane, as insubstantial as dryer lint, crept out from her chin and I grabbed it before it could dangle down to her breasts. My hands burned, and I swear my heart stopped. I stuffed the filthy thing down the kitchen sink and hid my tears hunting for a bag of ice in the freezer. The grateful look in her good eye rewarded me some, but I never grabbed a bane bare-handed again, let me tell you.

At the quay entrance, as Carol sped past, the forty or so of us gathered round Elsie. Her voice cut through the sleet. "Listen up, girls. We got way more this time than last."

"Bummer," the woman next to me said. She couldn't be more than eighteen. Rainwater ran steadily off her maid's cap and down her curls. I didn't want to tell her large amounts of banes were more than just an inconvenience. If she didn't even know that being a maid might involve more expectations from her male employer than other jobs did — well, let her enjoy her innocence while she could. That's how I thought back then, anyway.

"Not like the numbers are ever gonna drop." Elsie glared at the lot of us. "We just gotta hustle faster."

"We'll need a bigger warehouse by spring," a hunched woman called out, tears in her voice. "Even with clearing it out every week." Someone put an arm around her and gave her a squeeze.

Elsie jutted out her chin. "Leave the warehousing to me. Let's boogie." She glanced around, squinting in the low light from the lamp posts. "Minnie?"

The best looker of us all, Minnie stepped forward, her little red tam frosted with icy moisture. "All set. The bastard wants the usual arrangement and three hundred dollars, too. Says the bosses are getting suspicious. Thinks we're smuggling drugs or something."

We dug through our purses and shoved bills and coins into Minnie's hands until there was more than enough. Her heels tapped-tapped her indignation as she headed back over to the night watchman's hut. We watched the door slam shut, a sad will-o-wisp already welling up near the curve of her back.

Elsie's firm voice rang out. "Looks like it might be our last chance down here, girls. Let's stuff these ships to their goddamn nuts."

We snickered at her crude language and headed under the overpass and down the gravel of Garfield Ave., wobbling in our flats and pumps. Stale diesel fumes, the raw tang of ore, and Superior's dank odor triggered coughs that we muffled with our scarves.

In the near darkness, a few of us peeled off at a particular warehouse — the one that other women had been stockpiling all week. The fifteen of us assigned to the *Fitz* followed Elsie, while more women squeezed past us, heading to the *Anderson* and others.

The *Fitz's* gangplank of narrow steps and thin railings loomed up at us. With the crew on shore leave during resupply and it being a Sunday, our chances of being caught were the lowest we could make them. Women always learn to hedge their bets, don't they.

Carol had her back gate open and was hauling 'em out, handfuls at a time. We spread out along the dock, the gangplank, and the deck, quick as we could, lining up in our bucket brigade positions. The dull half-moon gave no help, so we steadied each other as needed. I slid into my place up on the slick metal deck. Back on the dock, Elsie started to hum Sam Cooke's *Chain Gang*, like usual. As others joined in, a large woman with beauty-parlor hair and silky furs pushed past me and took her place on the far side of the deck — I recognized her from weeks past, but she'd never spoken a word. She'd just silently take 'em from me and pile 'em on the deck, hour after hour, until her arms trembled.

I pulled Donald's heavy leather work gloves from my purse and then gingerly plucked out the banes I'd brought with me. The patients and nurses, both, had shoved a few dozen into my coat pockets as I was leaving. I ignored the tingling that came through the gloves and tried not to listen to the random whispers the awful things made between my ears,

landlord looming, grinning beneath scruffy mustache, "there's other ways to pay rent, you're a fine-looking woman, whaddaya say?

dreading saying the words, "It's a girl," watching Paul's face harden, scooting back in the narrow hospital bed, flinching at the years ahead

father's callused hand hard on my cheek, "damaged goods, you'll have to marry him now" wracking sobs

skirt whipped up, cold air on my legs, damp clamminess on my thigh, alley's brick wall at my back

—I scraped that last one off my glove hastily and practically threw it, earning a squawk from the woman in the mink. Other people's banes are always worse than your own.

The frowsy shop girl who perched on the gangplank below me started handing up more, first from Carol's station wagon, then from the handcarts women were wheeling up from the warehouse.

Back at the entrance, the night watchman's door slammed loud enough for us all to hear. Some tap-tap-tapping in the gloom and Minnie pushed past the shop girl and grabbed my sleeve. "Outa the way." Her finger hooked her mouth, and she drew out a small whimper of a thing reeking of unwashed cock, and hurled it at a coil of rope. Fresh ones hurt more than old, the pain still new and sharp.

Then we both stood shoulder-to-shoulder, passing them along to the mink-wearing woman or stuffing them as quickly as we could into nearby nooks and crannies, fighting against how they wanted to cling. The sleet turned to rain then back into sleet again.

Before long, my woolen Sears coat was soaked, and my feet hurt. To distract myself, I imagined the journey these banes would have. How they'd head across the Superior, into the center, too far to see the other side. How Glen would chuck them overboard during the long nights of the three-day journey, endlessly, wearily, unable to ask the other men for help. Not that the rest of the crew — most likely good honest men, who lifted their children high and bought jewelry for their wives — would have refused, had they been able to see what was right in front of them.

But, they couldn't.

The banes would sink, riding the currents downward, ghosting over wrecks, huddling on the bottom. Elsie's secret special girlfriend, Carol's daughter's shame, my own incident in the church basement. How many generations would it continue, how many millions of women?

"D'you think," I said, my breath a white cloud in the cold, "that it's true what some women say — that most men could see our banes if they cared enough, and tried hard enough?"

Minnie spit over the side. "Don't matter much, since they don't."

"Or that men have their own banes? And we can't see 'em?"

"Yeah, sure, and that's why cats stare at *nothing*."

We both paused for a moment and the woman in mink glanced over. Somehow that wasn't as funny as Minnie had meant it.

The piles kept growing. We packed them wherever we could, tightly, too tightly, dangerously compressed, dangerously high.

Elsie kept on goading us, even after she could see the deck had become a powder keg of agony, a tower of despair.

"Enough," I finally said. The woman in mink had tears running down her face.

Dockside, Elsie's face gleamed in the dim pool of light. "Keep goin'. Gotta empty that warehouse. You want all that bad karma stayin' in there?"

The other women in hearing distance nodded. She had a point.

When dawn raised its gritty head, we were finally done. I shoved my two newly-formed ones deep into the stack: a small snarled mess of night shift guilt that I'd left eight-year-old Helen at home in charge of my two younger ones — Ronald couldn't be woken for anything; and that, in her always-chilly room at the nursing home, old Mrs. Wozniak would be sodden in her bed by now. We shuffled off down Garfield, calling exhausted goodbyes in the thin rain.

Carol gave me and Elsie a ride home through shiny, slick streets, her wrinkled face slack with exhaustion, three of us silent.

A couple of days later is when I heard on WEBC radio that the *Fitz* had gone down. I let a meal tray fall as the DJ droned on about the storm, the twenty-nine deaths, and the captain's last known words: "We are holding our own."

There're lots of official reasons for the sinking of the *Edmund Fitzgerald*. A record-setting storm, hidden shoals, a flooded ballast, a mysterious starboard tilt — the men who studied such things back then said it was probably a combination of all of 'em.

Gordon Lightfoot's song blames some sort of *witch of November*. I laughed so hard first time I heard that, I startled a patient I was wheeling to the showers. I tried to explain the lyric to her, a proper sort who'd hid her lifetime of densely-packed banes behind perfect posture. She peered up at me from under her blue hair. "Women are always at fault, dear. Surely, you know that."

But I can picture how things might have happened. Glen on the deck, yellow slicker iced up, beard crusted with sleet. Tossing banes over the side against the spray, faint glimmers of gray caught by his lamp then gone. The pent-up anguish of so many clustered together eating at his soul. Unable to ask for help, certain the other men would scoff, working alone in the storm until the thirty-foot waves unfurled their power and swept him off, to settle amid the other lost sailors at the bottom of Superior, leaving evil still clinging to the deck.

Poor Glen, he tried to unburden the ship, do what he could in a hostile world, and died, having lost.

Much like all the women I ever knew.

We went on to find other ships, other warehouses, other ways. For a while, we had a whole trucking company hauling 'em from Duluth up north to the Yukon. Eventually I let younger women do the bulk of it and I took over in a supervisory capacity. Computers sure helped there.

Now, just about fifty years after the wreck, I'm still tired, worn out, used up. And now it's my turn to lay here in this small chilly room with its loud linoleum tiles. Over-busy women bustle about me, banes clinging to their shoulders, catching in their earrings, nestling in their hair — everyone stolidly ignoring them because that's the only way they can cope.

Good thing is, laying here, I've finally had time to think.

In five decades, what have I accomplished? I raised my three kids, and did a heck of a lot of cleaning, cooking, and tending to Ronald and old people before my hips wore out. Maybe that's enough, maybe it isn't. But putting a dent into the number of banes haunting Duluth women might have made a small difference, too, and that's sure a comfort in my old age.

Dumping them in the lake with Glen's assistance was only a stopgap measure — I'd always know that. And I'm truly sorry about all the men that died that day. Sure, we were desperate, but those lives had meaning, and vitality, and it was wrong of us to pack the *Fitz* so full. I haven't ever tried to pluck that one off, a pale dense mass pressing right at the base of my neck.

How are we going to manage from here on out? What with the population showing no signs of slowing, the rising anger I see in the new generation of women, and banes multiplying every which way, we need a better system for getting rid of 'em, just like for toxic waste. First place to start, I figure, is by studying the past. Listing all the ways women have tried, all the ways we've barely hung on. The ways that some men helped sometimes.

So, I'm getting it written all down, starting with how it was in Duluth back in '75. Spilling the beans, finally. Breaking the unspoken vow. One of the nursing home attendants is kindly doing it for me because of my arthritis, writing it in a fine hand in a coil-bound notebook. Her name is Nneka. She's from Nigeria and I want to weep at the banes *she* carries.

I'm going to ask her to scribble down more notes as I think of them, in the time I've got left. The things I've seen! The waste, the ignorance, the needless suffering. How we've all gone sideways, tipped over, nearly sunk, women and men alike.

Holding our own is not enough.

Keeping silent is no longer working.

We need to open our mouths and speak, even if it means we all drown.

* * *

>>> *The sinking of the freighter, Edmund Fitzgerald, in 1975 is more than a chart-topping song by Gordon Lightfoot: it's an iconic moment in the history of the Great Lakes. The disaster led to major changes in shipping regulations that included better equipment and tighter inspections. The wreck is now considered a heritage site.*

Holly Schofield

Holly Schofield travels through time at the rate of one second per second, oscillating between the alternate realities of city and country life. Her stories have appeared in such publications as *Analog, Lightspeed*, and *Escape Pod*, been used in university curricula, and been translated into several languages. She hopes to save the world through science fiction and homegrown heritage tomatoes. This is her second appearance in the Tesseracts series.

hollyschofield.wordpress.com

About the Editors

Susan MacGregor

Co-editor: Susan MacGregor is the author of *The Tattooed Witch, The Tattooed Seer, and The Tattooed Queen* (Five Rivers Publishing), a historical fantasy trilogy, set in an alternate 1550 inquisitional Spain (think gypsies, magic, flamenco, piracy, and Spanish colonization of the New World). The first book, *The Tattooed Witch*, was short-listed for a Canadian Science Fiction and Fantasy Association Aurora Award in 2014. A prior editor for over twenty years with *On Spec Magazine*, her short fiction has been featured in *On Spec,* as well as anthologies, *Divine Realms* (Ravenstone Books), *Northern Frights* 5 (Mosaic Press), *A Method to the Madness* (Five Rivers Publishing), *Urban Green Man* (Edge Books), *Equus* (Word Weaver Press), and more recently, *Fire: Demons, Dragons & Djinns* (Tyche Books), and *The Dame Was Trouble* (Coffin Hop Press). She's written one non-fiction book on writing – *The ABC's of How NOT to Write Speculative Fiction* (Copper Pig Writers Society), an SF writing primer, which she uses as the basis for writing workshops. In 2011 she co-edited *Tesseracts Fifteen: A Case of Quite Curious Tales* (Edge Books). *Tesseracts 22, Alchemy and Artifacts* is her second foray into editing a Tesseracts anthology. When she isn't writing or editing, you can find her rehearsing and performing professionally as a singer and dancer of flamenco, or finding calm through painting landscapes. Susan lives with her family in Edmonton.

Lorina Stephens

Co-editor: Lorina Stephens has worked as an editor, freelance journalist for national and regional print media, is the author of eight books (fiction and non-fiction), been a festival organizer, publicist, lectured on many topics from historical textiles and domestic technologies to publishing and writing, teaches, and continues to work as a writer, artist, and publisher at Five Rivers Publishing. She has had several short fiction pieces published in Canada's acclaimed *On Spec Magazine, Postscripts to Darkness, Neo-Opsis, Deluge, Strangers Among Us*, and Marion Zimmer Bradley's fantasy anthology *Sword & Sorceress X*. Her book credits include *The Rose Guardian, Caliban, Stonehouse Cooks, From Mountains of Ice, And the Angels Sang*, and *Shadow Song* (Five Rivers Publishing), *Recipes of a Dumb Housewife* (Lulu Publishing), *Credit River Valley*, (Boston Mills Press), *Touring the Giant's Rib: A Guide to the Niagara Escarpment* (Boston Mills Press). Lorina lives with her husband of four decades in a historic stone house in Neustadt, Ontario.

lorinastephens.com — Twitter @LorinaStephens

For more EDGE titles and information about upcoming speculative fiction please visit us at:

www.edgewebsite.com

Don't forget to sign-up for our Special Offers

If you enjoyed this read

Please leave a review on Amazon, Facebook, Good Reads or Instagram.

It takes less than five minutes and it really does make a difference.

If you're not sure how to leave a review on Amazon:

1. *Go to amazon.com.*

2. *Type in Alchemy and Artifacts edited by Lorina Stephens and Susan MacGregor and when you see it, click on it.*

3. *Scroll down to Customer Reviews. Nearby you'll see a box labeled Write a Review. Click it.*

4. *Now, if you've never written a review before on Amazon, they might ask you to create a name for yourself.*

5. *Reviews can be as simple as, "Loved the book! Can't wait for the Next!" (Please don't give the story away.)*

And that's it!

Brian Hades, publisher

www.ingramcontent.com/pod-product-compliance
Lightning Source LLC
Chambersburg PA
CBHW032220050726
47591CB00001B/200